Wild Game

• • •

Western Literature Series

Wild Game

■ ■ ■

FRANK BERGON

University of Nevada Press

Reno   Las Vegas   London

Western Literature Series

Series Editor: John H. Irsfeld

A list of books in the series appears at the end of this volume.

Names, characters, places, and incidents in this novel are either invented or used fictitiously. The author made use of information reported in court transcripts, newspapers, magazines, *Outlaw*, by Jeff Long, and *Give a Boy a Gun*, by Jack Olsen. The poem "A Crock Called Crockett" is a variation of "A Claude Called Dallas," by Lin Anderson.
The author is indebted to numerous Nevada Division of Wildlife game wardens and biologists, to ranchers, hunters, and trappers, and to many helpful readers. Special thanks go to Mark Bergon, Roser Caminals-Heath, Tony Diebold, Leonard Gardner, Marie Grace, Bill Heath, Jim Jeffress, Noel McElhany, Dave Mendive, Howard Norman, Zeese Papanikolas, Emily Rawlings, Jack Vernon, others who wish to remain anonymous, and most of all to Holly St. John Bergon.

The paper used in this book meets the requirements of American National Standard for Information Sciences—Permanence of Paper for Printed Library Materials, ANSI Z39.48–1984. Binding materials were selected for strength and durability.

Library of Congress Cataloging-in-Publication Data

Bergon, Frank.
Wild game / Frank Bergon.
p.   cm. — (Western literature series)
ISBN 0-87417-257-8 (alk. paper : hard)
I. Title.   II. Series.
PS3552.E71935W5   1995   94-41278
                                                                    CIP

University of Nevada Press, Reno, Nevada 89557 USA
Printed in the United States of America

1   3   5   7   9   8   6   4   2

To Short Watson and Darrell Winfield

Westerners and Friends

CHAPTER 1

On an unseasonably warm New Year's Eve in 1982, when he was still a wildlife biologist, Jack Irigaray sat at home in suburban Sparks, watching TV. A tawny western mountain lion with a black-tipped tail stalked across the screen. Jack's wife, Beth, lay in their bedroom, door closed, reading one of her occult books, *The Mysteries of the Past*. Her asthma was acting up. Their two little girls slept. Alone in the TV room, Jack poured himself a nightcap, two fingers of Drambuie, his first in three months. The heat of the alcohol clawed up his neck.

The mountain lion sprang from the snow—two hundred startling pounds of muscle—and pounced onto the back of an aging elk. Down the mountain slope, snow flying, the big elk lunged and bucked, the lion bouncing like a bull rider. The cougar clamped its teeth into the elk's neck. Up snapped the antlered head, legs buckled; the old elk tumbled into the snow. The lion's jaws locked on the buck's throat, squeezing the windpipe.

1

"We are all predators," a solemn voice intoned on TV. "The cougar hunts the elk. Man hunts the cougar. Life without bloodshed is impossible."

Why the hell couldn't they get anything right on TV? All his life Jack had watched animals hunt and kill. He'd seen violence, he'd seen death. But humans were the animals who regularly killed without need. The necessary violence of this cougar, he thought, was beautiful.

He got up for another splash of Drambuie. The phone rang. It was almost eleven-thirty, only a half hour away from the big ball dropping into the new year.

"Jack?" It was Bob Pritchard, the Washoe game warden, with an edge in his voice. "Billy Crockett is trash-trapping up in Little High Rock Canyon. I wonder if you can get away to check him out with me. Dale's hobbled up with the flu."

Normally Dale Ellison, the other Washoe warden, would join Bob. Now, though, Jack knew he had to go. Law enforcement wasn't his concern or interest, but the department, always shorthanded, counted on everyone—even fisheries and nongame biologists—to help out when needed. The two Washoe wardens had over nine thousand square miles as their beat. If they didn't move in on a poacher like Billy Crockett as soon as they got a tip, he'd leave a cold camp and no evidence. And Jack knew that if he didn't go, Bob would go alone. Bob was his friend. He'd helped out during Jack's last run-in with Billy Crockett. Jack still owed him for that.

"I'll be over as soon as I get into my uniform," Jack told Bob.

"Hey," Bob replied, sounding relieved, "I'll owe you one, Basco."

Jack had grown used to the nickname, although it had come about only in recent years. People from the West—Nevada or Idaho or California's San Joaquin Valley—knew right off from his last name, Irigaray, that he was Basque. Laxalt, Arrizabalaga, and Ybarguengoitia were familiar names around

Reno, but no longer of sheepherders. The solitary Basque herders of previous generations—those tough "Black Bascos," as they were derisively called—had pretty much vanished. Peruvians and Chileans had taken their places. Most of the Basques Jack grew up with peaceably sold cars, taught school, ran banks, wrote books, even hobnobbed with the president. When Jack was a kid, they were all just Americans, and not even hyphenated ones. His two little girls, who sang Basque songs and danced the *jota* at the Zazpiak Bat Club, were more conscious of their ethnicity. When he was their age, he was just another westerner—a Nevadan.

After putting on his uniform—work boots, green twilled jeans, and a khaki shirt with a Division of Wildlife bighorn insignia—he brushed his teeth and rinsed out his mouth with Listermint before pushing open the door to the bedroom. Beth sat up in bed with pillows bunched behind her head, her book propped on her knees. The bed table lamp lit up her curls. The long, naturally straight California blond hair she'd had when he married her had been cut, styled, and teased into a witch's snarls. An attractive witch, he had to say, not like some of the angry women in the group she'd begun to hang out with. Psychic power was what they claimed to study. Their purpose, Beth said, was to attune themselves to the beneficial forces of light and harmony so often obliterated by modern plastic and chemicals. White witchery is what they called it, but Jack felt it had blackened their lives.

He leaned over to kiss her good-bye. Her lips tightened. She wore blue pajamas, buttoned to her neck. He had given her a pink satin nightie for Christmas in the hope that she would shed the flannel PJs that made him feel like he was sleeping with a boy. He missed the fetching shortie night-gowns she used to wear.

"Jack," she said, "you can try to hide the smell, but you can't hide your eyes."

Her accusation caught him off guard, but he knew better

than to deny he'd been drinking. Growing up with an alcoholic father had made Beth alert to any slight shifts in expression, any fractured normalcy in silent eyes, those messages that passed for communication in alcoholic families.

"It was only a nightcap," he explained. "It's New Year's Eve." He tried to smile, but the need for apology rankled. He hadn't had a sip for three months, with no encouraging word from Beth. One nightcap, and he felt she was all over him.

"I have to go with Bob," he told her. "Billy Crockett has shown up again. We'll be back tomorrow afternoon."

Her hand surprised him with its strength as it curled around the back of his neck and pulled him down to her lips. The bed table light glinted off the blond down of her arm, taut and shapely from her workouts at the gym. It used to excite him when she came home from the gym and they made love, the cold smell of iron weights still on her hands. His stomach went feathery from the unexpected softness of her kiss.

"Be careful, honey," she said.

It was after midnight when he pulled off McCarran Boulevard into the Reno suburb where Bob Pritchard lived. The temperature was dropping. The neon of the downtown casinos winked in the distance. Most of the houses on Bob's block were dark. Elsewhere in the country, Jack thought, people were celebrating the New Year. Maybe things stayed quieter in Reno suburbs because the strain of celebration haunted the gambling casinos year-round.

A lamp in Bob's house silhouetted a Christmas tree in the bay window. It was a modest stucco house, the most a game warden could afford even after he maxed out on the government's puny salary scale. Jack knew that he and Beth could never have afforded their home on a game biologist's salary without help from her parents.

A woven wire fence fronted Bob's yard, the brown lawn cluttered with scraps brought home for the dogs from the

Nugget Casino, where rib-bone dinners were a specialty. In the mist the sun-whitened bones looked eerie. Jack pulled in front of Bob's dirty green Dodge pickup; months of scraping through sagebrush had rubbed the bighorn DOW decal off the truck door. Two barking mutts rushed to the fence, and the light behind the Christmas tree popped out.

"Happy New Year," Bob said, as he climbed into the cab after tossing some gear into the back of Jack's truck. It went without saying that Jack would drive. Bob's bad eye, poked out when the needle flew out of an air mattress on a camping trip, affected the night vision of his supposedly good eye. He drove at night anyway, but nobody in the department would ride with him. He was always running into things.

Bob was a big, energetic, jowly guy with the trimmed mustache of the Marine sergeant he once was. Like most people in the Division of Wildlife, he'd lived in Nevada just about all his life.

He put his Stetson on the seat between him and Jack.

"Do you have your pistol?" Bob asked.

Jack nodded. It was under the seat, the .357 Magnum he had qualified with during three months at POST in Carson City. He hated the damn gun, but orders had come down sending all department biologists to Peace Officers Standards and Training after a warden and a fisheries biologist had been shot up in Idaho. Jack wished he could just be a biologist and look after wild game, as he'd been trained to do. But the world had changed, and he had been dragged into its violence.

"We'll go up to Gerlach," Bob said. "Scotty Larsen is the guy who spotted Crockett in Little High Rock Canyon. We can get some info from Scotty, catch some shut-eye, and get an early start on Crockett."

Jack headed the truck north on empty two-lane Highway 445, keeping the lights on low beam, though no other cars passed. Reno vanished in the rearview mirror; black clumps of sagebrush and shadscale sped past the window. At the Bureau of Land Management wild horse station in Palomino Valley, miles out of town, the dark mustangs packed into the pens looked like stuffed animals, the result of the good intentions of horse lovers with their laws against rounding up excess mustangs for dog meat. BORN TO RUN announced the animal-lover posters with photographs of galloping horses. Now the mustangs bred like rats. Desert forage couldn't sustain them. They ended up crowded into these pens. Some freedom! It made Jack sad. Even Beth didn't understand that there were some things worse than death.

Bob snapped open a tin of Copenhagen and loaded his lower lip with snoose. He thrust out his hand, offering Jack a dip.

Jack shook his head. "I've been quit three months," he explained. But the enticing, ammoniac odor of tobacco was more than he could resist. "What the hell. Beth accuses me of chewing even when I'm not." He packed a wad into his lip and waited for the nicotine hit. He'd experienced homicidal rage during his first week of quitting, and since then Beth had interpreted any irritability as a sign that he was dipping again, hooking himself into the old cycle of withdrawal and relapse. Quitting alcohol had been a snap in comparison. Now, in the dark truck, a feeling like warm water flowed up his neck, stretching the residual glow of the Drambuie into his skull. The muscles in his neck and shoulders relaxed. He felt a sense of fellowship with Bob, bound by the clear, early morning demands of a man's job to be done.

"When we were first married," Bob said, "Cindy crabbed about me leaving spit cans all over the house, so she got me a pewter mug to use, and now everything's fine."

"You're lucky."

"I am," Bob agreed matter-of-factly, without smugness. "I am a lucky man."

Jack felt a twinge of jealousy, thinking of Cindy, Bob's green-eyed second wife. She was twenty-eight or -nine, a couple of years younger than Beth, but at least fifteen years younger than Bob. People had been surprised when Bob married so soon after the death of his first wife—he'd actually met Cindy at the funeral—but Jack was happy for him. He knew how much Bob had suffered during his wife's struggle with cancer. Bob deserved a turn of fate. Jack remembered the time when he and Beth, Bob, and Cindy had gone up to Pyramid Lake on the Fourth of July. Sitting on the shore with Beth, he'd watched Bob and Cindy in the water playing like kids. They smeared each other with the thick lake mud that sticks to human skin like damp charcoal. Splashing around in a tiny black bikini, Cindy threw her arms up to get away from Bob, and one of her bright, silky breasts popped free from her loose top. She glanced at Jack, smiled, and calmly tucked herself back into the skimpy bra. She and Bob held hands as they waded back to shore. Jack and Beth were sitting together on the sand, but they weren't holding hands.

Ahead of the truck, the black expanse of Pyramid Lake, surrounded by treeless hills, now loomed into view, devoid of the innocent emerald and turquoise hues that had flecked the water under holiday sunshine. As a boy, Jack had discovered he could never anticipate exactly what color the water might be in daylight; even its shades of blue shifted by the hour. That was half the fun of driving up to see it. The sight of the massive salty lake, sparkling in the treeless desert, was always an unearthly surprise. At night or in a storm, it revealed its underlying treachery; it was a moody sea, unpredictable, capable of overturning boats, and had spawned legends among both whites and Indians of monstrous, man-eating serpents.

It was after two when he and Bob pulled into Gerlach, the tiny desert town huddled precariously at the point of the V-shaped Black Rock Desert. Jack drove past the shapes of the gas station, Bruno's café, and the five bars that composed the bulk of the town's commerce. Only one building, Eddie Dodd's bar, still had a light on. Jack pulled up to Scotty

Larsen's home, the only log house in a town of shabby trailers, mobile homes, and desert shacks. Scotty's two-story log house stood out like somebody's misplaced dream of an Idaho hunting lodge.

"He said we could wake him up," Bob said.

Bob knocked. A window lit up. Scotty Larsen came to the door wearing a pair of old Levi's over gray flannel long johns and bare feet. A giant of a man—at least six seven and 240 pounds with a mop of curly graying hair—he grinned, his quizzical eyes casting their look of constant bemusement. "You boys looking for a party?" he asked.

Inside, all the way up to the high-peaked cathedral ceiling the split-log walls sprouted stuffed heads and bodies—bobcats, deer, elk, pronghorn, desert bighorn, a mountain lion, a wild boar, the skin of a grizzly—as well as old hand-forged traps and antique guns. For ten years Scotty had worked as a government trapper for the Animal Damage Control boys before becoming a hunting guide and independent trapper. His clients rarely went away empty-handed. On a good morning, Scotty could show deer hunters half a dozen trophy heads and let them take their pick.

He poured mugs of reheated coffee. "Cream? Sugar? Arlene's not going to get up, so I guess I have to do all the work."

Jack apologized. "I'm sorry we had to wake you."

Scotty grinned. "Hey—day, night, what's the difference when you're with friends?" He sprawled into a hunting-lodge chair under a row of his framed wildlife photographs. In the off-season he ran a photography and framing business out of his large garage.

Jack looked at the pictures just above his head. Three cute kit foxes poked their little pointy faces out of a den. A desert bighorn stared suspiciously in the direction of the camera. A frightened cottontail crouched in cheatgrass bathed in a sunset glow. Jack thought he remembered seeing that picture in *National Geographic* or *Nevada*. Scotty was in all the magazines. Jack could never figure it. One day Scotty was snapping pictures of cuddly foxes, bunnies, or birds; the next, he was blowing them away. Jack had once asked the trapper if he saw any contradiction in what he did. "No way," Scotty answered. "I just know more about nature than most people."

Sipping his coffee, Scotty wasted no time getting into what Jack and Bob wanted to hear. "I ran into Billy Crockett trapping up near the Sheldon Refuge in November," he said. "Crockett was doing it the same as he always did, hanging bait, you know. He came down this way and got into a row with Jess Nichols over territory. He's been up in Idaho for two years, and he comes back and thinks no one else should be trapping where he wants to. He pulled up some of Jess's traps."

"A tough guy," Bob growled.

"Maybe in his own mind, but he's lucky Jess was in a good mood. Crockett doesn't know what tough is till he sees Jess on a mad. It was the end of the season, so Jess didn't give a shit."

Jack started to laugh. "You're not trying to tell us that Jess Nichols would quit trapping just because it's the end of the season?"

"Hey," Scotty said, "those Nichols boys are good Democrats. They know how to work the system. Why should they work when the government will pay them for not working?"

Jack had had his own run-ins with Jess Nichols and his father and brothers. They lived on a hardscrabble family homestead northwest of Gerlach. Poaching was a way of life for them. Both Jack and Bob had cited all of them more than once. Now they both suspected that Jess had been getting into heavy-duty poaching ever since the department had reintroduced desert bighorns into the Granite Mountains. Jess could make big money as a guide for hunters during the offseason. Jack knew some out-of-state jerks would always pay a bundle to be able to kill all four species of bighorns and complete what they called the "grand slam."

"Just before Christmas," Scotty continued, "I came across

Billy Crockett again, and he had a dead lion in his camp. That pissed me off. I chewed him out and told him he knew he wasn't supposed to be trapping lions. Crockett said, 'What was I going to do? I wasn't looking for him. He got in my trap.' I said, 'Why didn't you choke him down and let him go?' He didn't know what the hell I was talking about. Later they had that lion skin stretched out on the pool table in Eddie Dodd's bar, and Eddie was bragging about Crockett like he'd killed it bare-handed. The skin was botched. Crockett didn't even know how to split the tail right. The guy's a pussy."

"Why didn't you call me then?" Bob implored.

"I would've," Scotty said, "but I misplaced your number. More coffee?"

Jack pressed back a smile when he saw that Bob wasn't amused. The truth, he knew, was that when it came to trapping, Billy Crockett wouldn't make a whitehead on Scotty Larsen's ass. But Scotty lived in Gerlach. For him to squeal on locals wouldn't make his life in town easy. His feuds with the Nichols gang kept him in enough trouble. He'd only called Bob after Billy Crockett had moved his camp far from town into Little High Rock Canyon where he was hanging deer and illegally trapping bobcats. Every illegal deer and bobcat was potential money out of Scotty's pocket.

Scotty went on, "When I told Crockett deer season was over, he said, 'That deer still thinks it's November seventh.' I didn't argue with him that time. He had a mean, crazy look in his eyes. He was packing a pistol and looked ready to reach for it. 'What's it to you,' he said, 'if I knock down a deer? I've got to live.' A single-engine plane flew over us, circled, and headed back toward Reno. Crockett got nervous and wanted to know what that plane was doing. I said it was probably just the BLM, but he shouldn't be surprised if the Fish and Game checked on him. He said, 'That's fine. I'll be ready for them.'" Scotty paused. "He meant it, too. You boys better be careful. There's something loose in that guy's head. He can be a mean son of a bitch."

"Did he have any cats?" Jack asked.

"I didn't see 'em, but I never went into his tent. He had traps set for them. He complained that it was too warm. The coyotes were already rubbing, and the bobcats weren't moving around. The bastard chains up the traps so the cats can't drag to cover."

"I can't believe I'd ever hear you feeling sorry for a bobcat," Jack said, remembering the picture he'd seen of Scotty with a season's catch of bobcat and coyote skins stacked almost chest high. Scotty would set out a three-hundred-mile trap-line and bring in as many as a hundred cats and two hundred and fifty coyotes in a good year. Professionals like Scotty made money by putting a lot of steel in the ground and making their rounds in trucks. The trick was knowing how to read the country, putting the traps in draws and under overhangs along game trails where bobcats were likely to travel. Billy Crockett wasn't like that. Working on foot or on horseback, he saturated a smaller area with traps and depended on luck for an animal to stumble into one. Chained traps were easier to check, but they left cats exposed. Caught in the open, a trapped cat would go crazy trying to rip its foot free.

"I never said trapping wasn't cruel," Scotty said, "but I don't make it any crueler than it has to be. If a cat can drag the trap, then it can get under cover in some brush and lick its foot. Then the cat's happy."

"I bet it is," Bob interjected. Bob looked angry, sparked no doubt by the news about Billy trapping a lion.

Jack stood up, trying to divert Bob. "We have to take off if we're going to get any shut-eye before it gets light."

"You boys can stay here," Scotty said. "The rooms are free." He meant the guest rooms for his hunting clients.

"If I got into a bed," Jack said, "I might not get out."

"We'll sleep in the truck up by the hot springs," Bob said. He stood up, too. "Thanks for the help, Scotty."

"I could use a soak," Jack added, thinking of how good it would feel to get into that geothermal water. His head had started to ache as the rush from the Drambuie and Copenhagen wore off.

"They're still fenced up," Scotty said about the hot springs, "ever since those two guys got drunk and scorched themselves to death in the hot pool."

Jack recalled the shoddy accident. The Gerlach hot springs consisted of several pools; one of them was boiling, but he'd soaked in the safe ones hundreds of times when he was a kid. He couldn't believe the pools were still closed up because two guys had drowned.

Bob grew irritated. "It's lousy," he complained, "that two dumb drunks get themselves killed and ruin things for everyone."

"That's your government for you," Scotty replied. "You boys work for it. Me, I'd just let nature take its course."

"Everything's changing," Bob said. "We've got a lot of dumb people coming into this country." Jack knew Bob was thinking of all the out-of-state hunters who would break the law to get a trophy.

Scotty nodded. "It's just like those drowned Mexicans they're always fishing out of the Truckee River. They get juiced up and forget they don't know how to swim."

"Let's get out of here," Jack said. "Thanks for the java, Scotty."

Scotty smiled. "Hey, it's New Year's Eve. We gotta have some fun, right?"

Jack drove his truck past the hot springs, the steam rising behind the wire fences above the pools. He parked off the road and killed the engine in some scraggly saltbush at the edge of the Black Rock Desert. A ghostly glow hovered above the massive salt flat, a frozen seabed stretching all the way to the horizon.

"You can sleep in the cab," Bob told Jack. "I got the bedroll in the back." Bob was still fuming as he crashed around in back, pushing aside shovels and tools to make room to stretch out his sleeping bag.

In the cab, Jack tried to lie on his side, his nose inches from the steering wheel, but he couldn't get comfortable. The seat was too short, his head jammed against the door handle. Booze, nicotine, caffeine—he was wired. His skull vibrated. Sweat greased his palms and armpits, but he felt cold. He might have slept outside, but the wind whistled, and he hadn't thought to bring a sleeping bag. A couple of coyotes in the distance sent up howls that sounded like the wavering cries of a pack sprinting across the desert at astonishing speed. He always found it amazing how coyotes could throw their voices. Nature's ventriloquists. He thought he'd never fall asleep; then he felt Bob shaking his shoulder. He heard the weepy cry of seabirds. The sky was gray with morning light.

"Boy, you were out," Bob said. "I'll drive."

Jack stumbled into the sagebrush to pee. Squawking gulls from Pyramid Lake circled above him. His eyes felt heavy, swollen. None of us belongs out here, he thought; all of us are misplaced.

Bob backed up the truck and rammed into a lichen-stained boulder. "Dammit," he said. Even in daylight, he had no depth perception.

As they drove north, Bob griped about Crockett trapping a lion. Before Crockett had left for Idaho, word had come that he was running a poaching operation out of Eddie Dodd's bar. Eddie had kept Crockett stocked with supplies in exchange for pelts as well as some venison he illegally sold to migrants in the off-season. That's when Jack had come across some of Crockett's traps baited with mustang meat. He'd called Bob, and the warden began to make things hot for both Eddie and Crockett, but he couldn't pin Crockett with anything more than a couple of misdemeanors. Then Crockett left the state.

"That's not his first lion," Bob said. "A tourist saw two lions rugged out on the bar pool table, but I couldn't get anyone to testify. You know, if someone's grandmother's getting killed, they'll sure call the police, but a poor deer or lion doesn't mean shit to them."

To Bob, murder was murder. In his view, if people were constrained in their slaughter of animals and birds, fewer grandmothers would be murdered. He even wanted all shooting of mountain lions to be outlawed. A couple of years ago when the season's legal kill of lions had topped two hundred, Bob had stomped around angry for days. "Add the fifty lions that the ADC boys knock off for the sheepmen, and you've got two hundred and fifty dead lions in this state alone." Arguments that lions had to be managed to protect the deer herds and sheep meant nothing to him. "Let the deer and lions work it out themselves," he said. "How many sheep are worth a lion?"

Jack knew that Crockett had joined hundreds of trappers who'd flooded into the deserts and mountains since the price of pelts had shot up. Despite Brigitte Bardot, the European market for furs was growing. A warden could only do so much. Tighter quotas on game animals gave guides like Jess Nichols a steady trade with illegal trophy hunters. At one time Bob had taken it as his mission to cite or arrest every poacher in the state. But he'd mellowed since marrying Cindy. Since he was one of two men trying to cover nine thousand square miles, the most he could do was make the occasional arrest of a flagrant violator stand as a warning to others. And the slaughter went on.

A little after nine Jack and Bob reached the mouth of Little High Rock, a rough volcanic canyon of steep basalt cliffs that cut through the desert for seven miles. They put on down jackets and tramped through shoulder-high sagebrush to where Scotty told them he'd seen trap sets. "Over there," Jack said, his eyes sharper than Bob's. Hanging from a greasewood bush, a brown sage-hen wing fluttered in the wind where it might attract a curious bobcat. The bait was tied to the brush with colorless nylon leader. Under the wing lay an unmarked trap set without spacers to protect the legs of accidentally captured hawks or eagles. Hanging visible bait—mustang meat, rabbit fur, sage-hen wings—was illegal because it attracted raptors, who depended on their eyesight rather than their noses. Here were four violations: no identification on the trap, no spacers, hanging bait, and illegal possession of game bird parts.

"Son of a bitch," Bob said, and pulled the trap. They went farther into the canyon, the basalt cliffs rising higher, and found another set of traps against the rimrock. A captured red-tailed hawk frantically flapped its wings trying to jerk its broken leg free from the jaws of the trap. Without its hunting claws this bird was doomed. The hawk blinked as Jack grabbed its neck and released the trap from the torn leg. Holding the hawk by the head Jack swung it around, its wings flapping as it tried to get away, until he heard the neck break. A bead of blood hung on its beak, and its eyes turned cloudy. He tossed the dead bird into the sagebrush.

"Let's go," Bob said.

They hauled the traps back to the truck and drove along the canyon's north rim, parked, and scoured the sage. Jack spotted another hanging wing. He felt himself getting as angry as Bob. Trash-trapping is what they called it—what Crockett did. Crockett wanted people to think he was a big-time trapper, but he always cut corners. It was easier to use body parts than to go to the trouble of scenting steel the way real trappers did, by using Cat's Passion or making their own scent from bobcat glands or coyote urine or rotted fish or whatever.

"Oh, Christ," Bob said. "He's got a pup." A kit fox, its mangled front paw clamped in the staked trap, tried to scramble across the exposed ground toward the brush, dragging the trap as far as the taut chain allowed. It had begun chewing through its leg just above where the jaws of the trap clung to its paw. The fox glared at the men with intense, frightened eyes and snarled. Bob reached down and jerked it up by its bushy tail, lifting it off the ground. It was a female. "Cut it," he said.

Jack snapped open the blade of his pocketknife and sawed into the bloody leg where the fox had been chewing. The kit fox squalled angrily in his ear. The sharp blade sliced through gristle, then the bone snapped free. The trap dropped into the dirt with the little paw still sticking out of it.

Bob swung the fox by her tail and tossed her several feet through the air. The fox hit the ground in a defensive crouch, her pointed ears erect, staring with dark, alert eyes. Jack looked at the fox. She looked at him. She rose and hobbled over the rocky ground, stopped, glanced back, then began a quick three-legged stumbling trot into the sagebrush, her silvery back and blond legs blending into the desert shades.

"She'll be all right," Bob sighed. "Let's go get that punk."

They walked back to the truck with the pulled traps and continued driving slowly along the rocky rim, stopping now and then to scan the canyon floor with binoculars. It was nearing eleven in the morning when they approached the far end of the canyon and saw a red Ford Bronco parked on the rim.

"Who the hell's that?" Bob blurted out.

A man stood behind the Bronco wearing a red deerhunter's cap with flaps and a woolen red-and-black checkered mackinaw. Bob and Scotty were big, but this man was fat. He was about thirty with rosy cheeks and an expansive pale forehead. He leaned backward to counterbalance the pull of gravity on his bulging stomach.

"How're you doing?" Jack said, not wanting to startle the man. "What's your name?"

"Larry Hughes," the man answered, sounding jumpy. His billowy khaki pants cuffed around new blue Gore-Tex hiking boots.

"Give me that pistol," Bob ordered, pointing toward the holster at the man's hip. "Butt first."

Bob swung open the loaded cylinder and shook the cartridges into his palm. He dropped the cartridges into the front pocket of the man's jacket and handed back the revolver.

"What are you doing with a .357 Smith?" Bob asked.

Hughes's ruddy face glistened. He was breathing heavily. "Eddie Dodd, the barkeep, loaned it to me. I needed it to signal a friend, to let him know I was here. I was bringing him some supplies from Eddie."

"Where's your friend?" Jack asked calmly, as though he were only casually interested in the answer. He didn't want the man to get any jumpier than he was.

"He went to reset some traps. I was just about to haul the rest of this stuff down." He nodded toward the Styrofoam cooler at his feet. "This is my second trip. I didn't know it was so fucking far down there."

Jack flipped up the lid of the cooler. It was packed with cans of Dr Pepper and Squirt, some chocolate-chip cookies in Saran Wrap, oranges, apples, and a plastic Cool Whip container.

"There's butterscotch pudding in there," Hughes explained, pointing to the Cool Whip container. "My wife made it."

"Does your friend Billy have any game hanging down there?" Bob asked.

The mention of Billy Crockett's name startled Hughes. "Look, you guys, I just came out here for a little outing, to look for some arrowheads and things. Eddie Dodd asked me to drop this stuff off. I don't know what's going on here. I'd like to leave right now."

"Were you planning to take back some pelts with you?" Jack asked. He saw it was too late to sidle up to Hughes calmly; the man was already too agitated.

"Oh, hell. Don't try to set me up. Just let me go down there and get my coin shooter and I'll be on my way. I don't want to be here when Billy gets back."

"Here he comes now," Bob said.

At first Jack couldn't recognize Billy Crockett striding along the rim. It had been four years since he'd last seen the trapper. Crockett had grown a beard and was wearing a long yellow rubber slicker, the kind Marlboro Men wear in ads. When Jack had known him Billy had always been clean-shaven. But he still wore his blond hair in a long neat ponytail swinging from under a high-crowned old-style buckaroo hat. Like Jack, he was about thirty now, but his round steel-rimmed spectacles gave him the look of a college boy, which is why Jack's uncle Pete had nicknamed him "Berkeley" when Billy had showed up looking for work at his ranch a decade ago. Under the unbuttoned raincoat Billy wore clean Levi's and an Eddie Bauer chamois shirt. His clothes almost looked pressed.

Crockett's nose, delicate at the bridge, flared into prominent uptilted nostrils. Sensuous lips curled into a smirk. Behind the steel-rimmed glasses his flat eyes remained rigid, like blue pebbles in ice.

"How do you get rid of a mule you don't want?" he asked nonchalantly. "I got two to give away."

Bob held out his hand, ignoring the question. "Give me your pistol, Billy."

Crockett hesitated a moment, then reached behind the lapel of his yellow slicker and withdrew the pistol from his shoulder holster. It was a .22 caliber, forceful enough to finish off a trapped animal without seriously damaging the pelt. A powerful .357 Magnum, like the one Larry Hughes was wearing on his hip, would ruin a coyote pelt. A less bloody way favored by trappers was simply to stomp on a coyote's rib cage with a boot heel and burst the animal's heart.

"We've got a report on you," Bob told Crockett, "that you've been knocking down game out of season. We want to check your camp."

"I have some meat hung up," Crockett admitted in a calm voice. "If I didn't, I'd have starved to death by now."

"Deer season is over, Billy," Jack said.

"If you guys came all the way out here just to cite me for knocking down a deer, I can't see it. Don't you have anything better to do?"

"You're setting illegal traps," Bob said. "Let's get going."

Crockett turned and glared at Larry Hughes.

The fat man lifted his hands in a defensive posture. "I didn't say anything, Billy. I didn't know they were coming out here."

Air burst from Crockett's nostrils in a dismissive snort. His accusatory look told Jack that he thought the fat man had squealed on him.

"A lot of guys could've told us you were out here," Jack said, trying to cover for Hughes.

Crockett smiled. "Remember what I told you, Jack, when I invited you into my camp?"

Clearly he was talking about the time, four years ago, when Jack had confiscated Crockett's guns and traps. Jack had come across some unmarked traps, and while following the trapper's tracks, he found a parked Jeep with two loaded rifles in the cab. At the time Jack had a feeling of dread that he was being watched, but loaded guns in a vehicle were a misdemeanor that allowed him to confiscate them. Then he saw the outline of a man in a buckaroo hat with a rifle looking down at him from the rimrock. Jack went to his pickup and called Bob, who drove out right away. Two days later Crockett showed up in town to get back his rifles. His hair hung in a single braid down his back. He was polite and soft-spoken, although he wouldn't admit that the unmarked traps were his. Jack told him he'd always been taught that when you get caught with your hand in the cookie jar, you should fess up. But Crockett wouldn't. He only asked in a polite, submissive voice whether he could have his guns back. Jack knew that without a confession he couldn't make any charges stick, and he thought that if he could get on Crockett's good side, the kid might straighten up. They talked about Jack's uncle Pete; Crockett said he'd never worked for a better man in his life. He'd still be buckarooing if Pete's ranch hadn't gone under. Jack told him he could do just as well trapping legally as illegally. "I'm just asking you to play fair," Jack said. Crockett then promised that Jack wouldn't ever see any of his traps baited or unmarked. They shook hands, and Crockett said, "You're always welcome in my camp, Jack, but leave your badge behind."

"You know I can't do that, Billy," Jack had told him.

His eyes had gotten hard. "Well, then stay out of my camps," Crockett had warned.

Crockett was still looking at Jack when Bob ordered him to lead the way from the canyon rim to the camp.

"Can I at least haul down some of this grub?"

Bob said okay, and Crockett swung the heavy Styrofoam cooler to his shoulder and set out at a quick clip. Jack and Larry Hughes followed, and Bob brought up the rear.

The trail switchbacked down the steep canyon wall. Jack was sweating when they hit a sloping scree field of volcanic rock. He took off his coat. The scraping sound of sliding stones echoed from the opposite wall as he scrambled and skidded down the scree field, trying to keep up with Crockett, even though the young trapper's feet swung out in a typical urban dweller's splayfooted duck walk.

On the canyon floor the sagebrush grew shoulder high. Prime cat country. A meandering line of red willows marked the banks of a creek. In a clearing Crockett had pitched a canvas sheepherder's wall tent, tall enough for a man to stand up in. His camp, as always, was orderly; wood was stacked neatly by a fire ring covered with a metal grate. On a foldout table, a frying pan, tin plate, and pots rested upside down on a dish towel. A washstand had been fashioned on a tripod of juniper branches. On another tripod in the shade hung the hindquarters of a deer. On the metal poles behind the tent hung another set of deer's legs from which he had carved slices of meat for himself or his traps. In the brush at the edge of the camp was a third set of venison quarters. On the ground lay a deer's head, with a four-point set of antlers. What the hell did he need with three deer, if he was only killing for sustenance? Jack knew Bob was thinking the same thing when he asked to see Crockett's trapping license.

"You're still an Idaho resident," Bob said.

Crockett objected. "I've got a nonresident trapping license for here."

"But you've got no license for these deer."

"I never said I did."

"I'm going to write you up."

"What's the point? I'm a hundred miles from civilization. If I obeyed city people's laws, I'd starve to death."

"Those laws still apply to you," Jack said. He wanted to cite Billy and get out of there, but he could see that the three slaughtered deer were causing Bob's temper to crackle.

"A man who lives off the land as I do should have some rights. Game laws don't apply to Indians around here."

"You're no Indian, buddy," Bob snapped.

Crockett remained calm. He seemed to feel a need to explain his way of life, to justify the rightness of his hunter's code. "It's a matter of survival," he said with unforced patience. "I can't buy groceries down the canyon. I either eat venison or a man's cow. And I've never stolen another man's beef."

"What do you have in the tent?" Bob asked.

Billy stiffened. "You're off limits there. This tent is my home."

"Maybe Larry can go in and get the pelts you have in there."

Crockett threw an angry glare toward Larry Hughes. "I don't know what he told you," Crockett said, "but I have a license to trap cats."

Larry protested. The fat man's pale face was splotched from the quick hike down the canyon trail. He looked ripe for a stroke. "I didn't say anything, Billy."

"You have a nonresident license," Bob said, sounding tough. "If you've got illegal game, I have a duty to arrest you."

"Let us see what you have," Jack said, trying to calm the situation. He hoped they wouldn't have to arrest Billy. Since they knew him, and where he lived, they had grounds to write a ticket instead. He hoped Billy would cooperate.

"If you don't have a search warrant," Crockett warned, "I don't want you in my home."

Jack stood between Billy and his tent. Larry Hughes backed away. The front of the tent was tied shut, so Jack couldn't see into it. "Come on, Billy," Jack said. "Let's not make this hard. You know this camp isn't your home. It's temporary. We have a right to search it."

"You show us what you've got," Bob told Crockett, "or we can go in ourselves."

"You're out of line," Crockett's voice snapped, hot now. "This is my home. You're not going in there."

"Okay, Jack," Bob said, "check out what's inside."

Bob stood with his back to the tent. Crockett faced him about six feet away. Jack untied the tent flaps. He wished Billy would quit balking. Whatever tough-guy scenario he had running through his head was only going to get him in more trouble with Bob. The warden wasn't going to put up with an over-age adolescent acting out some lunatic mountain-man fantasies—Bob had slammed the lid on tougher poachers than Crockett.

As Jack untied the flap strings, he heard Bob saying, "You know the law, Billy. We have the right to check out any camp." Then Crockett replied in a weak, pleading voice, sounding like a little boy, "Are you going to take me in?"

Inside the shadowy tent, Jack noticed a portable kerosene heater near a canvas cot. A blue North Point sleeping bag and a foam pad lay on the cot. The guy sure liked his comforts. The smell of warm canvas filled the tent. Against the sunlit back wall of the tent leaned two bobcat hides on stretching boards and a raccoon skin drying on a third board. Nothing necessarily illegal except that they had been taken with baited traps—a misdemeanor, though hard to prove. Then along the side of the tent Jack saw the tawny fur of what looked to be the rolled pelt of a mountain lion. Shot or trapped, a mountain lion was illegal at this time of year.

Outside the tent, Bob's voice burst into a shout, "Oh, no!" Jack whirled. Pistol shots cracked. Jack flung back the flaps of the tent and saw Crockett in a crouched police stance, firing a pistol gripped in both hands. The exploding handgun thundered, as Bob fell backward, his face spattered with blood, a coil of smoke snaking up from his chest. Larry Hughes slumped forward, his big body crashing through sagebrush. Crockett swung his arms back and forth, blasting bullets into both falling men. Then, still in his crouched stance, knees bent, he whipped the barrel of the abruptly silent pistol toward Jack.

"Come out here," he yelled.

Jack walked as if trying to push through the thick cloud left by the noise of exploding cartridges. He didn't know whether Crockett's pistol was still loaded. He thought he'd heard it last click on an empty cylinder, but Crockett kept it pointed at his chest. Bob lay on his back. His bloody head lifted up from the ground, his desperate eyes searching in Jack's direction, then plopped back. Jack realized with a stunning jolt of fear that he was helpless. He was defenseless. In the excitement on the canyon ridge he'd forgotten to strap on his pistol. He'd left the damn, hateful gun under the seat of the truck up on the rim.

Crockett ducked into the tent and reappeared carrying a .22 rifle with a leather shoulder sling. Jack watched without believing what he was seeing. "Billy, don't," he shouted. His hands floated up in a hopeless gesture. Crockett shot Bob in the head, then aimed at Larry Hughes, pointing the barrel an inch from the fat man's skull just behind the ear, as if finishing off an animal in a trap. "Billy!" Jack screamed, his fluttering hands futilely extended outward. Jack shut his eyes just as the bullet cracked through bone. Bob and Larry lay in the dirt motionless. Then Jack saw the rifle pointed at his face.

"No, Billy," he pleaded. "For Christ's sake, don't!"

"Shut the hell up. Get over here."

Jack stared at the bodies on the ground. "Why, Billy?" he pleaded. "For God's sake, why?"

Crockett looked at him coolly. "You had no business coming into my camp and violating my rights." He spoke as if delivering a rehearsed speech. "I swore I'd never get arrested again."

His flat voice, with its mechanical indifference, terrified Jack. Now it's coming, Jack thought. He sensed the .22 was about to fire; the bullets would thud into his chest, and that would be that.

"I don't want to hurt you," Crockett said with unexpected intimacy. "I have to get rid of these bodies, Jack. I need you to help me. Don't do anything to make me shoot you. Just do what I say, Jack. I don't want to kill you. You understand me, don't you?"

Jack didn't know from the tone whether he was supposed to respond or not. The question sounded like an order. Crockett had just murdered two men. Why not him, too?

"Cover up these bodies with sagebrush," Crockett continued in a calm, explanatory tone, "while I get the mules. I don't want anyone spotting them." He glanced up at the overcast sky, as if expecting a Bureau of Land Management plane to appear. "I'll be watching you." His words sounded like a kindly warning. "So don't try anything."

Crockett methodically reloaded his pistol without looking at Jack and slipped it into the holster on his hip. The .357 Magnum's customized quick-draw wooden handles disappeared as the flap of the yellow rain slicker slipped over the gun and the holster. Jack should've known. His uncle Pete used to tell him how Crockett would practice quick-draw shooting for hours at the ranch. Bob had confiscated Crockett's .22 but hadn't found the bigger, more dangerous hip gun under the slicker. But who would've thought a trapper would be walking around in the wilds carrying two concealed pistols?

Crockett picked up the service revolver lying on the cracked ground a few inches from Bob's outstretched hand. Bob must've reached for it instinctively as he tumbled backward.

Crockett put Bob's pistol in the pocket of his slicker. "This gun is going into the ground with this guy." He sounded disgusted. He then pulled the Smith & Wesson from the holster on Larry Hughes's waist. His voice lifted in surprise. "This gun's empty!" He stared at Jack as if expecting an explanation.

"Bob disarmed him on the ridge," Jack said.

"I thought he was a CI," Crockett muttered with a shrug. "You get to work," he told Jack; then ducking his head, he scooted into the tent.

Jack started pulling sagebrush to cover the bodies, his mind a confused web. Larry Hughes was dead because Crockett had mistakenly assumed he was an informant.

Bob was dead because he'd been too easy in searching Crockett. Jack figured that after he helped hide the bodies, he would be dead, too. A few minutes ago he was too stunned to be scared. Now he was just scared.

Despite the cold, gray afternoon, sweat slicked his hands. He had to tug hard on the sage to rip the roots loose from the dirt. Crockett came out of the tent with a shotgun and two more rifles. Jack recognized the guns he'd confiscated four years ago, a lever action .300 Savage and a reconstructed .50-caliber Hawkins, the muzzle-loader used by old mountain men like Jim Bridger, Jedediah Smith, and Tom Fitzpatrick—

Crockett's heroes when he'd first come to Nevada. They'd once been Jack's heroes, too, when he was a kid.

"What's that noise?" Crockett asked, startled. His previous calm self-assurance had vanished. He looked like a man who'd just walked out of a bar, blinking, confused with drink.

"What?" Jack couldn't hear anything except the desert wind and a clanging echo in his ears from the gunfire.

"Up on the rim. Don't you hear it?" Crockett's eyes looked frantic.

Jack shook his head. The guy's losing his cool, he thought.

"Maybe it's a plane." Crockett listened for a moment, his face anxious. He jerked his stare from the rim to the red willows along the streambed. "We got to get out of here. Get those bodies covered."

Crockett slung the .22 across his back and walked hurriedly away, leaving the other guns on the mess table, right in the open. Jack knew that Crockett had probably emptied them in the tent but just wasn't going to say anything. He'd love an excuse to blast away again. Jack realized that if he'd thought straight when he was in the tent he could've grabbed one of the rifles or the shotgun when they were still loaded. But if he'd been thinking straight earlier, he would've remembered to bring his own pistol. Then he'd probably also be dead, just like Bob and Larry.

Everything seemed a mishmashed series of unbelievable mistakes. The booze, the snuff, the lack of sleep had left his mind sodden. His hands trembled. Then he remembered his knife, bulging ominously on his thigh in the pocket of his green twilled uniform jeans. Sharp enough to slice through bone, the leg of a fox, a man's stomach. He'd need to get it out, ready. Not too soon, not too late. Or he'd be the next one dead.

Crockett hollered angrily from the other side of the red willows. "I can't catch this damn mule. Bring some feed from the tent."

Inside the tent, Jack found the grain sack and scooped oats into a dishpan. Oats scattered all over the ground, his hands shook so bad. He looked at the bulge of his knife in the silvery afternoon light. He put down the pan of feed and pressed his palms against his eyes to steady himself. Lighted whorls bobbed like illuminated snowflakes against the veined inner walls of his eyelids. He kept the pressure on his eyes until the skittering patterns of light diminished into darkness.

He heard Crockett call, his voice faint, tossed away in the wind. "Hurry the hell up, Jack." On the other side of the shallow stream, hidden in red willows, Crockett tried to catch two mules. Hobbled, but skittish from the gunfire, the mules lurched away as he approached. When Jack drew near, Crockett jerked the dishpan of oats from his hands and tossed him the halter. "Forget that big mule. We'll catch the little one. Don't let it see the halter. Put it behind your back."

Crockett held up the dishpan, scooped up a handful of feed, and let a waterfall of oats stream down from his fingers to entice the mule. "Here, you grain hog. Come and get it." The big mule hopped away, looking as spooked as a Nubian goat, but the little one became entranced with the vision of sparkling oats repeatedly streaming from Crockett's hand, like golden coins falling from the hand of a magician. Crockett called out sarcastically, "Here, oat pig, oat pig, oat pig."

When they finally caught the jumpy little mule, Crockett cracked it hard across the face with a juniper branch. The animal reared back terrified, and Crockett sent the toe of his boot into its belly, knocking the wind out of it.

He dragged the bleeding mule into camp, and Jack held it by the halter while Crockett threw on a packsaddle. "A mule's got no more sense than a goose," he complained, still panting. "I got burned with these two." He knelt by Bob's body, cut away the department patches and emblems from his shirt, and stuffed them into his day pack. Jack wouldn't look at Bob's face. He was surprised at how little blood lay on the ground.

Crockett ripped off Bob's eighteen-year service badge and stared at it contemptuously. "How could a guy work that many years for the lousy Fish and Game?"

Together they lifted Bob and swung him up over the cross-buck saddle. The little mule quickstepped aside, and Bob's body plopped facedown onto the ground. Jack saw then where all the blood had gone. Bob's back was soaked black. So was the ground where he had been lying.

After they got Bob lifted onto the packsaddle and tied down with a squaw hitch, Crockett, with his rifles strapped atop his backpack crammed with gear, led the mule up the canyon trail. Jack followed, out of breath, with the cooler on his shoulder and Larry's metal detector dangling from his other hand. The Styrofoam cooler was heavier than it had seemed when Crockett had trotted down the trail with it on his shoulder. Jack couldn't keep pace. He stopped to switch the cooler to his other shoulder and to get a better grip on Larry's metal detector, thinking how the poor fat guy had come out with his coin shooter, as he called it, to indulge in his hobby of collecting arrowheads, old cartridge casings, coins, bottles, and other Old West relics, only to get mistaken for an informant and murdered. Jack thought of how he might get out his knife up on the rim—he'd already made too many mistakes, so he had to do it right—then he encountered Crockett hurrying back down the trail. The trapper had already dumped his load and retraced his way about fifty yards from the rim. "Leave that stuff here," he ordered Jack, "and we'll get it on the way back. You're moving too damn slow."

On the floor of the canyon they rolled Larry Hughes out of the brush onto his back. A soaked area in the dirt where he'd been lying looked as though someone had poured a drum of oil onto the ground. The dead man's pants and shirt were slick with blood from his neck to his boots. From the front pants pocket, Crockett fished out the keys to the red Bronco. His hand came away greased with blood. "If I'd known this guy's pistol was empty, I would've taken Pritchard up on the rim," Crockett said. "But I thought they would get the best of me up there." His voice was again calm, meditative. "I know you won't think this way, but as far as I'm concerned, it was justifiable homicide. You had no right breaking into my camp like that."

"Then why not me, too?" Jack blurted out, his words snapping from the tension he couldn't hold back. "Why didn't you kill me, too?"

Crockett replied without hesitation. "I saw you didn't have a gun and were just along for the ride. You were good to me that time, and so was your uncle. He's the best man I ever worked for. Bob Pritchard was a son of a bitch." He grabbed Larry by the arm. "Here, let's get this tub of guts out of here. This guy was just too damn dumb to stay alive."

They got Larry Hughes stood up between them, but he was too heavy to lift onto the packsaddle, and the mule wouldn't stand still long enough for them to get the body leveraged against it. Crockett let go, and Jack found himself with his arms around the body, stumbling in a crazy dance, holding Larry up, chest to chest, cheek to cheek.

"Drop him," Crockett yelled. The body crumpled to the ground.

Jack looked at his hands, his shirt and pants, smeared black with blood.

"If you're going to throw up," Crockett said, "go over in the brush. Get away from me."

Jack tried to wipe his hands on the sides of his jeans, but they stayed sticky.

They dragged Larry onto a rock ledge and guided the mule into the depression next to the ledge so they could cantilever the body onto the packsaddle. Crockett tied Larry down under a webbing of rope. He worked fast and efficiently. "Go on and start up the trail," he told Jack. "I'll catch up."

As Jack led the mule out of the camp, he saw Crockett pour

kerosene onto the stained ground where the bodies had fallen. What the hell was he doing now? The little mule brayed and stumbled under a burden more than half its own weight. As Jack led it up the steep scree slope, it clopped forward, one unsteady hoof at a time. The fat man's body shifted, the ropes went loose, and the corpse hung sideways in a webbing of robe on the straining animal's flank. Then the mule toppled over, crashing down onto Larry, its four legs swimming frantically in the air, its swollen eyes popping from their sockets as the pack cinches across its chest and neck pulled tight. Jack whipped out his knife and cut the ropes from the choking animal. The mule with its wild, crazed eyes rolled free and scrambled to its feet.

Crockett jogged up the trail at a half trot. Behind him clouds of black smoke billowed. "Close your knife, Jack," he ordered, "and give it to me." Jack jerked with an impulse to lunge forward, but Crockett squared off against him and flipped his slicker away from his pistol handle, ready to draw. Defeated, Jack closed the knife and handed it to him. That was it. His hope had vanished. His flesh sagged on his bones with doubled heaviness as he moved to Crockett's orders. Now he had no alternative but to die.

"You thought you could stick me, didn't you?" Crockett snarled. "You double-crossing son of a bitch. You're like the rest. One more move like that, buddy, and that's it for you. Now get this fat slob's arms."

They tried lifting the heavy corpse back onto the packsaddle, but there was no way they could get it off the ground. The fat man was just too much weight, and the mule was too skittish.

"The only way we're going to get him out of here," Crockett said, "is to quarter him."

Jack looked down into the camp and saw the deer parts hanging on tripods. He knew his face reflected horror. The idea was monstrous. "You can't do that!" he shouted.

Crockett nodded, glancing away from Jack's anguished face. "I don't have the stomach for it either. We're going to have to hide him down in the willows."

They tied ropes from the mule to Larry's ankles and started to drag him on his back toward the creek. Larry's shirt scraping over the rocky ground ripped away in shreds. Then the body snagged against a protruding boulder, and the rope around Larry's ankles jerked his boots free. White socks covered his feet. The little mule, its load lightened, leaped forward, dragging the boots away from Larry's body, which lay hung up against the boulder, stained with lichen.

Enraged, Crockett pulled the mule's head around by the halter and cracked it under the jaw with his fist. He picked up a piece of firewood and began thrashing the mule, holding the halter with one hand and hitting with the other, while the mule backpedaled through the brush, dragging Crockett with him, until they both fell to the ground, crashing through sagebrush, Crockett still swinging, his face scrunched in anger.

He's going to kill me, too, Jack thought. As soon as we get this job done, he's going to kill me. But he's going to let me walk my own corpse to the rim first.

This time Crockett roughly tied the rope around Larry's neck and began dragging him facedown across the ground. Crockett hurried the mule, and Larry's body jolted and bounced over brush and jutting rocks. His belt buckle broke free, and his pants slid down, exposing his enormous buttocks. Jack ran forward, gasping, and tried to pull the pants up, wanting to leave the man some measure of dignity, but Crockett wouldn't slow up. He continued dragging the body, its neck stretching, along the willows toward some beaver dams.

"Rub out my skid marks," he shouted at Jack.

Jack started to scrape his boot sole over the dirt, trying to smooth the hoofprints and drag marks.

"Use your hands," Crockett yelled.

The mule dragged the body into some marshy ground along the willows as Jack worked his way back toward the camp on his hands and knees, smoothing and scuffing the ground as best he could, his vision wavering behind tears, or stinging sweat—he couldn't tell which. This is so crazy, he kept thinking. Blood lay all over the place now. How did this madman think he could get all the blood hidden?

Crockett returned to the camp with the riderless mule and turned it loose, smacking it on the rump so it would head up the canyon away from the body. "I cut that other bitch loose, too," he said about the other hobbled mule. "Come on. It's getting dark. We have to get out of here."

The winter sun like a white metal disk neared the south rim of the canyon. Jack stared at his digital watch. He read the numbers. He looked at the sun, then back at his watch with gathering shock. Bob and Larry had now been dead for nearly four hours.

"Stop," Crockett hollered, his head cocked in a listening position. "Someone's driving up on the rim. They're coming."

Jack heard only the call of a canyon wren. A nighthawk darted through the shadows on its evening feed.

"We'll have to be careful near the top," Crockett said in a whisper. "Let's go."

He led the way, loaded down with a full pack and sleeping bag, the kerosene can swinging from his arm. Jack wore Bob's day pack, stuffed with cooking gear and leftover food, and carried a folded blue tarp in his hand. They walked fast up the canyon trail, with Jack puffing hard. His arms and legs felt as heavy and unmovable as when he was at the county fair spinning around with his older daughter in a carnival ride called the Gravitron.

When he reached the canyon rim, Jack found only the trapper's pile of unloaded gear. Crockett was nowhere around. Jack walked quickly toward his truck, hurrying to reach the pistol under the seat, when Crockett's voice boomed out, "Don't even go near that truck."

The tailgate of Larry Hughes's red Bronco hung open, and Jack saw the soles of Bob's hiking boots jutting out from under the vehicle. Crockett walked up drinking a Squirt. He handed Jack a Dr Pepper. "Here," he said. "Take a rest. I don't want you having a heart attack on me."

Jack popped open the can of Dr Pepper. It had the metallic taste of blood.

Crockett leaned against the tailgate of the Bronco. "This is murder one for me. I didn't weight the body down there. They're going to find it easy."

It's coming now, Jack thought. This guy's thinking all the time. If he's so concerned about covering his tracks, he can't have an eyewitness to his crime.

"I'm sorry you're involved in this, Jack," he said. "If you'd come here alone, none of this would've happened. Why do lawmen have to be so pushy? Come on. They're not going to find this body. They can't nail me as a cop killer without a body."

The sun had vanished behind the horizon, leaving the sky opalescent blue in the west and inky in the east. Three hundred feet below, darkness blanketed the canyon floor. Jack looked down at a bat flying out of sight into the low shadows.

Crockett had emptied the cargo bay of the Bronco and piled all the gear into the backseat. He dragged Bob out from under the car. Jack helped wrap Bob in the blue tarp and lift him into the cargo bay, but the dead man's legs wouldn't bend—they'd already stiffened up—so his feet stuck out the open rear window.

Crockett pulled the Bronco forward, poured kerosene where Bob had lain, and struck a match. Deep orange flames quivered across the ground.

"You drive," Crockett gruffly told Jack.

Jack slid behind the steering wheel. "Where to?"

"Gerlach. Eddie Dodd's place."

His mind pressed with grief and confusion, Jack gave up trying to figure out Crockett's thinking. If Billy wanted to get rid of Bob's body—and him—why wasn't he heading north, up toward the Sheldon National Wildlife Refuge? No one would find two corpses in that desolate country.

Frost covered the windows. The kerosene flames diminished to a blurry yellow wink in the rearview mirror, then vanished. Jack turned on the wipers and the defroster to clear the windshield. Once off the canyon rim, he headed south on the dark, deserted road. He drove without thinking, letting his sluggish limbs respond mechanically.

Crockett jerked forward. "Is that a truck coming up there?"

Dazed, Jack searched the horizon. "I don't see anything."

"There. Coming over the hill."

But only stars popped into view, breaking through clouds.

Crockett leaned back. "I never asked anything from anyone, and I always paid for what I got. All I wanted was to be left alone, to live a natural life. I never took from nature more than I needed to live. My law is the natural law. Nobody else lives like me anymore."

Jack didn't say anything, and he had the feeling he wasn't expected to.

Crockett went on, almost talking to himself, "I never felt greedy like other trappers. If Scotty Larsen had his way he'd kill every animal on the mountain. Look at that big log house he built in Gerlach. Greed built that house."

All the way to Gerlach, Crockett got jumpy whenever he thought he saw an approaching car. Once he really did see lights, and he made Jack pull off the road, and he took the keys. "If they stop, you tell them I'm hiding in the brush and have them covered, so tell them to keep going." He got out of the truck, but the lights were those of a low-flying plane.

They reached Gerlach after several hours, but Jack no longer had any sense of time. Except for an hour or two of fitful sleep, he'd been awake now for some thirty hours.

They drove through the dark town and pulled around Eddie Dodd's bar to the barkeep's house. Crockett went up to the door, the porch light went on, and someone growled, "What is it?"

Jack, listless in the dark cab, heard Crockett say, "Eddie, I need some help. Some Fish and Game boys tried to bust me. I dusted one of them. The body's in the car."

"I don't want anything to do with it," Eddie Dodd said from behind the screen door.

Crockett called Jack into the house. Under the harsh kitchen light, Crockett's pale blue eyes looked jumpy. Dirt and blood smeared his yellow slicker. Eddie Dodd, his rotund body wrapped in a purple robe, his boozed-up nose almost the color of his robe, searched nervously around the kitchen for his horn-rimmed glasses. Jack watched him. This stubby drunk who always talked so tough in his bar, threatening to kill Division of Wildlife and Bureau of Land Management officers because they represented governmental tyranny, now shook like a penned rabbit. In the doorway his gray-haired wife, Sue, crossed her arms tight across her sunken chest, her bony fingers clutching the lapels of her velour robe. "We don't want any trouble, Billy," she whined.

"You won't get no trouble," Crockett said, sounding exasperated with the two of them. "Just do like I say."

He asked for a pick and shovels to cache Bob's body. He also needed to borrow Eddie's pickup so the body could fit in the back. His clothes and Jack's had to be burned. Jack needed to take a shower. He wanted Eddie and Sue to wash out the back of the red Bronco and to leave it down the street near Larry's house.

"Whatever you say," Sue Dodd said.

Crockett ordered Jack into the bathroom. "Be sure to wash under your fingernails," he added.

Numb, muscles slackened, Jack pushed his head under the steaming shower nozzle. Rust-colored water swirled around his feet. He scraped at his nails and around the cuticles. He had the nightmarish impression that his own blood was rushing down his legs, twisting into the drain.

He returned to the kitchen dressed in a pair of Eddie's corduroy pants, cinched up with a belt, and a polyester dress shirt. Dodd's shoes were too small, so he wore a pair of rubber snow boots. Sue Dodd tossed his soiled clothes into the flaming wood stove.

Crockett was ready to go. He had already moved Bob's body into the back of Eddie's pickup, and he'd washed off his rain slicker. He handed Jack a down parka.

He told Eddie he'd be back after he dumped the body. "But if I'm not," he said, "tell my parents when you see them that I love them."

At Crockett's orders, Jack drove the rattling old pickup out of Gerlach, then turned northeast on the rough dirt road skirting the Selenite Range and the Black Rock Desert. He didn't know how far Crockett thought they could go on that road. If there had been any recent washouts, they wouldn't get far. The tires thudded over the ruts.

"I think we've got a flat," Crockett said.

"It's just the road."

"Pull over. Let's see. Kill the engine."

Jack checked all four tires. They were fine. Crockett stood with his back to him, pissing, as he looked out over the massive salt flat, shimmering in its own strange lunar light. "This is as good a place as any," he said, turning around and buttoning up his fly. "Get one of those shovels."

They were only a few miles out of town, on the road to Sulphur and Trego Hot Springs. The Western Pacific and Southern Pacific tracks ran along the salt flat a few hundred yards away. This country was not nearly as remote as the canyon country they'd left. Jack realized that it made no sense for Crockett to haul Bob's body all the way into Gerlach and then bury it along the railroad tracks. Why hadn't he just dumped it under the volcanic scree of some side canyon near Little High Rock?

"Hurry up," Crockett ordered.

Jack reached into the bed of the truck and grabbed a shovel. He hesitated a moment and projected his imagination, like a camera, frame by frame, through the next half dozen seconds. He saw himself turning around, pulling the shovel out of the pickup, then cracking the handle across Crockett's head. If he missed, he would be shot. If he did nothing, he would be shot anyway.

The shovel felt heavy as a barbell as he jerked it from the truck bed and whirled around. Crockett faced him with a pistol aimed at his heart. Even as Crockett smirked, he looked sad. "Sorry, Jack," he said, and fired.

Jack's back smacked the fender of the pickup, but he heard no shot. It was like getting hit by a car. The shovel dropped to the ground, and so did he, into abrupt darkness.

CHAPTER 2

When Jack opened his eyes, bright winter stars in the millions surprised him, as if the night's glittering canopy had dropped to a few feet above his nose. The rattling whine of Eddie Dodd's pickup retreated in the distance. Then there was just the desert wind.

His feet felt cold, his left side numb—arm, shoulder, chest. A gurgling sound, like someone slurping soda through a straw from the bottom of a waxed cup, came from his chest. From the rale he knew he'd been lung shot. His breath quickened, and so did a new sound like rapidly crackling cellophane. A lung-shot animal could live a long time if it didn't exert itself. He tried to steady his breathing.

The coldness in his feet started to seep like chilled sludge up into his stomach. He was going into shock. He concentrated on not giving in. With his right hand he worked the zipper of the big parka up to his neck; he rolled onto his uninjured side and curled into a fetal position. A coyote cut loose with a yowl, echoed in the distance by others. Jack lay still, listening to the howls, the wind, and the rhythmic gurgling sound in his left lung. He felt a strange, disturbing distance from himself—from his body, his pain.

That's how Jim Sandoval, the sheriff's investigator and Jack's old school buddy, found him at midmorning. The deputy covered him with an emergency foil blanket and called for an ambulance. The desert sun warmed Jack's face. Jim Sandoval knelt and talked to him until the paramedics arrived; the deputy's wide, fleshy face, with its generous grin and Mexican *bandido* mustache, hovered in a cone of light. A halo of shadows flickered around his black curly hair. My angel, Jack thought.

When the paramedics lifted him onto the stretcher, the sparkling Technicolor desert—the flaring sun, translucent sky—faded into terrifying darkness.

He drifted in and out of consciousness for the rest of the morning, aware of doctors and nurses like so many disembodied faces and hands at work cleaning, patching, and taping him back together. Wheeled into a room and hooked up to a network of tubes, he watched someone else's blood in a plastic bag, mingling with his own—type O negative, he knew, that rare blood common to Basques, probably donated by someone whose ancestors had known his in the Pyrenees. All these people, invisible and visible, keeping him alive.

After the operation, Beth walked through the door like an apparition wearing blue jeans and a white cable-knit sweater. Teary-eyed and smiling, she held his hand. He felt safe, protected, and overwhelmingly sad. It had taken a near deadly wound to impel them to hold hands with affection.

The bullet, he learned, had sliced between his ribs, puncturing the lung. A tube went into his chest to drain the blood.

Doctors estimated that if all went well he could be out of the hospital in a week, although it would be much longer before he could go back to work. With rest, the deflated lung would heal itself. The freckled, red-haired surgeon who'd operated on him said, "You're very lucky."

Lucky? Jack wondered. Crockett had shot him with the small-caliber trapper's pistol he kept in his shoulder holster rather than the .357 Magnum he wore on his hip. The bigger gun would've left him as stiff as Bob and Larry Hughes. Even the .22 fired into his heart or head would've done the job. Crockett was too good a shot not to hit where he wanted. Jack found himself in the sad position of feeling grateful to a murderer for choosing not to kill him.

The Washoe County sheriff, Ben Nelson, and an FBI agent came into the room the next day. The FBI was on the case because of Jack. Murder could be left to local authorities, but forcing Jack to drive down the road was kidnapping, a federal offense. That was the red flag that waved in the Federal Bureau of Investigation.

Jack found it a strain to talk. Thank God, the doctors had kept out the reporters. The cops had already pieced together much of what had happened. The morning after Jack had been shot, Eddie and Sue Dodd had driven into Reno with their lawyer to report what they knew to the district attorney. They said that two hours or so after Billy Crockett had left their house with Jack, Crockett returned to the house alone and made Eddie drive him out to the salt flat. "You'll wear a lot of heat for this," he told Dodd. Billy carried a backpack loaded with food, two pistols, and a .300 Savage with a telescopic sight. When Eddie dropped him off, Billy said, "I botched the job on those other two, but they had it coming. You can call the cops in the morning and tell them they can find Jack Irigaray on the road to Trego Hot Springs." The last Eddie saw of Crockett, he was heading northeast across the Black Rock Desert.

By the time Jack was found and Eddie Dodd could drive into Reno, Crockett had been on the run for over seven hours, and nobody had any idea where he'd dumped Bob's body.

The FBI agent, Fred Banfield, a soft-spoken, brooding man with dark pouches under his eyes, asked Jack which way Crockett had driven after he shot him.

"I think he was going back to Gerlach," Jack said. "I couldn't see the truck."

"But you could hear it."

"Yes, but it was hard to tell which way it was going."

"Well, was the sound coming from the direction of your head or your feet?"

"I was shot. I wasn't thinking about directions."

The FBI agent glared as though he suspected Jack might be in cahoots with Crockett, just as maybe Eddie Dodd was. Jack knew the FBI didn't trust Dodd; no one did. Everyone knew he was the king of bullshit. They didn't even believe he was telling the truth about where he'd dropped off Crockett in the desert. And since they didn't have a body, Bob's murder was still just an allegation.

Fred Banfield and the sheriff asked Jack the details about the shooting, where it happened, and where Larry Hughes was hidden. Eddie Dodd had claimed he knew nothing about Hughes or where he might be found. Jack felt weak; he had trouble remembering exactly how many rounds Crockett had fired.

"Probably six," he said.

"So his gun was empty," the sheriff said. "He was unarmed."

"I'm not sure."

"Why aren't you sure?"

"He had the gun pointed at me. He acted like it was loaded."

"What provoked the actual murders?" the FBI agent asked.

"You tell me. Crockett claimed he wasn't going to be arrested again."

"He killed two men over misdemeanors?"

"That's what happened."

"Did you or Pritchard threaten him?"

"No. I didn't even have a gun."

"Well, then why did he shoot?"

"I don't know."

"You were there, weren't you?"

Jack felt as if he was going to throw up, and the floor nurse notified the special agent and the sheriff that they had used up the time the doctor had allotted them.

When Jack awoke, his chest throbbed. The nurse brought a pill. Outside the dark window of the hospital room flashed the purple neon of the Circus Circus Casino. People were drinking, laughing, gambling, and watching circus acts just a block away. The casino and St. Mary's Medical Center. Life and Death. This view from the hospital window had also been his father's when he had died. Jack wished the view out the window had offered his father—and now him—a brighter spur to get better than a neon vision of more drinks and another spin of the roulette wheel.

He watched the evening news on the small television that swung over his bed on a moveable metal arm. A news helicopter showed an aerial view of Little High Rock Canyon, a dark gash in the desert. Snow still hadn't fallen, but the temperature had dropped. Dusk shrouded the canyon. Crockett's white canvas tent slid into view. Forensic experts had arrived at the scene of the crime with their cameras, tape measures, labels, and clear plastic bags to collect evidence. The helicopter flew upstream. A hundred yards from the camp, Larry Hughes's body had drifted free of the red willows and floated facedown where the creek widened into a beaver pond, now iced over. From the waist down, except for his white socks and the shredded pants bunched around his ankles, Larry was naked. Men stood in the freezing pond chipping the body out of the ice.

A National Guard helicopter rose from the canyon floor with the corpse zipped into a rubber body bag. The chopper pivoted its dragonfly nose and headed south, the dark burden swaying from its underbelly in a sling.

The last image Jack had of Larry Hughes before he went into the body bag was of those bulbous white buttocks encircled in ice. That's what Larry's wife and children would confront on their living-room TV—a husband's and father's naked backside exposed for all the world to see. This was the dead man Jack had clutched against his chest, struggling to hold the man up, with arms tight across his back, as if he could drag him away from death by not letting him drop. Jack remembered the lifeless head flopping against his neck, the fat man's blood soaking into his clothes, sticking to his hands, seeping under his fingernails.

At that moment he felt such electrifying hatred toward Billy Crockett that he resolved to do whatever he could to be sure Crockett paid for what he'd done. Only one other shock his father's death—had struck similar light into his soul. His father had worked in casinos most of his life, moving from a job as a pit boss in Elko to managing John Ascuaga's Nugget Casino in Sparks. He wanted nothing to do with the struggle of living off the land, as his parents had done and his brother Pete continued to do. He dreamed of moving away from the desert and retiring with Jack's mother to a house on the California coast. After he'd found his dream home and cemented the sale with a down payment, his car had skidded on black ice and crashed in the Sierra. He had died in St. Mary's before Jack could reach him.

That's when Jack had resolved to become the professional his father had always wanted him to be. "It's important to have a career, not just a job," his father had said. "Do something you love." That's when Jack knew he'd be a wildlife biologist. He was in college, and his life and its purpose came into focus. He'd intended to go on to get a master's degree in wildlife management, but he and Beth got married, a job at the Stillwater hatchery opened up, Carrie was born, then Sarah—and then he'd begun to drift through life, while he and Beth drifted apart. Too many years had receded into a blur.

Jack knew he hadn't been fair to Beth, especially with the booze. They hadn't been on a real vacation together for years—visiting her parents in California was hardly a vacation for either of them. Beth's allergies prevented her from camping with him, but she loved scuba diving—they had qualified together when they were in college and had spent their honeymoon diving in the Mexican coral reefs near Zihuatanejo. That was eight years ago. He resolved to do it again, as soon as the hole in his lung closed up.

When he'd started work as a game biologist he'd slept as many as two hundred nights a year in the brush—that's why he'd taken the job—to be outside. Now the job kept him more hours at a desk than in the field. It was frustrating to stare at numbers and statistics about herd counts and animal population projections on a green computer screen until his vision blurred, while wanting to be in the desert and mountains, to see the animals themselves. He needed a change, but new openings in the division came up rarely—wildlife biologists and wardens changed jobs less often than most government workers. He'd heard, though, that the game biologist in Winnemucca was scheduled to retire. It was about time—the guy had hung onto the position for thirty years. He was an old-time glad-hander who did more for the ranchers and the hunters than for the animals. Many would look at a move to Winnemucca as a step down, but if he took the job, Jack knew he'd have more time in the field again. He'd be in charge of reintroducing bighorns into the northern ranges. The girls would have the advantages of a good small-town school. Beth could take up her nursing again without the hassle of working in a big city hospital. Reno was growing into an unlivable mess, according to all the reports. Just a few weeks ago, Beth had showed him an article in *Psychology Today* claiming that Reno's rate of alcoholism, crime, suicide, and divorce made it the most stressful city in the country. Beth put more faith in those reports than he did—the gambling and divorce industry skewed everything—but he was heartened to think that maybe she shared his thoughts about moving.

When Beth visited him the following evening, Jack was eating dinner with some difficulty—pain flamed through his chest every time he raised his arm. She had brought a large crayoned picture Carrie had drawn of Jack in bed surrounded by figures of numerous animals and birds—a deer, a rabbit, a coyote, a bighorn, an eagle, and a kit fox. Out of the cartooned mouths of Carrie and her younger sister, Sarah, ballooned the words, "Come home, Daddy!"

Carrie, almost six, was all spindly arms and legs. Jack thought her ability to draw was remarkable for her age, but he figured that perhaps lots of children could draw like that— with all the daycare and preschool kids got nowadays. Such talent was so far beyond what he and his schoolmates had been capable of that he always considered Bob Pritchard's ability to paint and draw somewhat magical; Bob's birds and animals weren't great art, but some little detail—the way he captured how a hawk cocked its head or a coyote lifted its paw—made them special. Jack had framed and hung two of Bob's drawings in his TV room.

Beth took off her green parka. She wore a baby-blue lamb's wool sweater, jeans, and sneakers. She brought Jack a pile of magazines—*People, Vanity Fair*, things like that. "Here's some mind rot," she said, "but I figure they're better than TV. I didn't think I should bring the girls yet. But they miss you."

"I miss them, too."

Beth noticed on the order form for the next morning's breakfast that Jack had checked scrambled eggs. She scrutinized his dinner with the critical eye of a former nurse and shook her head. "I can't believe hospitals are still giving people such unhealthy glop."

The evening meal didn't look great—gray beef streaked with whitish gravy and soggy kernels of corn. "It's not so bad," Jack said, and he meant it. People always complained about bland hospital food, but after what he'd been through, the first tastes had a salty zing that made his tongue tingle in happy awareness that he was alive.

"You shouldn't be ordering eggs," Beth said.

"Well, are pancakes with syrup and butter much better?"

Beth smiled wearily and again shook her head. When they'd met, she was doing clinical work for her nursing degree. After getting her BSN she had continued to work until a couple of years ago when Sarah was born. Jack sometimes thought that the trouble had started when Beth quit working. Not that housework and taking care of two kids wasn't work— he knew better—but he felt that the real world didn't press in on her in the same way as when she'd had to get up and go out to a job every day. It was different now than it had been for her mother and grandmother, with TV, microwaves, and other gadgets—not easier, but different. Anyway, shortly after she'd quit nursing, the animal rights activism and the white witchery stuff had started up.

When Jack told Beth of his desire to apply for the biologist's job in Winnemucca and of the advantages they all would have in a small town, she said, "We can talk about these things when you get out. I called your mother, and she and Steve are coming to see you tomorrow."

"Oh, God," Jack moaned. "Tell 'em to stay away."

"She's your mother."

"But he's not my father."

Technically, Steve was Jack's stepfather, but Jack had never taken a shine to the man. A retired accountant, Steve had married Jack's mother less than a year after her husband's

death—too soon as far as Jack was concerned. The newly-
weds had immediately moved to Grass Valley in California.
His mother seemed happy with Steve, and Jack came to be
glad for her. He didn't want his resentment at her sudden re-
marriage to last. He wasn't one to carry a grudge, but he had
no intention of cozying up to his stepfather.

He tried to get Beth back on track about the possibility of
moving out of Reno. "I'll bet you could get a job as a nurse in
the school system or for the county health department. I
know how you feel about hospitals."

"It's not just hospitals, Jack, it's medicine. Healing is more
than just popping a pill or getting a shot."

"Well, I'm glad for my pills and shots."

"You should be. Sometimes you need them, but they're
not everything."

A nurse who came to take away the food tray complimented
Jack on his appetite. "He eats good," she said to Beth, flashing
gold-rimmed teeth. After the nurse moved to the patient on
the other side of the sliding curtain, Jack said to Beth, "We
both need some time off. We haven't done anything fun together for ages." He was thinking of the trip to Mexico, but
he wanted to get everything planned as a surprise.

"It's true," Beth replied, "we haven't been making each
other very happy."

"Things are going to be different," he assured her. He took
her hand.

"Do you need me to bring you anything?"

He wanted to ask for a tin of Copenhagen. The meal had
left a longing for the calming taste of doctored tobacco. But
he didn't dare ask. "I'm fine," he said. "In fact, I wish people
wouldn't send me these flowers." He cast a sweeping glance
toward the potted plants and cut flowers on the counter and
along the windowsill. "They make me feel like I'm in a funeral
parlor. Except for those tea roses, of course."

Beth smiled. Sometimes with her big head of blond curls,

large mouth, and wide-apart eyes, she had the look of a lioness. She'd brought the roses, and he did like them. Yellow tea roses had been her favorite flowers when they were in college, and he still gave them to her on special occasions. Though the last time was when Sarah was born.

Beth gave him a peck on the cheek and left. He felt relieved to have her gone. What a strain things were between them, he thought. They couldn't even talk about hospital food without hovering on the edge of an argument. How had they let their marriage come to this?

He made it through the next day, feeling better, keeping his eye on the TV reports about the search for Crockett. Between eighty and a hundred armed men, many in bulletproof vests, were scouring Crockett's old haunts in the northern mountains and deserts between Gerlach and Winnemucca, some of the roughest, most remote country in the state, the newscasters stressed. Patrolmen had set up roadblocks in towns and were stopping men with ponytails and beards. The Division of Wildlife and the Forest Service had sent two Cessnas to comb canyons from the air. Two five-men FBI SWAT teams from Reno and Las Vegas appeared on the evening news in commando outfits boarding a helicopter to begin a systematic search of desert hiding places. Tracking dogs accompanied deputies in camouflage suits to the point where Eddie Dodd had supposedly dropped off Crockett. But the dogs, sweeping their trained noses frantically back and forth, picked up no scent from ground frozen hard as iron.

A photograph of Crockett, provided by the FBI, flashed on the screen. The previous day newscasters had presented only a vague description of Crockett along with one of those composite police sketches that always look like a hundred people in general and no one in particular. The black-and-white photograph from the FBI files had been taken in 1973 when Crockett was arrested for draft evasion. That's when he was doing ranch work for Jack's uncle Pete. Two FBI agents and a deputy sheriff dressed as ranch hands had apprehended Crockett in a buckaroo line shack northeast of Paradise Valley. For some reason, the newsman said nothing about that arrest. The program just showed the photograph of the hatless, beardless man, nearly ten years younger, and read a police description of him. The same description appeared in that day's *Reno Gazette-Journal*:

> Height: 5′10″; Weight: 180 lbs; Light brown hair (may be shoulder-length, worn braided or in a ponytail); Blue eyes, wears glasses, may have full beard. No known scars. Thirty years old, born 1–10–52. Subject is armed and extremely dangerous. Wanted for kidnapping, attempted murder, and 1st degree murder (2 counts). A reward of up to $25,000 is offered for information leading to his arrest and conviction.

When Jack read the description in the newspaper, he was stunned to realize that the physical description, except for the glasses and ponytail, could have fit him. Crockett's hair was lighter and probably should've been called blond, but otherwise he and Crockett were the same height and weight, had the same color eyes. In the past Jack had even worn a beard. They were the same age, born two months apart—but at opposite ends of the country. Jack knew Crockett wasn't a true westerner. Uncle Pete had told Jack that Billy had come from some state back east—Illinois or Indiana. What was Crockett's ethnic background? Although Jack's looks—fair skin, blue eyes, and light hair—didn't fit the stereotype of Basques, he'd been told his features were commonplace in the old country. That's why for years people mistakenly thought some racial connection existed between the Basques and the ancient Vikings. "I saw a thousand boys who look like you," his dark-haired uncle had told him after a European trip. There was no way Crockett could also be Basque. With that name and his looks, he was quintessentially American, probably a hodgepodge of Anglo-Saxon ingredients blended together on some earlier Appalachian frontier.

On the late-night news a reporter was shown interviewing Crockett's father, William David Crockett, Sr., a big barrel-chested man, in front of a mobile home somewhere in Tennessee. "We're all tore up over what happened," Crockett's father said, "but we're standing by our boy. He wouldn't do nothing he didn't think was right."

The next day Jack suffered a relapse. Nurses jabbed needles into his arm. He had a temperature of 104. He thought he felt Beth's hand on his forehead, but when he opened his eyes he saw Bob's wife, Cindy, her green eyes watery and her pretty face and pert nose blotched pink from crying. Jack tried to smile and comfort her, but it was useless. When she was gone, he kept seeing Crockett's face, his smirk—if only he'd grabbed the .22 in the tent, maybe he could've saved Bob. He could still see Bob on the ground, lifting his head, his fearful eyes searching for Jack's, before Crockett shot him in the skull.

The ruddy face of Father McGinnis, the parish priest, hovered over him, apparently scrutinizing his physical and spiritual condition. For a moment, Jack thought he was being offered the last rites, but Father McGinnis was just making his routine Thursday sick calls. Jack had stopped going to Mass in college but had started up again after Carrie was born. She would soon make her first Communion. Many friends his age were in the same boat. They had kids; they went to church.

Someone had left two circular tins of Copenhagen on the bedside tray. In his fever, he must've asked somebody for them. But who? Beth, Jim, Cindy, his mother, his stepfather, friends, coworkers—they were all a blur. Being sick in a hospital and facing visitors was hard work. He just wanted to be alone. He wanted to get better and get out of that room. He just didn't want to see any more sad smiles of well-wishers.

At eleven o'clock he flipped on the TV news and through a feverish blur watched sheriff's deputies rush toward an abandoned cabin near Rabbithole Creek in the Kamma Mountains. Like every other cave and cabin the armed deputies had searched during the week, it turned out to be empty. Sleet and snow now whipped across the desert. The Washoe County sheriff admitted that hope of finding Crockett was slim. "He's a tough little turkey," the sheriff explained. "He knows every badger hole and cave in the northwest part of the state. There's no telling where he is. He could live off the land for months."

"Even in winter?" a reporter asked.

The sheriff nodded. "He's completely self-sustaining."

What a crock! Jack thought. The sheriff didn't know a thing about Billy. He was just covering his ass because the guy had escaped. But at least he got part of it right. Crockett was a turkey—a turkey vulture.

Searchers had narrowed the range of their operations and were now concentrating on trying to locate Bob Pritchard's remains. Jack watched Jim Sandoval in bright blue coveralls and a red helmet rappel down a mine shaft, the rotting boards threatening to crash in on him as he descended into darkness. Jim had always been a daredevil, even in grammar school; once he'd raced his bike alongside the Southern Pacific and then jumped the bike across the tracks in front of the locomotive. If he weren't a cop, Jim would probably be getting into all sorts of trouble. On TV he was always the one in the lead as deputies rushed like commandos with their M-16s into collapsed mine buildings and caves looking for Crockett. That hot-dog Rambo mentality in too many cops had turned Jack off from law enforcement. But he couldn't help wondering what might have happened in Little High Rock Canyon if Jim Sandoval had been out there instead of him. Charge a gun and flee a knife was an old street-fighting adage. He'd had a knife and Crockett a gun, one that was probably empty, and he'd neither fled nor charged.

Jim Sandoval dropped by the hospital the next night. He was the first visitor Jack was glad to see since Beth. "I've been wanting to thank you," Jack told him, "for finding me, for saving my life."

"Glad to do what I could, Basco," Jim answered. "I wish I could find Bob, too."

"No one can say you haven't tried. I saw you on TV, rappelling down that mine shaft."

"All I turned up down there was a bunch of hibernating rattlesnakes, all tangled up."

"And nothing in the lake either," Jack added. "Isn't that right? That's what you get for listening to weirdos."

Jim grinned to cover his embarrassment. A psychic named Crystal had told police that Bob's body would be found in water. Jim and other scuba divers had plunged through the ice of Rye Patch Reservoir and swum along the weedy bottom of Pyramid Lake. "Does Beth know that dame Crystal?" Jim asked.

"She probably does. She knows them all."

"She's a hell of a looker for a flake," Jim said. "We had to follow her lead. You never know."

"The Trego Hot Springs would be a better bet than Pyramid."

"We checked them out, too. We sent sonar probes into all the reservoirs and springs. The National Guard pumped down the hot pool in Gerlach, and I dove into the rest. Nothing. We didn't find nothing."

Jack thought of the drunks in Gerlach who had jumped into the scalding pool and left behind only their bones boiled clean of flesh. He wanted to find Bob, but he didn't want to see his bones being fished out on TV.

Jack fretted to get out of the hospital. As the days went by, he lay in bed fending off visitors as best he could. At night he watched TV alone, his lip packed with snoose, using small paper cups as spittoons, padding frequently to the bathroom to empty them so the nurses wouldn't catch him.

He had mixed feelings about his inability to join the searchers. He wanted Crockett caught, but what could he possibly do that the cops weren't already doing? Normally, he would leave investigations and manhunts to the professionals—he had little use for the yahoos in this state who jumped at any chance to become gun-toting vigilantes—but he felt he had to do something to help find Bob and to track down his murderer, something, he realized, to redeem himself for all the damn mistakes he'd made, from leaving his pistol in the truck to failing to crack Crockett across the skull with the shovel.

Bob's wife, Cindy, came back to the hospital. She wanted to know exactly what had happened in the canyon. "I can't bear it, Jack," she said. "People say Crockett chopped up Bob and scattered him."

Her grief pressed on him. He wanted to deny her suspicions, but he remembered Crockett's threat about quartering Larry Hughes.

Cindy said she had put an ad in the newspaper pleading for Crockett to tell her where her husband could be found. "Why did he bother to haul Bob miles out of that canyon all the way into Gerlach?" she asked Jack. "What kind of man is he?"

"I wish I could tell you, Cindy, but I just don't know. It never made any sense to me."

As she left the hospital, Cindy said, "Well, I'll tell you. He's not a real man, or he'd help me. He's a psycho, hauling a corpse around that way. But whether he helps me or not, I'm going to find Bob."

Jack hoped somebody would spare her that pain. Larry Hughes had already been cremated, and his widow had spread the ashes over the desert where he'd spent his happiest times hunting for arrowheads and sun-stained bottles. Bob still lay somewhere out there, lost in that frozen wasteland, angry and unblessed. Jack couldn't accept the thought of Bob lying helpless and lonely in the snow, so far from anyone who loved him, pecked by buzzards, gnawed by coyotes.

At the end of the week, the manhunt for Crockett was called off. National guardsmen, state patrolmen, and deputy sheriffs went back to their routines. The FBI SWAT teams shed their camouflage suits and flew back to Reno and Las Vegas. Beth came to the hospital with Carrie and Sarah and drove Jack home. On the local news that night, Jack saw Eddie Dodd handing out free stenciled T-shirts at his bar that read across the front in big red letters GO, BILLY, GO!

CHAPTER 3

Things at home didn't go as Jack had planned. He felt rotten most of the time, his torn lung insistent in its ache, a hot pressure under his ribs. He spent the afternoons sprawled in the BarcaLounger like a beetle on its back. The TV flickered constantly, the droning sound low. Outside, snow piled up.

One evening little Sarah knocked over a kitchen stool behind him, and the crack of wood striking the quarry tile floor jolted his heart. He knew Sarah had been playing around with the stool. He'd heard the groan of its skids as she pushed it across the floor with her chubby little hands, but when it cracked against the tile, he jerked the recliner into a sitting position and felt something tear in his rib cage. "What the hell are you doing?" he yelled at her.

Sarah began to bawl. Beth came around the floating tiled counter that separated the raised kitchen from the TV room. She swooped Sarah up from the floor. "What's the matter, honey?" she asked the baby.

Sweat chilled Jack's neck. "Why's she dragging that damn stool out of the kitchen?"

Sarah sobbed, "Daddy's mean to me."

"Jack," Beth scolded, "you don't have to make the children cry."

Like a lot of nurses, Beth had a low tolerance for the sufferings of convalescents. Once the wound was patched up, the broken bone set, or the disease cured, she expected patients to accept any lingering pains as the price they should be glad to pay for being alive. She became inured to any subsequent moans or complaints. Not that he complained—he didn't— but he did involuntarily groan in his sleep, and at times he bolted up in bed from bad dreams. A counselor at the hospital told him to expect such things; the aftermath of a gunshot wound was long and traumatic. Beth mixed up some potions from her vials of homeopathic medicine and encouraged him to get out, to take walks, and even to go to the gym for a light workout. A workout? He felt he could hardly walk to the gym, let alone lift a barbell.

He looked forward to the calm of the afternoons, when Carrie was in school, Beth out of the house—at the gym or the store or with one of her groups—and Sarah asleep or at daycare, depending on Beth's wishes. He liked the days when snow tapped against the sliding glass doors between the rec room and the backyard. The flickering TV and the cats snoozing in the wintry light—Hod, Netzach, and Kether, all witches' names—kept him company. He tried "imaging" happier times, the method the hospital counselor advised to ward off the sediments of depression that gathered in deeper layers each day.

He thought of Beth and himself scuba diving in Mexico on their honeymoon. Downward they dove into increasing darkness until everything gleamed inky blue. Beth swam below him, her long hair hidden beneath a midnight-blue Speedo cap. Below her yawned a frightening vacuum of blackness. A dark cliff loomed into view. Bright, pop-eyed fish streamed out of a hole in the rock. Beth hovered calmly alongside the rippled coral with her arms and legs spread like an astronaut in outer space. The next second it looked as though the top of her skull blew off. The Speedo cap shot upward like a rocket propelled by a fizzy trail of bubbles. Beth's long blond strands uncoiled upward and outward like frantic tentacles. Jack dove down to her. They floated face mask to face mask, her lips swollen around the mouthpiece, as was normal when diving. Her pale hair stretched straight up, wavering like kelp in the current. She patted the top of her head, signaling that everything was all right. He realized that the pressure of Beth's bunched-up hair straining against the stretched elastic of the Speedo cap, and the bubbles of oxygen trapped beneath it, had caused the cap to shoot free like a snapped rubber band.

Back on the beach they were as giddy as kids; they were daring space travelers returned to a familiar, comfortable, oxygen-rich planet. That night they drank fruit drinks on a patio and held each other. Their touches were tentative and tender as if to communicate their shared discovery of how fragile they were. How lucky they were to have each other.

Late one afternoon, still intending to surprise Beth with a holiday trip, Jack called Ponderosa Travel to ask about flights to Mexico's Pacific Coast. More than ever he and Beth needed time away. He learned that the beach area near Zihuatanejo had been converted into a giant resort called Ixtapa, with a jetport and a string of high-rise hotels that dwarfed the little cove and fishing village where they'd spent their honeymoon. "Hardly anybody stays in Zihuatanejo anymore," the travel agent said. "Everyone stays in Ixtapa."

"Is that so?" Jack replied. "Let me think about it. I'll call back."

Friday evening he drove over to see Jim Sandoval at his home. It was his first venture out in the car, and he maneuvered cautiously through the snowy streets. Jim's door was opened by a tall willowy blond girl wearing a V-neck lavender sweater, who looked no more than twenty, her pouty mouth shiny with lip gloss and tomato sauce. The deputy sat at the kitchen table in a polo shirt that showed off his muscular arms and the black curly hair nestled at his throat. His thick bandit mustache jumped as he smiled, but he looked weary, his eyes red-rimmed. He nodded toward the flat cardboard box on the table. "Want some pizza, Basco?"

"Thanks, I already ate."

"Beer?"

Jack helped himself to a Corona from the fridge. The popped cap released a skunk smell. The bottle must've been sunstruck—a problem he knew with beer in clear or green bottles exposed to sunlight. But he didn't say anything. Before he'd learned the cause, he'd drunk so many sunstruck Heinekens in college, he'd assumed the taste was natural. He stuffed a crescent of lime down the neck of the bottle.

Jim introduced his girlfriend—Kristin was her name. Jack had met several of Jim's girlfriends since the deputy's second divorce; most were like this one. At backyard parties around swimming pools, Jack and his buddies became acutely aware of their flabby stomachs and their wives' childbearing sags whenever Jim showed up, as he usually did, with a young hardbelly like Kristin.

"I have to talk to Jack for a while, honey," he told the girl. He looked at his watch. "We'll go out in half an hour or so."

Kristin gave Jack a pouty look and left the kitchen to watch television.

Jack told Jim that he was concerned about everyone giving up the search for Crockett.

"We're following up every lead we get," Jim assured him. "We couldn't justify the expense of maintaining a full-scale manhunt on the desert, but we're on the case. The FBI is too. I've personally made Crockett my top priority. I have no intention of letting a cop killer stay free."

"What kind of profile do you have on him?"

"That's the funny thing. I always thought the guy was from around here, but he's not."

"I know. He's an easterner."

"That's right. He came out from Illinois when he was eighteen."

"He worked for my uncle in Paradise Valley for several years."

"I talked to your uncle Pete," Jim said. "Crockett was pretty much a loner—quiet, cordial, but a loner. He's only been arrested once, for draft evasion, but the charges were dropped. I've been back to his camp twice, looking for evidence, but we don't have much to go on. He kept a clean camp. The forensic boys found some scraps from a Pillsbury flour bag and a cellophane butterscotch candy wrapper."

"He had a thing for butterscotch. Larry Hughes was bringing him some butterscotch pudding."

"What doesn't make sense is all the trouble he took to haul Bob Pritchard's body out of the canyon and to try burning out the bloodstains on the ground. That didn't accomplish anything. Tests showed the blood soaked in the dirt matched the blood types of Hughes and Bob."

"And he left me as a witness."

"That's right, he left an eyewitness. He would've been much better off killing you, Jack."

Jim repeated what Jack had already read in the papers about the raid on the old Airstream trailer where Crockett lived, behind Eddie Dodd's bar. There they found Crockett's fancy spurs with big Mexican rowels, a pair of hand-tooled, red-topped Cristóbal Romero boots, and a small arsenal. "The guy had ten pistols of all kinds with speed loaders and combat grips," Jim said, "and about a dozen rifles—an M-16, an AK-47, an AR-15, a Ruger submachine gun—all kinds of knives, a bulletproof vest, and human-shaped police targets. I even found a gas mask and an Israeli tank helmet. He had cartridge reloaders and cases of about three thousand rounds of ammunition."

"They say he has caches of weapons hidden all over the desert."

"Where was this guy when Che needed him?"

"He's going to be hell on wheels to deal with. He had a bunch of books about commando strategy and quick-draw techniques."

"Yeah," Jack said sarcastically, "my uncle said he read quite a bit."

"He did," Jim replied. "He really did. We found a lot of Louis L'Amour novels, maybe twenty or thirty. *Soldier of Fortune* magazines. He also had two books—manuals, I guess you'd call them—*Kill or Be Killed* and *No Second Place Winner,* about gunfighting. That guy wasn't just a poacher. He had mayhem on his brain."

"Where do you think he is, Jim?"

"Well, he could be most anywhere. You can't believe the sightings we've had reported to us. I've stopped buses and trains he was supposed to be on. I've gone into casinos and malls where he was spotted. There are a lot of nutty people seeing things out there, but I guarantee you I've checked every lead I've gotten in this state. But now we're getting reports from the Yukon, from Mexico, from Texas—you name it. He's like Elvis."

"I don't understand how he's getting away, if the FBI is really tracking down these leads."

"It's because he's not at those places. I think he's still out there—in the desert. That's the country he knows, and that's where he's hiding. And that's where I'm going to get him."

"Jim, I want you to promise me that when you think you've found him, you'll tell me."

"Don't worry, Jack. When we get him—if I'm involved—you'll be there."

Kristin came back into the kitchen and pulled a bent wedge of pizza from the box. She looked down her nose at Jack in an insolent way as she tilted her head back and bit off the pointy red tip, letting the strings of cheese slide into her mouth. With the thumb of her free hand resting at the back of Jim's neck, she massaged the base of his skull. It was time for Jack to go.

Outside the door tiny snowflakes swirled in the porch light.

"I feel bad that we never found Bob's body," Jim said. "His wife is in an awful way about it. She's been putting a lot of pressure on me to keep looking."

"You've got to keep looking, Jim. You have to find him."

"We intend to. If only that bastard would just have the decency to let someone know where the body is."

"Why didn't he tell Eddie Dodd? He's just perverse. He's not gaining anything by letting Bob stay unfound."

"Except causing people a lot of grief."

Jack drove home and sat in the car in front of his house. The aftertaste of the Corona and lime made him want another. Since he'd come home from the hospital he'd taken a few nips now and then, usually in the afternoon when Beth was out, or at night after she'd gone to bed, just enough to help deaden the pain. He tried to stay away from the Copenhagen and found that he could get through the day with only three dips; then he got it down to two—one in the morning and another at night. Just that morning he'd thrown an empty tin away with the intention of quitting altogether. Now the Corona had gotten the old urge going again. All day he'd felt as if a knife were sticking between his shoulder blades, twisting, the muscles of his back wrapping tighter and tighter around the blade as the knife turned. The hell of it was that he knew a simple wad of Copenhagen under his lip would release that torment. When he got like that, he feared he could be yelling at the kids in a flash.

He decided to try to walk it off in the cold, to trudge through the snow. He'd come this far, and he didn't want to slide right back to square one. It was a little after nine o'clock. A jetliner came in low overhead, its loud roar rumbling along at a distance behind it as it dropped toward Reno's Cannon International Airport, the blinking lights on its wings intermittently bright and dull through an otherwise unseen haze of lightly falling snow. That's how he felt as he walked: he was an overburdened craft, dragging along an insistent roar at his back that he couldn't shake, his feelings flashing hot and cold. They talked about an addiction as a monkey on your back. He felt he had a rabid wolverine on his, one that when he went to bed would be chewing the base of his neck hamburger raw. And no one's fingers would be there to soothe it.

Up ahead at Greenbrae he saw the green and red letters of the 7-Eleven. He went in and bought a can of Skoal. At least that wasn't quite as potent. He could get through the night and let the Skoal go in the morning. Then on the way back home he picked up a pint of Jim Beam at the Pyramid Plaza. As the clerk rang up the sale, Jack felt himself riding an impulse and heard himself say, "Throw in a can of Copenhagen, too, would you?" That's it, he thought as he headed home, the barely visible snow pricking his face like flying sand—I'm hooked.

At the end of that week Cindy Pritchard called. Three weeks had now passed since the murders in Little High Rock Canyon. "There's a group of us going to look for Bob this weekend," she said. "Jim Sandoval told me you might like to know."

"I'll be there," Jack said.

When he told Beth about his plans, she was definitely not pleased. She'd just come back from a workshop with her animal rights group and was trying to get Sarah to drink a glass of soy milk. In the tussle with Sarah some milk splashed on the front of Beth's camel hair pants; she almost never wore skirts anymore, ever since joining her women's group.

"I wish you'd think about what you're doing, Jack." Her curly hair fell around her face as she bent over to dab her pants with a paper towel.

"I know exactly what I'm doing. I'm going to look for Bob."

He'd taken a snort before Beth came home and felt mellow enough to venture a joke. "Anyway, you're the one who says I should get out for exercise."

Her grimace showed she took the remark as a dig, not a joke. "When are you going to let this thing go? You're not going to find Bob. The search teams have looked all over. Put this thing behind you."

He tried to match her seriousness. "As long as there's a chance of finding him, I have to try."

"This isn't the movies, Jack. You've gone through enough."

"That's the trouble. I didn't *do* enough."

"You're just letting yourself get obsessed. You did everything you could that day. Most people would be dead right now. You kept yourself alive, and you can testify when they catch that murderer. That's what you can do, and that's what you should do."

He felt an impulse to say something about Mexico—to show that he thought about other things besides that day in Little High Rock Canyon—but he held back because he hadn't called back the travel agent to make plans for the trip.

Beth turned her attention to Carrie, and Jack shuffled through the pile of photocopied handouts she'd put on the kitchen table, directions for making homemade explosives in the war for animal rights. Jack thought he and Beth felt the same way about animals—most of the time—but this was going too far. These people weren't just blowing off steam; they were fanatics. That's all he needed to ruin his credibility in the state as a wildlife naturalist—to have his college-trained middle-class suburban wife arrested for bombing a fur store or a taxidermy shop.

"What's with this stuff?" he asked. "Talk about obsessions."

"This is only one thing in my life, Jack. I don't think about it day and night."

"Look, something's wacky here. You're getting mixed up with weirdos."

She swung Sarah from the chair and put her on the floor next to the scattered pieces of a Bugs Bunny puzzle. "Here, honey, why don't you show Mommy how you can put this puzzle together?" On her hands and knees, Sarah reminded Jack of how Beth might've looked as a child when her mother found her down on all fours eating kibbles from a bowl next to the family cat. "Back then," Beth had once told him, "I wanted to be a cat. Sometimes I thought I *was* a cat."

Beth rested her elbows on the counter and leaned toward him. "Things can't keep going on as they are. Your friend Bob would be alive today if Crockett didn't have a market for skins."

"Blowing up stores isn't going to make things right."

"But the *threat* of blowing them up might make people think about what they're doing. It's a one-sided war right now, and animals can't fight back."

Jack saw no sense in arguing the point. It wasn't the issue he objected to so much as that Beth's new commitments seemed to be hardening her. Even her features, the strain around her eyes, the tightness of her mouth, showed the transformation.

"Bob was my friend," he said, trying to bring them onto some common ground. "I couldn't live with myself if I didn't do something to help find him."

Her response blindsided him. "You're not going to do it with booze and a lot of agitated behavior. Bob is dead. It's yourself you have to find."

That night he slept terribly. Beth lay on her side, her back to him, breathing in a steady, peaceful unawareness of him or anything outside of herself. What trust people had to lose consciousness night after night in the presence of another! He thought of Jim lying in the comfort of Kristin's leggy embrace. When he finally fell asleep, he drifted into a disturbing, ragged dream. He saw Bob lunging with outstretched hands, trying to speak, trying to say where to find his body. When Jack opened his eyes, the afterimage of Bob faded into the room's darkness like a dissolving shade. Something about lions, "buried with lions," was all he could remember from Bob's agonized effort at communication.

He went into the TV room and stretched out on the Barca-Lounger. Trying to calm himself with Copenhagen, he abruptly felt his body go cold, like that night when he lay bleeding on the desert, listening to coyotes. Beth was right. He was letting himself get into a hell of a state. He thought he'd been doing a good job of hiding the drinking, but she just hadn't said anything about it until now. "You're obsessed," she'd said. "You're the master of your own fate," his father had always said. "Lions, buried with lions," Bob had said. Jack felt he had to get things under control. He couldn't let Bob down. He had to do what he could to find Bob and to get Crockett. He had to get things straightened out with Beth. He was losing her but hadn't lost her yet. He wasn't going to let that happen. That's what he'd resolved in the desert: if he lived, he wasn't going to lose her.

By the end of the week, both he and Beth had made an effort to be better with each other. Their tiff had touched something in both of them. They didn't talk about it, but they talked about other things in gentler ways. On Thursday night, at last, they made love. Afterward they lay in bed.

"You know what the booze does," Beth said softly. "Mom and I went through the same thing with Dad, but I won't let that happen to Sarah and Carrie."

Jack wasn't sure whether she was talking about now or last summer when he had started hitting the sauce pretty hard and she'd threatened to leave. That's when he'd quit, at the end of September. Since then, even after the shooting, he thought he'd been restrained. Moderate. He resented the comparison to her father. "I haven't done anything to you or the girls. Your father was a brute."

"No, you're not a brute. But you have to understand; you're just not there for us. Booze puts up a wall."

He'd heard it all before: You have to quit for yourself. You can't do it for anybody else.

He reached under the sheet and stroked her back, running his hand down to the base of her spine where she liked to be massaged. "I do understand," he said. "You'll see."

Beth rolled toward him. "Nothing will happen if you try to do it only for us. You have to quit for yourself." She put her arms around his shoulders and they kissed.

On Friday she had a smile for Jim Sandoval when he came by the house. Her face had regathered the good-natured softness of the college girl Jack remembered falling in love with, and she kissed him good-bye with that same anxious warmth as on New Year's Eve when he'd left with Bob to go after Crockett.

The afternoon was windy but the desert sky was cobalt blue when they arrived in Gerlach. About thirty volunteers for the search, both men and women, gathered in front of Bruno's bar and restaurant. Bob's neighbors, the Halstons, were there, along with some other friends, deputies from both Washoe and Humboldt Counties, biologists and wardens from the Division of Wildlife, and members of the Nordic Search and Rescue Squad from Tahoe. Scotty Larsen showed up with another trapper. Three men and two women from the Bureau of Land Management had prepared topographical maps marking the area with a series of concentric circles. Places previously searched had been X'd out. The search was to be systematic. Jim Sandoval had arranged for a Cessna to fly overhead as the searchers combed the ground. They all felt this would be their last chance to find Bob.

Cindy Pritchard wore one of Bob's old red-and-black-checked hunting caps with wool earflaps. Her face was flushed rosy from the cold wind, her normally bright green eyes dulled to the color of slate. "Thanks for coming, Jack." She clutched his hand. Bundled in a down jacket, she looked grimly determined, her ordinary pep girl bounciness and quick smile now subdued. Even the freckles across her nose, muted against her bright wind-stung face, had lost their jauntiness.

Bob's twenty-three-year-old son by his first marriage stood next to Cindy. "I know your being here means a lot to my dad," he told Jack, apparently indicating that he thought his dad— or his dad's soul—was somewhere watching them.

They divided into teams of four. Jack rode with Cindy, a man from the search and rescue team, and a woman from the BLM. Since the afternoon was short, they began checking out marked areas close to Gerlach. It was getting dark when they came to the place where Crockett had shot Jack. Jack was surprised that it was so near town. When he had lain out there alone that night sucking what he thought might be his last rasping breaths of oxygen on earth, he'd felt as abandoned as if he were on the moon.

Jack spent the night in Bruno's Motel with Jim Sandoval in a room next to Cindy's. Jim snored like a bandsaw. Jack wondered if that was why Jim had to keep changing girlfriends. The searchers had filled up the motel, and the spillover stayed in vans and the Halstons' RV. Several people with sleeping bags lay on the floor at Scotty Larsen's. Aware of Jim's snoring most of the night, Jack wished he'd taken up Scotty's offer to stay in his guest room.

Saturday morning was gray and wet with blowing sleet. A dozen more people had driven out from Reno. Everyone spread out in 4 × 4s to search their assigned areas. Frigid air stung the membranes of Jack's bad lung. He searched the map for someplace connected with mountain lions. "Buried with lions," Bob had tried to tell him in his dream. There was the Fox Range, Buffalo Hills, Chicken Spring, Antelope Basin, Horse Canyon, Burro Mountain, Eagle Rock Spring, Goose Spring, and even Poodle Mountain, but nothing named for lions. Mountain lions roamed the Selenite Range, and as they worked their way around the east side away from Dry Mountain toward Mud Spring and Selenite Peak, Jack hoped Bob had meant that place where Crockett had possibly bagged the lion whose pelt Jack saw in his tent. But at the end of the day the only dead things the searchers found were a frozen steer carcass, its matted hide stiff as plywood, and a sun-bleached headless skeleton of a deer.

Jack felt discouraged when the group reconvened in Gerlach that night, but Cindy clung to her hopefulness. They still had places to search, she said as they pored over maps spread out on the motel floor; the places left were those Crockett most likely had time to drive to, if Eddie Dodd was telling the truth.

"I'd like to talk to that son of a bitch myself," Cindy said angrily.

"I've already talked to Dodd," Jim Sandoval told her. "You might as well go out and talk to a buzzard."

"I'd like the chance to talk to his wife," Cindy said, "woman to woman. I can't believe she's as much of a creep as he is. I just know Crockett has been in touch with them."

A sign in the window of Eddie's Bar had said CLOSED when they'd arrived on Friday afternoon, and the sign was still there Saturday night. The man at the Texaco station told Jack that Eddie and Sue Dodd had gone out of town for the weekend.

"The scumbag knew we were coming," Cindy said. "Why isn't he in jail, anyway? He helped Crockett escape."

Jack's own rage, fueled by the day's frustrations, quickened in response to Cindy's anger. "He destroyed evidence," he added angrily. "He burned my clothes, gave Crockett food, drove him out to the Black Rock, and didn't let anybody know what had happened until it was too late to do anything about it."

"Money, too," Jim added. "Dodd denied it at first, but during a polygraph test he admitted he gave Crockett two hundred dollars that night."

"Well, why the hell isn't he in jail?" Jack yelled at Jim. "He left me out in the desert to die, for Christ's sake."

"The D.A. decided he had acted under duress," Jim explained.

"Oh, barf," Cindy blurted out. "He sure didn't make those GO BILLY T-shirts under duress. He's still helping Crockett."

The weather the next day brought fierce sheets of hard-blowing snow. The desert had no horizon, as if the salt flat had tipped upward into an impenetrable white wall. Deputies grounded the Cessna. The pinching pain in Jack's lung wouldn't let up. Several of the searchers drove home in defeat, but Cindy, more grimly determined than ever, said she would check out the remaining spots even if she had to do it alone. The few people left joined her. "We're not going to find anything," Scotty Larsen told Jack.

He was right. They returned after five in the dark, glumly whipped. Cindy burst into tears. She and Jack stood outside the motel by a BLM pickup. She pushed her face against his parka, the woolly top of her cap bristling under his chin. He put his arms around her shoulders. "I just thought," she said weakly, "if we could find poor Bob, and bury him right, we could all start to heal."

Jack felt she spoke truly for what was driving him as much as her. "You have to find yourself," Beth had snapped, but he knew his heart's wound would remain open as long as awareness of Bob's unrest stabbed at it. That was just life, not obsession. Cindy shared it. Why couldn't Beth understand? Maybe it was a primitive drive shared with his Ice Age ancestors, those people in their Altamira caves whose self-awareness as humans coincided with their awareness of death, giving rise to injunctions to bury the dead and avenge murder. How could he feel healed until Bob was at peace, the murderer struck down? He could go through the motions, but he just couldn't forget what was unfinished.

He'd seen a light in Eddie Dodd's bar as they'd driven into

town. The CLOSED sign was still in the window, but a butter-yellow Jaguar and a battered Chevy pickup were parked in front. While the searchers said good-bye and climbed into their vehicles, Jack walked over to the bar, its tan and pink walls faced with desert stone like an old-time rock jail. He didn't even try the front door but walked around to the back. Dodd's pickup was parked by Crockett's shabby Airstream trailer with its peeling aluminum skin. Jack twisted the knob and the back door swung open.

Inside the bar, a woman in a safari hat sat on a stool next to a small man who was flipping through a pile of photographs. Jess Nichols, the grizzled trapper with flaring Gabby Hayes whiskers, sat alone in the back nursing a beer. Two locals shot pool at the table where Dodd had once displayed Crockett's lion pelts. The cord from a jukebox lay on the floor unplugged. Two old-fashioned slot machines stood against the wall. Behind the bar, Eddie Dodd, looking owlish in his horn-rimmed glasses, put down his liquor glass when he saw Jack. "We're closed," he snarled.

"That's what you're saying," Jack said, "but I see different."

"This is a private party. Get the hell out."

Jack walked up to the bar and slid onto a stool. "Forget the tough talk, Eddie, and give me a beer."

Dodd's hands dropped out of sight behind the bar. "Listen, pal, if I have to get tough, you'll know it."

"I'm impressed. Can the acting and give me a beer." Jack really did want a beer. He was just about ready to walk around and draw his own. Jack remembered Dodd's mousy fright that night when he had scurried around his house carrying out Crockett's orders. Now, bolstered with booze, Eddie Dodd had returned to his normal blowhard self, a puffed-up frog. There wasn't a game warden or deputy sheriff in the county Dodd hadn't threatened to kill—behind their backs and in front of his barroom buddies.

"Your tough-guy act stinks," Jack continued. "Give me a beer or I'll get my own."

"Nuts to you, copper. In two seconds, you're going to get what you don't want."

Jack almost hoped Dodd would pull his bouncer's club up from beneath the counter, when the woman at the bar said, "Give him a beer, Eddie."

The big woman in the safari hat became familiar to Jack when she smiled, a whole-faced smile framed by a lot of laugh lines, shiny black eyes, and abundant black hair. She wore a turquoise-colored pantsuit. He'd seen her at a few Basque festivals—her maiden name was Jenny Zubillaga. Now she was married to Earl Morrison, the small man sitting next to her; he was the owner of the Jaguar franchise in Reno. Jenny Morrison still worked as a loan officer at Nevada Trust, where she'd negotiated the home mortgage for Jack and Beth several years ago. "How are you doing, Jack?" she asked.

"Is this guy a friend of yours, Jenny?" Dodd asked.

"Let's say an acquaintance," Jenny answered. "Give him a beer."

Earl and Jenny Morrison were avid chukar hunters. Jack had heard that on their stops at Dodd's bar they'd gotten to know Billy Crockett, and Jenny had developed a motherly affection for him—at least that's what Jack had been told. Earl went along with Jenny's interests and whims. She called the shots, and he walked in quickstep behind her.

Dodd acquiesced. "One beer and you're out."

Jack eyed the leather dice boxes on the counter behind him. "I'll flop you for it."

"No flops," Dodd said. "Cash money or nothing."

"What's the matter? Don't you always win at Liar's Dice?"

Dodd shut the handle of the beer spout before the mug was half full. "Okay, wise guy. You can crack wise outside." He poured the beer into the sink.

Jack noticed a wanted poster of Crockett taped on the mirror above the liquor, but covering Crockett's picture was a cutout photo of Bob Pritchard. Jack thought of the pain that picture would cause Cindy. He told Dodd, "I just want you to know you're going to pay if you're hiding anything about Crockett or Bob Pritchard."

"I'm shaking in fear."

"You're going to be more than shaking, Eddie. I just want you to know that. If I find out you've talked to Crockett and you don't have him tell us where we can find Bob, I'm going to skin you."

Everyone knew that Crockett had sought to please his surrogate Nevada daddy by molding himself into Dodd's fantasy of the hard-ass mountain man who took no shit from anyone. If Dodd really thought Jack would skin his nose, maybe he'd try to talk Crockett into telling him where the body was. At least that's what Jack was hoping.

"Your threats don't scare me," Dodd said, but his bluster had weakened. He was nervous.

"You better leave, Jack," Jenny Morrison ordered. She wasn't smiling. "You're asking to get bopped."

Outside the bar window Jim Sandoval peered in and rapped his knuckles against the dirty glass. Jack slid from the stool and went over to open the door for him. Jim's badge was pinned to his shirt, his service revolver strapped to his hip. The deputy followed Jack into the bar.

"Both of you, get out of here," Dodd shouted. "You're breaking and entering."

"What are you gonna do, Eddie?" Jack asked. "Call the cops?"

"I'll show you what I'm gonna do." His hands dropped back behind the bar.

"You tried to kill me once," Jack shouted. "You left me out in that desert to die. You're going to pay for that."

Jim grabbed Jack's arms. "Come on, Jack. You're doing no good here."

"This bastard didn't have the decency to tell anyone where I was." His lung burned.

Jenny intervened. "He thought you were dead, Jack. He didn't know you were still alive."

Jack was startled. He simply hadn't considered that when Crockett had said that Jack Irigaray could be found on the road to Sulphur, Dodd had assumed he'd meant Jack's corpse. The impression Crockett had given Dodd was wholly calculated. Why would Dodd think Crockett had only wounded him? If Jack were dead, as Dodd thought at the time, then whether he revealed the body's whereabouts right away or in the morning wouldn't make Jack any less dead, and it would give Crockett more time to escape.

"I shouldn't have told the cops anything," Dodd snarled. "Then you'd be where you belong right now."

That made Jack mad all over again, but Jim held his wrist. "Knock it off, Eddie," Jim said. "We're leaving."

"You're damned right you are."

"It's Jim's idea," Jack told him, "not yours."

Jack's eye caught a pile of photos on the bar in front of Earl Morrison. He reached over and snapped up the one on top. Jenny tried to reach across her husband and get the picture away, but Jack jerked it from her.

It was a photograph of Crockett holding up the head of a dead bighorn with enormous curled horns. Jack could see the rock-faced front of Eddie's bar in the background. He turned the picture over. It was dated with the film developing company's stamp: March 1980. Jack knew Crockett had never drawn one of the few lottery tags to hunt bighorn, and even if he had, March wasn't the season.

"Don't you ever come back in here, Irigaray," Dodd said.

Jack threw the picture onto the bar. "Tell your poacher, it's his head that's coming off next time."

Outside, Jack was trembling. He felt the pressure of Jim's hand on his back pushing him toward the motel. "That son of a bitch," Jack complained. "That dirty son of a bitch."

"That wasn't smart, Basco. In fact, that was real dumb."

Jack was thinking about the poached bighorn. Dodd had taken the picture. Crockett had shot that bighorn and gone to all the trouble of hauling it into Gerlach to show Dodd.

"I get it now," Jack said.

"You should've gotten it earlier," Jim said. "Dodd had a pistol in his hand when you were shaking him. It's a good thing I came in."

Jack had thought Dodd was reaching for a bouncer's tranquilizer, a club, not a gun. He tried to reassure himself. "He's a blowhard."

"That's true, but a scared blowhard can shoot you."

"Crockett's the one who does his shooting for him. Did you see that picture, Jim? Crockett did the same thing with Bob as with that poached bighorn. He drove all the way into Gerlach with Bob's body just to impress Eddie Dodd with another trophy."

Jim looked for a moment as though the idea was too crazy to be believed; then he got the point. "Nothing else makes any sense."

"Everything that guy does makes sense in some twisted way. If we're going to get Crockett, we have to figure out how he's thinking."

"That's what we're trying to do."

"How can you figure a guy who won't drop a dime for a phone call to tell a widow where her husband's body is?"

"He's a mean son of a bitch," Jim said.

Cindy hurried up to them in front of the motel. She had changed her clothes and taken off her hunter's cap. Her thick hair, pinned back at the sides with two barrettes, spilled around her face in dark curls. Jim left them alone.

She clasped both of Jack's hands between her palms. "I'm not going to give up, Jack. But I know now we're not going to find Bob until Crockett's caught. Will you help me?"

"Jim and the sheriffs and the FBI are going to do that. It's only a matter of time." He didn't want her to start doing something on her own, like his own foolishness in the bar. He didn't even want her to talk to Susan Dodd. He thought of the poster in the bar with Bob's face on it.

"I know that," Cindy said. "But will you talk with me about this?"

"Sure. I'll talk with you."

"Tomorrow. Will you call me tomorrow?"

"I can do that," he said.

She raised up on her toes and surprised him with a quick kiss on the cheek. "It's just that I'm alone now, Jack. I'm scared to be alone with all this."

Jack made an uncomfortable effort to comfort her. "Bob had a lot of friends. You saw that this weekend."

"I know, but people have their own lives. You'll call me tomorrow?"

He assured her again that he would, and went off to find Jim. The deputy was down on one knee by his Jeep Cherokee checking the air pressure in the tire with a silver gauge. He looked up as Jack walked past him. "Hey," Jim called, "where are you going?"

Jack pointed toward the lights of the shabby bar: BRUNO'S COUNTRY CLUB. "I need a drink. Bad. Come on, I'll buy."

CHAPTER 4

Jack called Cindy and drove over to see her on Tuesday after-noon. It turned out that her obsession surpassed his own: Billy Crockett—who was he? why was he? Cindy had collected files of newspaper clippings and videotapes of TV news reports. She'd filled another folder with information she'd dragged out of Jim Sandoval. She'd gathered newspaper articles, underlined the names of people who knew Crockett, and had begun to visit them. In a spiral school notebook she recorded each contact and what she'd learned. Jack shared her excited belief that if they could figure out who Crockett was, they'd find out where he was.

"Look at this garbage," Cindy said.

She handed Jack a Gannett News Service article. It began: "The desert of northern Nevada is one of the most barren, hostile regions in North America. Yet people who know

William David Crockett, Jr., say he is as comfortable living in this forbidding desert as most people are in their living rooms."

A survival expert from Idaho was quoted as saying that Crockett could easily live in the winter off plant life alone, such as sego lily bulbs, biscuit-root plants, and several varieties of streambed plants. Rabbits, quail, and partridge roamed the range. Crockett could supply himself with fresh meat by setting simple snares before going to bed each night. If he was hiding in a cave or abandoned mine shaft, he could survive on mice and pack rats. "The rodents are high-protein, tasty meats," the survivalist said. "In dry, snowless country, morning frost alone is enough to supply him with drinking water. He can wipe frost off plants with a handkerchief and squeeze it into a container. He can chip ice from rocks and melt it over a fire. If he's as good in the outdoors as I've read he is," the survivalist concluded, "he's got it made."

But Crockett also carried a pistol and a high-powered rifle. A friend reported, "That SOB can shoot the eye out of a needle at two hundred fifty yards."

A columnist claimed that Crockett had told a witness to the shootings that he would never be taken alive.

"That must be me," Jack said. "I'm the only witness, and I never reported that."

Someone who'd known Crockett in Humboldt County claimed: "Guys like Billy would have been at a premium a hundred years ago. He would have made a first-rate guide or scout. He took a canoe trip down the Yukon River with little more gear than a gun, an ax, and some rope. He's lived the kind of life most of us only wish we could live."

Cindy had tracked down an American folklife book by two Smithsonian Institution anthropologists titled *Buckaroos in Paradise: Cowboy Life in Northern Nevada*, published ten years ago. Two photographs showed Billy in a high-crowned buckaroo hat, steel-rimmed spectacles, with a bright scarf around his neck—a kid with peach fuzz on his chin dressed up like a cowboy. In one picture he played cards in a bunkhouse; in the other, he sat astride a horse in a branding corral along with two Paiute Indian buckaroos.

"That's when he was running cows for my uncle's outfit outside Paradise Valley," Jack told Cindy.

"Look at his face compared to the other guys," she replied. "He's still got baby fat."

From Jim Sandoval, Cindy had obtained a complete list of the possessions that deputies had seized in Crockett's trailer behind Dodd's bar. Besides guns, books, ammunition, and cowboy gear, they'd found an Aladdin hair massager, a Water Pik toothbrush, maps of Canada and Mexico, a Spanish-English dictionary, and several framed prints of Charlie Russell's watercolors of cowboy life.

"I got the name of Crockett's dentist from the paper," Cindy said. "Apparently Crockett had a thing about his teeth and came in all the time for checkups. He had an obsession about his gums, even though they were perfect."

"I guess he didn't chew either," Jack added. He felt the comforting pressure of the circular snuff container in his hip pocket.

"Or smoke."

Cindy showed Jack her spiral notebook where she'd recorded her conversation with the Reno dentist, Dr. Davis. "I hunt a lot," the dentist had told Cindy, "and came across Crockett out in the desert lots of times. I've known Billy for years. In my office he was friendly and polite, but out in the desert he always gave me the cold shoulder. Probably because he always had deer or something he'd shot out of season in his camp. There's no secret about that. He either didn't want you to see what he'd killed, or he didn't want you implicated if he got in trouble. I don't know which. I do know Billy be-

lieved he had a right to kill animals out of season without
regard for game laws."

"We've got two Crocketts," Cindy said.

"One out there on the desert eating weeds and rats."

"And the other one hiding with friends and sucking soft
butterscotch candy."

At the end of the week Jack went to see his uncle in Paradise Valley to talk to him about Crockett. As he drove out of
town, he passed the bare cottonwoods lining the Truckee
River. A dusting of snow on the hills highlighted striations of
rock and patterns of sage. The sky ahead brightened into a
paler shade of white as he headed east into what was still left
of the West, or the West he had glimpsed as a kid. He stopped
to buy some tax-free snuff at the Paiute I-80 Smoke Shop, a
tan cinderblock building with metal bars that swung over the
door and windows at night. Behind the glass doors of the
cooler lay rolls of plastic-wrapped, refrigerated Copenhagen
and Skoal, tons of snuff, stacked like logs. He picked up a roll
of eight cans.

A young Paiute woman in white fringed boots and black
jeans worked behind the counter.

"You must sell a lot of this stuff," Jack said.

"It goes pretty good," the woman answered.

Back on the road toward Brady Hot Springs, the land flattened out into a white playa—salt or snow, the eye couldn't
tell—empty of houses, fringed at the edges with stunted gray
clumps of greasewood and saltbush. The sky opened up.
Plumes of steam hovered above the hot springs in calm stationary columns as if in a country without time, without a
horizon. Light and space stretched all the way into the pale
stratosphere.

Jack loved the sense of release on the road, the feeling of
buoyancy, the expansiveness. As the desert wind, sharp and

invigorating, sliced through the half-open window, the years fell away and he was a boy again. "Black care rarely sits behind the rider whose pace is quick enough," his uncle used to say, quoting his favorite president, Teddy Roosevelt.

Unlike Jack's father, Uncle Pete had stayed on the land all his life, running cattle and a few sheep in the Santa Rosas, the Owyhee, and other tracts of public land outside Paradise Valley. Open range, the ranchers called it, though they had to pay grazing fees to the BLM and the Forest Service. When he was young Jack had liked to visit Uncle Pete, to ride from the ranch into the hills, to carry a pail of steaming milk into the house on a cold morning, to drive a herd of bawling cows toward the cutting corrals. He'd worked for Uncle Pete two summers when he was in high school, and during that time he'd wanted to grow up to be like his uncle. And yet, despite all Jack's youthful admiration for his uncle's way of life, he'd come to feel that in Uncle Pete's eyes he—like his father—never quite measured up to what a man should be. Jack had adopted his father's view: the real world was one where people taught school, sold cars, ran restaurants, managed casinos, wrote books, and even governed the state. The tough, lonesome world of Basques herding sheep in desolate hills and buckaroos following chuck wagons and sleeping in bedrolls was part of a bygone era.

In later years, his uncle continued to exist at the edge of Jack's awareness, an outmoded figure tottering on the rim of extinction. Yet whenever Jack drove into the high desert, he always felt Uncle Pete behind his shoulder, glancing squint-eyed down on him from that elevated rim. There, in that harsh, blunt country, the airy mental construction of his father's denials and city-centered judgments collapsed in the wind.

West of Winnemucca, near the tiny desert burg of Imlay, a weird monument, three stories high, molded out of discarded railroad ties, steel cables, rusted disc blades, hubcaps, guardrails, dead animal bones, windshields from wrecked cars, old manual typewriters, all cemented with concrete, rose into a mushroom-shaped organic fusion of junk and cement. Around it stood life-sized wooden sculptures of Indians and ice sculptures of animals—deer, horses, and even a mountain lion. Jack had heard that some out-of-state Indian lived in this place with a bunch of adopted kids. This towering jumble of concrete, ice, and trash was supposed to be a monument to the American Indian.

Jack pulled into his uncle's ranch in Paradise Valley a little after one. He'd stopped in Winnemucca to make a reservation at the Cozy Motel to avoid having to spend the night with his uncle—and to prevent Pete from having to invite him. It was enough to spend a long afternoon under his uncle's scrutiny while trying to pry out information about Billy Crockett.

Scattered in the snow around the yard of his uncle's house lay the refuse of earlier ranching days—a rusty spring rake, wooden-spoked wagon wheels, an old buckboard—all that was left after his uncle's cattle outfit had gone belly-up. In the mid-1970s Pete might've tried to take out loans and expand his outfit, but since his sons and daughters lived and worked in cities scattered between Phoenix and Seattle and weren't interested in carrying on with the ranch, he'd sold his slumping enterprise for a song, keeping the ranch house, along with the collapsing barn and sheds, and the horse pasture. After paying off his debts, which left him close to broke, he'd gone to work as cow boss for the Flying Circle J cattle outfit—until his horse fell on him in the hills a year ago. He now lay stoved up in the house with a mangled leg and blood clots on the brain. He was seventy-six.

Jack parked by an enormous ridged-bark cottonwood whose punky limb had broken under him when he'd climbed it as a boy. Between the chicken pens and rabbit hutches, the yellowish corpse of a dog lay flattened in the snow. It looked like a mastiff, maybe a Rhodesian Ridgeback, but Jack couldn't tell for sure; its snout was shoved into a pocket of snow.

Jack heard his uncle's strong, hoarse voice through the screen door but couldn't see him through the dark wire mesh. "You came on a good day. You can help me bury that mutt."

The screen door swung open, squealing on its hinges, and Uncle Pete, stocky and bow-backed, held it ajar, standing there in a frayed green-plaid cowboy shirt, tattered Levi's, and white socks. The brush-cut mustache and hair flying straight up from his head were as white as his socks. A line marking the lower edge of where his hatband had rested for decades sharply separated his pale forehead from the rest of his scoured face. He spit a line of Copenhagen to the side of the wooden steps. The lids of his eyes snapped at Jack like a turtle's.

"I had to pop that mutt last night. He killed nine of my rabbits."

Inside the sparse living room by a wood stove fitted into the big fieldstone fireplace, Jack sprawled in a spotted cowhide chair with a bent willow frame, a mug of reheated coffee steaming in his hand, while Uncle Pete, sitting on the couch with his cane nearby, continued his narration of the previous night's assault on his rabbits. "I heard dogs barking about three or so and went outside. There was a little moon show-ing, most of it was behind cloud cover, and I saw something lunging at those upper rabbit hutches. I figured it was a dog. Another one hunkered down in the shadows by the new hutches I just got. I hadn't got around to securing them like I should—they seemed pretty strong—but they weren't strong enough to keep those dogs from tearing into those new rab-bits. I only had my .22, and there wasn't even enough moon-light to see the sights on the barrel, but I threw a shot at the lunging dog. I guess I hit him pretty good. The other ran off right away. The one I hit was growling and hunched up at me when I came to it. My rabbits were scattered all around it. I finished him off. I know you don't like to think animals kill just for the thrill of it, but there it is. Those dogs had no intention of eating those rabbits. They were just killing them."

Jack hadn't been out of the car for ten minutes or taken more than two sips of coffee before he fell under attack. "Don't expect me to defend a couple of stray killer dogs," he told his uncle. "They can do a lot of damage, especially with sheep."

"Any canine can turn into a killer. Coyotes, too."

Jack objected. "They get the blame for what dogs have done, but coyotes like to eat what they kill." He never would've said that around his uncle years earlier any more than he would've suggested that his uncle's cattle and sheep might be overgrazing public lands. "Overgrazing" was a word BLM and DOW officials wouldn't dare use at a public meeting until recently.

"You know as well as I do," Pete persisted, "that coyotes will go on a rampage."

Jack remembered the first summer he'd worked for his uncle. One morning they found over a dozen sheep with their throats ripped. Either dogs or coyotes were the culprits, but the Animal Damage Control trapper came with 1080 to poison the coyotes.

"We know now," Jack told his uncle, "that most of the time when you get those slaughters, like your rabbits, they're domestic dogs on a tear."

Stretched out on a circular braided rag rug by the fire, Pete's half-toothless Australian shepherd slept with her chin on her crossed front paws. She was Pete's favorite, the mother of numerous dogs he'd used with sheep and cattle. Now, after she'd spent years of winter nights sleeping outside on hay bales, he'd broken the rancher's code and let her come inside by the fire while she waited out her last days.

Uncle Pete had spent his whole life struggling with what was wild or only half-tame, like his stringy range-fed cattle.

Jack knew Pete was right about some coyotes; young ones could cause trouble—just like teenagers getting into mischief—but grown up, they were mainly interested in eating, not killing. His uncle knew as well as he did that any person's much-loved, gentle dog, even old Alice by the fire, could turn murderer when night came and she tasted the thrill of the chase. One of the most shocked faces Jack ever saw was that of a suburban dog owner whose beloved pet had been accused of mayhem in the night.

"Come on," Uncle Pete said, "let's bury that dog. Who cares what the coyotes do now? There aren't any more sheep or calves left in this country. The government has already killed off all the stock—and the ranchers, too. Your coyotes and lions can take over the world."

Relieved to be shut of this discussion, Jack followed his uncle outside to bury the rabbit killer. The silvery sky was lumpy, trying to make up its mind whether to snow or to clear. Nine young rabbits lay mangled around the hutches.

Jack looked at the dead dog. "It has a collar," he told his uncle. "Do you want to see whose it is?"

"I already looked. There's no tag."

Jack dug a shallow grave for the dog behind the barn. Uncle Pete wanted nothing to do with the rabbits, though Jack was sure they were fit to eat. "Toss them out back for the birds," Pete said. The sight of rusted barbed wire in rolls, the chassis of an old butane Allis-Chalmers tractor, and rusted disc blades cluttering the yard reminded Jack to ask about the monument of junk near Imlay.

"Some guy named Frank Van Zant built that pile of crap," Pete explained.

"I thought he was an Indian."

"Oh, he calls himself an Indian—Rolling Mountain Thunder, or something like that."

"So he isn't Indian?"

"Everyone's an Indian these days. I hear he claims to be

half Creek, but he grew up white. He sure left a mess out there, didn't he?"

After burying the dog, Jack followed his uncle back inside, and they reheated more coffee. Pete's old cleaning lady, Carmela Rodriguez, drove up in her ancient Buick to move the dust around in his house. What once was an all-day task when Jack's aunt was still alive had diminished to a few hours of puttering every Friday afternoon.

"Éste es mi sobrino," Uncle Pete told Carmela, introducing Jack.

"Ya me acuerdo." She remembered the summers when Jack had worked on the ranch and had spoken Spanish with her. He'd taken Spanish in high school and then had kept it up for two years in college, but he still wasn't fluent like his uncle.

"Nosotros también hablábamos vasco," Jack said, reminding Carmela how they'd also picked up a few words of Basque from a herder that summer. Uncle Pete's first language as a child had been Basque, but he claimed not to remember it.

"¡Es imposible!" Carmela said, continuing in Spanish: "The Devil himself spent seven years trying to learn Basque, then gave up."

Pete told Carmela about the dogs and the rabbits. She just shook her head, glad the dogs hadn't been able to break into the older hutches and that most of the rabbits had survived. "Malos perros," she said. "Bad dogs."

"Jack thinks only dogs will kill like that," Pete told Carmela. He just wasn't going to drop it. "I could show him how a lion will kill sheep and take only one bite out of each of them, and even after he saw it with his own eyes, he wouldn't believe it. But that's what a lion will do."

"Sí, sí," Carmela agreed. "El león es muy malo."

It was late afternoon and getting dark when Jack finally got around to bringing up Billy Crockett. He and his uncle sipped more reheated coffee, black as pitch. Jack's mother used to joke that the way to make classic buckaroo brew like Uncle Pete's was to take a pound of Hills Bros. coffee, wet it real good with water, boil the hell out of it for an hour, and then drop a horseshoe into the pot. If the horseshoe sank, add more coffee.

"When I first met Billy," Uncle Pete said, "I'd already heard about him. He came in with two buckskins, riding one and leading the other with all his gear. People had spotted him along the highway near Imlay, dressed up like some mountain man out of a movie. He rode those horses right across the salt flats in summer, I'm told, and tourists on the highway stopped to take pictures of him. Of course, the sun is so bright off those alkali sinks that their pictures wouldn't come out, so I guess when they got home they must've thought they'd tried to photograph the ghost of Jed Smith or Kit Carson or some other mountain man come back to haunt this country.

"When he showed up here, he said he wanted to be a buckaroo, but I put him out fencing with old Beltran Atxaga. You can always find cowboys with their fancy buckles and spurs and big hats, but you can't always find a good fencer. That kid turned out to be a worker. From can't-see to can't-see he hauled fence posts on his back and stretched wire, hardly stopping but to take a piss or drink some water. He kept to himself. He was always polite, kind of shy, and neat—even when fixing fence he put on a clean shirt every morning. The only thing really odd about him was that he wore a pistol strapped to his waist, even when he was fencing."

"And you let him carry a gun?"

"What did I care? This is a free country—or anyway, it used to be. He got his work done, and he never acted up. He seemed responsible. People got used to it. He even went into town to get his mail wearing that weapon. We just thought he was a kid playing cowboy."

Jack knew from the FBI reports that Crockett's high school

classmates in southern Illinois remembered him as a shy, quiet kid who always had a dream of going West. He'd reportedly promised his mother that he would finish high school, and he was no sooner graduated than he was on his way to the Rockies. His family had bounced around a lot; he had seven brothers and sisters, and his father, a strict parental taskmaster of Appalachian stock, had worked as an electrician, a maintenance man for a Ford assembly plant, a chemist for a fertilizer company, and a state contractor for bridge and highway repairs. The family bounced from Tennessee through Ohio, West Virginia, upstate New York, Michigan's Upper Peninsula, and finally to southern Illinois, where Billy's father tried to make a go of it as an independent farmer with a few dairy cows.

"Milking cows wasn't Billy's idea of buckarooing," Pete said. "He was such a good worker through the summer that I put him out with a wagon crew for the fall roundup. He was so excited he shook like a dog shitting peach seeds. He'd had some experience working with a cow outfit in southern Oregon, so he knew a few things, but those big outfits in Oregon are like dude ranches compared to down here. It's a good thing Billy had that experience, though, 'cause he wouldn't have made it here otherwise.

"Nothing came real easy to Billy, but he worked hard at learning. He'd practice roping for hours. By the time kids around here are twelve they can do naturally what Billy was trying to learn at twenty. Once he spent two hours trying to trim and shoe a horse himself, but he cut too deep into the frog, and the horse came up lame and threw the shoe to boot. You can't say Billy had the natural itch of how to head a steer or start a colt, but he was first in line to try. And he got to be pretty good. At least he could do the job—what I mean: he was dependable, and that was a damn sight more important than having some hotshot hand who was drunk up at Simone's or the Pussycat when you needed him."

Jack cut in. "I heard he never raised hell or got into fights."

"He didn't have to, what with that gun he carried all the time. The guys just left him to himself. I never heard of him being in a fight. Once some guy in the Gem Bar started ragging on him for drinking fruit juice—the bartender had made Billy leave his pistol out in the truck under the seat—and Billy either went outside and pulled out the gun, or told the guy he had a gun—one of the two—and the guy backed off. I figure if Billy ever did get into a real fistfight with one of these experienced hands, he would've gotten his ass handed to him. But he wasn't looking for trouble so he didn't find it."

"Fights usually start when guys are drunk, but if Crockett didn't drink . . ."

"I think I heard of him going on a toot once, early on, but he seemed embarrassed about it, and it never happened again. He'd go to the bars, but he always drank fruit juice or Dr Pepper, though he'd usually stay away from the sweet drinks. He worried about his teeth, although I'll tell you, he sure loved candy and pie. He's the only buckaroo I knew who bought dental floss. Sometimes he'd even go to town and buy some of that health food crap. But he wasn't a pantywaist." Not like you, his uncle's squint-eyed pause seemed to say. "I don't want you to get the wrong idea. Billy was never a mountain man, like people say, but he wasn't a pussy either. He was always doing things to toughen himself up. Little things, like shaving with water so cold he had to break the ice in the pan, or going on a long hike instead of resting on a day off just so he could carry a heavy pack thirty or forty miles and sleep out in subzero weather. I asked him once if he got cold sleeping out in winter, and he said, 'Deer and cougars don't complain about the cold.' He had some idea of how old-timers used to be out here, and he went about rigging himself into that idea. In Elko he tracked down an old-style Garcia saddle with a high cantle and horn. He learned from a rawhider on the Circle A how to braid a riata and make horsehair macarties. He bought himself a pair of old-fashioned chaps—Angora goat-hide woolies—and a lady's-leg spade bit with silver inlay. He studied those paintings by Charlie Russell and duded himself up to look like he could fit into one of those pictures. Once, he told me, he made a trip up to Cody, to the Buffalo Bill museum there, just to look at those Charlie Russell paintings in the original. 'That was the life,' he said, 'back then.'"

"What about women? I heard he never had any girlfriends." Jim Sandoval had said that Crockett was a loner. He hadn't developed relationships with men or women, except for a few older women like Sue Dodd or Jenny Morrison and some ranchers' wives who used to mother him.

"He didn't go whoring, if that's what you mean," Pete said. "When the other boys went to buy some pussy over to Penny's or one of the houses, he stayed out, even on rodeo days or the Fourth. There were a few girls who took to him—I don't know if you could call them real girlfriends—but he would go fishing or camping with them. There was one gal he seemed to like pretty good; she was from back east, and they saw each other for a while."

"What was her name?"

"Georgette . . . something. She was working at Winner's then. Now she's a dealer in Sparks, over to the Nugget. I don't know if it was so much that he didn't like women as that there wasn't room for them in what he was trying to be. Not too many women are going to want to sleep out in freezing bedrolls or slog through snow in the mountains when it's colder than a well-digger's ass. He had a saying: If you had a good woman in camp, you'd never want to leave. If she wasn't good, you'd never want to come back. He was always a gentleman around women. I think he sort of had a highfalutin notion about what a woman was supposed to be. If she didn't fit his notion of a lady, then she was a slut."

"He grew up Catholic," Jack offered as a possible explanation for Crockett's extreme attitudes about women. He knew from Jim Sandoval that Crockett's classmates didn't remember him dating in high school.

Pete seemed surprised by this information. "If he was Catholic, I never saw it. He never went to church or said anything about religion. He hardly ever cussed, which would be damn strange for a real Catholic. Maybe his mother was a churchgoer, but from what I know about his family, his father wouldn't have been one. His father could've been a good Catholic, though. He was a big-mouthed, beer-bellied braggart, something like Eddie Dodd over in Gerlach—just the opposite of Billy."

Jack saw no point in pursuing the subject of Billy's Catholicism with Pete. His uncle misunderstood him as implying that Crockett was somehow churchy. Uncle Pete's idea of being a Catholic merely meant you got married and buried in a particular ceremony, and you partied it up on certain holidays. The Church was something you just happened to be born into. Otherwise it didn't affect your life in any profound way, especially if you were a Basco.

Jack had once read that Christianity had come so late to parts of the Basque country that even in the nineteenth century the mountain Basques in Bizkaia hadn't yet heard of the birth and death of Christ. Perhaps that's why, as with a lot of ranchers—and the descendants of old mountain Basques—his uncle's religion rested on the belief that good judgment and physical competence were signs of virtue. You either knew or didn't know how to handle a cantankerous horse, doctor a sick steer, irrigate a hay field, wallow a truck out of a mud hole, buck bales without pulling your back, protect your stock from predators and yourself in a blizzard, rope and cut a calf, start a colt, build a barn, drive and fix any machine with a gas, diesel, or butane engine, as well as kill, butcher, and dress any kind of hooved or feathered domestic stock or wild game in the state. Possession of such skills needed no comment. To live without them in Paradise Valley was its own hell. Beyond these things, there wasn't much worth worrying about, nothing worth bothering with—least of all anything beyond the veil.

Jack got up to throw a couple of aspen logs into the wood stove. The dried white bark curled back in the yellow flames. "Maybe there's a lot of his father under the surface," Jack said about Billy, "under wraps. I hear they both have short fuses."

Pete reflected for a moment. "Billy pretty much kept his temper under control—around people anyway. There were only a couple of things I didn't like about him. He was too hard on animals. I mean, you've got to be tough with some of these thick-skinned, ornery mustangs that end up in a cavvy. A horse ain't someone you socialize with, despite what these animal lovers like your wife think. But Billy went too far. I've seen him crack a horse with a two-by-four just for being frisky. I mean, no one takes shit from an ornery horse or a balky steer, or they'll walk all over you, but deep down you've got to like them in some way. They're your bread and butter. I don't think Billy really understood animals."

Pete pointed toward the dog stretched out by the fire. "Once he was walking across the yard, and Alice here was laying in his way. Instead of walking around her, Billy gave her a kick in the ribs."

Alice, hearing her name, opened one milky blue eye, without lifting her chin from her crossed paws, and stared. Pete went on, "I told Billy if I ever saw him kick Alice again I'd kick his nuts right up into his eyeteeth."

"What'd he say?"

"Nothing. His throat reddened up. I know he thought I must be going daft, talking about a dumb mutt that way."

"What was the other thing?"

"What other thing?"

"You said there were a couple of things you didn't like about him."

"If you'd give me two minutes to finish up one thing, I'll tell you. What is this? A police interrogation?"

"Sorry."

"How about a snort? The day's about done in. I don't have much to offer you but a little dago red."

"That'll do."

Jack got up and filled two small fruit jars with wine from a gallon jug. He gave one to his uncle and settled with the other into the cowhide chair. The wine had a nice moldy homemade bitter taste. It warmed him up.

Uncle Pete took a sip and made satisfied smacking sounds with his mouth. "Billy was always knocking down game," he said. "In season or out of season, it didn't matter to him. Now I don't mind if a man bags a deer or pronghorn now and then for food. Hell, none of us would've made it through the down times if we didn't. There are plenty of deer and antelope anymore, but Billy overdid it. He'd show up at a line camp with deer out of season when we didn't need them. He knocked down wild horses, too. That was too much. I got the idea that he liked killing just to kill."

Jim Sandoval had learned that Billy got his first shotgun when he was ten and bagged his first deer when he was twelve. Poaching became a habit for him and his brothers, winning the praise of a father who disapproved of bureaucratic red tape and game laws. Restrictions on hunting, in his father's view, were just bullshit; they didn't apply to subsistence hunters like themselves.

"All that came to an end," Pete said, "when the FBI arrested Billy for not answering his draft-board notice. They tracked him down when they come across his picture in that dumb book about Paradise buckaroos. He was sleeping over to the Little Owyhee line camp when they come up and arrested him. The deputy from town, Guy Williams, was with them, and he told me later that Billy gave 'em no trouble. As they were driving to town he chatted about this or that just like he was out for a ride with you or me."

That had been at the tail end of 1973. Jack knew that part of the story pretty well; at least he knew what had happened after the arrest, although he didn't know Billy's side of the story.

Pete filled him in. "Billy had ignored his draft notice not because he had anything particular against the war but because he didn't think the government had any business telling him what to do. I had to play hell to get his social security number out of him. He said he didn't take nothing from the government, he didn't expect nothing from it, and he didn't see why it should take from him. I told him if he didn't give me his number he could go work someplace else. I don't care if it's a right number or a wrong number, just give me a number. Even all those Paiute buckaroos I had working for me bitched less about taxes than Billy did—and they had more reason to gripe. I've had some of the biggest thieves in the county on my payroll—you can see their pictures right there in that book where those anthropologists made heroes out of them—but they paid their social security, and I filed their W-2 forms even when the government couldn't figure out whether they were wetbacks or Indians or Okie drifters or what the hell."

Jack had heard that the FBI had flown Crockett back to Illinois to face the draft dodger charges. Crockett had borrowed five hundred dollars from Pete and another five hundred from an Oregon rancher for his defense, but his case never came to trial. With the war winding down, draft evasion cases around the country were being dropped, and the Selective Service itself faced congressional extinguishment. Crockett's lawyer found a legal loophole: those previously indicted for draft evasion in Billy's district had received two notifications, but the government had no proof that Billy, always on the move, had ever received a second notification from the draft board, so the government quietly dropped the charges the day before a jury was to be selected.

Those were the facts as Jack had heard them from Jim Sandoval. The stories spawned around Eddie Dodd's bar were

something else. The cops had roughed up Billy, the bar stool-
ies said; the Feds had humiliated him as they dragged him
from state to state, throwing him into drunk tanks at night
and common cells with petty thieves, bums, perverts, and every other form of lowlife. The FBI knocked the heels off his
boots. They "lost" his buckaroo hat and forced this soft-
spoken, hardworking, square-shooting, horseback-riding
buckaroo to walk—walk bareheaded!—through public places
in leg irons and waist manacles. For another half a year they
harassed him, though he was out on bail, depriving him of his
freedom and livelihood, just as if he were another cowardly
greasy-haired, dope-smoking draft dodger.

"He was different when he come back," Pete said, "that's
for sure. He came back to work off what he owed me, but I
couldn't keep him on no more. I was going under. All the new
regulations from the BLM, the restrictions on grazing, and
the environmental protection laws were killing us. They were
closing down the range. I had to start breaking up my outfit
and selling out. Finally the Federal Land Policy and Management Act put the last nail in the coffin for me. It wasn't low
prices and higher grazing fees that killed us. I could've gone
on not making money—when the hell did I ever make money
in this business?—but closing down the open range to free-
roaming cattle made it impossible for outfits to work in the
old way. The BLM had college kids who didn't know a steer
from a heifer telling us how we were supposed to ranch. The
only way to make it was like those big outfits that hauled cows
from place to place in semis and scooted them into portable
metal loading chutes on Honda trail bikes. What fun is that?
If you can't ranch right, the hell with it.

"Billy eventually paid me back. He picked up jobs here and
there, irrigating hay, ripping ground—he drove D-7s and D-9s
for some of these potato farmers around here—drilling wells,
driving trucks, even carpentering. Then he got into trapping
and drifted over into Washoe County. Like everything else, he

worked at it. Trapping didn't come natural to him, but he was a perfectionist, and he wanted to learn how to do it in the old way. I think that's why he ignored all the regulations about exposed bait or stamping his traps with ID numbers. He just wanted to do things the way the old-timers did. These new bureaucratic laws have nothing to do with the natural way trappers have worked in this country for the last hundred and fifty years."

"You said he was different when he came back."

"Well, he stayed to himself even more, brooding all the time. He only mentioned the draft thing to me once. He said, 'No one's going to get the drop on me again.' And then he really got into guns. It wasn't that Old West stuff so much anymore. He was like a commando or one of those SWAT guys, shooting at human-shaped targets with both hands, emptying his guns and slamming them full again with speed loaders. I remember thinking to myself, Someday this kid is going to kill somebody."

The snow outside, in the afternoon's last light, deepened into a blue sheen. Pete snapped on the standing lamp by the couch.

"Let me get you something to eat," he said.

"I should be going. I was planning to grab a bite in town."

"It'll only take a minute. Nothing fancy. I was just going to make an omelet tonight."

Pete hobbled into the kitchen on his cane. With his big carving knife, the blade worn from years of use, he diced up some ham, chopped an onion, and peeled and cut a potato into translucent-thin slices. In what seemed only a few seconds he had the whole batch, along with a fistful of minced garlic, popping and sizzling in a big cast-iron skillet, the tangy smell filling the house. Pete's hands flew around as though they'd grown younger, as during those early mornings when Jack was working for him and they had to get up at four and Pete whipped up breakfast. Jack remembered one summer morning when he and Pete were on foot in the dark pasture gathering horses. The herd broke into a gallop, and Pete yelled for Jack to head them off. Jack ran toward the horses, but when he saw that he was having no effect on their barrel-ass gallop, he slowed up a bit, just to keep them from running him over and crushing his skull. But then he and Pete had to walk clear to the other side of the pasture to get the horses, and though his uncle didn't say anything, Jack could tell from his look that Uncle Pete was disappointed in him. He realized later that he should've kept running hard and the horses probably would've turned, and if they hadn't, at least he would've been doing his job with some spunk when they knocked him over. No doubt that's what Billy Crockett would've done.

Jack noticed a book by his uncle's couch. The writer, the son of old Tom Winters, a Paradise Valley rancher, now taught school at the University of Arizona. The book had caused a little stir in the valley when it came out last fall. The Winters boy claimed he hadn't taken over his father's ranching operation because he'd recognized the environmental destruction that cattle had caused in the fragile Great Basin desert.

"Did you read this book?" Jack asked his uncle.

Pete nodded. "That kid just had a problem with his father. He'll never be half the man his dad was. You want to take it with you?"

"I can get a copy."

"Take it. I don't want it. When it came to ranching, that kid was a loser."

"Well, maybe he wasn't much of a rancher, but he became something else."

"If he didn't want to take over the ranch, then why didn't he turn down old Tom's money? If ranching was so tainted, why wasn't his inheritance tainted, too?"

"I'll have to read the book and see what I think."

"You know, I've worked these hills all my life, and I've never read a book yet that tells what it was really like out here."

Pete whipped up some eggs in a bowl and poured them over the sputtering ham and vegetables. Jack could tell from the clean, fresh smell that the eggs had just been gathered that morning. Uncle Pete scooped the omelet onto plates; Jack poured more wine, tossed some salt and pepper over the steaming plate, and dug in. With the first bite, he was a kid again, in the cold early morning, ready to saddle up and ride into the dark.

After Jack helped wash the dishes, he told Pete he was ready to head into Winnemucca to the motel. They stood in the large bunkhouse living room.

"I wonder if I could borrow a rifle from you," Jack asked.

Pete swept his hand toward the rifles on the walls. "Take your pick."

Jack took down a lever-action Winchester Centennial .30-30.

"That was your grandfather's," Pete said. "Your dad didn't want his guns, so they're here. That's a beauty. Billy had one like it but with an octagonal barrel."

"He's carrying a .300 Savage now."

Pete pointed toward the .300 Savage just above the empty pegs from where Jack had removed the Winchester. "That Savage was your grandfather's, too. You might take it along as well. I've got no use for it."

"Thanks. I will."

They walked together toward the door. "I didn't know you were interested in these guns," Pete said, "or I would've given them to you long ago."

"I didn't have a use for them till now." Jack didn't say any more. He knew Pete understood why he wanted them. As he carried the rifles toward the door, the heft of their stocks in his palms, Jack recognized their familiar feel from the days when he'd hunted as a boy. He had a momentary feeling that he indeed would like to plug Billy with one of these guns, the rifles of both his grandfather and his uncle, and haul the corpse back to show Pete, just as Billy had done with Bob. It was the kind of fantasy he might have had as a kid, when he'd think ahead to showing his uncle some wild game he'd shot, to win his respect.

The phone rang and Pete went back in to answer it. It was the man who owned the dead dog they'd buried. Carmela had told the man what had happened. "He apologized," Pete said. "He was sorry about my rabbits."

In the mudroom, old Alice, with a stiff-legged limp, waddled around the corner toward the clattering sound of her dinner as Pete poured dry kibbles into a metal bowl. He and Jack stood at the screen door watching the dog eat.

"You know," Pete said, "you've got to wonder what might've happened to Billy if all these cow outfits hadn't folded. Buckarooing wasn't a bad life, if you weren't married. The money didn't seem like much, but you didn't have many expenses either, so you always had two or three hundred bucks to blow in town when you wanted to. How many guys these days have that kind of cash money in their pocket just to blow?"

"I know I don't," Jack said.

"And things are going to get tighter, too," Pete added, "for the working man." He glanced through the screen door into the darkness as though trying to see something in the far distance. "It was a good life out here," he went on. "The work was hard, but you could do your job without some bastard hanging over you. That's why Billy come out here in the first place, to be free—that's all a guy wants out of life. But you can't tell anybody, if they don't already know it, what it was like to live out in these hills when they were open lands. Until those agents started coming around a few years ago, I got up every morning of my life, and I looked out at that sky and hills, and I knew I lived in a free country. There wasn't some son of a bitch out there waiting to tell me what to do. Your kids will never know what that was like. No one anywhere in America will ever again know what that feeling was like. It's over now."

Pete turned back into the house. He never said good-bye; he always just turned away, in the same casual way as he'd greeted Jack without a formal hello or any indication that they hadn't seen each other for some time, as though their appearances and disappearances, like the comings and goings of the days and the nights, needed no special comment.

Jack walked out to his pickup. The sky blazed with aluminum-colored stars. In the firmament of the West, he thought of his uncle Pete, and maybe even Billy, and he thought of those faraway, collapsed stars that still flare in the heavens, though already dead or dying.

CHAPTER 5

At the end of March the FBI picked up Billy's trail in North Dakota. Jack had gone back to work in February and was spending a lot of time at a computer preparing hunting quotas for the year. In mid-March he flew for three days with a helicopter pilot checking on the survival rate of fawns born the previous June. He counted between five and seven hundred head in each mountain range in the county. Bucks had dropped their antlers, making them indistinguishable from does, so as usual he based his spring estimate on the number of fawns per hundred adults. He came up with averages and ratios. He calculated a percentage of fawns that had survived predators, drowning, pneumonia, or other accidents or diseases over the winter. He couldn't figure the exact number of deer in the mountains, but he could tell whether a population looked healthy or not.

Lions were more difficult. They were so secretive, he hardly ever saw one from the air. He depended on track counts after a fresh snow to come up with his BG, or "best guess," estimates.

Until the end of March, Jim Sandoval and the FBI had only BG estimates on Crockett's whereabouts. Sightings had come in from almost everywhere between the Yukon and the Gulf of Mexico. Then a report arrived from Mott, North Dakota, about a man named Jack Atxaga who was working on a road crew and driving a snowplow for the county. A fellow worker had noticed a striking resemblance between Jack Atxaga and a picture of Billy Crockett in an issue of *Startling Detective*. The social security number the man gave his employer varied only a couple of digits from Billy's actual number. It appeared that Crockett had taken Jack's first name as his own along with the last name of the Basque fencer he'd worked with at Uncle Pete's ranch. Under his alias, Billy had applied for the county job on January 24, which meant that he hadn't spent much time hiding in the desert. He'd hightailed it out of Nevada and landed in North Dakota about three weeks after the murders. One of the names he'd given as a reference to his new employer was Jack's uncle, Pete Irigaray.

Why Billy gave Pete's real name as a reference mystified Jack at first, until he realized that Billy must've felt some kind of allegiance to what he considered truthfulness; it was hard for him to tell an outright lie. That's why he was so persuasive to some people: he could believe in the truthful part of his half lies. He probably also figured he wasn't going to hang out in North Dakota long enough to be traced. By the time the FBI got the report at the end of March, Billy had gone. He'd told a fellow worker that he was off to see spring come into the Rockies. That meant that the Feds were left with nothing better than BG estimates about his flight. But at least he was leaving a trail.

Jack tried to keep his mind on his work. Jim Sandoval told him to be patient; a report would come in about Crockett and they would get him. Jack went from work to home, had a drink, ate dinner, sipped a few more drinks alone, fell into bed, got up, and trudged off to work again. He and Beth clung to a troubled truce; she went her way and he went his. He saw Cindy now and then, but there wasn't much they could do besides commiserate about what wasn't happening. She'd almost given up on finding Bob, but not on capturing Crockett. In March, when she thought Crockett might still be in the desert, she hired a professional bounty hunter from Wyoming to track him down. Along with the $25,000 public reward for Crockett's capture, Cindy offered an additional $10,000, plus fifty dollars a day for expenses. She asked Jack to meet the manhunter before she closed the deal. Jack wanted nothing to do with it. He'd heard the guy was a boozer and a blowhard, and he told Cindy she was just pissing away her money. The report about Jack Atxaga's appearance in North Dakota finally convinced her that Billy had indeed fled the state, and to Jack's relief, she then broke off her negotiations with the hired gun.

Jack was doing a survey of sage grouse at their spring strutting grounds when his lung acted up. It had never felt completely well, but this new inflammation suggested that all the blood hadn't been drained in the hospital. Wendell Phillips asked to see him. Wendell was the supervising biologist of the region, so technically he was the boss, and though that's what Jack called him, he never really felt bossed. Like the wardens, the district biologists pretty much made their own schedules. They came and went as they pleased, carrying out their duties as they saw fit.

Wendell sat behind his desk wearing his predictable Mr. Rogers cardigan sweater and Mr. Rogers smile. Wendell was someone everybody called a "nice guy." He had "accepted the Lord," as he once told Jack, right after college. Active with his wife and five kids in their Christian fellowship, he regularly taught Sunday school. But there was another side to him. He'd been known to go out single-handed and slam poachers with violations and fines, even though he was just a biologist. Like Billy Crockett, he devoured Louis L'Amour novels. He once told Jack that L'Amour's stories were made up, but the western details were accurate. That's why he liked the books. He once found an obscure creek near Elko mentioned in a L'Amour novel. That, Wendell claimed, showed that L'Amour did his research; he went out there and saw that creek. He was a good writer.

"You're not looking too spry," Wendell told Jack. "If you're not well, I can arrange a leave."

"I'm feeling okay. The doctor says I've just got a little pleurisy."

"I want you to feel free to come to me if you have any problems. I'd rather have you take time off now and come back healthy than hang in and make yourself sicker."

Jack thought it amazing how a smooth-skinned, pink-cheeked, high-foreheaded Christian like Wendell with his liquorless and tobaccoless good health could make him feel so guilty. Wendell's sympathetic, probing stare over the top of his glasses seemed to say: You know what I'm really talking about. You know that I know you're hitting the bottle, and it's taking its toll.

Beth started to get on his case, too. Jack was fed up. She was like Wendell. It got to the point where it seemed a crime for a man to take a normal drink.

"You know you can quit," she told him one night after the kids were in bed. "Dad did. Your uncle did."

"Pete still drinks," Jack reminded her.

"Not like before. He's as good as quit."

It was true: Pete had tapered off in late years, especially since he got stoved up with clots on the brain.

"You can't compare me to Pete when he was my age," Jack said. "He really knocked them back."

Beth frowned. "You sound proud of him. Why would you want to be like him?"

The question confused him. When he was young, he *had* wanted to be like Pete—someone who worked hard, played hard, and didn't bellyache. In contrast, Jack's father, discontented with his jobs in casinos, repeatedly talked about the day he could leave Nevada and live on the Mendocino coast. Pete never whined that way.

"I'm not like Pete," he told Beth. "Maybe that's the problem."

"No, the problem is that you've always felt you should've been like him and those other ranchers. But you've got to face it—you can't be that way, and you shouldn't be. Look what happened to Billy Crockett."

"Are you comparing me to Crockett?"

"Well, yes," Beth said, "I am. He acted out what you dreamed about."

Jack felt he was talking to a stranger. Had her desperation pushed her to provoke him? Or did she really think this way?

"I don't know what the hell you're talking about. Billy Crockett is a killer."

"And you're not. But you're a drinker, and he's not."

"Now you're on that again. Am I drunk now?"

"You've been drinking."

"One! I had one drink. You've got to be fair, if we're going to work this out."

"And you've got to stop this denial."

Denial! Those trendy terms always flipped the switch in Jack. "Who's denying what?"

"You're denying that booze changes you—one, two, three drinks, it doesn't matter. It's only going to get worse."

"Who's changed? I'm not the one who turns my back on you at night."

"What I'm saying is that you've got to get some help. Otherwise it's reaching that point—"

"The point, the point. What's the point?"

Her answer came with effort. "I'll have to leave you."

That weekend he didn't touch a drop. He and Beth went to Louie's Basque Corner with some friends for dinner, and he didn't even drink a picon punch.

In bed that night Beth said, "It can be this way between us. I want you back all the time."

"I haven't gone anywhere."

"Don't be flip. I know it's not easy, but we could make it this way every day. You have to think about why you just don't give it up."

Jack had been considering what she'd said earlier about him and Uncle Pete. About Billy Crockett and himself. Something bothered him, something in what she'd said that he couldn't put his finger on.

"You tell me. You seem to have the answers."

"I don't. But you've said it yourself—about a demon eating at you, saying you've failed."

"Well, I've admitted that. You're the one who said I didn't fail."

"I'm not talking about what happened in that canyon with Bob. I'm talking about before, how you always felt you fell short."

"To do what? Be like Billy Crockett?"

"Maybe, a little bit. Or like Pete. Why else would this whole thing be eating at you this way?"

Spring slipped into summer and Billy turned up again, this time in northern California, on the Mendocino coast, near Fort Bragg, where Jack's sister taught school and her husband worked for the state Fish and Game Department. Sensing a hot lead, Jack called his brother-in-law Dave to find out what he'd heard. Billy, Jack learned, had been sighted in the woods where Crockett's two brothers worked for a logging outfit. The problem was that the report came in August and Billy had been seen in June. The informant, a bark stripper for the logging outfit, said he hadn't put two and two together until he'd seen a reward notice for Crockett in the August issue of *Outdoor Life*. He then remembered seeing Billy with his brothers.

"He might be gone by now," Dave added, "but then again, he might not be. None of us are wearing our uniforms around here. We don't want to attract another murder."

Through the fall, several look-alikes around the country were arrested and released. Billy was seen running a fishing boat off the Florida Keys; he was spotted mushing a dog team in Talkeetna, Alaska; he was photographed at a Seahawks game in the Seattle Superdome; he was seen singing with the Apaches for Jesus country band at the Jicarilla Reservation Little Beaver Roundup in Dulce, New Mexico; he was found dead floating in the Sacramento River with his pockets turned inside out. He was seen by several people on TV as a contestant on *The Dating Game*.

"He's back," Jim Sandoval told Jack one night on the phone. It was late November, a little more than a month shy of the first anniversary of Bob's murder in Little High Rock Canyon. "We've known something was up since the end of October. Some of his old cohorts in Paradise Valley and Gerlach have been mouthing off, bragging how Billy will never be caught. They've been helping him out. He's hiding out somewhere, but the FBI is sure people have been taking him supplies."

Jack called Uncle Pete, who said, "The only thing I can tell you, Jack, is that I've heard rumors that Billy has been around, but I haven't seen him."

He knew his uncle wouldn't lie. If Pete didn't want him to know something, he would just say, "I'm not going to tell you," or "It's none of your damn business."

Jack drove to the Nugget to find the blackjack dealer

Crockett had once dated. The casino manager, his father's old friend, had told Jack on the phone that her name was Georgette Spinelli. Jack arrived about twenty minutes before the end of her shift. He hoped she might've heard something about Crockett's whereabouts, or better yet, something from Crockett himself.

Jack sat at the video poker bar and watched her from a distance. She was in her late twenties with smooth olive skin, black curly hair, and dark liquid eyes shaped like tilted teardrops. Broad-shouldered, she was as tall as Jack. She wore a pleated white blouse, a Williamsburg blue vest with a paisley design of sparkling gold leaf, and a blue bow tie the same shade as her vest. Sleek black slacks showed off long, muscular legs. She wore shiny black flats. A white towel hung from a loop on the table in front of her, and other towels lay folded and stacked behind her, but Jack never saw her use them to dry her hands. He liked the way she casually placed her right hand on the felt table, loosely pointing her fingers toward the player whose turn it was to stand or draw. She waited with her scarlet lips pushed out, as though looking to be smooched.

Ten minutes before the end of her shift Jack took a chair at her table, slid his glass into the drink holder, and played a few hands. He lost all but one of them. That's how he felt when he tried to talk to her after her shift. He still held a losing hand.

After she got her coat, they walked outside and stood in the lighted parking lot trying to talk against the roaring traffic on the I-80 overpass that traversed a low roof of the casino complex.

"I haven't seen Billy for years," she said in a pleasant, husky voice, cadenced and calm. "I went out with him a couple of times, but our romance—if you can call it that—fizzled out pretty quick. How did you find me anyway?"

"My uncle's Pete Irigaray. Billy used to work for him. He told me."

She nodded. "You're only the second cop who's asked me about him. After he shot those two guys I thought I was going to get grilled, but only one FBI agent came around. I had a feeling I was being watched, though. That's why I left Winnemucca."

"I'm not a cop. I'm a game biologist for the DOW. Crockett shot my friend, and I'd like to see him caught."

She sort of shrugged in her coat, a heavy green parka with a hood, as though Jack's distinction was nit-picking. She had one of those wonderful sexy noses that looked as though it had been broken but really hadn't. "I can't help you," she said. "I haven't heard a thing about Billy except what's in the news. The only thing I will tell you is that anyone who tries to get him better be careful. If you find him, don't think you're going to take him alive. He's going to shoot the shit out of you, or he's going to die trying."

"If you hear anything, will you let me know?"

She shrugged again. "Why should I? You're all the same— boys in a pissing contest."

Jack felt his neck heat up. "Crockett's a murderer!"

"Okay, okay." A husky laugh rumbled deep in her chest. She had a sweet smile that warmed her eyes. "You did care about your friend, didn't you? I can see that. I may call you after all."

"I'd appreciate it." They'd inched closer together as they talked in order to hear above the traffic. They stood face to face, eyes level. A faint musky scent lingered in the air between them, an appealing smell he identified with some kind of hippie perfume.

She pulled the hood up over her curly hair. "You know," she said in a disinterested tone, "you might call me, too."

He watched her climb into a red Firebird and shoot out of the parking lot with a quick, accelerating rip of rubber.

Two nights later he was home watching TV when a woman called. She didn't sound like Georgette; her voice was too high. She didn't sound like someone disguising her voice either—he could usually tell—but he couldn't be sure.

"If you want to catch Billy Crockett," the woman said, "check out King Lear."

"If you're telling the truth," Jack replied, trying to hide his excitement, "you should let the police know who you are. There's a reward. You might have something coming."

"I don't care about an award."

"Tell me your name. Who are you?"

He expected her to hang up at that point, and she did.

The tip about King Lear Peak sounded right to Jim Sandoval. "We know he's out there somewhere," he told Jack. "There's just been too much strange activity around Gerlach and Paradise Valley. Some hunters saw a man who looked like Crockett in a pickup with an Indian heading southwest from the reservation at Fort McDermitt. An outfitter sighted him through binoculars. I think he's in the Jackson Mountains or the Black Rock Range."

"That's quite a ways from Gerlach or Paradise," Jack said, thinking how hard it would be to track down Crockett in those remote mountains up near the northern border.

"Not so far for someone to run supplies out to him every couple of weeks or so. We're thinking of doing some surveillance flights to see if we can pick up any signs out there, but we're pretty short-handed at the moment."

"When can you take off?" Jack asked. "I'll go with you."

"I was hoping you'd say that."

On Saturday night about midnight Jack met Jim at the airport. The sky was dark as a pit. Jack climbed into the backseat of the Cessna next to the infrared probe. Jim settled into the front seat, and they took off, heading south, then banking east. The glittering lights of Reno fell away as they climbed north toward the Black Rock Range. Although Jim was a good pilot, Jack didn't like flying at night. Unable to make out the land below, he felt lost. He'd had a couple of drinks to settle his jitters, but they weren't doing the trick. The aftertaste only burned his throat and sparked a chilly sweat. He felt jumpy, like on the night he'd gone out with Bob to look for Crockett.

Through the squawking headset Jim's voice, tinny and far away, told him to open the window and stick out the Probeye. Wind slammed into the cockpit as the shuttering plane banked hard and tipped toward the blackness below. Wrestling the Probeye box onto the edge of the window, Jack gripped the side-handles and pressed his face against the vibrating eyepiece. He felt as though the probe and gravity were about to pull him through the window.

Jim shouted through the headset. "See anything?"

Through the eyepiece, the blank neon-green screen shimmered. "Negative," Jack shouted.

They circled and dove toward the dark mass of the mountains. How the hell had they used this machine in Vietnam, Jack wondered, without getting shot down? The liquid nitrogen in the gadget supposedly responded to infrared heat sources from enemy camps and truck engines hidden in jungles during the war, but the Probeye was only truly effective when it was dropped to within a thousand feet of the ground in the darkest nights after the air had cooled. Out here an airplane flying at a thousand feet risked smashing into a mountain.

The Cessna lurched upward, flinging Jack into his seat. The chattering engine shuddered as it strained away from a mountain wall, only yards away, it seemed. Again Jim circled and plunged downward. Jack thought he was going to throw up. When he was on the ground and spotted a small plane blinking high in the sky at night, he sometimes thought how nice it would be soaring up there through sounds of silence, as the song says. In truth, it was like being inside a goddamn cement mixer.

A corner of the quivering green screen exploded into a bright flare.

"Positive," Jack shouted.

"The Pinto Hills," Jim shouted back.

They banked east. Jack could make out the escarpment of

the rugged Jackson Range as the plane dropped down and rolled into a sideways flight. They combed the mountains from south to north and then back again. Once more, a lime-colored splash of brightness registered on the screen. Another hot spot. Jack yelled the news to Jim.

"Roger," Jim replied. "King Lear."

They circled, and the hot spot again sparkled for a few seconds on the screen. Farther south they hit new pay dirt; a bursting neon flame startled Jack's eye, then faded like a dissipating Fourth of July rocket into an eerie green sky.

When they returned to Reno, the Cessna thudded onto the runway, lined with blue lights, and sped like a drag racer down the strip. Jack helped Jim tie down the wings. His skull trembled from the motion of the plane. The tarmac rolled like the floor of an unanchored boat as he walked with Jim toward their trucks.

"That spot in the Pinto Hills is probably just that old hermit who lives by the hot springs," Jim said. "No telling who's in the Jacksons. Could be hunters, at least in the lower spot. It's unlikely any hunters would be up high in this cold weather. That camp on Lear looked near the peak."

"The only way to know," Jack said, "is to check it out."

"The FBI isn't cooperating. Ever since we determined that Crockett was back in the area, they've clammed up."

"Who needs them?"

"They've got the resources. They could send a Huey in there with a SWAT team. But they're doing things their own way. They've cut off working with us. You give the bastards information, then they don't reciprocate. Their excuse is they don't want any leaks. Why should we tell them what we know if they're just going to leave us in the cold?"

"Then we should handle this ourselves."

"The problem is getting in there. Whoever's up on the mountain could see anybody coming twenty miles away."

"Maybe someone should do it alone."

Jim frowned. "That's not smart, Basco. If Crockett's up there, he'll shoot the shit out of you before you can get near him."

"I've heard that somewhere before," Jack said.

Jack told Beth the same thing he'd told the receptionist at the office: he'd be in the Granite Range for a couple of days checking out places to transplant bighorns from the Santa Rosas. He investigated the whereabouts of local hunting outfitters who might be in the mountains, but none was contracted to be in the high Jacksons. During the day Jim Sandoval flew by himself and sighted a canvas tent where they'd picked up the heat source in the lower part of the range. That wouldn't be Crockett—he wouldn't let himself be that exposed. The other hot spot in the Pinto Hills, as they'd suspected, was near the geothermal springs where the old desert hermit named Bristlewolf Kreske lived in a dugout. Everyone considered him crazy and stayed away from him. That left the camp on King Lear Peak. Jim hadn't seen anything in the area during the day. Odds were that if someone was up there, it was Crockett, hiding out.

Jack loaded his old Kelty frame pack with wool clothes, a sleeping bag, granola, beef jerky, trail mix, and binoculars. He planned to travel light and bivouac in a cold camp. But he got to thinking about those cold mornings without brew, and he added a backpacker's kerosene stove for coffee. From the rifles Uncle Pete had loaned him he picked the .300 Savage because it had a strap. His .357 Magnum went in a holster around his waist. He wasn't going to be unarmed this time. The ammunition he needed along with canteens of water made the pack a little heavier than he'd hoped, but he could manage it. Perched high on King Lear Peak, Billy could spot a squad of deputies or a SWAT team miles away. Traveling alone, Jack felt he had a chance of sneaking up on him.

He thought about taking along a Louis L'Amour paperback

he'd picked up, to read in camp, just to see the kind of stuff Crockett was so crazy about. The cover blazoned a blurb from John Wayne: "The best Western I've ever read." Jack opened the book to the first page and read about a man named Hondo Lane: *"He was a big man, wide-shouldered, with the lean, hard-boned face of the desert rider. There was no softness in him. His toughness was ingrained and deep, without cruelty, yet quick, hard, and dangerous. Whatever wells of gentleness might lie within him were guarded and deep."*

Jack was surprised. Wendell had said this guy was a good writer! He tossed the book onto the night table by the bed. No use carrying any unnecessary weight.

He took off at midmorning. His plan was to leave the truck near Rattlesnake Canyon in the southern Jacksons and start his trek to King Lear Peak at night.

The sun was low when he pulled off the dirt road that petered out between Black Canyon and Rattlesnake Canyon. The eastern edge of the Black Rock Desert, less sterile than the stretch near Gerlach, bristled with scrubby greasewood and saltbush. He made his way on foot to where Jim had spotted the canvas tent at the mouth of Black Canyon. A Volkswagen van was parked by the big army surplus tent, but no one was in sight. Jack took off his pack and pumped a cartridge into the chamber of the rifle, just in case.

"Anybody home?" he shouted.

Something rustled inside the tent. The front flap wiggled open and a young man with a dark goatee and thinning, messy hair stepped out. He wore camouflage pants and a dirty long-sleeved river driver's shirt that had once been white. He nervously blinked in the harsh late-afternoon glare of desert sunlight as though he'd just waked from a nap.

"Anybody else with you?" Jack asked.

"My wife and kid," the man muttered.

"Pull back the flaps."

A young woman in jeans and a purple down jacket stepped

out carrying a boy in a stocking cap who looked about three. Behind her Jack could see that the tent all the way to the back was empty. He slung the rifle onto his shoulder.

"Where you from?" he asked. He showed the man his badge.

"L.A.," the man said. He looked relieved now that the rifle was hanging from Jack's shoulder. He blinked. "What day is it?" he asked.

"Thursday," Jack said. "Let me see your license."

He shook his head. "Don't have one. We're just on vacation, hunting coyotes."

Jack followed the man to the van, where he pulled open the big sliding door on the passenger side. Unfastening the twist ties from some black garbage bags, the man showed Jack the skins inside. Coyotes. Jack was relieved not to see any carcasses of wild game in the van. He didn't want entanglements to keep him from looking for Crockett.

Jack asked, "Have you seen any hunters around?"

The man shook his head. "No—yes, some guys passed in a truck yesterday, or the day before. Three of them, I think."

"What kind of truck was it?"

"A Chevy. Brown."

Jack decided not to ask any more questions. He figured the guy and his wife slept during the day and used a recorded call at night that mimicked the cry of an injured rabbit. That would bring the coyotes yipping. The woman would flash on the lights of the van, and the man would blast away at the charging animals, their eyes glowing red in the glare of the headlights. A cat's eyes glowed green. Some sport. Wardens called hunters like these JOSAs. Just out screwing around.

Jack made his way north along the western slope of the range toward the old Red Butte mine and Navajo Peak. The cottony clouds overhead took on a lemon glow as they began their sundown play of colors, passing into salmon pink that deepened into an orange hue followed by a dusky rose until finally the whole sky flamed scarlet in a fiery rage against the dying of the light. Then the color popped out as from an exhausted bed of coals, leaving the sky streaked with clouds the color of gray ash. Jack spotted a coyote's prints in the sand and followed them along a draw until the tracks strangely divided into three sets of tracks. He realized that three coyotes had been trotting along single file, as they sometimes did, playing follow the leader, the animals in the rear flawlessly placing their paws in the tracks of the leader, who picked the way through the rocks and brush of the rugged terrain. It made travel easier for those in the rear to follow a trail already blazed, but the illusion of one coyote suddenly multiplying into three was nearly perfect. No wonder Indians considered the coyote magical.

Through binoculars Jack glassed the rocks ahead and picked up the shadowy shapes of the three coyotes under a rimrock feeding on a carcass. They scattered when he approached, trotting away with their tails low to the ground, until they reached a safe distance and squatted on their haunches, watching him, no doubt waiting until they could return to their meal.

They'd been feeding on a dead deer, a five-pronged buck, shot through the neck and lungs. Wide, deep-treaded tire tracks and boot prints scoured the ground. No one would shoot such a fine buck and just leave it there, unless they were out for a trophy head. Not to be caught over their limit, trophy hunters would shoot a deer and leave it behind when they discovered it didn't meet their expectations. They would then go on to shoot another deer.

Jack followed the tire tracks for about an hour. He discovered another deer carcass, larger than the last, headless, lying in some stunted junipers. His hunch was right. No meat had been taken from the decapitated buck.

The best thing to do, to catch Crockett, was to forget the deer and keep on his way, but he thought of how Bob would feel, and he started to get angry. Deer innocently went about their business in this rough country with graceful tenacity. Why should they be so defenseless against those who wanted to blast them apart just for the hell of it?

He kept on the trail of the truck until he spied firelight from a camp nestled in the rimrocks below Navajo Peak. The overcast sky held enough diffused light from a hidden moon for him to make out the large Chevy pickup with a camper on the bed and an extended cab with folding backseats. It looked like the same kind of truck Jess Nichols drove, the one that had been parked in front of Eddie Dodd's bar on the day when Jack had questioned Dodd during the search for Bob.

Jack worked his way up the ridge to look down into the camp. He slipped off his pack. Three men hunkered around the fire on small folding canvas seats. Hunched against rock, he rehearsed what he'd learned during training at POST: Keep your strong side away from the suspect.

A man with a full gray beard in a slouch hat poured amber liquor from a gallon jug into the tin cups of the two men dressed in Day-Glo orange hunting caps and down parkas. The bearded man was indeed Jess Nichols. The bottle reflected sparks of firelight. Jess placed it on the ground, leaned forward to speak to the other men, then stood up and walked toward the back of his truck. He heard me, Jack thought. The man had ears like a hound. He was going to the truck for his rifle. Jack immediately stepped into open ground and hollered down into the camp, "Hey, Jess, how you doing? It's me, Jack Irigaray."

At the back of the truck, Jess pulled out a ring of keys and locked the camper. Jack shouldered his rifle and walked down into the camp. Jess told his clients, "This is Jack Irigaray. He's a biologist for Fish and Game, the best damn biologist in the state." Jess raised the big bottle of Old Crow toward Jack. "How about a shot?"

"Fine by me," Jack replied.

Jess introduced his two clients, Pat McCarthy and Doug Winston from Pennsylvania. All three men looked pretty well liquored.

"You hunting?" Jess asked Jack.

Jack nodded. "For Billy Crockett. We think he's hiding out around here."

Jess grinned, and the other two men abruptly mimicked his feral smile, their bodies visibly loosening with the knowledge that a warden wasn't checking on them.

"I heard Crockett was up in Canada," Jess said.

You damned liar, Jack thought. "You know as well as I do he's come back."

"I haven't seen him," Jess said. "I've heard nothing but rumors. I believe there's more chance he's still in Canada."

Pat McCarthy reached for the bourbon and asked with affected innocence, "He that guy that smoked those two game wardens?"

"One game warden," Jack said. "The other guy was a buddy of his, just helping him out."

"Jack was with them," Jess told the two men. "If he'd been there alone, nothing would've happened. The game warden caused all the trouble."

Jack held back his anger. "What do you know about it, Jess?"

The guide tried to defuse the tension with his grin. He was a wiry, ratty-looking guy in his fifties who appeared younger when a smile broke through his beard. "I knew Bob Pritchard. He carried too much badge for his own good. If he had his way he would've put every trapper and hunter out of business. Crockett wasn't much of a trapper, but he wasn't that bad a guy. When you corner a man like a caged animal, he's gonna strike back."

Jack sipped the whiskey from the tin cup. He figured that the hunters were after prize racks and that they would be shipping them back to Pennsylvania. If they had illegal tags, as he suspected, and he cited them now, it would be just a misdemeanor, and there was no way he could prove they'd shot and abandoned the two deer he'd found. It was better to wait until they tried to send their game trophies home and then nail them. The Lacey Act made it a federal crime to transport any illegally taken wildlife across state lines. It was the only law that had any teeth in it when it came to this kind of poacher.

"I found a couple of deer on the way up here," Jack said. "Someone took the head of one but left the meat. Did you see them?"

He sensed the two hunters tightening up. Their glowering faces, fortified with booze, flashed resentment. Jack had grown accustomed to such looks. Men who ordinarily wouldn't think of stealing a candy bar back home could become threatening out in the brush where mountain-man fantasies ranged unhindered. The wild ranges and deserts made laws seem irrelevant except, of course, for what people assumed to be the law of nature: the survival of the fittest. A man with a badge walking into a camp became an obscenity to everything wild and free.

Doug Winston started to shake his head in denial, but Jess Nichols, his small eyes flitting angrily toward the man, intervened. "We saw one buck back there, a five-pointer. Looked like someone shot it long-distance with an off caliber, like a twenty-five aught six. Maybe they couldn't find the carcass. It's sad, the waste of it. Guys like that shouldn't be let out here. I'd love for these fellows to get a deer like that. I always taught my boys that whatever they killed they had to eat, and whatever they shot they had to find."

Jack walked to the folding table near the fire. Turning the spigot of the five-gallon plastic water container on the table, he rinsed out the tin cup and handed it back to Jess. "I have to be going. Thanks for the drink."

"You bet," Jess said. "Good luck. I hope you get Crockett. I can't shed any tears over Bob Pritchard, but Billy had no business killing Larry Hughes. That fat boy was a damn fine fellow."

Jack walked north for an hour and then rolled out his sleeping bag under the rimrock of a side canyon where he found some water running. He ate dry granola and made a cup of coffee. He felt beat. The prehistoric lake bed of the Black Rock Desert stretched into the west in calm silence. Clouds glowed silvery with diffused moonlight. In the darkness of the distant alkali flat, steam from Buckbrush Springs misted the air. Jack crushed a bit of dried rabbitbrush between his fingers and sniffed its lemony scent.

The desert felt tranquil and unpeopled. Jack knew better. Out among greasewood and saltbush, swooping owls and pouncing coyotes casually went about their nightly business of catching mice and rats. The desert basins, so empty to the eye, swarmed with scurrying rodents, more than most people could imagine. All the rats and mice and rockchucks outweighed in bulk all the hawks and owls and coyotes that hunted them. Poachers like Jess Nichols's clients had it all wrong. The law in the desert wasn't one of interminable battle or bloody massacre but the calm, muted pursuit of life. For the most part, peaceful coexistence was the real law. Predators didn't fight each other. In fact, the survival of the fittest rested on the avoidance of fighting. Those coyotes Jack saw would continue cooperatively feeding on that deer carcass without turning and snarling and snapping at each other over the last scrap, as domestic dogs would do. They had learned that survival depended on getting along. A lone mountain lion, spotting the tracks of another cat in the snow, would turn away and seek out new territory where it could hunt alone, even if it could easily overpower the other lion. Healthy deer had little to fear from stalking cougars. The old and sick were their common prey. In the spring, young deer were also vulnerable, but by fall they could romp away from a lion along with the rest of a healthy herd. Coyotes preferred to scrounge after carrion rather than undertake the hard work of chasing a healthy jackrabbit. But what they did kill, they cleaned up. A full belly satisfied coyotes more than the need to kill. Only humans, thrilled with slaughter, were a threat to both predator and prey out here.

Jack remembered how as a boy he'd trapped muskrats along the Steamboat and Sparks ditches draining into the Truckee River. He would set ten traps, catch one or two muskrats a week, and sell the skins to the Garcia Fur Company. He felt like Jim Bridger in the wilderness. He'd probably read the same books about Bridger and other mountain men as Billy Crockett had when he was a kid. Those free trappers, as they called themselves, or "white Indians," who ranged the Rockies and the Great Basin in the 1820s and 1830s in search of pelts and adventure had inflamed his boyish imagination to incandescence. In daydreams he had often pictured himself as a mountain man in greasy fringed buckskin, riding with a Hawkins rifle into the Green River rendezvous with Jedediah Smith. Later he even imagined trying to take up such a life, as best he could, someplace else, maybe in Alaska, hunting and trapping, living alone in a cabin.

But one day, when he was a senior in high school, he found a muskrat's leg in one of his traps. He thought of the animal somewhere in the willows licking its bloody stump. A change in feeling had been gathering from week to week, month to month, as he'd stripped pelts from dead animals and tossed their glistening carcasses to the birds. While he stared at the bloody leg, trapping abruptly seemed horrible to him. What honor lay in taking an animal's skin and leaving its body as waste?

The next year he was hunting deer in the mountains south of Austin. He shot a doe near a spring at about fifty yards, but it didn't drop. The doe stood there, swiveled her head back, and looked at him. Then he saw blood drip from her mouth. Usually he was a good shot. People said, "You have an eye like your uncle Pete." But on this day he was shaking, and when he again fired at the doe, trying to hit her in the neck, he missed. Seven shots—he missed them all. The deer bounded into the aspen thicket around the spring. He went down to find it, and he heard a sound in the thicket, that terrible sound a thrashing body makes in brush while dying. When he came up to the doe, it was dead, but he never hunted deer again.

He'd continued to shoot birds—doves, quail, chukars, pheasants, ducks—until he was out alone chukar hunting one Christmas Day. He went to retrieve a bird he'd dropped in flight. He came across a patch of stained snow. The sight of bright red blood on clean white snow got to him. That was the end of hunting for him.

Often he was glad he and Beth had never had a boy. He suspected that he would've felt the need to teach a son something about hunting. Many in the department still hunted. Bob and he had been the odd ones out. The young nongame biologist in the office, a Berkeley type with round rimless glasses, as passive a soul as anyone could meet, kept a garden and took a deer every year because he wanted his son and little daughter to know something about where their food came from, that it didn't automatically and painlessly materialize in plastic packages in supermarket coolers. Jack couldn't say that was a bad thing. He knew the blood and nerves of his prehistoric ancestors still stirred in his own. Humans had been forged in Ice Age hardness, and out here was where they still could feel most alive, most at home. But people had fashioned another niche for themselves with their inventions and gadgets, where they lived in comfort but no longer felt at home. It was called the pursuit of happiness.

He could appreciate how Billy Crockett wandered out here in his own pursuit of happiness. Beth was right, to a point.

Once, he had envied Billy's dream. As a boy, he'd lived for the thrill of being in open country. But Uncle Pete was right, too. Things had changed. Everywhere the country bore the press of humans. Abandoned mines lay within easy walking distance. Tracks crisscrossed the basins and salt flats. Domestic stock and four-wheelers roamed the hills. Hunters sought open space and bumped into windmills and irrigation ditches and sheep. Jack and his cohorts kept track of pronghorn and deer herds as though they were cattle. They moved bighorns from one range to another and watched after them. Mountain lions wandered the high rimrocks with telemetric collars around their necks. The wilderness had become a game park. The wild, free country those JOSAs and poachers sought existed only in their minds. They had no right to slaughter whatever they wanted. Bighorns had clattered through these mountains for ten thousand years. By the 1940s they'd been wiped out. By what right? Now bighorns once again romped in their native homeland. What right did Billy Crockett have to knock one off just because he felt like it? Wild game needed protection from all the JOSAs, poachers, and punks like Billy Crockett. Jack felt he might not shoot a deer, but he sure as hell was willing to put a slug into William David Crockett, Jr.

He poured the remains of his second cup of coffee into the dirt. He was letting himself get too agitated to sleep. He wished he'd brought along a pint. The taste Jess gave him was nice, but not enough. It had been weeks since he'd gone without more than one drink in the evening. But he knew that to carry a bottle while tracking a killer was not a brilliant idea. At the same time, he knew that maybe Beth was right, although her words had irritated him. The desire to kill Billy Crockett and the demon inside him were one and the same.

His digital watch flashed 5:18. He'd overslept. He stuffed away his sleeping bag, strapped on his pack and rifle, and set out in the darkness. His plan was to work his way up the narrow gorge below the nameless peak south of King Lear, traverse the saddle between the two peaks, and drop down to where Jim and he had spotted the camp on the western slope. He wanted to have elevation to come down on Crockett. The more accessible route up McGill Canyon with its broad alluvial fan at the mouth and wide walls was too dangerous. From the peak's southern ridge, Crockett could have a hawk's aerial view of Desert Valley to the east and the Black Rock Desert to the west, his gaze sweeping the arid playas all the way to the Bloody Runs and the Black Rock Range. Jack would be too exposed. The bushwhacking route he was taking was rougher but safer. He only wished he'd hit the trail earlier.

Beyond a stand of leafless cottonwoods, he picked up a dry streambed that divided and cut to the northeast into steep cliffs. He scrambled up jagged rocks that in the spring and summer would be a gushing two-tiered waterfall. It was tough going. The scraping of stone made him nervous. A rock took off bouncing and clattering down the stony chute. He hunched behind a lichen-stained boulder for several minutes before resuming his climb.

A clump of junipers gave him a place to rest just above a mossy rock pool. Water cascaded in a narrow stream over a ledge and rushed past dogwood and red willows webbed with wild grape vines. The sun broke through a rocky notch above him, bringing out the weird bruised purple and greenish colors staining the cliffs. The range was treeless, except for occasional Utah junipers, beaded with a few white berries.

Sweat chilled his eyelids. He climbed higher into a wind off the northern ridge. At noon a surprising amphitheater broke open to his right, exposing a steep talus plunging a thousand feet down to a clutter of rocky rubble. He felt like an eagle hanging on air.

Something screamed past his ear; then he heard the shot, a burst from a rifle that echoed and reechoed in a ringing whine off the cliffs. He stumbled back, turning to break his fall, his palms slamming hard against the slope, his cheek scraping rock. He found himself behind a boulder, remembering Uncle Pete saying that if someone shot at you, and you heard the blast, you hadn't been hit. The rifle strap caught on his pack as he tried to pull it free. His scraped palms turned wet with blood. He fired a shot up into the cliffs in the direction of where he thought the bullet had come, then scrambled on his elbows and knees toward a protective ledge below him.

An answering shot came down, chipping rock from the boulder where he'd fallen. Between two jutting pinnacles on the cliff overhead, he caught a glimpse of a neon orange hunting cap as the shape of a man darted from one pinnacle to the other. Jack fired off a shot, knowing he wouldn't hit the man but wanting him to keep at a distance, then he made a run down the talus, his feet slipping and stumbling until he dove for cover where the rock face split into a dark cavity. In the stony crevice a single, scraggly bunch of rabbitbrush clung to yellow sand. He felt disoriented. What was rabbitbrush doing up this high? Its dry, pale blossoms, burst of seeds, appeared incandescent in the thin air, intense with life, a luminous apparition. His heart lurched like a terrified animal. He scanned the high rocks, looking for the orange cap. Had Jess Nichols circled above him in an attempt to knock him off? Jess must have known that the casual encounter the previous night was only a mask for Jack's suspicions of what the hunters were really up to. Jack's dead body up here could conceivably be passed off as a hunting accident. Or was Crockett uncharacteristically wearing a Day-Glo orange cap simply to disguise himself as one of any number of hunters who could be on the mountain?

The route down the mountain looked like a free fall of tumbling boulders and shards, much steeper in its descent than when Jack had climbed it. His scraped palms smeared the rifle stock with sweat and blood. He had to get down the mountain. An unexpected weightless sensation in his arms and head made him want to rest against the rock and fall asleep. His breathing roared in his inner ear like a distant bellows, an autonomous machine detached from human control. He felt his consciousness straining to float up and away from his body, indifferently leaving behind its sack of bones and flesh to fend for itself. He concentrated on his hands, forcing them to squeeze the slick stock of the rifle, to assure himself that what he touched was real.

A threatening stillness hugged the rocks as though they had become animate beings tensed with fear. He listened hard for the scrape of Crockett's boots. Now he was sure the man above had to be Crockett. Jess Nichols was capable of rage, but not enough to sustain a calculated attempt to murder a government biologist. It had to be Crockett. Had he fired and missed on purpose? Jack looked at his watch. It wasn't there. His reddened left wrist was swollen. The watch strap must've snapped off when he hit the ground.

Pushing with his elbows, he slid on his stomach feetfirst out of the crevice, keeping the rifle pointed upward, eyes strained toward the cliffs. He wriggled down, letting his feet feel their way on the rocks, stopping now and then so he could scan the stony slope up toward the ridge. He saw that he'd almost made it up to the saddle before Crockett must've spotted him. The steepening slope now left him standing perpendicular, pressed against rockface, but he continued to let his feet find holds as he kept the rifle and his attention directed upward. It was so much harder going down.

Then he was falling over sharp shards and scree, his face and stomach hitting and bouncing against rock as he tried to grab at something, anything, with his right hand while his left still gripped the rifle. His feet thudded hard against level rock, stunning him from his soles to his skull as though he'd jumped from a roof onto hard, flat ground. He found himself standing upright on a protruding ledge, shaken but no longer falling.

Carefully, he continued to creep downward. The slope became less steep. He turned and started to run, at first cautiously then faster, jumping and stumbling past ledges and jagged outcroppings until he reached the stand of junipers above the rock pool of still, tranquil water. He didn't stop to rest but continued down the mountain, expecting any moment to feel a slug of lead slam into his back. He didn't know how long it took to reach the mouth of the gorge. Exhausted, he had no sense of time. His body ached, his scraped face stung. His hands felt as though he'd burned them on hot briquets. His bad lung throbbed.

Following the base of the Jacksons, he trudged south for the next couple of hours until he reached the place where Jess Nichols and the two hunters had camped. They had gone, their truck tracks heading north. He walked on until he saw the tent of the coyote hunters ahead. The sun was dropping. He skirted west onto the desert to avoid the tent and make his way through sand dunes and over salt flats. He'd had enough of rocks for the day. The sun now hovered about four fingers above the horizon, less than an hour away from vanishing.

When he stopped to take a compass reading to locate his truck, only the bald red dome of the sun peaked above the Black Rock Range. He headed southeast in the direction of the canyon where he'd parked. The sky started its celestial light show, and by the time he reached the canyon, the cloudy expanse stretching westward looked like a bubbling flow of scarlet lava.

Relief ran through him like cool water when he finally spied the dark shape of his truck. It appeared like an old friend patiently awaiting his return. He felt like crying in gratitude. He ached all over, so instantly tired that he felt even the last hundred yards would take all his dwindling strength. He trudged on until he saw that the truck hunkered in the sand, a wounded beast. Shredded holes in the thick-treaded Desert

Duellers showed where bullets had punctured each of the four tires.

Jack stared out into the darkening desert. That damn Jess Nichols! He and his imbecilic thugs had circled around and blown out the tires. To the west it was fifty miles to Gerlach; to the east, fifty to Winnemucca. A fading rosy glow smeared the tops of the western peaks. Night blackened the east. Jack took a drink from his canteen. The water tasted cold and sweet. It made him realize he was still alive. Crockett had eluded him; the bastard was still free. But so was he. Crockett had had two chances to kill him, one almost a year ago on the desert and now one on the mountain, and he'd escaped both times. Something venomous stirred in him. He was alive. The game wasn't over. Weary but determined, he started the long trek across the desert for help. He chose to head east, though the way was darker.

CHAPTER 6

In February Jack helped nail Jess Nichols and the Pennsylvania poachers on the Lacey Act. He'd told Division of Wildlife law enforcement investigators about the decapitated deer and his suspicions. Jess Nichols had illegally bought resident tags from some locals for the out-of-state hunters. Tom Morini, who was in charge of Operation Game Thief, tracked down the taxidermist in Stillwater who'd mounted the three heads, each sporting a trophy rack more than thirty inches wide. The heads had then been shipped to Pennsylvania. The whole investigation took two months, including weeks of paperwork and phone calls before the desk boys could build a case. But in litigious times, they had to be careful. One slip, and the indictment could get tossed out of court.

When the Feds raided the home of Pat McCarthy in Pennsylvania, the poacher had dragged two of the heads out the back door. He protested his innocence. He might've gotten away with it if the Feds hadn't persisted in their search and found the mounted heads in the snow behind some trees. The other guy, Doug Winston, had the third trophy in his den. All three deer heads now lay on the floor in Tom Morini's office, staring up forlornly with marble eyes.

When Jess Nichols went to court in March, he was stripped of his license as a guide, handed a $3,000 fine, and given a three-year probation. Big deal! Jess had charged the hunters $5,000. The fine was a trifle. In court he pleaded ignorance: "Your Honor," he told the judge, "there's so damn many laws and regulations anymore, this country is nothing but a dictatorship."

Jack went to see Jess after the trial, but the little beady-eyed rat wouldn't admit to shooting out the truck tires. He just smiled. "That's sad, Jack. I seen some coyote hunters out there. I bet they're the ones who done it."

By the time that Jack had finally got his pickup out of the desert and made it home, the pleurisy in his lung was pretty bad. His face was torn up from the rock fall, his wrist sprained. The rest of his body ached as though he'd been clobbered by a Land Rover. The exhilaration he'd felt on escaping death in the desert flipped to black depression. Over and over again, he retraced his route up the mountain and his route down it. A few minutes one way or another might've made a difference. Maybe if he hadn't overslept, he might have got the drop on Crockett. He walked around as though muffled in woolen blankets of anger and despair.

Beth worked on him with her "radiant touch" therapy. He took off his clothes and sprawled on the bed while she lightly touched stress points up and down his legs, back, arms, and stomach. Her soft fingertips felt like feathers. She said it was an enhancement of a technique called biomagnetic healing. The idea was to stimulate the body's own natural recuperative powers by activating its healing energy. For all his skepticism,

Jack sensed a warmth flowing through his skin under Beth's touch, and he felt better after each treatment. Who was to say?

The phone rang while they were in the bedroom. A woman left a message on the machine telling Beth the place of their group's monthly outdoor meeting. Jack had no idea what went on out there in the desert under the full moon. Beth had grown up religious, her mother a believer in novenas, stigmatas, bleeding Sacred Hearts, apparitions of Our Lady, and palpable, cinder-breathed demons. Perhaps that was the only way Beth's mom had to deal with a drunken husband. Jack feared Beth was headed in the same direction. Maybe it was genetic.

"Don't try to equate what I'm doing with my mother," Beth said before going off for her meeting. "I'm not superstitious." She'd always separated herself from her mother's fanaticism; that's why Jack had such a hard time understanding her New Age connections.

"It seems just as loopy to me," he told her. "They're both so irrational."

"There are lots of things rationality can't explain."

"I know that." He thought about his dream of Bob. "But it can explain nuttiness."

"Don't undermine what I'm experiencing. I'm too old to fall for nutty behavior. I'm a tired mother with a husband who drinks too much, and if I can find some strength in a group of women like me who believe in powers of the spirit, then I'd appreciate some support. All I want is to make things a little better than they are, but I have to start with myself."

For a second, Jack saw the grieving face of a woman whose simple ambition to become a nurse, help people, and mother a happy family had crumbled. He lifted his hands, but the gesture startled her. Her mouth tightened in momentary fright, as though she thought he was going to hit her—memories of her father?—before her eyes read his and she stepped into his arms.

He wanted to say he was sorry, but it wouldn't come out.

"I want us to make things different," she said. "But it's not happening."

"How?" Jack protested. "I've been trying."

"Trying to hide things. Trying to be Clint Eastwood up on that mountain. What a crazy kid's thing to do. Now you have another excuse to drink, don't you? Forget about that idiot Crockett. Just let him go, for Christ's sake."

Since coming down from King Lear Peak, Jack had become more resolved than ever. He no longer cared what Beth thought. Nailing Jess Nichols gave him confidence that they could nail Crockett, too, now that he was back in Nevada. "I can't do that. Not now, anyway. I know we're going to get him, and then this thing will be behind us."

"You just don't understand, do you?"

"I need *you* to understand, too. It's only a matter of time. We're going to get him any day."

But Crockett had vanished again. By the time Jim Sandoval led two deputies up King Lear Peak, all they found was a stone fire ring where someone had camped. The FBI refused to make surveillance flights, claiming the territory was too extensive and the sites too numerous to check out. Jack felt that the search had reverted to square one.

Then in April everyone's attention got caught up with three murders in the northern desert. Bristlewolf Kreske, the hermit who lived in the dugout at Pinto Hot Springs, shot and killed two college kids, a guy and a girl, who were exploring the area with an old placer map that had been handed down in the girl's family. It was just a vacation adventure for them, but Bristlewolf, paranoid about BLM threats to evict all desert dwellers as trespassers, shot them as they hiked up to his dugout. Bristlewolf had formerly spent his days working in his garden and cornfield, studying the Bible, and painting scriptural quotations on rocks. It was said that in the army he'd been used for LSD experiments. He'd once told Jack that he only carried a .30–30 to protect himself from a wolf that kept following him. He said the wolf waited for him every night just over the hill.

On the day that Bristlewolf shot the two kids, one of his few friends, Fermin Yndart, a retired Basque sheepherder and prospector who regularly bathed his arthritic legs in the hot springs, drove out on his three-wheeled ORV for his weekly soak. Bristlewolf killed the old herder as he drove up to the dugout. He left all three bodies lying by the hot springs.

After his arrest—he didn't put up a fight—Bristlewolf was sent off for a psychiatric evaluation. He wouldn't say a word. At his show cause hearing the only thing he said was that his name wasn't Kreske. He wouldn't say what it was. He had legally changed his name to Bristlewolf in 1977. The grand jury returned a three-count indictment of first-degree murder. Bristlewolf now sat silently in his jail cell awaiting trial.

At the end of April it happened. Somebody snitched on Crockett. An informant called the FBI and said Billy was hiding out in Wyatt Green's trailer in Gerlach. Jim Sandoval called Jack at five-thirty in the morning on the last Sunday in April.

"So we've got ourselves another snipe hunt," Jack said. His sarcasm sprang as much from a fuzzy head, aching from Saturday night drinking, as from sixteen months of frustrating leads and searches.

"This is it," Jim replied. "I've been on the FBI's ass to get me into the loop. They've had their eye on Gerlach and Paradise Valley for the past two months. They know he's in Wyatt's trailer, but he might split."

Wyatt Green lived alone in a dilapidated trailer northeast of Gerlach near Granite Point. About Crockett's age, Wyatt was a rawboned guy with a luxuriant handlebar mustache who worked as a fencer and general handyman. Whatever job he picked up, he insisted on working alone. He frequently sat in Eddie Dodd's bar wearing a tractor cap and nursing a beer without speaking to anyone. When asked if he wanted another Keystone, he might nod. He'd worked as a firewood cutter for a time in Talkeetna, Alaska, one of the places where a false sighting of Crockett had occurred.

Wyatt took measures to protect his privacy; in Alaska, he returned to his log cabin each night and left every morning by a different route. In Gerlach he strung a wide circle of high barbed-wire fencing around his trailer and a graveyard of old cars and trucks. Crudely painted signs threatened trespassers. He was an ex-Marine, wounded during the Tet Offensive, and like Crockett, a gun fanatic. The two had target-practiced together, talked guns. Odd bedfellows, the vet and the dodger had apparently become tight enough for Wyatt to risk harboring the fugitive.

Jim Sandoval told Jack to be at Crosby's Lodge at the Pyramid Lake Marina by eight o'clock. Room 3. "Take your own truck," Jim said, "not the department's."

Jack drove onto the Paiute reservation, past shabby prefab houses and mobile homes, rusting cars, and chainlink fences. Weeds and rabbitbrush sprouted in the cracked dirt of front yards right up to the walls of Indian houses and trailers. He turned onto Desert Flower Road, its name being the only thing pretty about it, and drove down toward the lake to some cottonwoods and a cream brick building with a simple yellow sign: MOTEL.

Only three unmarked cars and trucks were parked in front of the motel and store. He thought he was early, but when he knocked, the motel door swung open, and he walked into a room crammed with men and guns. He recognized Sheriff Ben Nelson and FBI Special Agent Fred Banfield, who'd interrogated him in the hospital. Highway Patrolman Larry Groppenbacker, a longtime friend of Bob's, sat on a bed next to Jim Sandoval. SWAT commander Roger Hansmeyer leaned against the wall. Members of two FBI SWAT teams filled the rest of the room. No one wore a uniform.

Special Agent Fred Banfield seemed to be running the show. "I didn't think it was a good idea for you to be involved," he told Jack, "but Jim insisted, and we need the manpower. The sheriff said he was willing to deputize you."

"I feel I should be here," Jack replied. "This guy shot me."

Fred Banfield frowned. "I don't want you to bring anything personal into this operation. We have to work as a team."

They were waiting for the Las Vegas SWAT team and a Huey helicopter to arrive. Jack found it hard to understand how Banfield felt shorthanded. He'd already staked out a deputy sheriff and an FBI agent on Granite Point with a telescope overlooking Wyatt Green's trailer. Two deputies in Reno stood ready with a Cessna to provide high aerial reconnaissance of the area.

A map on the wall showed the plan of attack. Three SWAT teams and the Huey helicopter would form a moving horseshoe that would swoop toward the trailer from the southeast. Vehicles posted on the roads to Empire and the Black Rock Desert would block exits to the north and south. Jack and Jim Sandoval were supposed to block the dirt road running northwest from Gerlach in the unlikely event that Crockett could make a break along Granite Point toward the Smoke Creek Desert. Jack didn't like the plan. He felt left out of the action.

"I'd rather Jim and I split up," he told Fred Banfield. "I could watch from farther north." He tapped the wall map where a black line marked a dirt road running to Bloody Point.

"I want you where I put you," Fred Banfield snapped. "If Crockett comes your way, you'll have your shot at him."

"I don't want anyone to have a shot at him," Jack heard himself saying. "He knows where Bob Pritchard's body is. We have to take him alive, or we'll never find Bob."

Fred Banfield blinked, but if Jack had introduced a new idea to him, he didn't let on. "That's our intention," he agreed, "to capture him. We don't want him dead."

"Then wouldn't it be better just to circle the place, so he'd see escape was hopeless? You're planning an attack. He's going to fight back."

Fred Banfield glowered. "We're doing what's efficient with the manpower we have. If you're not going to cooperate, I'm going to ask you to stay out."

Jim Sandoval jabbed an elbow into Jack's weak lung. Jack shut up.

All morning the men sat in the stuffy room waiting for the Las Vegas SWAT team and the helicopter. About noon, someone knocked on the door. Another deputy sheriff entered with Dale Ellison, the Washoe warden who'd had the flu the night when Jack and Bob had gone out to check on Crockett. Jack wondered what would've happened if Dale had gone with Bob that night. Would they all be in this mess right now? He wondered which of them, sitting in the room at this moment, might be dead at the end of the day.

The men began to unwrap sandwiches and pop open sodas. Jack hadn't brought a lunch, and Fred Banfield suggested that he go buy something next door.

The marina store was divided into a grocery section and a bar. Tacked to the wall above a kids' coin-operated rocking horse, hundreds of Polaroid snapshots showed fishermen holding enormous Pyramid Lake trout caught during the previous season. On the far wall, above video poker machines, hung dozens of stuffed and labeled cutthroat trout, all heavier than fourteen pounds. The mounted fish looked like painted wood.

Jack passed gallon jugs of Old Grand Dad and Wild Turkey. The store shelves turned out to hold more liquor than food. He picked up a six-pack of Dr Pepper and two salami and cheese sandwiches encased in plastic wrap. He bought an additional box of rifle cartridges for his .300 Savage in the truck.

Back in the room, at two o'clock, the phone finally rang.

Fred Banfield announced that the Huey helicopter was at the Reno airport, ready to go. The Cessna had taken off for a reconnaissance flight. The deputy and agent staked out on Granite Point had reported by radio that they'd spotted a man working on a truck near Wyatt Green's trailer.

Jack complained to Jim Sandoval, "If we don't get going, Crockett will be long gone."

At three o'clock, the Las Vegas SWAT team still hadn't arrived, but Fred Banfield ordered all men who were going to set up roadblocks to take off. They were to wait in Gerlach for further orders on their portable two-way radios. As Jack left the room, men on the SWAT teams began to take off their street clothes and put on bulletproof vests and camouflage fatigues.

Jack rode with Jim Sandoval. A little after four in the afternoon, they drove through Gerlach, passed Eddie Dodd's bar, and headed out of town on the road toward a place called Planet X, where some aging hippies spent their days making pottery and dry sailing on the salt flats. Jim pulled his Cherokee off the road and drove overland to a ridge where they could look down on the desolate flat and Wyatt Green's trailer, about three-quarters of a mile away. When Jack glassed the barbed-wire enclosure, his binoculars magnified the legs of a man extending from under a flatbed truck. The hood of the truck yawned open. The man on the ground wriggled out wearing coveralls and a Cat cap. He bent over the exposed engine. He climbed into the truck, started it, and drove forward, then backward about ten yards, only to get out and resume tinkering with the engine.

The man had Wyatt Green's lanky build, but Jack couldn't make out the face under the cap.

A dry wind whipped up dust devils on the alkali flat. The sky was cloudless, an Easter-egg blue. The sun, a fiery spring gold, hung above the hills. It seemed like any other lazy Sunday afternoon with threshers and sparrows flitting in sagebrush while a man puttered over his truck.

By five-thirty the sun had slid dangerously close to the horizon, polishing the desert a coppery gold.

"Where the hell are those suckers?" Jack asked. "It's going to be dark in another hour."

Jim nodded. "If Crockett's down there, he'll get away for sure in the dark."

From behind Granite Point, an old black Ford pickup crept toward Wyatt's trailer, moving so slowly that no dust kicked up from the tires. Wyatt Green swung open the wire gate to let the pickup into the yard. A bareheaded man in blue jeans and a checkered shirt, shorter and stockier than Wyatt, got out. The two stood in the yard talking. Then Wyatt walked back to the flatbed truck, and his companion disappeared into the trailer.

"That's Crockett," Jim said. "It's a good thing we didn't start the raid earlier. He wouldn't have been home."

Jack's new digital watch read 5:50. He and Jim had been told to keep their radio off until they actually saw the raid begin, but there still came no sign of the SWAT teams or the helicopter. The sun was just about touching the western peaks.

"What are they waiting for?" Jack asked.

"I've been thinking," Jim answered. "If Crockett makes a break this way, it might be better if one of us is on that bluff over there." He pointed toward the rise to the north of the road. "That way we can catch him in our crossfire."

"Go ahead. Let's just not shoot each other."

Jim carried his Ruger submachine gun and rifle to the top of the bluff about two hundred yards away. A high drone in the sky caught Jack's ear. He glanced up, squinting. Flying at about fifteen thousand feet, tiny as a fly, a twin-engine Cessna circled in the fading light. In another twenty minutes all light would vanish. Around and around the Cessna circled. Shit, Jack thought, remembering how spooked Crockett got about planes. If Billy heard that plane, he might be out of the trailer before the raid even started.

An explosion of dust tornadoed up from the earth as a Huey helicopter burst over the ridge of Granite Point and roared toward the trailer, its siren screaming. Two sand-colored Suburbans raced out of Gerlach, trailing funnels of dust, speeding toward opposite flanks of the barbed-wired enclosure. The clattering helicopter banked and swung low to the ground, about four hundred yards from the trailer. One after another, five men jumped from the chopper into the sagebrush. Swirling dust engulfed them as the Huey lifted, pivoted, and roared back toward the trailer. The siren cut out, and a loudspeaker blared: "FBI. CROCKETT. FBI. SURRENDER WITH YOUR HANDS UP. FBI. COME OUT WITH YOUR HANDS UP."

Two four-man SWAT teams to the southeast trotted beside their advancing vehicles, hugging the sides behind the protection of winged-open doors. The group from the chopper scurried through sagebrush toward the trailer from the opposite direction. The man tinkering over the truck in the yard flopped to the ground on his stomach in a stationary, spread-eagle position.

Shattered glass erupted from the trailer as Crockett hurtled through the window, hit the ground, rolled, and lunged behind a white camper. He lay prone, a rifle in his hands, then scrambled to his feet, casually sauntered to the old Ford pickup, and climbed into the driver's side. Dirt spewed from the back of the truck as it swiveled in a sharp U-turn, gathered speed, and shot past the trailer in the direction of the fence. It crashed through the fence, strands of barbed wire fluttering out from the radiator grill like Christmas tree tinsel.

With heart thumping Jack put on a Day-Glo orange parka and switched on the portable radio strapped to his waist. The calm voice of the SWAT team commander told the helicopter, "Redeploy. Suspect heading north."

The black pickup bounded over a gulley, lifted into the air, and came down on a slope, where it spun into another U-turn and careened southwest. It sped away from the chopper team and picked up the dirt road for a hundred yards or so, then cut into rolling mounds of sage and rabbitbrush a half mile away, racing back toward Jack.

The Huey dropped through the air, hugging the tail of the speeding truck like a cutting horse. The helicopter swung back and forth trying to steer the pickup toward the SWAT teams. The truck bounced through brush and over hummocks of alkali. The sound of gunshots cracked over the radio and in the air. "Taking fire," the helicopter pilot reported.

"Green light," the SWAT commander calmly ordered. From the belly of the helicopter a sharpshooter opened fire. Other flashes and bursts erupted from the SWAT team flanking the pickup. The ridge across from Jack ripped with the rachety roar of Jim's Ruger submachine gun. The black truck swerved away from the bluff, speeding toward the Smoke Creek Desert.

Jack started the Cherokee and spun onto the road, staying parallel with the truck. He gained ground, making better time on the hard-surfaced road, pulled a hundred yards ahead, then turned into the brush to cut off Billy's pickup. He jumped from the Cherokee. The pickup, veering away, bounced over the rough hilly ground. As Jack fired twice at the door of the turning truck, his heart was wild, his hands shaking, just like the time when he'd tried to hit the wounded doe. He held his breath, his lung on fire. He kept his aim low, hoping not to hit Crockett in the chest or head. He fired twice more at the truck.

The black pickup thudded to an abrupt stop, tilted at an odd angle in roiling dust with its right front tire submerged in a gully wash. The top of the passenger door on the side away from Jack swung open. Jack caught a fleeting glimpse through the sagebrush of a hobbling man, then nothing. Jack strained to spot movement in the brush, shrouded in shadows. It was like trying to look into a foggy sea. The earth was losing light fast, leaving the sky pearly while the desert gathered darkness.

The Huey had picked up the most distant SWAT team and now hovered above the ground a quarter mile beyond the truck, dropping the men like lumps from its belly. The dark shapes of the other SWAT team advanced on the truck, one man at a time appearing above the brush as the silhouettes lurched forward, popping up and dropping like scorched grasshoppers on a hot day. Jack jogged in the direction of where he'd seen Crockett stumble out of sight, about a hundred yards away.

Over the radio a voice shouted, "I have a man in orange in my sights." Jack knew he was the man the fool was talking about.

"Don't fire," Jack yelled into the radio. "It's me. Game warden. Game warden."

"Roger," came the reply.

He ran hunched along a gully and trotted over a rise about fifty yards from the truck. The leapfrogging shapes of the SWAT team bounded through the sagebrush. They'd passed the spot where Jack had seen Crockett disappear. He switched off the radio so he couldn't be heard approaching. The spooky quietness from the desert amplified the plops of his boots as he ran. Why hadn't these fuckers started the raid earlier when Crockett had first returned and there was still plenty of light? Crockett could've scurried a quarter of a mile away by now, or he could be lying somewhere in the brush waiting to pop his pursuers. Any moment Jack expected to hear an explosion of gunshots and the cries of men starting to die. Rustling noises sounded behind him. The heads of another SWAT team bobbed through sagebrush like swimmers doing the butterfly stroke. Jack felt disoriented. He whirled toward where the black pickup had stopped, trying to get his bearings. He could no longer see it. Then he turned and spotted the black metal top of the cab. It was behind him. He'd overrun the damn truck by thirty yards.

For the first time since the raid began, he felt afraid, his boots fused to the ground. He didn't know which way to turn. He heard the rasp of his own breathing. A shape lunged up beside him. He jerked the rifle around. A man in a camouflage cap and fatigues pointed his M-16 at him. It was Roger Hansmeyer, the SWAT commander. The forms of four other men emerged from the sagebrush.

They looked at each other like startled, lost boys, when no more than fifteen yards behind them a weak voice squeaked, "Hey, don't shoot. I'm over here."

The SWAT team burst past Jack. He turned and saw them spread out, their M-16s pointed toward the ground. He ran up behind them. A flashlight spread a cone of brightness onto Crockett's face. He lay sprawled on his back, his hands and elbows lifted above his waist in a gesture of surrender, the .300 Savage by his side. Blood smeared his forehead from a long gash he'd probably gotten when he'd crashed through the trailer window. Caked with dirt, the wound no longer leaked blood.

Roger Hansmeyer barked, "Keep your hands up. Don't move."

Crockett smirked. "I'm not planning on going anywhere, sir."

Other SWAT members ran up. One picked up Crockett's rifle. Others rolled him onto his stomach and cuffed his wrists behind his back. Blood soaked the bottom of Crockett's left pant leg and his white tennis shoe. Roger Hansmeyer pulled up Crockett's pant leg and exposed a ragged bullet wound just above his ankle.

Jack's hands shook. He realized that he'd walked within ten yards of where Crockett lay in the brush.

An FBI agent patted Crockett down, removed a speed loader, and recited Miranda to him.

Crockett, his face on the ground, growled, "I know my rights."

Over the radio, Roger Hansmeyer ordered the helicopter to

drop into the area to pick up the prisoner. He told Fred Banfield to notify St. Mary's hospital that Crockett would be arriving with slight wounds.

The agents helped Crockett up from the ground to load him into the Huey. As he came to his feet, his wounded leg straightened and he seemed to wince, but his lips tightened, and his face again registered bland indifference. It was the first time Jack had ever seen him without his glasses and his buckaroo hat. Crockett's eyes looked unfocused. His hair was darker, almost black, cropped short, the ponytail gone. His beard was neatly trimmed. He looked more like a stunned kid than a man in his thirties.

On his feet, he kind of smiled at Jack. "Hello," he said. "How're you doing?"

"Better than you."

Crockett surveyed the roaring helicopter and the fifteen or so men crowded around him. His mouth curled into that familiar smirk, as though pleased with all the attention he'd generated.

As he started to hobble toward the helicopter he leaned toward Jack. "I could've popped you, Basco. That makes three times. Don't forget."

Jack wanted to throttle him. He didn't know if anybody else had heard, against the chopper racket and all. But Roger Hansmeyer said, "Anything you say can be held against you."

Crockett nodded. "I was addressing my friend, sir."

"Get in the chopper," Roger Hansmeyer ordered.

"Say good-bye to your friends on your way out," Jack told Crockett. "Now Bob's friends are going to see that you hang. You better tell us where he is."

Crockett's shoulders tensed defensively. His pale, unfocused eyes momentarily flickered with fright, but his face quickly hardened and remained impassive.

As the helicopter lifted from the ground, Jack whirled his back against spitting sand from the prop's backwash. The chopper, its lights blinking, climbed into the night above Gerlach and headed toward Reno.

Roger Hansmeyer grumbled, "Some tough guy! I thought they told us we were after a mountain man."

With Jim Sandoval, Jack walked over to where some SWAT boys, chattering like magpies, were examining the black Ford pickup. Eleven bullets had struck the door on the driver's side. Jack hadn't fired that many. One shot had knocked out the distributor cap and the engine's electrical circuit. An agent took pictures of two pistols on the seat of the truck.

The agent handed the camera to Jack. "Here, take our picture."

Jack objected, "It's too dark."

"It has a flash."

The SWAT boys posed in front of their trophy, the shattered Ford pickup, with their M-16s crooked in their elbows or cocked up on their knees, their excited faces sweaty. Jack snapped the picture. The bulb flashed. Their eyes glowed red in the viewfinder.

Jim Sandoval urged Jack. "Let's get out of here."

They drove back to the trailer where Fred Banfield and the sheriff watched over Wyatt Green, who was sitting on a cot in handcuffs. An agent with a camera snapped pictures of the rifles, traps, stretching boards, and cartridge loaders crammed into the trailer. The agent took photos of two books on a table: *The Criminal Use of False Identification* and *The Paper Trip: A New You Through a New ID*. A jar of black hair coloring sat on the table.

"Why would that fool come back here to hide out?" Jim asked.

"This is where his friends are," Jack replied. "He must've found out he couldn't make it on his own."

"He had a better chance staying in California with his brothers."

"Maybe, but I'm sure they didn't cook pies like Sue Dodd."

Jim offered to buy Jack a beer at Bruno's.

"I have to make a call first," Jack said.

In the phone booth outside Bruno's he dialed Cindy Pritch-ard's number. A sheriff's Blazer roared down the road. In front of Eddie Dodd's bar, the driver switched on the siren and swept the beam of his searchlight past the windows of the bar, a mocking salute to Dodd and his cronies. Through the back window Jack caught sight of Wyatt Green in his Cat cap as the vehicle roared past.

"Hello, Cindy?" Jack said. "We got him. We caught Crockett."

The sound of her breath fluttered in the phone; there was an exhalation of relief. "Is he alive?"

"He has a couple of little wounds, but he's alive. Too much alive."

Jack thought they got disconnected. The phone sounded dead.

"Cindy?"

A sob broke in his ear. Her voice sounded like a little girl's. "Thank God. Now we can find Bob."

CHAPTER 7

Crockett's preliminary hearing took place at the end of the month. Jack testified. At the arraignment Billy was charged with two counts of first-degree murder, attempted murder, kidnapping, using a firearm to commit a crime, hiding evidence, and resisting arrest. The FBI had dropped charges of interstate flight. "Too much trouble to prove," Jim Sandoval told Jack, "and the punishment wouldn't amount to anything. They wanted to clear the way for the big stuff. We've got him on murder one. He's a dead duck."

The prosecutor also dropped charges of illegal trapping and hunting. Those were just misdemeanors. The dead deer hanging in Crockett's camp, the hawk and kit fox in his traps, and the bobcats and lion whose skins Jack had found in his tent became expendable in the proceedings of justice. "They're still murders," Beth said. "We just have to wait for a new day when people can see that."

Wyatt Green went scot-free. He claimed that Billy had showed up at his trailer on Friday night with a gunnysack of traps and some guns, needing a place to stay. Except for Sunday afternoon when Crockett had borrowed the black pickup to set some traps in the hills, he'd stayed inside the trailer.

Wyatt was asked, "Didn't you know he was a fugitive?"

"No, sir."

"What did you talk about?"

"Guns, trapping."

"Why did you let him stay in the trailer?"

"He needed a bed."

The prosecuting attorney determined that Wyatt couldn't be found guilty of harboring a fugitive if he wasn't aware that the man was a fugitive.

"Unbelievable," Jim Sandoval said.

"That's the system for you," Jack responded. "Capable of anything, except common sense."

As with Eddie and Sue Dodd, no attempt was made to charge anyone with complicity. Contrary to the original belief that Crockett had used his mountain-man skills to hide out after the murders, the FBI determined that he'd actually trekked across the desert to Paradise Valley and holed up in a friend's house, watching the news on television until the manhunt died down. He then fled to North Dakota, backtracked to California, where he'd hung out with his brothers in Fort Bragg, and then returned to Nevada, where friends supplied him with food and guns for the short time he hid in the Jackson Mountains. He then spent the rest of the time hiding in the homes of aiders and abettors around Winnemucca, McDermitt, and Gerlach.

"What would this guy have done without his friends?" Jim Sandoval said.

"Got caught sooner," Jack said. "He couldn't have made it without his buddies."

The prosecutors felt that numerous indictments would

simply galvanize existing support for Billy and generate hard feelings among a lot of otherwise good citizens. Sympathy for Billy was already a problem. The *Reno Gazette-Journal* reported that the attending physician at St. Mary's Medical Center, Dr. Michael Harper, had found the wounded captive "extremely polite." Billy had apologized to the doctor for troubling him with an insignificant wound, which it was, though it kept him in a wheelchair. A jagged piece of metal from the door of the pickup had pierced the flesh over his Achilles tendon. "He was a courteous, well-behaved young man," the doctor reported, "very cordial to the nursing staff. I can understand why his friends like him so."

"The guy is a consummate con man," Jim Sandoval said. "He can snow these idiots."

Jack held a photocopied letter that Jenny and Earl Morrison had circulated to seek help for Crockett's defense:

Dear Friends,

We are assisting in the Defense of William David Crockett, Jr.

We understand you are willing to help us. We need character witnesses who would be willing to appear in court. If you cannot appear, please write a letter testifying to his good character.

In addition, we are seeking funds to help with his defense. If you are able to make a contribution, make your check payable to the William Crockett Defense Fund. You will receive a receipt by return mail. Save your receipt so you will have it for tax purposes.

We hope you will be able to help us.

Thanks again.

Jenny & Earl

"What's with these people?" Jack asked. He remembered Jenny Morrison's hostility toward him that afternoon in Dodd's bar, but he hadn't suspected that she had such a deep allegiance to Crockett. It embarrassed him that Jenny was a Basque.

Jim Sandoval said, "People claim that once in a Paradise bar Jenny mentioned she was interested in buying some local potatoes. Crockett was ripping ground for a potato farmer at the time, and after overhearing the conversation, he left the bar and later returned with a sack of potatoes on his shoulder—a gift for Jenny. No charge."

"So he bought her friendship with a stolen sack of potatoes."

"That was the start."

After his capture, Crockett refused to say anything about where he'd hidden Bob's body. Jack went to see the defense attorney Crockett's father had hired. He was a tall, fair-faced guy in his thirties named Michael P. O'Grady. A Reno boy who'd graduated from Boston College Law School, O'Grady had reddish hair and wore aviator-style glasses that gave him the confident, unexpressive look of a young airline pilot. His cool manner reflected assurance: Everything's fine, ladies and gentlemen. I'm in control here.

"I'm sorry I can't help you, Mr. Irigaray," O'Grady said. "Your insinuation about my client's knowledge of this alleged body is unfounded. We'll address all charges properly in court."

"Cut the gobbledygook," Jack said. "It's no skin off Crockett's nose to say where he hid Pritchard. He's just causing people a lot of suffering."

"I won't jeopardize the protection of my client. He's entitled to due process."

"If you know where that body is, and you're not saying, then you're breaking the law yourself. Lawyers can't harbor evidence. You can be arrested."

O'Grady flushed up to the ruby roots of his hair. "And you, sir, have just opened yourself to threatening the defendant's attorney."

"Look, I'm just asking you to show a little human kindness for Bob Pritchard's wife and children. They've already suffered too much because that scumbag didn't have the decency to let them know where he dumped the body."

"I refuse to address unfounded allegations."

Jack could tell that O'Grady was uncomfortable. The lawyer could be in hot water if it came out that he knew where Bob was but wouldn't answer the direct inquiries of a law officer. He'd already refused to answer Jim Sandoval, and now he was stonewalling another inquirer.

Jack tried another tack. "It's to Crockett's advantage to let a grieving widow know where to find her lost husband. The public will see it as a sympathetic act if he does it out of a concerned, humane impulse. You can make it appear that way."

That approach didn't wash either. "You must consider two facts," O'Grady said. "A: you've been making unfounded allegations and threats against me. B: no accusation of illegality can be found on what a person neither knows nor wants to know. I don't know where that body is, and I don't want to know."

That was the end of it. Jack waited all day and through half a bottle before calling Cindy that evening with the bad news that she would have to wait until Crockett's trial to learn where Bob was hidden. It was the hardest thing he'd had to tell her since the murders.

"Do you think," Cindy asked, her voice constricted, "that he might say he just buried the body and doesn't know where?"

"It's possible."

"Can he get away with that?"

"I suppose he could give a general area and say that he couldn't be more exact. He could claim he was in a panic and hurrying to escape."

"What if he really did what some people say?"

"What do you mean?"

Her voice sounded far away, scared. "You know, chopped up Bob and scattered him to the coyotes."

She'd been dwelling on that thought ever since she'd heard that Crockett had suggested quartering Larry to get him out of Little High Rock Canyon.

"I don't think that's a real possibility. He had a pick and shovel, and his plan that night was to bury Bob. We just have to believe that Bob's at rest, even though we don't know where."

Jack then called Jim Sandoval. "I want a chance to talk to Crockett."

"I can't do that, Jack. It could get us into all sorts of trouble for harassing a prisoner. You'll just jeopardize yourself as a witness."

"It's not illegal for him to have visitors. Jenny and Earl Morrison have visited him. You can have another deputy there as a witness to what happens. You can tape the conversation. You can film the damn meeting if you want."

"I'd have to check with Crockett's lawyer."

"No, you don't. You don't have to check for every visit. If he's willing to talk with me, he doesn't need his lawyer."

Jack didn't let up until Jim gave in and agreed to meet him at the jail in the morning. Jack would let the deputy ask all the questions, and he'd keep quiet, unless Crockett specifically agreed to talk with him. Another deputy would also chaperon the event.

In the morning Jack sat on a metal chair in the visitors' area, surrounded by gray cinderblock walls. Behind a glass partition, Crockett hobbled into view on a pair of crutches, wearing a surprisingly bright parachute-orange jumpsuit—it reminded Jack of the orange jacket that had almost gotten him shot on the day of the raid. He had imagined himself talking to Crockett face-to-face through jail bars. Instead, a milky Plexiglas window separated them. Crockett's hair was cut short, his beard neatly trimmed.

Jim spoke to the prisoner over a telephone. "We're here to ask you where Bob's body is. It's to your advantage to tell us."

Jim held the phone away from his ear so Jack could hear Crockett's reply. "My lawyers told me not to talk to anyone."

"Ask him if he'll hear what I have to say," Jack said.

Crockett nodded before Jim repeated the words. Jack took the phone from Jim.

"Billy," he pleaded, "telling us where that body is won't hurt you. It will help. Pritchard's wife will be grateful to you. I'll be grateful. You know she's in a lot of pain not being able to bury her husband."

Crockett's washed-out blue eyes seemed to be directed toward a spot somewhere on the wall behind his interrogators

Jack continued. "Let's end this game, Billy. You said you could've shot me when I walked by you in the sagebrush. Well, I could've popped you in that truck—I had a bead on your head—but I didn't do it. I let you live so you could tell us where Bob's body is."

Billy hung up the phone. Behind the dusty glare of the Plexiglas, his eyes assumed the vacant, unseeing stare of a corpse lying faceup in a dirty pond.

"You indecent son of a bitch," Jack shouted, loud enough to force the sound of his words through the thick glass.

Jim gave a wave of dismissal to the deputy standing next to Crockett. "Knock it off, Jack. Save it for the trial."

Crockett's hunched orange back retreated from the window. As he waited for the metal door on the far wall to slide open, he leaned his shoulders into his crutches, swiveled his face toward Jack, and smirked. Then he swung his body through the open doorway.

"Okay," Jim Sandoval said. "I gave you what you wanted, but I shouldn't have. I knew it would come to nothing."

"Has he talked to anyone?"

"Sure. Not about the body, if that's what you mean—at least nothing I heard—but he talks. His parents drove out here all the way from Tennessee. Billy was polite with them, but he firmly told his father he didn't want him at the trial. He said he didn't want him to have to go through it. I know the real reason is that his father is a big-mouthed braggart, like Eddie Dodd. He's been making all sorts of tough-guy threats and complaints to the papers. Billy knows having him around won't do him any good."

"And Jenny Morrison? She's been in to see him a lot, right?"

Jim nodded. "She's usually circumspect in what she says, when I'm listening. She wasn't so careful, though, when telling him who probably snitched on him."

The FBI had given no clues about the anonymous informant who'd turned in Crockett, but the $25,000 reward had been secretly paid. It was commonly assumed that the snitch was a person around Gerlach, someone Crockett knew, probably even a friend. Crockett's father mouthed off to reporters that he thought the snake in the garden was Eddie Dodd. The bartender, he claimed, had made a deal with the Feds in exchange for their dropping accessory charges against him. He'd turned in Billy to save his own neck. Wyatt Green was under suspicion for the same reasons; no charges had been made against him either.

Jenny Morrison pursued a short list of possible traitors and somehow came up with telephone records of several calls from Gerlach to the FBI during the week before Billy's arrest. Through her connections in the bank, where she worked as a loan officer, she discovered a sudden swell in the account of Jess Nichols.

"I wouldn't put it past Jess," Jack said. "He and Billy have had their run-ins. Twenty-five thousand easy bucks would be a big temptation for Jess."

"It could've been any number of people. Small rewards were made to other people for information early on. But word's out around Gerlach that Jess is the one who's in trouble. Jenny Morrison claims she'll take care of him herself if Crockett can't."

"She's a blowhard."

"You're also on her shit list. She told Crockett that you were the one who shot him when he was trying to escape."

"He's had his chances, and I've had mine. Now I'm going to take care of him at the trial."

"You've got your work cut out for you. Jenny has a load of witnesses and testimonials lined up for Billy."

"At least one of 'em won't be my uncle."

When Jack had talked to his uncle on the phone, Pete had said, "I know Billy too well to do him any good. I told his lawyers that I'd be glad to testify. But what was I going to say? That Billy was a hard worker, that he knocked down wild horses, that he shot deer and antelope out of season, that he kicked old Alice in the ribs? They weren't interested."

The Gerlach and Paradise Valley lowlifes testifying for Billy would be easy game for the prosecutor's ridicule. A few other people of good standing would have credibility, but none of them had been witnesses to the actual murders.

"Character witnesses can't usually stand up to an eyewitness," Jim Sandoval said. "Look what happened to Bristlewolf, and there were no witnesses at all to those murders."

The old hermit, who had come to trial in June for shooting the two college kids and his old Basque friend, had been found guilty of three counts of first-degree murder. The trial was swift. The sentence was life imprisonment without chance for parole.

Jim went on, "But Bristlewolf wouldn't speak at his trial. Even the public defender had little sympathy for him. That's not going to be the case for Crockett."

"I can't wait to see how Crockett's smarmy smirk goes over with the jury. There's no way he's going to hide who he really is. It'll come out."

"Just keep your cool," Jim advised. "Everything depends on you. The trial's going to come down to your word against Crockett's."

Jury selection began in the middle of September. The prosecutors, using all their allowable peremptory and cause challenges, had hoped for a predominantly male jury of law-and-order types, but the pool of prospective jurors was composed mostly of women. After three and a half days, they ended up with a final selection of ten women and only two men. The prosecution worried about Crockett's appeal to the jury's maternal and romantic instincts. Except for one woman in her sixties and another in her fifties, the others were closer to Crockett's age. In fact, like Jack and Billy, the two defense attorneys and the two prosecutors were also in their thirties—the age, Jack remembered reading somewhere, of people who created most of the world's troubles.

Jack didn't attend the trial's opening days. The defense had invoked the rule to keep him out of the courtroom until he testified. But Jim, Cindy, and the newspapers kept him informed. Cindy and Larry Hughes's widow were the prosecution's first witnesses. They recalled the last moments with their husbands and the shock of learning about the murders. If the opening draw of the jury was a bad one for the prosecutors, Cindy Pritchard and Melissa Hughes gave them a rebound—they were two grieving queens. Their value doubled when the judge, against the objections of the defense, allowed them to remain in the courtroom as spectators after their testimony. In full view, the widows sat, victims of violence that the wives on the jury could identify with: there but for the grace of God go we.

The judge did place restrictions on Cindy and Melissa in response to the defense's objection that their presence would prejudice the jury. They couldn't sit together, talk to the press, or exhibit any emotion during the trial. If they did, he'd throw them out.

"When I feel like crying," Cindy told Jack that night on the phone, "I tell myself I have to watch my P.D.E., and that kind of makes me smile inside. I knew a gal once who dated a guy at West Point, and they weren't allowed to hold hands on campus or show what the army called P.D.A.—public displays of affection. With me it's public displays of emotion. When I think of it that way, it becomes kind of a game, and it keeps me from crying."

On the day of her testimony Cindy got her first glimpse of Crockett in person. He'd shaved his beard and was wearing a cream-colored cowboy shirt with fake pearl snaps.

"I'd steeled myself by looking at his pictures," she said, "so I'd be ready when I saw him, but he still surprised me. I didn't expect that he'd be so small, so boyish. He has those little eyes and little hands. How could he do that to Bob and Larry?"

"That's what his lawyers are hoping the jury will wonder," Jack replied.

"When I got out of the box, I turned and stared at him, and he looked down. He's no man compared to Bob."

The flop of the dice or spin of the wheel—the luck that plays its part in any trial—kept the prosecution on a roll. Scotty Larsen testified about Crockett's methods of trash-trapping, the rapacity and wastefulness that had caused Scotty to alert Bob Pritchard. The six-seven, two-hundred-and-forty-pound trapper made no attempt to hide his disdain for someone who would violate the sense of fair play that governed real trappers and real hunters.

"I warned Crockett that Fish and Game was likely to show up, and he told me, 'I'll be ready for them.'"

Scotty described the details of the night when Bob and Jack had arrived at his log cabin to awake him at two in the morning. "I've had my own run-ins with Bob Pritchard," Scotty said. "He was stern when it came to protecting animals, but he was a fair guy. He knew the country like the back of his hand. He loved the desert and the animals in it, and he respected those of us who made our living off the land."

Crockett wouldn't look at Scotty during his testimony.

The prosecution showed the jury a TV videotape of Larry Hughes floating in the red willows at the bottom of Little High Rock Canyon. They exhibited colored photographs of his half-naked body, the bullet holes in his chest, the rope burns around his ankles. The defense objected to the graphic pictures, claiming they were meant merely to inflame the jury.

The prosecutor, Kirk Peters, a compact, unsmiling, bullet-headed former Marine who had fought in the Golden Gloves, agreed that the evidence was indeed graphic. "These pictures aren't out of *Better Homes and Gardens*," he told the jury. "This is a murder trial."

The judge let all the evidence stand except the close-up picture of Larry's bloodied head with the jagged bullet hole behind his ear.

The prosecutor had come into the trial swinging. He had no interest in finesse; he was ready to slug it out. During his previous prosecution of the hermit Bristlewolf, he'd tried to show the jury a photograph of Charles Manson to demonstrate that the cult leader's crazed eyes looked exactly like those of the old hermit, but the public defender and the judge had stopped him.

In his opening statement, Crockett's red-haired lawyer had pleaded his client's innocence on the grounds of self-defense, but the prosecutor, with his videocassettes, photographs, and testimony of investigators and ballistics experts, aggressively maintained that what had happened in Little High Rock Canyon was nothing less than a brutal execution, as calculated and remorseless as a gangland slaying by a thug who sported a submachine gun for Bugsy Siegel.

In a risky attempt at an early strike against the scenario of self-defense, Kirk Peters called Crockett's friend Eddie Dodd as a prosecution witness. Depending on what he said, the barkeep could smash up the prosecution's game plan, but Peters, and his more subtle, dapper coprosecutor, State Assistant District Attorney General Elliott Bingham, took the chance.

On the fifth day of the trial, Bingham politely gave the old boozehound Dodd every possible opening to claim that Crockett had justified his shooting of Bob in self-defense. But the barkeep merely reported that Billy had awakened him in the middle of the night to say, "I need some help, Eddie. I dusted a Fish and Game boy. He tried to bust me. I need to cache the body."

Eddie Dodd's testimony followed almost word for word what he'd told the police that morning after the murders. He described how Crockett had asked for a pick and shovels to bury the body, how Jack Irigaray had taken a shower and changed clothes, and how Crockett had cleaned his slicker and ordered Dodd and his wife to wash the blood from the Bronco after he left, which they did. Dodd also admitted that he'd given Crockett money and that his wife had burned Jack's bloody clothes.

"Did the defendant say anything else to you?"

"Yeah, he told me to tell his parents he loved them. He also said he didn't want to make any trouble for us. He didn't want us to have to wear a lot of heat."

"Did he say anything more to you about what had happened in Little High Rock Canyon?"

"Well, he said he did a sloppy job, but they had it coming. They deserved it."

"Did he give any reasons why they deserved it?"

"I already told you. They busted into his camp and tried to arrest him."

"Is that all he said?"

"That's it. He just said, 'I dusted one of them.'"

The prosecutor pressed Dodd to be certain that his recollection was complete. "Do you recall the defendant, William Crockett, on that night telling you anything other than what you've testified to us today?"

"No, sir," Dodd insisted. "I sure don't." The barkeep's smug glance at Crockett showed that he thought he was helping.

The prosecutor's gambit had worked. Dodd had given no indication that Crockett in any way had claimed the need to defend himself against Bob, Jack, or least of all Larry Hughes.

The defense did its best to discredit this testimony. Crockett's attorney, Michael O'Grady, launched into an investigation of Dodd's drinking habits.

"Did you by chance have anything to drink on the day in question?"

"Of course," Dodd admitted. "I had a few drinks—a few Seven and Sevens, a few martinis. Nothing special."

"How many drinks is a few?"

"I don't count 'em."

"Would fifteen be an unreasonable number?'

"Oh, that would be easy—before lunch."

Laughter rumbled through the audience of spectators, the first comic respite during the grim proceedings. Dodd responded to the laughter with the puffed-up, swaggering stance he maintained in his bar. He appeared to be delighted with himself. He went on to say it had been just an ordinary day for him.

"Would you describe this Seven and Seven," O'Grady asked, "as a mild or stiff drink?"

"Probably like a milk shake to a kid," Dodd said, his watery eyes bright.

A loud laugh burst from Crockett, as he joined the mirth of the spectators. Still smiling, Crockett shook his head, as if to say, What a card! It was the first sound to come from him during the trial. His only other smile had appeared at the beginning of the trial, during the prosecutor's opening description of Billy's leap through the window of Wyatt's trailer and his attempted escape from the helicopter and SWAT teams. At that time the prosecutor maintained that Crockett's actions, especially his shooting at the helicopter, manifested his "consciousness of guilt," but Crockett's smug smile was one of macho pride. Otherwise, behind his round, wire-rimmed glasses he quietly watched the proceedings with the eyes of a dead fish. He seldom blinked.

O'Grady pressured Dodd to admit that the drinks had left him confused that night, disoriented, in fact, *drunk,* but the judge sustained the prosecutor's objection—the word "drunk" was objectionable, calling for either a legal conclusion or the opinion of the witness. Dodd claimed that if he was disoriented at all, it was because of Billy's shocking appearance in the middle of the night, not the booze. He always consumed at least a quart of rye in the course of his daily work.

"I'm pretty hard to disorientate," Dodd announced proudly. "I'm no alcoholic."

He denied that he was like a father to Billy. "He knows more than any father could teach a son." He said that his relationship with Billy, who didn't smoke, drink, or trouble anyone, was a "one thousand and one percent pure friendship."

Dodd repeated that Billy had told him nothing other than what he'd already reported.

The attorney pressed him. "Do you recall Mr. Crockett ever stating to you that night, 'I had to do it.'"

Dodd answered, "No."

"Are you sure about that?"

"As sure as the sun," Dodd replied.

"Is it possible," the attorney persisted, "that Mr. Crockett could have made a statement like that?"

Kirk Peters shouted, "Objection." The judge supported him. Dodd was excused, his testimony completed, a triumph for the prosecution.

It was day six of the trial when Jack testified. He'd spent the previous night going over and over in his mind the details of the murders. He knew that he only had to recount what actually had happened as clearly and honestly as he could. He had nothing to hide, nothing to construe. The facts would speak for themselves. Self-defense was never an issue in Little High Rock Canyon. Crockett just hadn't wanted to be arrested or even cited.

When Jack walked through the metal detectors of the crowded courtroom he was surprised to see so many armed deputies in the room. Four guards stood behind Crockett, and another four or five at the door and along the walls. Cindy sat by herself in a smart black dress with buttons down the front, her legs tightly crossed. When Jack looked at her, she averted her eyes. Crockett, wearing new wire-rimmed glasses and a baby-blue cowboy shirt, remained rigid. He sat at the end of the defense table, turned catercorner toward the jury. His lawyers obviously wanted the jurors to have a clear look at his face.

"Bob Pritchard called me just before eleven-thirty," Jack began, "on New Year's Eve." In response to Kirk Peters's questions, he told the jurors, the judge, the spectators, and Crockett exactly what had happened during that thirty-hour period almost two years ago. With as many precise details as he could provide, he took his listeners step-by-step down the canyon trail to Crockett's camp. He explained that if someone possessed illegal pelts or wild game, officers were obliged by law to arrest him if he had a nonresident's license. A state resident could be given only a citation.

Jack described his position in front of Crockett's tent when Bob told him to begin the search. "I untied the flaps and entered the tent. Inside I found two bobcat pelts on stretching boards and the folded pelt of a mountain lion. I heard Bob shout, 'Oh, no,' and then pistol shots. I rushed outside and saw Bob falling backward, smoke coming from his chest.

Larry Hughes stumbled forward, then spun around. Crockett was in a crouched, police stance, holding a pistol with both hands, firing a volley into both men. He then went into the tent and returned with a twenty-two rifle. He shot both men in the head by the ear."

Jack told the jury of his dreadful realization that he'd forgotten his pistol under the seat of the truck. With pain and relief, he described the awful events that followed during that long afternoon.

The prosecutor asked, "While you were busy trying to hide the bodies, did the defendant show the slightest remorse?"

"Objection," O'Grady shouted.

"Go ahead," the judge said. "You may answer."

"No, sir, he did not. In fact, after he opened the chamber of Larry Hughes's sidearm, he said, 'If I'd known this guy's pistol was empty, I would've taken Pritchard on the rim, but I thought the two of them would get the best of me up there.'"

"Did Mr. Crockett show any awareness of his crime?"

"At one point, he said he considered the shootings justifiable homicide, but up on the rim he said, 'This is murder one for me.'"

"Did he offer any reasons for his action?"

"Yes, he did. He said, 'I swore I'd never get arrested again. Why do lawmen have to be so pushy? You had no right to break into my camp that way.'"

Jack knew it was important to get the fact of Crockett's previous arrest into the trial. The prosecution was precluded from mentioning it, since it was a past event that would prejudice the jury, but Jack was allowed to report what he'd heard Crockett say.

He recounted the trip, in the Bronco with Bob's body in the back, from the canyon to Eddie and Sue Dodd's home where he showered, following Crockett's orders to scrape the blood from beneath his fingernails. He told of driving with Crockett in Dodd's pickup to the edge of the Black Rock Desert, where Billy ordered him to get a shovel from the truck bed. Bob's body lay in the back. When Jack turned around with the shovel in his hand, Crockett held his pistol aimed at his chest, saying, "Sorry, Jack," and then fired.

The courtroom assumed a predawn hush, as if spectators had just watched a rope being cinched around a man's neck. In the hallway, Jim Sandoval said, "That's it for Crockett, Jack. You nailed him." That night Jack met Cindy for a drink. He then continued his celebration alone at home.

The next morning, he felt a little heavy-headed but okay when the defense attorney began his cross-examination. "From your testimony," O'Grady said, "it appears—but correct me if I'm wrong—that there are a number of things that you don't recall about what happened on that day of January first."

The question blindsided him. "How do you mean?"

"It appears, but I stand ready to be corrected, Jack, that your memory of events on that day differs from what you've previously testified."

It was true that he'd given previous accounts of what had happened: twice from his hospital bed, later in the sheriff's office, then at the preliminary hearing, and now in the courtroom—five testimonies all together. Except for his confusion in the hospital, he thought the reports had been consistent, the basic facts always the same. O'Grady, however, began to pick away at what he called "inconsistencies" in Jack's testimony.

The defense attorney presented a sketch Jack had drawn for the police that showed Pritchard and Hughes standing in front of Crockett's tent in positions different from those he'd reported in court.

"They're basically the same," Jack said. "Hughes stood at an angle to Bob's left side."

"Basically, but not exactly? Is that correct?"

Jack remembered Jim's warning to keep his cool, but it took an effort as O'Grady politely continued to chip away.

"Now, as I indicated, Jack, our purpose is not to embarrass you or trip you up, but it's very important that we have a certain understanding of what you recall. When you entered the tent, you untied the flaps, is that correct?"

"Yes, that's right."

"Did they tie together on the seam?"

"Well, they tied together in the middle, yes, on the seam."

"Did they overlap or come together?"

"I'm not sure about that. They were bunched where they were tied."

"You're not sure? Do you feel that your recollection is clear in respect to everything that was said and occurred on that day?"

That's how it went. O'Grady asked if Jack had had anything to drink that day, and he admitted that he'd had a couple of nightcaps on New Year's Eve but only coffee at Scotty Larsen's. He didn't want to guess what should or shouldn't be said. His intention was simply to be honest.

The attorney probed into his drinking habits against the objections of the prosecutor. O'Grady asked how much restful sleep he'd got that night in the cab of the pickup. Jack had to admit that during the whole ordeal he was awake for almost thirty hours. The attorney pressed him on the uncertain answers he'd given to the FBI in the hospital about the number of shots Crockett had fired.

"You told FBI Special Agent Banfield that you weren't sure, is that correct?"

"I guess so. I was sedated then. It was hard to remember."

"But now, almost two years later, do you feel more sure?"

"I was in the tent when Crockett started shooting. It was hard to count, but I do remember seeing him fire at least four shots."

"Now, when you were in the tent, you say you heard someone shout, 'Oh no.'"

"That's right. Bob shouted, 'Oh no.'"

"Can you be absolutely certain that it was Mr. Pritchard, and *not* Mr. Crockett, who shouted, 'Oh no'?"

Jack had recognized Bob's voice—he was sure of that—but he had to confess that he hadn't seen Bob cry out because he was inside the tent, and that admission introduced the possibility that either Crockett or Hughes could have shouted.

O'Grady continued to push on whether a shot had preceded the shout, or vice versa, and whether it was possible that Bob had drawn his gun first and Crockett had responded by shouting, "Oh no."

Jack tried hard to concentrate. O'Grady's magnified blue eyes swam in and out of view behind the glare on his rose-tinted aviator glasses. Cindy's small blurred face appeared behind the lawyer's ear.

"Now this is important, Jack. Do you recall testifying at the preliminary hearing that when you saw Mr. Pritchard's gun on the ground, you concluded that he had to have had the gun in his hand at one time?"

"That's correct, after he was shot."

"The gun was in a position you concluded it wouldn't have been in if it had just fallen out of his holster."

"Correct—about eight or ten inches from his hand."

"Did you see the pistol in Mr. Pritchard's hand?"

"No, I didn't."

"And how many shots did you say were fired at this time?"

"I wasn't counting. It sounded like one continuous loud roar."

"Was your mind pretty much a blank as to what happened there?"

"Well, I'm sure I was in shock, a bit."

"Now, do you recall testifying, Jack, that you were in the tent and unable to see who had drawn and fired first?"

He felt himself losing it. "Bob was no quick-draw artist. The gun was on the ground after he was shot, and it wasn't smoking."

"Did you examine the weapon on the ground?"

"No, Crockett picked it up and said it was going to be buried with Bob."

"Could you observe, at the time you saw Mr. Pritchard fall, whether or not he was alive?"

"I did see Bob's head come up once and then lay back down. That was the only movement I saw."

"Now, Jack, you have never testified to that before in any of your statements."

Jack saw Cindy's face stiffen in the distance. His neck grew hot. "Well, I said it a number of times. It is true. I did see that."

O'Grady's eyes swelled behind his lenses. "You're sure? Because it is in none of your testimony, and you gave two statements within sixty-four hours of these events."

The next day on the stand Jack felt rattled as O'Grady forced him to admit that there were other words and events that he hadn't witnessed. No, he hadn't heard Bob threaten Crockett. No, he hadn't heard everything Mr. Pritchard might've said to Mr. Crockett while he was in the tent. Yes, Mr. Crockett had said he considered the shootings justifiable homicide. Yes, Mr. Crockett had also said, "This is murder one for me." In earlier testimony Jack had reversed the order of these statements.

O'Grady held out a copy of the transcript from the preliminary hearing. "Does this appear to you to be a true and correct copy of the statements you've previously given?"

"Well, yes, but I remember now that we were up on the rim when Crockett said, 'I didn't weight the body. They'll find it for sure in the morning. This is murder one for me.'"

"Do you recall what you testified earlier, Jack?"

"Which time?"

"I'm going to read from your preliminary testimony, Jack, and please correct me if I misread anything. The sequence here is somewhat important, Jack, so I'm going to ask you—"

The prosecutor interrupted. "Your Honor, I'm going to object to counsel characterizing his questions. He doesn't have to keep reminding people how important his questions are."

O'Grady made a polite bow toward the prosecutor. "I apologize. I'll refrain from making such comments."

Jack admitted that the reason Crockett gave for not shooting him was that he wasn't armed.

"He would not shoot an unarmed man," O'Grady said, "one who was not a threat to him, is that correct?"

"He shot me."

"When Mr. Crockett did shoot you, out in the desert, the situation was different, was it not?" O'Grady asked. "Did you not have a shovel in your hands at the time?"

He felt his face flush as he remembered his intention to swing the shovel at Crockett, but when he'd turned around the pistol was already aimed at his chest.

"Do you deny swinging the shovel at Mr. Crockett's head?"

"Yes, sir, I do."

"And during Mr. Crockett's alleged escape attempt, is it true that you shouted into the two-way radio that you were a game warden?"

"Well, yes," Jack said, confused now. A sound distracted him, like the rumble of an air conditioner kicking on. "At the time it seemed the most efficient thing to say, to make it understood who I was. The SWAT team thought of me as a game warden. I was about to be shot, and I wanted to make it clear whose side I was on."

"But you are not a game warden?"

"No, I'm not. I'm a game biologist."

"Game wardens are trained law enforcement officers, is that correct?"

"Yes, that's right."

"Although you are a biologist, do you think of yourself as a law enforcement officer, a game warden?"

"Objection, Your Honor," the prosecutor said.

"Sustained," the judge said.

The next day Jack read in the *Reno Gazette-Journal* that his whole testimony was perceived as convoluted and contradictory. He felt fractured. The negligible inconsistencies O'Grady had emphasized in no way altered the important fact: Jack had seen Crockett fire two bullets into the heads of two helpless men. But the newspaper article noted how many times Jack had said, "I'm not sure," or "I don't know," or "it's hard to say" about insignificant details.

He had to blame the judge for a lot of what had happened, for allowing the defense to engage in speculative questioning, and for constantly overruling the objections of the prosecution. His honor, Third District Judge Lee Reilley, a beefy-faced pol in his late sixties with brush-cut white hair, was anything but a hanging judge. He was known always to give the defense every break; the last thing he wanted was a mistrial that would cost the taxpayers. He'd rather have the system work quickly through compromises or reduced charges or even acquittals than have a hung jury or lengthy appeals. Off the bench he was considered a jovial man who liked cocktail parties, political benefits, and off-color jokes. On the bench, he made the efforts of prosecutors a nightmare. With him the system and its loopholes prevailed more often than did justice; for him, hard-nosed prosecutors pressing for the harshest verdicts only gummed up the works.

It came home to Jack, once again, that a trial was just a play, a theatrical cycle of conflicting accounts, that could only approximate what had actually happened months or even years earlier. It was a slippery mess of impressions and interpretations that in no way could exactly reproduce past events. He felt that his mistake had been choosing to recount honestly those hours on the desert with all their uncertainties and complexities. He would've been better off simply memorizing his original testimony to the police and repeating it word for word, the way Eddie Dodd had done. It would've saved a lot of thinking and struggle. He knew that just as a consistent set of figures, even if they didn't accurately reflect actual expenses and earnings, would get someone out of an IRS audit quicker than an honest but incomplete accounting, so, too, a simplified, brightly consistent story, even when dishonest, would sway a jury more effectively than one whose loose ends and shadows came closer to what used to be called the truth.

CHAPTER 8

For the next week, Jack stayed away from the trial. He had work to do, and anyway, after what had happened, he didn't want to go into that courtroom for a while.

He came home one night to find Beth at the kitchen table with her head in her hands.

"Are you all right?"

She didn't say anything. Then he heard the raspy breathing.

"You better get back on your medicine," he said.

Every fall it was the same, but since she'd begun self-treatments with her own homeopathic medicines, her asthma, when it came, seemed worse.

Carrie and Sarah stood in the kitchen doorway; they'd both tied garish bows in their hair. "You kids go to your room," he said. "I need to talk to your mother."

Sliding her hands from her face, Beth said, "It's all right. You kids get yourself some cereal."

169

Jack offered, "I'll cook something. What is there?"

"They can have cereal. Cook yourself something. I'm going to lie down."

He scrambled eggs for the kids, had a drink, and then went into the bedroom. Against the pink pillow Beth's face looked ashen. "Just leave me alone. It helps not to talk."

"Maybe you should go to the hospital."

Her head swiveled back and forth on the pillow. "No, I'm feeling better. I'll get up soon. I need to make some calls."

Now that fall hunting season had started, she'd been on the phone a lot, organizing a protest. A list of names lay on the night table.

"Can I get you anything?"

She closed her eyes. "Spend some time with the girls."

Her order annoyed him. "I always spend time with them."

She didn't say anything.

"I told you things would get better. We just have to get through this trial."

She still didn't say anything.

"Well, things are better, aren't they? At least you can admit that."

Her constricted breathing reminded him of the rale in his lung after he'd been shot. She made a harsh, scraping sound as she sucked in oxygen, eyes closed, her voice a rough whisper. "No," she said, "they aren't."

The hell with it, he thought, as he mixed another drink in the kitchen. Whether he tried or not didn't make a tick's ass bit of difference to her.

He went to read to the girls. Sarah wanted the book about a bunny whose mom had been blasted away by a farmer, and Carrie wanted the story about a porpoise who'd saved a little blond girl like herself from drowning. The drinks hadn't helped his black mood. He wanted a story about a wolf who ate kids, but there wasn't a hailstone's chance in hell that such a book existed in the house.

After tucking the girls into bed, he called Cindy to ask about the trial. Her voice was bouncy and excited. "Lady Luck has moved into our corner."

The prosecution had called a ballistics expert to testify that a bullet had hit Hughes in the back after an earlier shot had spun him around. The details were important, not just because they showed that Billy had shot a man in the back, but because they helped the prosecution establish the likelihood that Hughes, unarmed and defenseless, was still alive when Crockett blasted him in the head. The same was true for Bob.

The next day, though, Jack learned that the expert's conjectures about the angles of the bullets depended on the sketches he himself had drawn, and the defense attorney established that these sketches were inconsistent with Jack's later testimony. The ballistics expert agreed that if the positions of the men were different, then the wound in Hughes's back might've been an exit wound, meaning the bullet through his body probably would've killed him. In any event, the defense managed to throw doubt on the prosecutor's claim that Hughes had probably been alive when Crockett clipped him behind the ear.

The defense also damaged the prosecution's claim that Crockett had showed "consciousness of guilt" by firing at the Huey during his attempted escape. Under cross-examination, the FBI made the shocking admission that Crockett's rifle and pistols hadn't been examined to determine whether they'd been fired. The weapons had been photographed and tagged, but the barrels hadn't been checked. Jack guessed those SWAT boys were more interested in having their picture taken than in gathering evidence. Or maybe the FBI just neglected to request a lab report. Either way, the evidence that Crockett had resisted arrest by firing at pursuing lawmen melted away.

A week later the prosecution concluded its case and the

defense team took over. O'Grady went on the attack by calling a number of character witnesses to the stand. Buckaroos who'd worked with Crockett, his former employers in Oregon, Dr. Davis the dentist, Jenny and Earl Morrison, and others from Paradise Valley and Gerlach testified what a good guy Billy was.

"A swell guy," Cindy mockingly said one evening in the bar down the street from the courthouse. "He's such a *sa-well* guy."

"I should've done a better job," Jack said. "I let him off the hook."

"You told the truth, Jack, and everyone knows it. Jim Sandoval says these picky technicalities are common to every trial—we just aren't usually aware of them. In the end they won't hold weight. The real show is yet to come."

She meant Crockett's testimony. She showed Jack an article in a journal for muzzle-loaders and wanna-be mountain men, called *Black Powder,* that had already summed up the popular belief about Crockett's character: "Like the solitary mountain lion, Billy Crockett prowled the lonely rimrocks and desolate wastes of Nevada alone, avoiding people and staking out territory where survival depended on toughness and the instinctual skills of the self-sufficient predator."

"What bunk!" Jack said. "People don't know the first thing about mountain lions or Crockett either. They just want to hear what they already believe."

During the second week in October, a month into the trial, Billy took the stand. Spectators crammed into the warm, musty courtroom. The judge ordered the air conditioner turned on. Since Jack couldn't sit with Cindy—one of the judge's conditions for her staying in the courtroom was that she not be seen with any Division of Wildlife officers—he sat in the back by himself. Crockett's two older brothers, wearing checked lumberjack shirts, had arrived from California. Both were taller and burlier than Billy, who looked dandyish in his lime-green cowboy shirt, laundered Levi's, and cowboy belt with a silver buckle. Although in jail he'd insisted on having meat with every meal, the food wasn't to his liking, so he looked to have lost about twenty pounds, giving him the trim, fit tautness of a bronc rider.

More journalists swelled the press crowd, not only newspaper writers, but reporters from *Time, Newsweek, Rolling Stone, Outdoor Life,* and *People.*

A klatch of eight or nine housewives had forgone their midday viewing of *The Young and the Restless* and *The Bold and the Beautiful* to witness a real-life soap opera. One newspaper wag had dubbed them "Billy's Belles." They smiled at Crockett and slipped him encouraging notes. In the courthouse hall they chattered among themselves and eagerly relayed their impressions to reporters. One Belle summed up the group's infatuation during an interview on TV: "He's sweet," she said about Billy, "but he's tough. There aren't many western men like him anymore in this country. Of course, I'm lucky to be married to one—one of the few that's left. You can see that Billy's a gentleman, in an old-fashioned way, but he's not going to let himself be pushed around. What woman wouldn't admire a man like that?"

Billy walked casually to the witness stand, his feet swinging out in that urban splayfooted walk Jack remembered from the rim of the canyon. Billy sat down and coughed, covering his mouth with his palm. He leaned forward and whispered something to his defense attorney. O'Grady handed him a cellophane-wrapped cough drop. He took his time carefully unwrapping it and delicately put it into his mouth. He smiled at the jury. "Excuse me," he said. "A cold's trying to catch me."

Billy's Belles tittered, apparently delighted with this display of vulnerability and wit from one so legendary yet so human.

Crockett's lawyer began by asking Billy about his work on ranches in Oregon and northern Nevada.

"Exactly what is buckarooing, Mr. Crockett?" O'Grady asked.

Billy paused. With measured, thoughtful deliberation, this boy from southern Illinois, who hadn't seen the Rockies until he was eighteen, began to speak like someone who'd grown up in sagebrush glued to a saddle.

"Well, it's just—buckarooing is a man doing his job, working cattle on horseback, doing whatever work needs to be done ahorseback regarding livestock and such."

He'd left buckarooing, he claimed, and picked up odd jobs as a well-driller and cat-skinner for a potato farmer after the bottom fell out of the cattle industry. "I was interested in the old cow outfits and working ahorseback, but then things changed. The old cow outfits went to hell. That's when I took up trapping."

Composed, confident, idealistic, he blossomed into a man from another era, depicted in those Charlie Russell watercolors he'd hung on the walls of his trailer. Confronted with heartless change, cast adrift in heedless times, he'd pursued life as a trapper with the dedication of a monk. It wasn't just a job; it was a way of life, spawned out of dreams in nobler times.

Little wonder an Associated Press reporter described Crockett as a "clinical specimen of a lifestyle none of us have experienced. He seems the real thing."

The real thing! Jack grew outraged. Billy said nothing about his first arrest, his citations for trash-trapping, the hours he'd spent hanging around Eddie Dodd's bar, his months of living in a shabby trailer, and his weeks of firing pistols at human-shaped targets. He owned guns, he maintained, to protect himself. "When I'm out," Billy said, "I always wear a revolver. Always. I spend most of my time alone. I have no one to fall back on except myself. I've been hung up several times alone and needed a handgun. I've killed my camp meat with them.

Once I had to cut myself away from a fallen horse. If I'm ever away from camp and break a leg, I sure as hell want to have a gun with me."

On the day in Little High Rock Canyon, he'd carried two handguns. "Pritchard took my shoulder pistol, but he didn't ask for my hip gun. I made no attempt to hide it. It made quite a bulge under my coat. Pritchard didn't say anything about the hip gun, and I didn't say anything about it to him."

Crockett said he could tell Jack Irigaray was unarmed, but Pritchard had removed the safety strap from the pistol on his hip; he also carried handcuffs.

Jack glanced at Cindy, but she stared straight ahead.

"Pritchard said he wanted to check out my camp for wild game. I told him my camp was open. He was welcome in it, but he didn't need his guns and handcuffs."

"How did he reply to that?" O'Grady asked.

"He moved his hand to his pistol and said, 'I'm going to tell you something right now, Crockett. If you want to get along with me, you'll do as I say. We've got a report on you that you've been knocking down game out of season.'

"I told him I had some meat hung up. I had to eat. And I told him, 'If you guys came a hundred miles out here just to give me a citation for meat, I can't see it.' I needed meat for subsistence. I had no transportation. This was my home, where I lived. I couldn't walk down the canyon to a food store. But Pritchard and Irigaray acted like I'd robbed a bank or something. Pritchard read me the riot act about shooting deer out of season. I couldn't make any headway with him. He seemed on the fight right from when he got out of his rig, like he was primed."

O'Grady asked, "What do you mean by that statement?"

"Well, I noticed that every time I moved or said something, Pritchard's hand went to his gun. I didn't understand it. I kept thinking in my mind, Hell, why's he so hot? I'd never been approached that way. I'd admitted I'd knocked down game and my camp was open. All the way down into the canyon, Pritchard flanked me with the safety strap unhooked. From the things he said, I was led to believe that Larry Hughes had turned me in. Hughes still had a gun on his hip, and I thought he was working with the lawmen to set me up; otherwise why would he be armed? When Pritchard saw the deer quarters hanging on the tent poles, he started to fly hot."

Billy spoke directly to the jury, looking steadily at them. "I was bewildered at the time, somewhat apprehensive. Pritchard was getting hotter. I tried to explain the situation to him, that I'd been on my own, and it was unreasonable to arrest me for subsistence hunting in the remote area I was in. I thought if I could get a conversation going, he might cool off."

Jack wondered if the jury remembered what he'd told them: Billy had more meat hung up than he needed for months, almost three hundred pounds of it.

The prosecutor objected: the defendant was engaging in narrative rather than answering questions. But the judge overruled the objection and let Crockett carry on.

"When Pritchard threatened to search my tent, I told him, 'I believe you need a search warrant. This tent is my home.' I didn't know where this guy was coming from, threatening to arrest me before he even saw what I had or didn't have. I tried to calm things down by suggesting that he cite me for the venison, and leave it at that, because I didn't believe he had any authority to break into my home without a warrant."

"Were you willing to accept a citation at that point?" O'Grady asked.

"You bet," Crockett replied. "I sure was. I suggested it. But he insisted on searching. He was flying hot with me, and well, maybe I raised my voice, too, to tell him I didn't want him in my tent. This was my home, where I lived. I thought he was out of line."

O'Grady asked, "What did he say to that?"

"He said, 'You can go easy or you can go hard, Crockett. It doesn't make any difference to me.'"

Jack struggled to comprehend what he was hearing.

"You can go easy or you can go hard," the defense attorney repeated. "What did you understand him to mean by that?"

"Well, like I said, I was getting increasingly worried about the gun deal at this time, the way he kept moving his hand to it, with the safety strap cleared. It looked to me like he was itching to use it."

That was the moment when Bob told Jack to search the tent. After Irigaray ducked inside, Crockett claimed that he told Pritchard he had cat pelts, but he carried a valid license. He also had a hide from a lion that had accidentally gotten into a trap. "What was I going to do with that fur?" Crockett said he had asked Pritchard. "Just let everything rot out here and go to waste? I had no transportation to take it to town."

Billy said Bob had replied, "We're confiscating those pelts, Crockett, and taking you in."

"I told Pritchard I couldn't go. I said, 'I've got my livestock here. I've got my mules. I can't just up and leave them. I've got all my equipment and gear here, too. It's all I have.'"

According to Crockett, Pritchard then became more belligerent. He told Billy again that he could go easy or hard, and it didn't matter which way to him. Crockett tried to tell him that he couldn't abandon all his gear and stock.

"Then you can go hard," Pritchard had snapped.

The defense attorney asked Crockett, "What did you understand him to mean by that?"

"Well," Billy said, "hard, that's only one way. That's dead."

O'Grady paused as the spectators made a unitary gasp, then he swiveled toward the bench. "Your Honor, I would like to request a recess."

During the noon break, Cindy Pritchard, her cheekbones

pink with anger, caught Jack in the hall. "I don't know if I can take this. It's outrageous, his claims that Bob went out there looking for a fight."

Jack felt glum, thinking of the difference between Billy's narration and his own. "He's well rehearsed. You can tell he's been over this story again and again."

"Oh, it's all so phony," Cindy exclaimed. "All this phony macho bullshit. You can just see the little gears turning in his mind as he calculates what he's supposed to say. It's all so canned and phony and disgusting."

Jack felt he had to calm her down; people were staring. "You better mind your P.D.E."

"The hell with it. I wouldn't hang around here another second if I didn't need to know where he hid Bob's body."

Back in the courtroom, Jack noticed the blackjack dealer with the attractive boxer's nose, Georgette Spinelli, sitting among the spectators, chewing gum. She wore a white ruffled blouse and a kind of tight magenta jumpsuit with straps and a front bib that tucked up under her breasts like a ski suit. Metallic eye shadow covered her lids like paint. When Crockett saw her, his eyebrows jumped in that sudden involuntary way that psychologists called the "eyebrow flash"—that quick, instinctual signal of pleased recognition—but Georgette, other than momentarily skipping a beat in the rhythmic movement of her jaw, showed no reaction.

The defense resumed questioning Crockett about the moment after Bob had made his threatening remarks. "At that point in time, what happened?" O'Grady asked.

"Well, after Pritchard said to me, 'You can go hard,' I said, 'You're crazy, Pritchard, you're out of line. You can't shoot a man over a game violation.' And he said, 'I can carry you out, Crockett.' Then he went for his gun."

O'Grady interrupted. "He said he could carry you out?"

"Yes, sir, that's what he said."

"And he went for his gun at that point?"

"He did."

"Then what happened?"

"Well, I just reacted to it. I went for mine."

"And then?"

"We fired."

"Did he fire at you?"

"He fired one round at me. Then I fired—his gun went off, you know. I fired again. Then I saw Larry Hughes crouched down, going for his gun, and I fired at him, spinning him around. I threw another two shots into Pritchard and one into Hughes. Then I ran into the tent and grabbed my twenty-two. I came back out and shot them in the head. They were on the ground. Pritchard was on his back and Hughes on his stomach."

"Were they alive?" O'Grady asked with a tension that indicated he had no idea what the answer might be.

"No, I don't think so. They weren't moving."

"Then why did you shoot them in the head?"

"Well, I was wound up. I was afraid. I thought this man was nuts, wanting to kill me. I was a little crazy at that stage. I didn't know what I was doing."

"Would you say you were afraid for your life?"

"I would certainly say so. Right from the start, up on the rim, there was a lot of belligerence and hostility on Pritchard's part. It was irrational. The way he flanked me all down the canyon, then the gun threats. I gave him no reason to act that way. I tried to keep the situation in hand. I tried to get along with those men. Any time I moved, his hand was on his gun. Then he said, 'I can carry you out,' and that's when he went for his gun. I was afraid for my life. I just—I did the only thing I felt I could've done to save my life because that man wanted to kill me."

Crockett said he picked up Bob's pistol from the ground not far from his hand. Larry Hughes's pistol was still in his holster.

The defense attorney asked, "Was Mr. Hughes's pistol loaded?"

"Yes, sir, I believe it was. I grabbed both guns fast, I didn't want Jack Irigaray to get them. I was still protecting myself."

"It wasn't possible that Pritchard had taken the bullets out of Hughes's pistol and given it back to him?"

"That doesn't make any sense. Pritchard didn't do that to me. He took my shoulder pistol. It seems he would've done the same to Hughes, if he wanted to disarm him. Why would he act one way with me and another with Hughes? A cop is usually consistent."

O'Grady probed Crockett's need to defend himself. "You say you took the weapons to protect yourself from Mr. Irigaray? Why didn't you shoot him, too?"

"I knew he was unarmed. He hadn't threatened me. I would never shoot an unarmed man who hadn't threatened me."

But he had taken precautions: he had confiscated Jack Irigaray's knife; on the canyon rim, he had kept Jack away from his truck in case he had a weapon stashed in the cab.

"Why didn't you leave the bodies where they were and turn yourself over to the authorities?"

"It would've been suicide to turn myself in. That's what I thought then and I still think now—even more so, what with the lynch mob mentality I've seen the state try to cultivate. I see now I made a mistake in touching those bodies, but I was thinking then I just had to buy some time. I felt my life depended on it."

When he described the trip to Eddie and Sue Dodd's house and then the drive out to the salt flat, he said, "Jack Irigaray came at me with a shovel, and I fired at him to protect myself. But I shot to wound, not to kill him. I got back to town as quick as I could and told Eddie Dodd where they could find Irigaray."

Jack saw that Billy had lucked out. Instead of bleeding to death that night in the desert, as he easily could have, Jack had survived. Crockett now seemed a reasonable man; he'd used only enough force to disable his attacker. And he'd even said, "Sorry, Jack."

Still, Billy showed no remorse for shooting Bob and Larry; he'd made no apology to the widows who sat in the courtroom looking at him. When O'Grady gave him an opportunity to express regret, he botched it.

"Now, Mr. Crockett," O'Grady said, "you told Jack Irigaray at Little High Rock Canyon that this was justifiable homicide. You told Eddie Dodd in Gerlach that you had to do it. Did you therefore want or intend to kill Bob Pritchard or Larry Hughes?"

Crockett replied without hesitation. "All I wanted to do was to keep those men from killing me. I responded in the only way I could have to save my own life and to prevent them from killing me."

The next day the prosecutor, Kirk Peters, tried to turn Billy's own words against him to show that he was a stone-hearted murderer. The former Golden Gloves champ took off his blazer and rolled up his sleeves. He'd kept himself in shape. With his bullet head, flat nose, and compact middle-weight body, he stood ready to go. He probed Crockett about his admission of guilt when he'd said, "This is murder one for me."

Billy calmly replied, "What I actually said was, 'They'll say this is murder one, but to me it's justifiable homicide.'"

Crockett put a similar spin on his statement "If I'd known this guy's pistol was empty, I would've taken Pritchard up on the rim, but I thought the two of them would get the best of me up there." He now claimed, "What I said was, 'If they'd taken me on the rim, they would've killed me up there.'"

Billy had no hesitation in coming back hard at the prosecutor. He acknowledged that he'd openly and knowingly violated game laws. Kirk Peters asked, "Why do you feel that you were above the law in killing deer out of season? Why couldn't you have brought in your supplies like anyone else?"

Crockett snapped, "Not anyone else that I know lives like I

do or under the conditions I do. It's not practical to pack in the meat you need to carry you through a winter. You can't bring in cut and frozen meat. It won't keep. Meat has to be hung in carcass form to keep."

Peters's jaw jutted at Crockett. "You could have made arrangements to be supplied."

"Even if I could've made arrangements," Crockett fired back, "I couldn't have afforded it. I was on my own out there."

The judge, who had consistently overruled the prosecutor's objections, now sustained those of the defense, so that Kirk Peters's line of questioning constantly got derailed. The prosecutor then tried to establish Crockett as someone self-trained in gunfighting techniques. He was no ordinary trapper.

"Do you recall that Jack Irigaray testified that you were in a crouched position when shooting?"

"Yes, I recall that," Crockett answered.

"Was Jack correct?"

"No, he was not."

O'Grady snapped, "Objection, Your Honor. Reference to another's testimony is inappropriate."

The judge agreed. "The defendant should be allowed to testify to what he knows, not to what someone else knows or has testified to. That's invading the province of the jury."

It would've helped the prosecution to investigate Billy's previous arrest, not to reveal that he was a slacker—that wasn't important—but to help explain his grudge against the law. Jack had reported Billy's statement, "I said I wouldn't get arrested again," but the prosecution wasn't permitted to pursue this motive for resisting arrest. Kirk Peters made it clear that Billy had foreknowledge of what could happen in Little High Rock Canyon when game wardens arrived. Billy had told Scotty Larsen, "I'll be ready for them." Trained and warned, he'd premeditated what he would do. That was first-degree murder.

"The pistol on your hip," the prosecutor asked, "was a Ruger Security Six?"

"Yes, a .357 Magnum," Crockett specified.

"With combat grips on the handle."

"*Custom* grips!" Crockett sharply corrected him. "I made 'em myself."

"How did you learn to quick-draw this pistol from your hip holster?"

Before Crockett could answer, his lawyer objected. "The question is argumentative and speculative."

"Sustained," the judge said.

The prosecutor pressed on. "Where did you learn to out-draw an individual who is drawing his gun?"

The defense again objected. The judge concurred, "The question assumes facts not in evidence."

At this point the prosecutor asked the bailiff to bring forward evidence to show that Crockett had long preoccupied himself with handgun combat. Peters intended to introduce the books found in Crockett's trailer, *No Second Place Winner* and *Kill or Be Killed,* the manuals he'd used to prepare himself as a quick-draw gunfighter who, as he'd bragged, would "never get arrested again."

Before the books could be introduced, O'Grady flew up to the bench, full of objections, requesting that the matter be discussed away from the jury.

The judge ordered the jury removed from the courtroom. Crockett's lawyer argued, "Your Honor, the defense has demonstrated through the testimony of witnesses that the defendant's character is peaceable and quiet. His own testimony has shown that he was not the aggressor in this situation. These books are wholly irrelevant to any issue in this case and are merely introduced to inflame and prejudice the jury."

The judge leafed through the books and nodded. "These publications appear to be legitimate books for legitimate purposes, and to have the jury speculate that they were read for other purposes is too dangerous. The court is going to sustain the objection."

The prosecutor's face took on the impassive mask of an experienced pugilist unexpectedly stunned by a violent combination. Jack was stunned, too. Had the judge chosen to believe Crockett's story, that he was a trapper of equable disposition victimized by a provocative, aggressive game warden who had overstepped his authority? How could the jury know the truth about the murders if they didn't know Crockett's history?

Other crucial evidence, especially Bob's pistol, was conveniently missing, buried somewhere in the desert. The barrel couldn't be checked to see if it had been fired, as Crockett claimed. Hughes's pistol was also lost. Crockett maintained that he'd disposed of the pistols and his own weapons—the .357 Ruger Magnum and .22 Marlin—at some point during his escape across the Black Rock Desert.

"I couldn't tell you within more than five miles where I dumped the guns," Crockett said. "I was heading across one of the flats, just trying to get away, and wanted to be rid of them."

"So you did not bury the guns with Bob Pritchard."

"No, sir. I told you I dumped them after I buried Pritchard."

I glanced at Cindy, leaning forward in her chair. Kirk Peters asked Crockett, "Can you give us an approximate location of where you buried Mr. Pritchard's body?"

Billy smiled. "Why, certainly," he said, as though he'd never been asked such a question before. "Quite easily, I'm sure."

The prosecutor offered Billy a topographical map of the Gerlach area. "Can you show us on this map where you buried the body?"

Billy took the map. "I'd be happy to. Would you like me to mark the location?"

The murmur and commotion in the courtroom came from

those, like Cindy and Jack, who'd waited nearly two years for this moment. The jury looked confused over the fuss.

Billy carefully scratched an X onto the topo map. "Right here."

Within minutes Jack was in Jim Sandoval's Cherokee, siren blaring, speeding behind the car of another deputy and the sheriff, on the road to Gerlach. They wanted to beat the reporters who would be on their way as well. With the windows rolled down, wind roared into the truck. The late afternoon air was mild; only the light betrayed the season. The October sun burnished the desert. Rabbitbrush and cheatgrass took on the rusty glow of autumn.

"I can't believe the place he marked," Jack shouted above the wind. "So close to Gerlach."

"I can't either," Jim shouted back. "But who knows if he's telling the truth."

They flew past Pyramid Lake, its calm deep-sea blue flecked white with distant pelicans from Anaho Island. Just past the town of Empire, south of Gerlach, they turned off the road and followed the sheriff's car onto a stretch of salt flat and headed toward the sandhills marked on the map. Bruno's motel and Dodd's bar stood within sight, less than a quarter of a mile away. If Crockett had really buried Bob here, so close to town, then he must've deliberately waited before returning the truck to Eddie Dodd in order to cause people to think that he'd traveled a considerable distance. When Jack had taken part in the search for Bob, they'd scoured this desert, but they hadn't spent much time looking near town.

Jim paced off the distance marked on the map. Sheriff Nelson ordered the other deputy to cordon off the area as a crime site. Jim began digging and sifting sand through a screened box. Reporters arrived and stood behind the ropes.

Jim scraped sand away from the scuffed toe of a laced boot. He got down on his knees with a trowel and carefully cleared a space around the entire corrugated Vibram sole. Out of the top of the boot extended a white bone.

The two investigators worked at the grave. Pieces of green twilled pants turned up, then some vertebrae and a few rib bones.

"Looks like coyotes got some of him," Jim said.

Bob's grimacing skull appeared face up in the sand. Jim gently tilted it and pointed to the bullet hole just behind the left ear canal.

Jack had seen enough. He told Jim to meet him at Bruno's when he was finished. Jim rolled the skull back to its original position, and another officer began taking pictures of the jumbled bones. After all the investigative fiascos the trial had turned up, they were being careful to follow procedures according to the book.

It only took a few minutes for Jack to walk across the flat to Bruno's. Near the town's old wooden water tower in front of the bar, facing in the direction of where Bob was buried, stood a homemade billboard that Jack had looked at dozens of times but hadn't really seen until now: GERLACH HIGH SCHOOL—HOME OF THE LIONS.

CHAPTER 9

A banner hanging in Bruno's bar portrayed an image of the Gerlach High School mascot. It looked like the golden MGM lion in the movies, thick-furred, broad-headed, and ready to roar. Jack had stared right at this African king of beasts on that weekend he'd searched for Bob's body. He felt spooked. Would he have made the connection with his dream and the ghost's message—"buried with lions"—if the mascot were a western mountain lion, or if the high school teams were the Gerlach Cougars, as they should've been called in allegiance to their Nevada homeland? He didn't think so. Not once had he considered that Bob's body lay on the edge of town. Neither had anyone else.

Crockett's choice had been calculating. Everyone had assumed he'd hidden the body at least a half-hour's drive from Gerlach. But the flats near town were as good a place as any to bury something. The unstable sands shifted with the wind

187

or rain—any change in the weather—leaving the surface smooth or wind-ridged. The change could happen overnight. Crockett had taken a chance. He'd lucked out again. Weather had come in, obscuring his tracks.

Everyone knew the story of how Jess Nichols and his brother, years ago, had robbed a boxcar of kitchen appliances on the Empire tracks, and in an attempt to hide the goods, they'd buried them in the flats near town, planning to wait for the investigations to die down before going back to dig them up. But the wind blew, sands shifted. The contours of the land assumed new shapes. Jess and his brother couldn't find the burial site, although it was within a few hundred yards of the train tracks. The toasters and blenders were still out there, somewhere, rusting in their cartons, until that future day when the wind might uncover them for some passerby.

Bob's bones came home to Cindy in a cardboard box. She planned to have them cremated and scattered over the northern desert, near the Oregon border, where Bob had spent so many childhood days camping.

When Jack joined her for a drink, she mused about Bob's lifelong love of that country. It was a wild land of sweeping savannas and ranges reminiscent of Africa.

"Bob was really born in the wrong century," Cindy said. "He would've been happier if he'd never had to come indoors. He was always restless in the house, champing at the bit to get in his truck and go. He was happiest out in the hills, just spying on antelope and bighorns through his binoculars."

They sat in the fading twilight of Cindy's living room, without turning on the lamps. Cindy poured herself a drink. Even though she was inside, she wore a cream-colored corduroy baseball cap with a long bill, tipped up, so dark curls peeked out on her forehead. The cap matched her white cotton sweatshirt with sleeves pulled up to her elbows, and a pair of casual white jeans, cut off just above her knees. Something about her short, compact body, her muscled calves, as she walked in that outfit, made Jack think of a Japanese judo instructor.

She refilled his drink and sank down next to him on the couch. He felt they were groping for a ritual to honor Bob. The box holding his bones rested on the mantel above the fireplace.

Months ago, at the outdoor memorial ceremony for Bob, about three hundred people had showed up, including maybe a hundred wardens and biologists from as far away as Idaho and Utah. It had been a sad, hollow, unsatisfying ceremony, without a body to bury or ashes to scatter. They had done their best to summon up Bob's spirit. Wendell Phillips spoke about the time Bob slept alone in ten-below-zero weather guarding the herd of bighorns penned up outside Summit Lake. Jack talked about the way Bob worked into the night with a magnifying glass and Rapidograph pen, drawing sketches of mountain lions and desert mice, eagles and sage sparrows, the tiniest animals as important to him as the largest.

Cindy reflected, "I don't know what it was about Bob and animals. I didn't really see it, the extent of it, until after we were married."

"They were a lot like people to him."

"That doesn't really explain it. They intrigued him. They— I don't know—they fascinated him in a way that nothing else did. He admired them, the mystery of them. He could sit out and watch a hawk perched in a cottonwood, doing nothing, just ruffling its feathers once in a while. He could do that for hours."

Maybe Cindy had to talk this way, to review her life with Bob in the presence of his bones, so that she could let him go. Jack let her take the lead and followed along.

"When he was married to his first wife and still in school, he spent a summer doing some kind of wildlife survey up in Alaska in the Brooks Range. He left his wife and son here. He told me if he hadn't been married, he would've just stayed up there in Alaska. That country was still so remote, a lot of the peaks didn't even have names back then."

"His real niche was down here," Jack said, thinking of his father's advice about finding a career that mattered. "In a lot of ways he was a lucky man." He glanced at Cindy, but she was staring off.

"He was a tough Marine," Cindy mused, "but there was that big soft spot in him people didn't know."

At times, it was easy to forget that Bob had been a Marine. He hadn't talked about it. He'd come back from Korea with a Silver Star and a Purple Heart, but he had never told anyone how he'd earned them. Jack had asked once, and Bob had started to answer, but he got sidetracked, or pretended to. Jack had never brought it up again.

Cindy went on, talking as much to herself as to him. "Maybe Bob didn't have finesse, but people knew he was straight. He would've even given me a citation if I'd broken a game law. Once he banned his son from hunting for the remainder of the season for forgetting to take a shell out of the breech when he put the shotgun in the car."

Jack found himself trying to justify what they both knew: Bob could be a pain in the ass. He told Cindy, "Bob always said, 'As long I wear a badge, it's going to be a clean badge.' His best friends would say that when Bob came across them in their camps he checked their licenses and tags, and then after spending the night with them, he would check them all over again in the morning, and then—"

"It was for the animals," Cindy interjected. "He banded birds when he was a kid; he knew how fast they were disappearing. He used to talk about how few animals were left in the country. He was going to do everything he could within the law to help them."

"That's why a guy like Crockett got to him. His wastefulness was more than Bob could take."

Cindy curled both hands around the drink resting on her knee. She gazed off through the room's hovering darkness to the bay window. Across the street a man leaned on a rake and looked thoughtfully down at a small pile of autumn leaves burning in the gutter as he unwittingly polluted the town. Kids on bicycles, with excited shouts, streaked past the window doing wheelies in the street.

"Bob always told me that someone was going to get killed," she said. "Game wardens have so many close calls. But I didn't worry that much about him. He had a good head. I knew he could keep things under control."

"Usually he could."

"Still there was something. All those accidents. Like when he lost his eye . . ."

She didn't have to say more. Bob was accident-prone; everyone knew it. That time, on a family outing, when he was blowing up an air mattress for his kid, the needle had flown out of the plug and into his eye. That was why he had to use a magnifying glass when he drew. He could only work for ten or fifteen minutes at a time before his good eye went blurry, too.

"I was with him that time," Jack reminded her, "out in Orovada when we were talking to some ranchers and Bob started chewing on treated wheat stalks. He got so sick at one point when we were driving home that he was holding his stomach and said, 'For Christ's sake, Jack, please, shoot me.'"

Cindy laughed, tipping her nose and hat brim up at the same angle. In the dim light, her perfect teeth brightened her face and the freckles across her nose. "Remember the time in Battle Mountain when that hunter shot a big rattlesnake? Bob went to step on the snake's head and reached down to cut off the tail—so the hunter wouldn't have the rattles to brag about—and the damn snake bit him."

"His hand swelled up something terrible."

"Then when he got an antivenin shot, he had a reaction and broke out in hives. He was a mess, but he still laughed about it."

Jack knew that Cindy was now considering what had happened at Little High Rock Canyon. "Bob had bad luck at times," he said, "but not when he was dealing with people. He went by the book and he was careful. I was the one who screwed up. I forgot my gun in the truck."

Her voice turned fiery. "The real problem was that you and Bob weren't tough enough with Crockett. You were too nice to him. You should've frisked him right to his asshole. You went easy on him, and you didn't find that other gun."

Startled, he tried to diffuse the blame. "Crockett says that gun was apparent, but it wasn't. I can't believe that his lawyer tried to make it seem as though Bob only confiscated one pistol so that he'd have an excuse to shoot Crockett."

"Why can't they see the truth, Jack? Why do people buy into this hogwash? Crockett knew he was going to try to kill Bob from the moment he met him up on the ridge. He had over an hour to plan it before he actually did it."

Cindy abruptly stood up, as though to turn on the lamp by the couch, then twirled around, putting her glass on the coffee table, and sat on Jack's lap. She put her arms around his neck. Her forehead pressed against his chest, just under his chin. Her lips moved against his shirt, her voice muffled. "Will you please hold me, Jack? Just hold me for a while. You don't have to say anything."

He held her until it was completely dark. Her tears wet his throat. When they stood up she kissed him on the cheek. Then at the door she surprised him with another kiss, this time on the mouth, and she pressed against him. "Thanks for being such a good friend, Jack. I feel something's behind us now. No matter what happens at that damn trial, something's over."

He felt a pressure in his head. They'd found Bob. That was finished. They'd passed a barrier, crossed a border, reached a summit. Now he feared what might begin.

The next day, he called the travel agent at Ponderosa Travel and made reservations for two round-trips to Zihuatanejo in

February during Carrie's winter school break. A week's vacation was coming to him, and he could take it then. He told Beth that night what he'd done.

"Did you already pay for the tickets?" she asked.

"No, I have time. They'll hold the reservations, but the longer I wait, the more chance the rates might go up."

"How much would it cost to take Carrie and Sarah?"

"I thought we could leave them with your parents, or with my mother. Carrie'll be out of school."

"Well, I guess we could. It's only a week. Let me think about it."

At the courthouse the next day, Judge Reilley gave in to the defense's demands to allow a string of witnesses to testify about Bob's character as a brute. Earlier the judge had ruled out anything about Bob that Crockett would not have known. Now he was caving in. He said, "Since the defendant has put into evidence the issue of self-defense, the victim's prior conduct is now an issue." The judge limited testimony to acts of aggression or violence that had occurred in the last five years.

Gary Valdez, a buckaroo who'd worked for Jack's uncle in Paradise Valley and who claimed to be like a brother to Crockett, took the stand. Crockett's lawyer asked him, "Do you know if Mr. Pritchard enjoyed in the community a reputation for dangerousness or violence or turbulence or aggression?"

"All of them," Gary Valdez shot back with a smile. "But most people used other words."

"What other words would those be?"

"Most people said he was an asshole."

During cross-examination, the prosecutor asked Gary Valdez about his personal encounters with Bob, and it turned out that they'd never met.

"You never had any negative encounter with the victim?"

"No. I didn't have to. I'd heard enough to know what he was like. He pushed around his badge and his gun."

Next a Winnemucca plumber named Ross Edwards testified. He had been tracked down by Jenny Morrison, who'd sent out letters, made phone calls, and scurried around the state in her yellow Jaguar in search of witnesses. The plumber testified that Bob had barged into a hunting camp in upper Washoe three years earlier and cited him and his friends for exceeding their chukar limit.

"He was extremely aggressive," the plumber said. "I got the impression he was trying to provoke me. His attitude was rude and abusive. He acted like we'd committed some major crime, like animals had more rights than we did. His hand kept going near his gun."

The prosecutor produced papers to show that the hunters had been cited that day by the other Washoe warden, Dale Ellison. Dale took the stand to confirm that he had indeed cited the hunters. The witness was mistaken about the incident. Bob had been on Mount Rose, two hundred miles away.

Only one witness actually claimed that Bob had pulled a gun on him, but the judge ruled out his testimony because the supposed event had occurred in the mid-sixties, twenty years earlier. Still, the man's story, though officially stricken from the record, had been told. The jury heard it.

"Who the hell's on trial?" Cindy asked Jack after the testimony. "Crockett or Bob?"

"All of us," Jack said.

During the closing arguments, Crockett's attorney did his best to undermine Jack's testimony. "Seventy-five percent of the state's case depends on Jack Irigaray's statements," O'Grady told the jury. "When you deliberate on the defendant's motive, ask yourself: Is there evidence in the record that the defendant has ever been arrested for a Fish and Game violation before? If there were such evidence, wouldn't the state have presented it? Does that comport with the statement that Jack Irigaray attributed to the defendant that he would never be arrested again?"

Jack saw from Kirk Peters's staggered, wary expression that Crockett's lawyer was hitting low, and the prosecutor was helpless to do a thing about it. Of course, Crockett hadn't been arrested for a game violation, but he'd been cited, several times, by Bob, Wendell Phillips, Dale Ellison, and even Jack himself. He'd been arrested for draft evasion, but the prosecution could say nothing about it, for fear of a mistrial. If the jury disregarded Crockett's statement, "I'll never be arrested again," then the motive for premeditated murder flew out the window.

As prosecutor, Kirk Peters had the closing position, and he threw his best shots. "The state of Nevada calls for a conviction of first-degree murder for someone who kills a peace officer acting lawfully. The defendant claims that the officers couldn't lawfully search his tent, but—ladies and gentlemen—I must emphasize that peace officers have a statutory right to search any camp because it is only temporary. They don't require a search warrant. That's the law. Because the defendant possessed illegally trapped pelts and a nonresident license, the officers had not only a right to arrest him but also a legal obligation to do so. That's the law, too. Even if Mr. Pritchard had said, 'You can go easy or you can go hard'— which he did *not* say—but even *if* he did say it, then why didn't the defendant go easy? By his own admission he was in violation of the law; by his own admission he resisted arrest; and by his own admission he shot and killed two men, one of whom was, in fact, an unarmed, ordinary citizen and his friend. If the defendant had nothing to conceal, why did he then hide the bodies and refrain from telling anyone of their whereabouts? Is it justifiable homicide to kill two wounded men, lying helpless on the ground, by shooting them in the head? Ladies and gentlemen, such an act is murder in the first degree."

The trial was over. Jack was cautiously optimistic. If seventy-five percent of the state's case rested on his testimony, then almost a hundred percent of the defense's position rested on Billy's fabrications. Even if the conviction dropped to second-degree murder, and Billy escaped the death penalty, at least he would be in the slammer for up to seventy years.

By the fifth day of jury deliberations, Jack wasn't so optimistic. Something had snagged.

"They're fighting in the jury room," Jim Sandoval said. "People are crying. The bailiff had to walk two women around the courthouse to calm them down."

The jury asked for further instructions from Judge Reilley, which he refused to give. It looked as though the judge had a hung jury and faced what he least wanted, a mistrial, and that is exactly what the worried prosecution began to ask for. The defense objected, as did Crockett; they wanted the trial completed even after one juror was dismissed for supposedly introducing Crockett's previous arrest into the discussions.

"Somebody screwed up the material the court gave to the jury," Jim said. "It included papers about Crockett's previous arrest."

The juror who pointed out the information about Crockett's draft evasion became a scapegoat and was dismissed at the request of the defense. The judge ordered the offending papers removed from the room. On the sixth day of deliberations, a substitute juror, with Crockett's approval, took up the empty spot, and the process continued.

When Jack stopped by Cindy's house for a drink after work, he was relieved to find her in a tough mood, so different from the other night. He was the one who was somber.

"Forget it, Jack," she said. "Whatever happens happens. Nothing is going to bring Bob back."

"I'd like to see justice done."

"The important thing is that we've found Bob."

A new container sat on the mantel. The bones had been cremated, and the ashes waited in a small white plastic box until Jim Sandoval could take them up with Cindy and Bob's two children to be scattered over the Sheldon National Wild-life Refuge in northern Washoe. In dismissing the approaching verdict, Cindy was just preparing herself for the worst. She was agitated. She tossed down her drinks, and he did, too.

"We found Bob," Cindy said, sitting next to him on the couch, "and the trial brought out the truth. That's what matters. Talk to anyone. They know. It's laughable to think that Bob was the kind of person to go down there, in front of two witnesses, looking for a shoot-out. But Crockett *was* that kind of person."

"Bob never had a chance to shoot," Jack said. "Even with his bad eye, if he'd drawn his pistol and got off a shot at five or six feet, he wouldn't have missed. But I don't think he ever pulled his gun on anybody."

Cindy corrected him. "He did, once, years ago. I wish it could've come out in the trial. He was serving a year as deputy sheriff in Humboldt County. Someone was loading a dead steer into a pickup and wouldn't stop. He had a rifle. Bob pulled his pistol but never fired. The man gave up. Bob was so upset about the whole thing he went right to one of the county commissioners and explained what had happened. He told me that after that, no matter what happened, he would never pull his gun again except to prevent someone from being killed. If he had it to do over again, he'd let the man have the damn steer."

"All this should've been brought out," Jack said. "I saw him let a man keep a poached deer. The guy was out of work and needed to feed his family. Bob told the man, 'Just don't let me hear that you've told anybody down at the bars about this, or I'll cite your ass.'"

"He did that more than you know."

"Remember how he always said, 'There's nothing I'd rather see dead than alive, even a poacher'?"

Cindy grew meditative. "That was because of the war. His

whole feeling about animals and letting things live came out of what happened to him in the war."

Cindy stood up from the couch. She was dressed in white again, the same sweatshirt and cutoffs she'd worn the other night but without the baseball cap. Her luxuriant curly hair fell around her head, rich and dark. Even in the dim evening light it had the sheen of damp coal.

"Oh, let's knock this off, Jack. We can't just keep retrying this damn case. Here, let me get you another drink."

She came back with the glasses—they were both drinking Scotch, his on the rocks, hers with soda—and after putting her glass on the coffee table, she slid onto his lap, as she had the other night, and folded her arms around his neck. In the darkness her black pupils had dilated to the rims of her green irises. "For two years," she said, "we've been tangled in this mess. We've got to get on with our lives."

"It'll be easier to do that from now on," he said.

"I don't know if it will be easier, but it will be better."

She was losing him. She wasn't just talking them toward bed.

"What do you mean? What are you planning to do?" he asked.

She tightened her arms around his neck. "Not just me," she said. "What about us? What are we going to do?"

"Us?"

She started to laugh and gave his neck a shake. "Yes, us, you numbskull. You know how I feel about you, how I've always felt about you."

Ever since the sixth grade, when someone told him that little Barbara Shaw had a crush on him, such revelations had startled him. Cindy's word "always" was the surprise. He hadn't expected such long-term seriousness. Even with Beth, he thought he'd made the overtures in college until she confessed she had had her eye on him much earlier. The shock came partly from feeling unworthy, knowing himself as he did. But he'd come to accept that, as with medflies, salamanders, olive baboons, and the females of most species, women controlled the game of love; men might play the role of suitors, but it was the females' biological role to make the actual decision of suitability. In high school, after making a fool of himself courting girls who had no interest in him, he just let nature take its course. Let them decide. Still, things always took unexpected turns.

Cindy played with the hair on his forehead, twirling it into a curl, letting go, and twirling it again. His stomach went light.

"I don't know about this, Cindy."

"You don't know about what?"

"This. Us. Whatever."

"What's there to know?"

He looked at Bob's ashes on the mantel. Cindy pushed her head against his chest and drew up her knees. Her bare legs, tan from the summer, shone as though rubbed with cream. Her compact body under her loose clothes, snuggled in his lap, resting there with the dense smoothness and roundness of a baby harp seal.

"I promised Bob," she said, "that I wouldn't do anything until I found his remains and could bury him right. Oh, I wanted you so much. But I kept my promise."

"But he's not buried." A lame thing to say, he knew, but it was the truth. Bob on the mantel and the memory of his ghost in the dream made Jack nervous. Maybe he would've felt different if those ashes had already been scattered. He sensed something wrong. Bob's message about being buried with lions turning out to be true still spooked him.

"It's over," Cindy said. "Bob wouldn't want us to strangle our lives. You were his friend."

"We have to think about what's happening. I have to think about Beth, too."

Cindy jerked her head up. "Oh, barf," she said. "Everyone knows you and Beth are on the rocks. The only thing that's surprising is that you haven't split up yet. I know you've been miserable with her. Everyone does."

How much did Cindy know? Beth had never been particularly fond of Cindy; she thought she was feather-headed, but the two attended the same aerobics class and worked out at the same gym. The exercise room had replaced the beauty parlor as the petri dish breeding gossip for their generation.

"Well," Jack said, "I am married to her. Things are getting better. We're going to Mexico soon, and things will be even better after that."

Cindy slipped her hand into his shirt and smoothed her hand back and forth over his chest. "This isn't about Beth. This is about us, you and me. I know we can make each other happy. Why should we continue being miserable when we can make each other so happy?"

He couldn't really separate what was happening with Cindy from his life with Beth. Nothing like this had happened during the nine years they'd been married. But Cindy's words hit home. He recognized the truth of them. He knew Bob, too. As Cindy said, Bob would have wanted what was best for her and for him, for them to be happy.

Jack kissed Cindy, and her hands slithered inside his shirt and over his bare back. He loved the taste of her, her smell, her heat. His hands went up under her sweatshirt. He thought of that afternoon at Pyramid Lake when she'd bounced out of the water, her skimpy black bikini slipping on her wet skin, her breast and rosy nipple exposed in the bright sunshine.

The tip of her tongue stroked his ear. Goose bumps rippled down his neck. Her breath echoed in the hollow of his ear like the inside of a conch shell. She whispered, "Let's go to bed."

He pulled her close. "It isn't you," he said. "I have to decide about Beth first. I have to know about her before I can know about us."

"Then kiss me," she said, and he did.

When he left Cindy's he headed for Barney's Bar on B Street to think things over. It was quiet and dark there, and no one, except maybe the bartender, knew him. Jack started drinking shots.

"Hey, buddy," the barkeep said, "you better slow up."

The liquor burned Jack's throat and heated his thoughts. Maybe he'd made a mistake. Maybe he should go back to Cindy; but, no, he'd done the right thing for now. Her talk about being happy gave him the willies. What a seductive image! The focused desire for happiness had once made him more miserable than any other. It's what kept people like Billy's Belles watching *The Young and the Restless* and *The Bold and the Beautiful*, as though some idea of happiness was the brass ring everyone was supposed to be striving for. He no longer believed in it as a thing to chase. Occasionally in his life, happiness had sidled up to him, catching him by surprise when he was consumed in doing something worthwhile. He could even recall times from his past when he'd been happy without really knowing it. But he'd discovered that to go whoring after happiness, as if it were some prize announced on a glittering, meretricious casino marquee, was a shoddy venture, destined to leave him smashed up in heartbreak hotel.

Still, Cindy had made him feel happy. Her kisses, her body pressed against him, her unapologetic declarations of desire left him excited.

He walked with an airy step up to the door of his house. The night air was brisk and moist, tingly on his face. All the lights in the house were off. Beth hadn't even left the outside porch light burning for him. The witch had even locked the door. He scratched at the lock with the key until it slipped in and released the bolt. He groped for the light on the inside wall. Something feathery brushed across his hand—one of the cats leaping from the table? A tumbling, crashing sound broke the quietness as the lamp came on and he saw splattering across the floor shards of the black ceramic Mexican bull he'd bought in Oaxaca, ruined.

A light clicked on in the hallway. Beth appeared in her pajamas, her hair a mass of yellow curls backlit by the hallway glow. Through the thin cloth of her PJs, he glimpsed the shadowy outline of her legs, the curve of her waist, the heft of her breasts. He'd come home wanting to climb into bed with her, to hold her full body against the heat of his own, skin against skin, flesh against flesh, wanting to find her where she was moist, silky warm.

She yelled, "What the hell are you doing?"

"The cat—" he started to explain.

"Oh, Christ, look what you've done."

He saw his plans for love shattered like the black ceramic pieces on the floor. "Don't blame me, goddammit. Why'd you leave all the lights off?"

"Stop shouting," she yelled. "The children—"

As though she'd just been announced, Sarah cowered in her little pink nightgown behind Beth's legs; her terrified eyes sent a surge of regret from Jack's stomach to his heart.

He dropped to his knees and reached out to her. "Come here, honey." He'd calmed his voice, trying to smile.

Sarah pulled back and clutched Beth's pajamas. "Daddy smells funny," she said.

"Leave her alone, Jack. You've frightened her enough."

He got to his feet and glared at Beth. Then he saw Carrie standing behind her sister. "Don't try turning the kids against me," he said.

"I don't have to try. You've done enough already. This is it, as far as I'm concerned."

"Oh, as far as you're concerned." He mimicked her mincing voice, angry at both her and himself for letting the night's loving plans somersault into a hateful mess.

"Get out of here, Jack. You're destroying us all."

"I'm going to *my* bed," he said sternly.

"Not with me, you're not." She turned and pushed Carrie and Sarah ahead of her down the hall. The door to the kids' room slammed, the lock clicked.

The door to their bedroom stood ajar, the lamp on the night table lighting the rumpled comforter and the sad blue sheets of their empty bed.

CHAPTER 10

In the morning, Jack skirted Beth without a word and was out of the house early, feeling angry and full of regret. He spent the day at work thinking that he probably should've slept with Cindy, for all the love that awaited him at home. Maybe Cindy and her friends were right: he and Beth were just carrying on a silly charade; their relationship was dead. But something in him didn't believe it, and there were the girls. What had happened last night, he swore, would never happen again.

Word came late that evening that the jury had reached a decision. He was in the courthouse the next morning. After seven days of stymied deliberations, the substitute juror had made the difference. Once she'd joined the jury, the stalemate had broken.

Jack and Cindy furtively glanced at each other; then she smiled, and he knew there were no hard feelings. Her smile said that they could pick up where they'd left off. They sat apart in the full house and awaited the report from the foreman of the jury.

The clerk read the verdict: "Guilty of voluntary manslaughter." Jack felt slammed in the head. The jury had decided that Crockett hadn't murdered anyone; he'd only engaged in the "unlawful killing of a human being without malice upon a sudden quarrel or heat of passion."

The jurors also found Crockett guilty of concealing evidence and using firearms to commit a crime, but they acquitted him of kidnapping, resisting arrest, and attempted murder. The judge set the day of sentencing for December 1.

On the TV news that evening the foreman of the jury explained: "We just figured Pritchard drew his gun and Crockett was a better marksman, that he was put in a position of self-defense. Crockett was a faster draw. He won out."

The only juror who'd held out for a conviction of first-degree murder was the one dismissed for introducing extraneous evidence.

"We might've acquitted Crockett," the foreman went on, "if he hadn't run into his tent, got his rifle, and shot those two men in the head. Those head shots seemed excessive force to us. Otherwise we likely would've reached a verdict of justifiable homicide."

A woman from the jury also appeared on the news. "Many western men are too independent to be pushed," she declared. "They're going to react to protect themselves. What Crockett did was wrong—there were better ways to handle things—but I'd hate to see a world where men were afraid to stand up for their rights."

Cindy had hit it on the head. There were two Crocketts: one in Little High Rock Canyon, the other in the courtroom, and the storyteller in the witness chair had won out. He'd spun the jury back to a mythical time of Old West showdowns when Hondo Lane stalked the streets at high noon. Jack had come out the loser. Even though he'd done his best to tell the truth, the jury hadn't believed him. He felt like a fool.

Wendell Phillips appeared on TV in his Division of Wildlife uniform. "It's open season on game wardens," he grimly warned. "The jury has told us that our wardens are expendable, and the enforcement of game laws is meaningless. If you don't want a hundred-dollar citation, just put a bullet in the warden. The last man alive is telling the truth."

Jack wished he were as eloquent as Wendell. When the reporters had caught up with him, he was furious. "This only proves," he'd said, "that in this country, if you want justice—real justice—you have to do it yourself."

He regretted his words, or at least saying them in public, when he saw himself on TV, glowering, dark, hung over, more a murderer in appearance than Crockett himself.

The only good news was that Billy wasn't satisfied either. His lawyers had been hoping for a verdict of not guilty on all counts. "But when police officers or law enforcement officials are injured or killed in a shooting," O'Grady complained, "the jury tends to give too much credence to the prosecution. Of course, we will appeal this case. The prosecution never proved that those men were alive when they were shot in the head."

Jack strained to believe what he was hearing. O'Grady's argument was as crazy as those that claimed Crockett's head shots were okay because they had put the wounded men out of their misery, just like killing wounded animals in a trap.

In a prepared statement to the *Reno Gazette-Journal*, Billy's father, William David Crockett, Sr., raged: "I don't know how a man who's lived in the mountains the last fifteen years can be tried by a bunch of schoolteachers. I don't know how a man that's never been hungry can try a hungry man that had to protect himself while he was hungry. Any man who uses the court to destroy his fellow man commits treason against the state and destroys all that should be sacrosanct."

Jim Sandoval showed Jack a photocopy of a letter Billy had written to his father and given a deputy to mail. In large, childlike script, Crockett wrote:

> My lawyers did a good job but they were rolling a rock up a hill with cops involved. I caught winks from the jury, so things were looking up but having an eyewitness worked too much against us. I'll still whip this deal one way or another. I know you sold some of your guns to help with the trial and I'll make it up to you. It'll take me some time to get staked again, but not around here. I'll have to cut out of this country because if I hang around here they'd make it hot for me and I'd have to drill another one of those bastards.

Crockett could be sentenced to fifty years for voluntary manslaughter, he could also go free, or—as he apparently expected—he could serve two to three years and then be paroled. Based on what he'd seen of Third District Judge Lee Reilley, Jack feared that Crockett might walk.

"This judge ought to be investigated," Jim said. "His credibility is shot. He let this whole trial turn into a prosecution of Bob."

"And every game warden who's ever done his job."

Cindy, despite the display of a stiff upper lip the other night, looked devastated by the verdict. Jack tried to find her in the courtroom hallway, but she'd fled, probably to avoid reporters. He tried to call her that evening, but she wasn't home. He couldn't get ahold of Jim Sandoval either, so he went to Barney's and drank alone.

The next day at work the receptionist brought in an envelope. Mrs. Pritchard, she said, had dropped it off. Jack was surprised to see that the letter was typed.

> Dear Jack,
> It's very hard to write. I'm crying my eyes out, and it's hard to see the keys. What happened in that courtroom

was terrible, worse than I ever could have imagined. I want him back. I want Bob back. Oh Jack, it's unbearable. I wish you were here to hold me. But you have your own life to live, to work out. I respect that. The other night you were absolutely right in your words and actions. My behavior was out of line. I hope to God Beth knows nothing of this and will forever remain free from knowing it. I love her, too. But I am glad I misbehaved for I meant what I said, I mean it today, and I'll mean it tomorrow. What we've shared over the past months is terribly intimate to me. It is very clear in my mind how close I feel to you and how much I want to make love with you. As I lay curled in your lap feeling so near you, I realized you have your own deep hurt as well. I see it in your wonderful, sad Basque eyes. I want to rub your hurt away, Jack. Oh, Jack, Jack, Jack. I love your name. It is straightforward and honest like Bob. Rest assured, however, lest you never come to house number 136 again for fear of being attacked by some sex-starved widow, that I will keep my behavior in line, at least most of the time. There is so much I want to tell you, to share with you. There are so many facets of your life I don't know. Next to Bob, you are the most decent, wonderful man I have met in my whole life. But you shouldn't drink so much. I love you, Jack, and I want you to know that no matter what happens, I will always love you. Good-bye.

    Cindy

    P.S. Enclosed is a packet of matches, for obvious reasons, unless you have a surefire hiding place for this.

He folded the letter and put his forehead on the desk. Sadness welled up in his chest, crowding his throat. What pain he'd caused people. What a mess he'd made of his life.

That evening after work he drove to Cindy's, but no one

was home. From Barney's he tried calling, but there was no answer. The next day he got ahold of Jim Sandoval.

"She went to L.A.," Jim said, "to spend some time with her sister. She told me to tell you."

"I didn't think she'd leave town before scattering Bob's ashes."

"She's having trouble letting go. I offered to fly her up this weekend, but she said she wanted to do it in the spring, when Bob's daughter could be here. She said spring is a more hopeful time."

"When is she coming back?"

"I don't know. I really don't. Spring, I guess. When she heard the news about Crockett this morning, she said she didn't know if she ever wanted to come back."

"What news?"

"You didn't hear? Crockett's out of jail, on bail. The judge let him go for a measly one-hundred-thousand-dollar bond. Here they had him in chains with a dozen armed guards watching him, and now he's as free as a hawk. This judge is something. I'll be surprised if Crockett shows up for sentencing."

The next day Jack learned at work that Crockett had last been seen driving away in Jenny Morrison's yellow Jaguar. Reports came that he was up in Gerlach, then Paradise Valley. Two weeks later, someone snitched through the STOP POACH-ING hot line that Crockett was hunting in the Santa Rosa Range, where a herd of bighorns had been planted, the ones Bob had guarded through the freezing night. Out of season, with no license or tags, Crockett had shot a protected ram.

Someone else called to say that Billy was back trapping illegally in Little High Rock Canyon. He was camped there with a woman.

Orders came from upstairs for the wardens to ignore the reports. DOW supervisors claimed that Crockett's flouting of the law while awaiting a possible fifty-year prison term seemed unlikely, but if the reports were true, then he was even crazier and meaner than people thought. The Division of Wildlife didn't want another dead warden. Crockett was going to prison anyway.

But not right away. Judge Reilley reset the sentencing date for January 4. So Billy had another month to hang out with all his old buddies and to see himself lionized. Jack sensed no end to this travesty of justice.

On January 4, 1985, after grim, gray weeks of waiting in December, Jack arrived at the courthouse. So did Billy, dressed in a tractor cap with a John Deere logo, a sheepskin coat, a white western shirt with snaps, and a blue silk cowboy bandanna around his neck. He'd grown out his beard and put on weight. No guards accompanied him as he walked into the hallway with his Paradise Valley buddy Gary Valdez. Billy's Belles huddled in an excited cluster. Crockett nodded and gave them that smirky smile as he passed into the packed courtroom.

Both the prosecutor and the defense attorney had a final chance at the sentence hearing to bring forth a string of witnesses in an attempt to influence the judge's decision. Division of Wildlife officers countered the earlier accusations about Bob, while defense witnesses testified to Crockett's good character. The judge called a recess. In the hall Jack saw Billy chatting with two women who'd served on the jury.

Jack went up to him. Billy looked a little nervous.

"I have something to tell you, Billy."

"I'm busy, Jack. I'm talking to these ladies."

A deputy grabbed Jack's arm. "I think it's better if you go inside."

Wendell Phillips appeared on the other side of Jack. "Let's go inside, Jack. It's okay for us to sit together during this sentence hearing. The trial's over."

Jack pulled his arm away. "I have something to tell this punk."

Crockett smiled at Wendell. "Thank you, Mr. Phillips. This man is out of line." He turned his back and walked away.

Jack wasn't sure what he'd meant to say; except he felt the need to let Billy know that someone was onto his lying game. He also wanted to let Crockett know, as he stood amid his supporters, that someone wished him the worst.

Inside the courtroom, after the last witness had stepped down from the box, Judge Reilley shuffled through a stack of note cards. He cleared his throat and looked directly at Crockett over the tops of his silver-rimmed spectacles, wrinkling his broad brow. His snowy brush cut stood up on his head like clipped porcupine quills.

"Mr. Crockett," the judge said, "I believe you know you have been given a fair trial. The jury, after seven days of deliberation, returned a verdict of voluntary manslaughter. Since that verdict, I have lived with this case every day and night for the last two months. I have reread all the transcripts, studied the presentence investigation, and sought the assistance and arguments of your attorneys, and the state's attorneys, in order to refresh my memory.

"I must tell you, Mr. Crockett, after having done all this, I can decisively tell you—sincerely tell you—that I do not believe the issue of self-defense ever arose at Little High Rock Canyon."

Billy's face remained stony. Jack wished Cindy were there. He glanced at Billy's Belles and some women of the jury. He couldn't believe that the judge was practically telling the jurors that the rationale for their verdict was bogus. Then the judge shifted gears with the clashing unexpectedness of a man jamming a moving car into reverse.

"By saying this," Judge Reilley continued, "I do not mean by any stretch of the imagination that you are a bad person.

The evidence is to the contrary. People who know you think very highly of you and would trust their lives and money with you. That's clear. You have been responsible to the court while you were out on bail, so I am not criticizing you as an individual.

"But I sincerely believe that the issue of self-defense never arose at Little High Rock Canyon. Let me be clear about my reasons. You had been warned by Mr. Larsen that law enforcement people might check your camp, and you said you would be ready for them. You also knew at the time that the worst thing you had done, if anything, was to commit a misdemeanor in violation of the game laws.

"When Mr. Pritchard and Mr. Irigaray descended into the canyon with you, you knew they thought they had disarmed you on the rim. They had also disarmed a third party, Mr. Hughes. It is contrary to common sense to believe that a peace officer of Mr. Pritchard's experience would ever attempt to shoot someone he thought was unarmed over a misdemeanor; and to think he'd do so in the presence of not only another officer but also a third person, Mr. Hughes, is an insult to common sense.

"When I consider your expertise with firearms, it is my judgment that you drew your gun simply because you did not want to be taken in, not to save your life. You shot Mr. Pritchard before he even drew a gun. You did that, and you could do that, because of the fact that he did not know you were armed. You then, of course, turned and fired and killed Mr. Hughes, a friend of yours. The fact that you did not even give Mr. Hughes the chance to demonstrate that he was unarmed and bore you no harm, or to drop his gun—even if it was loaded—is totally inexcusable. You are not in a position to argue that you had to kill him to secure your own life.

"Mr. Pritchard at this time had already been shot. You had your gun drawn and had the capability to do him in at any time. Instead—and I do not like to dwell on this ugly fact—

you went into your tent, you took your rifle and shot both men, prone on the ground, both in a motionless position.

"Your subsequent statements and actions corroborate, in my judgment, the fact that you did not exercise self-defense. At no time did you tell your friends, Mr. and Mrs. Dodd, that you killed these men in self-defense. You told them, 'They had it coming.' In all of his testimonies, Mr. Irigaray has been consistent in statements attributed to you, which you have not denied but merely reinterpreted. I mean your statements that you would not be arrested again, that Mr. Pritchard's gun was going into the ground with him, and that this crime was murder one for you. It is inconceivable to me that Mr. Irigaray, himself wounded and in the hospital, would concoct these statements in their detail. Your statement, according to Mr. Irigaray, that you would've taken Mr. Pritchard on the rim, but he would've gotten the best of you up there, comes very close to indicating premeditation. If this indeed happened, you had all that time when you were coming down from the rim to think about this situation. Never did you tell Mr. Irigaray or your friends, Mr. and Mrs. Dodd, that Mr. Pritchard had drawn his pistol. Your actions were not motivated by an actual threat to life or limb but by your desire to ensure your freedom."

The judge poured himself a glass of water but didn't drink any of it.

"Your subsequent thought processes," he continued, "were also very orderly. You knew what you were going to do about hiding the bodies and disguising the crime, and you gave clear instructions to Mr. Irigaray to help carry them out. These acts are not indicative of a person who is out of his mind. Practically all of your actions at the scene, particularly getting the twenty-two and coming back out and shooting those men in the head, were offensive, not defensive acts."

The judge began to cough. He drank from the glass of water, then wiped his brow with a handkerchief. His face was the color of muddy red clay. He shook his finger forcibly at Billy.

"You cannot equate shooting men in this way with killing animals, like maybe you've done in trapping. The court cannot do it, and you cannot do it. We are talking about an extremely violent type of crime."

Judge Reilley drank some more water, then went on, "After you shot Mr. Pritchard, you said, 'This gun'—meaning Mr. Pritchard's—'is going into the ground with this guy.' You then ripped off his badge and departmental insignia and said, 'How could anyone work that many years for the lousy Fish and Game.' I think these acts and statements are very relevant in this case.

"We have had much testimony concerning your good character and what type of person you are, but there is some kind of a resentment, or antigovernment philosophy, in your thinking. It probably has something to do with how you were raised—I don't know—but it's clear that you are not someone who has been disadvantaged all his life, who has been on drugs and dope and abused and mistreated and now needs rehabilitation. You are a well-read individual. You are intelligent. You are a well-liked, loyal person. I do not think we can talk about rehabilitating someone who appears very capable, honest, and moral except for the crime that he committed. I'm sure this dichotomy also puzzled the jury for the many days they were deliberating: trying to decide how these things could transpire with this type of person."

The judge went on speaking for maybe forty-five or fifty minutes, tracing Crockett's actions from Little High Rock Canyon to the Black Rock Desert where he shot Jack. He talked about Crockett's days as a fugitive, his attempted escape from Wyatt's trailer, the weapons he carried with him. Then he circled back and focused on Crockett's brutal treatment of the dead bodies. "You dragged Mr. Hughes's feetfirst, and then you turned him around and dragged the body facefirst by the neck. I have seen those pictures, and I know what

I've seen. Then you dumped Mr. Hughes's corpse into the creek." The judge paused. "Did you ever think about what effect this action was going to have on the people who found Mr. Hughes's body, not to mention his family?"

"You buried Mr. Pritchard in a shallow grave. There was no testimony that you covered this grave with rocks or took any precaution to make sure animals could not get at the body. Worse than this atrocious act was your long refusal to reveal the whereabouts of the body. Once you were free, there was ample time for you to let somebody know the general location of that body for the sake of the family. That has been a puzzle to me all the way through this trial. I have never been able to figure it out.

"You come from a close-knit family. You are a Catholic. You know what kind of pain and suffering Mr. Pritchard's family must have been going through. It is very difficult for the court to understand how you can be described as a decent person and yet do these types of heinous things."

The judge tapped his index cards on the bench like a gambler squaring up a deck after shuffling. He pushed the stack aside and folded his hands. His face was flushed, moistened with perspiration.

"Mr. Crockett, this court finds that the killing of Mr. Pritchard was totally unjustified, and that you killed Mr. Pritchard with little or no remorse. It is also the judgment of this court that the killing of Mr. Hughes was morally reprehensible and without justification. Your actions were devoid of any remorse or feeling of regret.

"This court sentences you to ten years in the state penitentiary for shooting Mr. Pritchard, ten years for shooting Mr. Hughes, ten years for using a firearm in these crimes, plus six months for concealing evidence, all sentences to be served consecutively for a maximum of no more than thirty years."

Jack was elated; so were Jim, Wendell, and Dale when they all met that evening for a celebratory drink. Not that Crockett had gotten what he deserved, which should've been death or life imprisonment for murder, or at least the full fifty years for manslaughter, but because they'd expected so little, they were happy that he'd gotten slammed with thirty years. The down side was that the sentence was indeterminate. Crockett could come up for parole in seven to ten years, if he was a model prisoner. The judge had told him, "I'm putting you in a position to prove to society that you are the type of person you claim you are. It is going to be difficult for you to be paroled— you might as well face facts—before you have served at least ten years, but the parole board can exercise its discretion to shorten your sentence of thirty years."

Jim Sandoval said, "To a guy like Crockett, ten years cooped up in prison could be like fifty to someone else."

"Let's hope so," Dale Ellison said.

"We're lucky we got what we did," Wendell Phillips said. "You know Crockett expected to walk."

Jack had wanted to ask Wendell something since the beginning of the trial. "Why didn't you testify against Crockett, at least at the sentence hearing? You cited him. You know what he's like."

"The prosecution didn't want me to," Wendell replied. "They were trying to paint Crockett into a portrait of evil. A tough guy. That was their big mistake. As soon as he stepped into the witness box, the jury could see he didn't fit the image. The prosecution wanted me to testify that he was big, bad, and ugly. I told them I couldn't do that. He's small, quiet, and ugly."

"You got to hand it to him," Dale Ellison said. "For a guy with a hair-trigger temper, he never lost his cool during the trial."

"The real problem," Jack said, "is that we still haven't seen justice done."

That remark dampened the high spirits around the table. Jim and Wendell nodded in agreement. Dale just looked down into his beer. Jack threw a few bucks onto the table and stood up. All three of them looked surprised.

"You leaving so early, Jack?" Wendell asked.

"Got to get home. Beth will be waiting."

Jim Sandoval gawked in disbelief.

The truth was that Jack didn't want to get soused in front of these guys. With a couple of more drinks he would be past the point of caring. He'd kept the booze pretty much under control since the night of the bad scene with Beth, when he'd come home tanked up from Cindy's. He didn't want that to happen again, especially for the girls' sake. If he was going to drink, he'd do it alone, after everyone went to bed, and he'd do it slowly, quietly, and privately.

Driving home, he repeated to himself, "Thirty years, thirty years." He began to make up a song to the tune of Tennessee Ernie Ford's "Sixteen Tons," singing aloud, "Thirty years, thirty years, and what d'ya got? Ten years in hell for a rat that's caught."

The more he thought about it, the more wonderful the sentence hearing seemed. It showed that the judge had believed him, not Crockett.

He'd worked himself into a fine mood by the time he got home. Inside, Beth met him at the bedroom door. Packed suitcases lay on the bed. Dresser drawers were yanked out, emptied.

"What in hell are you doing?" he asked.

"I'm leaving you," Beth said. "What does it look like?"

He glanced around the house. "Where are the girls?"

"They're with a friend. I'm not hiding them from you. I'm protecting them from you."

"What do you mean, protecting them?"

"I knew you'd come home from this trial drunk, after I heard the sentence."

"I'm not drunk. I had two beers."

"You're drunk. You've been drinking. I told you it was over

between us, but you just won't hear it. You can ruin yourself—us—but I won't let you destroy my daughters."

"Oh, can it. You sound like you're trying out for acting school."

"Don't trivialize what I'm saying. I waited through this trial with you, expecting that maybe something would change, but it hasn't, and it won't. I told my therapist I would give us until the end of the trial, and that's what I've done."

"Your therapist? What are you talking about?"

A puzzled look came into Beth's eyes, as though she thought he should know what she meant. Then her face relaxed with what seemed the recognition of something that she'd neglected to tell him. "I've been seeing a therapist for the last six months. Every week. I'm not acting out of some impulse. I've been considering things carefully, and I know what I want. I want a divorce."

He didn't know if he was more angry because she wanted a divorce or because she was springing this news right now, when he'd come home in a good mood, looking forward to seeing her. Or was he really mad because she'd been sneaking around behind his back telling some shrink what a jerk he was? And he hadn't known a thing about it. She could've been off having an affair for all he knew. He felt tricked. She said she'd waited for the end of the trial to make this grand announcement. Cindy had said she'd waited until they'd found Bob before coming on to him. What was it with these women, setting up private deadlines that affected his life, but that he knew nothing about?

"So this is it," he said, "just like always. No discussion, no input from me. It's just what *you* want, a unilateral decision, and I have nothing to say."

"Oh, it's not unilateral. We've both done this to each other, and you know it. It's just that I'm making the decision to clarify what's happened between us. It doesn't make me happy. Don't for a second think that this makes me happy."

"Then why are you doing it? Or is there someone in the wings to make you happy?"

"Forget it. Don't try to turn things around on me. You're free to go off now and spend all the time you want with your little Cindy."

"You're ridiculous," he said. "There's nothing between me and Cindy."

"'I hope to God Beth knows nothing of this,'" she said, quoting Cindy's letter in a mocking little girl's voice, "'and will forever remain free from knowing it. I love her, too.' What a schemer she is."

He recalled leaving Cindy's letter in his shirt pocket, easy for Beth to find. Maybe he had wanted her to find it. The letter, he thought, if anything, cleared him of any double-dealing. He should've known by now that evidence only proved what someone wanted to believe.

"You can think whatever you want, Beth. But the fact is I'm not involved with Cindy, and I'm not running off with her."

"And there's no one else in my life," she said flatly. "But I'm leaving you. It has to be done. I'm not helping you at all—to change, to get off this booze."

"Well," he said, and he felt his chest puff up, the heat of alcohol in his head, an actor's derisive grin on his face, making him feel that he must've looked something like Billy with a smirk on his lips. What he wanted to say was, "Well, don't let the door bang you on the ass." That's what Jim Sandoval had supposedly said, pointing to the screen door, when his wife had announced that she was leaving. But Jack couldn't do it. The snide remark withered. The smirk died. He could hardly say anything at all, except, "I know it, Beth. It's over. I'm sorry, I really am."

From her startled expression he recognized that although they'd changed, their love hadn't. They'd just grown unworthy of it. They were both losing. The pain, he knew, was just beginning.

CHAPTER 11

Since Jack didn't contest the divorce, it took a week and a half for it to go through. By mid-January of that year, thanks to slick Nevada law, he and Beth were split. She wanted the furniture but not the house. Too many bad memories, she said, for her and the girls. She moved into a garden apartment, and he was allowed to have the girls with him every other weekend. It seemed best for them, at their age, to spend the bulk of time with their mother, although it hurt Jack not to see them more.

Beth had emptied the living room and den except for the BarcaLounger and the TV. The house looked pretty bare, but that's how he liked it. He didn't want the memory of her lingering in things. Having to sleep in an abandoned bed was bad enough, but he bought new sheets, and usually by the time he crawled between them, his mind had whited out.

In the garage he found two blue plastic milk crates, which

he placed next to the BarcaLounger as side tables to hold his drinks. In the evening, stacked one on top of the other, they served as a kind of TV table. They suited him fine. At some point he intended to get new furniture, but he was in no hurry. He didn't plan to have anyone over. He wasn't out to impress anyone. He just wanted to be alone.

But friends didn't think the same way. They called to invite him to dinner, to set him up with dates. Jim Sandoval called to join him for a celebratory drink. "I can still remember the day I got my last divorce," Jim declared, emphasizing each word: "*It . . . felt . . . great!*"

Jack felt anything but great. He found a bottle of Country Flower Bubble Bath that Beth had forgotten in the cabinet under the sink, and its lilac smell snapped a picture into his mind of her in the tub caressed by diaphanous bubbles. One night, when he pulled the truck into the garage to jack it up and change the oil, the headlights illuminated her dusty snorkel mask and green rubber fins hanging on the wall. She was everywhere and nowhere. He thought of the trip to Mexico that would never happen.

In June his sister Marlene came crashing into the house with her two suitcases, her chalky white capped teeth, and her streaked hair flying. She was in town to attend her Sparks High School class reunion. Jack was alone that weekend, so she bunked in the girls' room. She had dark, dreamy eyes like Uncle Pete's; her dense eyebrows clashed with the blond and reddish highlights in her thick hair, recently added to evoke memories of her senior year in high school when she'd been all blond, except for those black eyebrows: in that era, prevailing tastes hadn't encouraged Basque girls to accentuate their ethnic good looks. She went off to her reunion in a dress that looked one size too small. Jack had to wonder how wise her husband, Dave, had been not to accompany her to the reunion.

But Jack heard his sister come in alone a little after four in the morning, and while he was still in bed that Sunday morning a vacuum cleaner howled in the den. Before he'd awakened, she'd gone out to Target to buy a new Hoover.

They ate a late breakfast of huevos rancheros while sitting on high stools and facing each other across the floating kitchen counter.

"Nancy Stephenson was at the reunion last night," Marlene said. "Remember her? The pep girl with the bazookas that all the boys were just crazy about? She married Ed Hopkins, the basketball player, but she's divorced now. She turned out all right. Now she's got her own real estate business. She remembered you. I'm sure she'd just love it if you called her. But you might be getting some calls yourself. I put up a sign in the ladies room with your number on it. 'No witches wanted,' it said. 'No feminists need apply.'"

Jack had heard it from both sides. Marlene and Beth had never hit it off. Marlene thought his wife's asthma was just one part of her manipulative, self-centered personality. Beth thought his sister's cutting jokes expressed her own bitter unfulfillment.

"You never had a chance with Beth," Marlene said, "once she got hooked up with those man-haters. Find yourself a real woman and get your life into shape. And get the fuck off this booze."

His sister went speeding back to Fort Bragg in her pink Mustang and left him with bags of groceries, a washed and waxed kitchen floor, a new vacuum cleaner, and Nancy Stephenson's phone number.

He never called Nancy, and she didn't call him. He'd heard that Cindy Pritchard had returned from L.A. in the spring and scattered Bob's ashes up north in the Sheldon National Wildlife Refuge. Jack found himself thinking about Cindy more and more. He thought of the letter she'd written. He thought of the night when they'd held each other, his hands up under her white sweatshirt, the feel of her pliant skin, smooth against his palms.

It was about nine o'clock on a late June night and he'd been out in the backyard sprawled in a webbed lawn chair under the stars, amid chattering crickets, plunging deep into a bottle of Early Times when he decided to give Cindy a call. He intended to ask her to go up to Pyramid Lake on the weekend. He imagined her in the slinky black bikini she'd worn on that sunny, sky-blue Fourth of July long ago when Bob was still alive and he and Beth were still speaking.

She no sooner answered than she said, "Let me get the other phone." It didn't take long for him to realize that there would be no trip up to the lake. "I've been seeing Jim," she said. "He's here now."

Jack loved the way women used that word "seeing"—they could stick it in like a knife. He bet she and Jim were indeed *seeing* a lot of each other.

"Well, congratulations," he said sharply, wishing he hadn't.

"Don't be that way," Cindy said. "You know how I felt about you."

It wasn't that he'd expected her to wait around pining for him. What burned him was that the guy who'd got there first was Jim Sandoval. Now Jim had exchanged a twiggy blond's lanky embrace for Cindy's short muscular clasping limbs. Variety was the spice of life, and Jim's was well seasoned.

But Cindy had been through enough, and Jack didn't want to make her feel bad. Disguising his hurt, he told her, "I just wanted to hear how you were doing."

"I'm doing better. I'm not reconciled to what happened, but I'm making it day by day."

"That's good. Maybe we can get together sometime for a drink or something. To catch up. Have a chat."

The cold edge in her voice told him that it wouldn't happen. "Jack," she responded, "why didn't you call earlier?"

The message was clear, but he thought he heard a tinge of regret as well as dismissal.

Thinking up things to do with the girls every other weekend became a chore at times. After all, the circus came to town only once a year, and most of the other things he came up with caused Carrie to remark, "How boring." Before the divorce, he'd never quite realized how much time Beth had actually spent with them. Thank goodness they belonged to the kids' dance group at the Basque club. During the summer he hauled them around to various festivals where they performed. They looked cute in their red skirts, black vests, and white bonnets, dancing with little boys in milk-white pants and red berets.

In July he drove them to the Elko Basque Festival, and they stayed in a motel. They watched the pelota games, the wood-chopping contests, and the strong-man competitions. The summer air smelled of spicy marinated lamb cooking over open fires. A burly Basque from Idaho won a crude contest by rolling a heavy granite ball from one shoulder to the other behind his neck more times than anybody else.

"Stupid," Carrie said.

Jack saw Jenny Morrison at the festival with her Zubilaga relatives, but he avoided her. She competed in the *irrintzi* contest, where competitors tried to see who could best cut loose with the wavering, bone-shattering war yell, something between a scream and a laugh, that Basques had wailed for centuries in the Pyrenees. Jenny sounded like a spooked coyote. Jack was glad she didn't win.

When they returned to Sparks, Sarah threw a fit at Jack's house because Carrie had spilled mustard on her red dance skirt. "It'll wash out, honey," Jack said. He felt like a tinderbox from staying dry all weekend while everyone else at the festival downed kegs of beer and jugs of wine.

"I want to call Mommy," Sarah wailed.

"Go ahead and call her. But she can't help you. You'd be better off if you let me wash it out."

While Sarah dialed her mother, Carrie taunted, "Tattle-tale crybaby."

"Shut up, Carrie," he snapped. "You're just making things worse."

When Sarah got her mother on the phone, she paced up and down the kitchen on her stubby legs dragging the cord behind her as she yapped into the mouthpiece about how Carrie did this and Carrie did that, and Daddy didn't do a thing except make everyone unhappy, and she wanted to go home. On and on she complained until her mother hung up.

"See," Jack said, "even your mother doesn't want to talk to you when you're being a brat."

Sarah clutched the dead phone in front of her chest, about to cry, but then she started to giggle like a little gremlin, looking for all the world like one of those devilishly possessed children in the movies as her glee evolved into a rumbling, deep-chested laugh beyond her years. She seemed delighted with herself as she announced to no one in particular, "I talk too much."

After he dropped the girls at their mother's he returned home and twisted the cap off a new golden bottle of comforting, bitter booze.

In the fall he made a weekend visit to Paradise Valley ostensibly to see his uncle. Instead he stopped in Winnemucca for a couple of drinks, then found himself turning into the dirt street on the edge of town by the Humboldt River. In the dark mist, he passed the Pussycat with its cat's red blinking eye. He'd been alone long enough. He parked at the end of the shabby strip in front of Penny's Cozy Corner. Through a boozy haze, he watched the neon cat jumping up to the roof. It looked like a mountain lion leaping upward over and over but never landing.

He'd been thinking: Why not leave things to the experts? People left everything else in their lives to specialists, be it a broken tooth, a broken car, a broken watch. Why not a broken heart? Why go through the charade with someone of buying drinks, dinner, a movie, a dance, when everyone knew what you really were buying? With professionals at least everything was up-front, and then you got somebody who knew what she was doing.

Photographs of rodeo cowboys, many of them autographed, covered the walls in Penny's. A printed sign taped to the mirror behind the bar said, HAPPINESS IS A GOOD LAY. Four guys who looked as though they'd just come from a road construction job drank at the bar. Two pasty-faced, milky-skinned girls with sharp noses, one in white shorts and a white pullover, the other in a shortie satin robe, sat at the bar smoking.

Jack ordered a shot with a beer chaser. Behind the bar, the tired-looking, gray-haired granny in flowered pants and a baggy yellow pullover looked more like a cleaning woman than a madam. "These two lovely young ladies," she said, introducing the girls at the bar, "are Liza and Ann Marie." The one in the white shorts looked at Jack indifferently and recrossed her fat legs. She puffed on her Marlboro, flashing long, sharp oxblood fingernails.

His own look of indifference brought an apologetic tone to the barkeep's voice as she refilled his shot glass. "We'll have seven girls in here by this weekend," she said.

The two girls picked up a conversation about spiders. They'd seen several earlier that day. "You tell Gloria to get those spiders," Liza said in a whiny voice. "I'm not going to work in a place with fucking spiders."

Jack was about to leave when he saw a tall black girl in her early twenties in the lounge to the side of the bar and in front of the jukebox. She wore a tight low-cut dress, barely covering her butt. Maybe it was the booze—he thought she was a knockout. "What's a nice girl like you . . . " The tight dress was brilliant salmon, the glowing color that gathered in eastern clouds during an October desert sunset. Silver studs ran down the side of her dress to reddish fishnet stockings. Black hair tumbled down her back in glossy curls, stopping just short of where the tight curve of her dress stretched against rounded, taut buns like those of a bullfighter Beth had openly admired one afternoon long ago in Texcoco.

"That's Susanna," the barkeep said.

When he followed Susanna from the bar, her long glistening hair bounced against her back. As she climbed up the stairs, carpeted with a green shag rug, she reached behind and tugged down the hem of her skirt with two fingers to keep her underpants covered. In the VIP suite, blue lights lit the water in the Jacuzzi. On the edge of the pool perched a clear Plexiglas bench for blowjobs. Susanna showed him the shower and pulled open a standing metal closet where he could hang his clothes.

"Is this where the spiders are?" he asked.

Susanna let out a little screech and jumped back. "No," she said. "We have a nice place. It's a clean house."

She spoke with a British accent. Jack asked her where she was from.

"Wisconsin," she said. The back of her hand brushed against the front of his pants. "Oh, excuse me, Jack." She smiled. He felt sixteen years old again, his stomach fluttering with frantic moths.

When they sat on the waterbed to negotiate finances and his various options, his excitement drained. Susanna was saying something about half-and-half being extra. She sounded annoyed. "Each girl would've told you her specialty, if you'd just asked. Around-the-worlds are Liza's specialty, not mine. Maybe you'd prefer the Fantasy Room."

"What's wrong with this room?"

"Nothing, but if you want to watch movies, we have to use the Fantasy Room. Tell me what you want to do. Do you want to watch some hot movies with me?"

What am I doing here? he thought. All he really wanted right then was another drink, but Susanna said she didn't allow drinks in the rooms, especially in the VIP suite. He offered to buy her a drink at the bar, and then they could come back to one of the smaller rooms. He didn't see any point in renting the suite.

"That's fine, Jack," Susanna said, spitting sarcasm. "Just fine. You can buy me all the drinks you want."

Downstairs he bought several drinks. Then he bought the bar a drink, the way Uncle Pete used to do. A group of five or six men, out-of-towners, came in and sat in the lounge. Susanna moved from the bar to talk with them, but soon returned to the stool next to Jack. "Guys in groups," she muttered. "When guys come in groups, they usually just drink."

Jack ordered a round for the new guys in the lounge, but he'd run out of cash and needed to use his VISA. "Give those fucks a drink," he told the barkeep.

"You're quite a man, aren't you, Jack?" Susanna said. "You're just one hell of a big man, aren't you?"

At one point Jack got the idea of taking Susanna back with him to his motel room, which would've been fine, except that Susanna wasn't around. She was in the VIP suite with someone else. In retaliation for this betrayal he made an offer to the sharp-nosed girl in shorts whose bare white thighs now looked more inviting than Susanna's lanky black ones. But his VISA, he discovered, was no good for such things. Cash money was the only thing that would talk now.

"Hey, what the fuck's going on here?" he said. "You been trying to fleece me? You want to get this bar busted up? No one's fucking fleecing me."

A hand swept his drink away from him. He felt himself pulled from the stool and pushed out the door into the river fog by some bruiser who had emerged from the smoky air. Jack stumbled past the neon lights of the Pussycat and Simone de Paris. His stomach became a bubbly caldron. He stood in sagebrush. The glint of the shallow river caught his eye as he threw up. He awoke on the damp ground under a cottonwood. Slimy mud clung to his shoes and streaked his pants and shirt. He just wanted to get into a clean bed. He walked toward the motel sign in the distance, forgetting that his truck was parked in front of Penny's.

The next morning, he got sick again before he went to look for his pickup. The dirt strip of shabby shacks and false-front trailers, devoid of neon, stood bleached in harsh sunlight. He glanced at the window of Penny's, opaque with yellow dust, and darted into the truck, slinking away like a battered river rat.

He felt so bad he stopped at the Gem Bar—where Billy used to sip fruit juice when he worked for Uncle Pete—and ordered a screwdriver. By noon he felt better—physically— but the black holes of the previous night oppressed him. He did recall Susanna saying something like, "You're quite a man, aren't you, Jack." In the old days, Uncle Pete probably would've banged the whore a couple of times, thrown some cash on the bar, bought the house one last drink, and gone home to sleep like a rock. Billy wouldn't have gone into the place at all. Jack wondered, What kind of man did that make him?

On the way home that afternoon he got hit with a DWI citation. He didn't even see the damn cop until the cruiser loomed in his rearview mirror, blue and red lights flashing, siren screeching.

The next week, Wendell Phillips asked to see him. In the past, Wendell had diffused his role of the "boss" by indirectly introducing "problem issues" in the course of other discussions. This time he called Jack in solely to talk about his drinking. Wendell was just doing his job, as he said, but Jack still resented it.

"I'd like you to think about going to AA," Wendell said, "for your own good."

The humiliation of Wendell's lumping him in with a group of whining alcoholics offended Jack more than any threat to his job. He felt belligerent.

"If you don't like my work," he told Wendell, "if I'm not

doing my job, then fire me. But don't go telling me how to live my private life."

Wendell didn't back off, but he wasn't provoked either. He wasn't unctuous. "There are some things you're going to have to decide for your own good, Jack, and for the good of your daughters. Otherwise you're going to find yourself down where a lot of other fine men have. I'm telling you that you've lost control of your drinking. It's damaging your life. It's hindering your work. You can do what the hell you want about it."

"All right, I can accept that. I'll take care of things." Jack meant it, until Wendell's Sunday-school teacher's smile pissed him off again. "But I'll do it in my own way," he added, "not at AA meetings."

Wendell quit smiling. "You've let this Billy Crockett deal take over your life. What happened to you and Bob was terrible, but look what you've done. You've let one day change your entire life, not because of what actually happened on that day but because of your obsession with it."

Wendell, a nondrinker, hadn't a clue about why people really drank, but he needed a cause-and-effect explanation to fit his Christian scheme of moral psychology. Jack knew that wasn't why he really drank. He drank before that day in Little High Rock Canyon, and he had drunk after it. The best thing to do was to talk about something Wendell could understand.

"Injustice triumphed in that trial," he told Wendell. "Crockett literally got away with murder."

"I know that," Wendell replied. "We all know it. But there's not a thing you can do about it. So why are you punishing yourself for something a punk named Billy Crockett did?"

That night Jack really tied one on. Usually when he had to go to work the next day he sipped his drinks, slowly, steadily, bitterly, before he stumbled to bed or conked out in the Barca-Lounger. After the talk with Wendell Phillips, he went home and chugalugged drinks from a tumbler. Fuck you, Wendell. Fuck you with flowers.

In the den on one of the milk crates sat a copy of *Rolling Stone* with a big story about Billy. Jack had read the article twice, thinking that no one could write that way except some easterner who'd seen too many bad cowboy movies when he was a kid on Long Island. The article made Billy into the last of the lone rangers, the wildest king of the wild frontier.

"Justice has not been served," Jack said aloud.

He heard the echo of Wendell's voice saying, "There's not a thing you can do about it."

Judge Reilley had tagged Billy as a murderer, even if he hadn't hanged him, but what difference did that revelation make to *Rolling Stone* with its picture of Billy in his silly trapper's hat and with his Hawkins rifle, riding into a sunset like a kid playing mountain man?

Better to have lived in another time when Crockett would have got what he deserved. Jack remembered the book about the old California bandit Joaquín Murieta he and Beth had been reading to brush up on their Spanish before they'd gone to Mexico. The world of that book made sense. Those people knew how to wield vengeance, to take an eye for an eye, a tooth for a tooth. If he'd been half a man, he would've done the same. At that moment, as if he'd been transported back to the desert, the room fell away and he saw at the end of a dark tunnel a brilliant image of the black Ford pickup bouncing through sagebrush on that late Sunday afternoon. Jack saw the driver's face in profile, framed in the pickup window, his snub nose, sandy hair, the glint of his glasses. The bouncing head came into focus, centered in the sights of a rifle, burnished copper from the sundown glare. Was it Billy, or was he seeing himself? Over and over in the cavern of his mind, Jack fired and fired, exploding that hateful, smirking face into shreds.

CHAPTER 12

Beth announced that she was going to move with the girls to L.A.—get them away from Jack. It was 1989, four years after the divorce, and four years after Crockett had gone to prison. Jack's drinking hadn't got better. He had just gotten better at hiding it—or so he thought. He'd discovered a rhythm that let him stretch a binge into three days every other weekend when the girls weren't with him. Otherwise, he kept it throttled, maintaining a steady purr, idling through the days in comfort, until the free weekends when he could let things rip.

With Beth's threat, he was at a lawyer's in a shot. He didn't want to lose his daughters. The lawyer said evidence of his drinking wasn't going to help, if things came down to a fight. He'd better straighten up.

Jack ordered furniture for the house. He attended an AA meeting. He went to the Gap for some new clothes, bought some aftershave, and thought about calling Nancy Stephenson to complete his public image as a healthy, responsible, sex-driven American male and potential mate. Instead, he called Billy's old girlfriend, Georgette Spinelli, remembering how she'd looked at the trial in that tight jumpsuit four years ago. He asked her out for a drink.

"Well, why not?" she said over the phone in that sexy hacksaw voice of hers.

He told her that he'd had a rough four years since the trial. He hadn't been able to reconcile himself to Bob's murder, his own near death, and the adulation that had surrounded Billy—all of which was true. He just wanted a chance to talk to her about Crockett. Maybe if he could break up this hardened image of Billy Crockett in his mind, he could get on with his life.

"I probably don't know him any better than you do," Georgette said. "I told you before, we didn't have much of a relationship. I'd rather not talk about it."

"Can I talk about what I think?"

"Well, why not? If you're the one I remember, you were sort of cute, weren't you?"

He picked up Georgette on a Monday night because she'd been dealing that weekend at the Nugget, and Monday was her night off. At her suggestion they went to the Hacienda del Sol near the Peppermill Casino where, two weeks earlier, a confused mountain lion, because of the drought, had wandered down from the Sierra and padded across the parking lot in broad daylight.

Georgette wore a creamy V-necked T-shirt and a pair of maroon slacks. The two previous times he'd seen her she'd also worn pants—the tight dealer slacks in the blackjack pit and the snug magenta jumpsuit at Crockett's trial. He was a little disappointed, having hoped for an unhindered glance at those long legs.

A neon parrot glowed through the warm September night above the Hacienda marquee announcing FOOTBALL TONIGHT.

As Jack pulled past the yellowed fake adobe building with the red-tiled roof and into the packed parking lot, Georgette asked, "What are you wearing?"

He looked down at his tan chinos. "Wearing?"

"The smelly stuff." A wad of gum snapped. Her pouting lips, painted glossy white, pooched forward as if awaiting a kiss. Her enormous dark eyes stared from sunken caves of metallic eye shadow.

"Oh, just Old Spice," he said.

The edges of her nostrils tightened. She started chewing again. "That's what Billy used to wear," she said, "when he thought he was out on the town."

Why the hell hadn't he bought some Canoe or Russian Leather, the sweet smells Beth had given him when they were in college, rather than the first bottle he saw when he was on his buying spree? It had been years since he'd worn any smelly stuff.

More to the point, he wondered why the hell he'd agreed to come to the Hacienda, a noisy meat market jammed with young roving eyes and strutting limbs, mostly people in their twenties. It was impossible to talk. Shouts barked above the din of Monday Night Football on the TV. A red-shirted 49er scored a touchdown to screams and clapping palms. At the bar, a red neon sign spelled MARGARITAS. Stemmed crystal glasses glinted upside down from the low ceiling rack over the head of the bartender, who winked at Jack and shouted, "Hello, Georgette baaaaby."

They had no sooner found a table next to some scruffy plant life by the window when a woman with cropped carroty hair, dragging along a bruiser in a muscle T-shirt, asked, "Can we join you, Georgette?"

Jack didn't care. His plans for the night were shot. He would've had better luck conversing in the middle of a steel foundry. Perhaps in an attempt to give the joint some tone, he ordered a Rob Roy. The two interlopers ordered beers and

Georgette a double shot of straight Herradura; then they all decided to change orders and join her in the tequila. Sucking limes, licking salt, tossing down shots, they grew as loud as their neighbors. The carrot-haired woman and muscle man were waterskiing buddies of Georgette. The bruiser owned a new speedboat. "You'll have to join us, Jack," he shouted. "When Pyramid's like glass, it's awesome."

Georgette could really knock 'em back. Shot after shot went down the hatch.

As Jack pulled out of the parking lot onto South Virginia he saw the lights of the Fantasy Inn and the Adventure Inn and marquees advertising ROMANTIC ADULT ACCOMMODATIONS and EXOTIC THEME ROOMS. He thought of the Fantasy Room Susanna had mentioned at Penny's with its four-poster canopy bed, TV, VCR, and dozens of XXX-rated movies to choose from. Why would anyone go to a whorehouse to watch movies?

He had his own fantasies about Georgette. She leaned her head against the window and folded her long hands in her lap. He resented the floor-box gearshift that kept her pinned to the opposite side of the seat. At least when he was in high school the wide, expansive front seats offered a chance to assess the degree of a date's ardor. A leg pressed against his was a welcome sign. A hand on the thigh cocked the trigger.

But Georgette splintered his burgeoning fantasies. "I'm beat," she sighed. "I need to get home." He wondered how long it had taken her to cozy up to Billy.

He called her for a date the following Monday, but she was tied up. Two weeks later, they went out again, to a quieter bar, and he learned about her divorce. His still hurt, he told her. He thought that the ache of missing Beth would have been gone by now. The problem was that he didn't feel unmarried, except when he was pretty boozed up, and then he felt pissed.

Georgette seemed more resigned. But she was also younger, and a longer time had passed since her split-up. She wore her hair twisted and pinned up so that loose strands swirled wildly. "I got married in Reno and divorced in Reno," she said. "My husband ran a warehouse for a fir door business. Imagine a fir door business, here on the desert. People are crazy. They'll buy anything. I did all the office work at the warehouse. All my husband wanted to do was hunt. That's why he came here. He said Nevada had the best trophy deer in the country. I'd go camping and bird hunting with him. He was six seven, a Vietnam vet, really fucked up."

"Billy Crockett must've seemed a squirt next to him," Jack said.

"Yeah, I guess so," she replied. "Billy's about your size."

Jack ignored the dig. "So you went camping and hunting with Crockett."

Georgette nodded. "That's why he was interested in me. I liked to camp back then, but not anymore. Who wants to be that dirty all the time? I'll take waterskiing any day."

Jack had learned that on the previous Monday, when Georgette was too busy to go out with him, she'd gone waterskiing with those friends he'd met at the Hacienda.

"Billy wasn't such a bad guy," Georgette continued. "But he had his problems. I just don't think there's anything he'd rather do than hunt."

"Not even have sex?"

Georgette squinted her big teardrop-shaped eyes. "Not even have sex," she said.

Her ex-husband had been the same way. Guns and hunting were what he lived for.

"It's funny," Jack said, "how we keep making the same mistakes over and over again." That's what Beth had always said.

"Are you implying that I'm a mistake for you?"

"No." He had no intention of explaining how different she was from Beth. "I was thinking of how you divorced one hunter and took up with another."

"They were so different," she said. "For Billy, hunting and trapping were his way of making himself into something."

"A man who murdered people."

Georgette gave that casual shrug, as she had under the lights in the Nugget parking lot years ago, as if to say, So what?

"I don't think Billy was a killer in the normal sense," she surmised. "I was never afraid around him. But he had an idea of himself."

"Just a kid's fantasy."

"What? To be free? To be tough enough not to take shit from anyone? Most of the men I know have those dreams, at least out here, even when they're trapped into running a warehouse, the way my husband was. I bet you do, too."

"Well, yes," he admitted, "maybe at one time."

"Not at one time," she said. "Now. Why else are you so pissed at him? Why else were you chasing him around on King Lear?"

Georgette went on to say that years ago, when she was living in New York, she'd had her own dreams of being a dancer. She'd been born in New Jersey, near the Pine Barrens, but had gone to a Quaker boarding school in upstate New York. After high school she moved into the city to become a star. "It was a rough life. You had to get other work," she said. "One day I went to Times Square to see about a modeling job. I was in this shabby office with a grungy little guy who said he had an opening for someone to model pantyhose. I couldn't believe it. 'Me?' I said. 'With these muscular dancer's legs? I could never model pantyhose.' The next thing I knew this troll was standing behind me and yanking up my skirt, holding the hem above his head as he looked me over. 'Your legs are great!' he said. 'But your ass is flat.'" Georgette giggled. "It's a good thing I had on underwear."

Almost a decade and a half had passed since Jack's last encounter with the rituals of dating, and he wasn't certain whether Georgette was just telling a story, fishing for a compliment, or coming on to him—or all three. You couldn't be sure; women talked like men these days. He chose to offer the compliment, skewed as it was. "That guy needed to go to Vision World."

She looked puzzled. "What do you mean?"

"You know—your ass. It's terrific."

Saying things like that came a lot easier after three or four shots of Siete Leguas in a seedy bar. But he'd never been that blunt to anyone before. He hadn't even talked that way to Susanna that night in Penny's.

"He was right," Georgette said about the talent agent in Times Square. "I was only nineteen then. I really didn't fill out until I came to Reno. But things didn't pan out here either. I got *too* filled out. Those girls in dance lines are really pretty flat, if you look at them. It's as hard to get a job dancing here as in New York, though you wouldn't think it should be."

They left the bar and walked up Sierra Street to the Truckee River.

"That's where I threw my wedding ring." Georgette pointed down toward the drought-diminished stream where many tipsy veterans of quicky Reno divorces, just like Marilyn Monroe in *The Misfits,* had followed the custom of flinging their symbols of bondage into the Truckee. "What did you do with yours?"

"It's home," he said, not adding that it sat on top of his dresser, a daily reminder of his failure.

"Why don't we get it and toss it in here?" Georgette seemed to be testing the tenacity of his ties to Beth, or his memories of her. He hoped she might be asking "my place or yours," but her tone was too cool. She kept him at a distance.

"I don't know," he said. "Those things cost money."

"You're just like Billy," she sighed. "So tight you squeak."

He liked Georgette, and he thought she liked him, but he didn't seem to be getting anywhere with her. Wary from their divorces, they tentatively tested each other, afraid to get hurt—that was part of it, he was sure—but he held back mainly because he didn't want to get hooked up with a murderer's cohort—except when he was drinking. Then she held back, distrustful, no doubt, of what he was up to. But his original plan to learn about Billy from her, and maybe to get his demon off his back, had shifted. Now he just wanted to see Georgette. He knew his sister would've been mortified to learn he was going out with a girl like Georgette instead of the wheeler-dealer Nancy Stephenson. But Georgette was fun to drink with and sexy as hell. He hoped they could get it on without smothering each other—that was the main thing. Finally he invited her over to the house for dinner. He thought he might as well let some gal see all that new furniture he'd bought, even if nothing came of it.

She answered without hesitation. "Oh, that's sweet. Of course I'll come. I was wondering when you were going to invite me over."

Jack scrambled through a folder of old recipes he'd kept since college days. He came up with a torn piece of notebook paper, stained with dried egg splatterings and greasy smears of butter from previous evenings fifteen years ago when he'd assembled the casserole for some other girlfriend. The scrawled pencil notations had faded over the years. At the top of the flimsy paper, creased with folds, he'd long ago printed the name of the dish in bold block letters: SHRIMP THING.

It was an old recipe copied from *The Settlement House Cookbook*, a magical concoction that allowed him to throw together a bunch of half-inch buttered cubes of white bread, beaten eggs, cooked shrimp, milk, grated cheddar cheese, and—presto!—a perfect, puffy soufflé emerged from the oven.

Georgette loved it, or at least she said she did, though by the time they got around to eating dinner it was almost ten o'clock and they'd put away a good amount of tequila and wine.

They ate in sexy darkness, the table lit by the flames of new blue candles. Georgette's black eyes and pouty lips burned a glowing hole in his alcohol-veiled vision. Even her bumpy tough-guy nose achieved luminous delicacy in the candle-light. Beyond the screen of the patio's open sliding glass door, crickets chirped in the warm autumn night. On Jack's new portable CD player Bonnie Raitt sang "Have a Heart."

"She went to high school with my sister," Georgette said about Bonnie Raitt. "She was nothing special, just another girl sitting out on the lawn playing her guitar."

"You must've known she had a good voice."

"Oh, sure. There were usually people sitting around listening to her. But a lot of girls had good voices." Georgette looked momentarily cross-eyed, staring at the candle flame, as though gazing into the light for the source of some secret. "Bonnie had a kind of drive."

Jack thought Georgette must've been thinking of herself, of her own potential as a dancer in those days. Bonnie Raitt had become a star and Georgette the consort of a murderer. Not that it seemed to bother her.

He pointed the bottle of Glen Ellen white toward her long-stemmed glass, asking, "More wine?"

She surprised him by absently shaking her head no. She stared off into the darkness somewhere above his head, over his shoulder. He was getting nowhere with this woman. Her aloof, preoccupied expression always appeared toward the end of their dates. With the amount of booze she put away, he expected that she would warm up a little bit. But she always seemed to know when to quit. Then he would be left alone to finish off the night in a drunken rage.

Georgette stood up from the table, hitting the edge with the front of her thigh, shaking the candles. Shimmering shadows on the walls caused the house to wobble. Here it comes, he thought. She wants to go home.

He stood up and caught his balance with his palm on the table. He was tipsier than he thought. He tried to forestall her exit. "I've got dessert," he said. "Fresh peach cobbler. Made it myself."

She seemed to give a smirk, one that brought back to mind Billy's face. Too much booze, he feared. The room's darkness pressed against the edges of his vision, forcing his sight into a narrowing tunnel. Ghosts flitted in the peripheral darkness. A sense of other voices, other persons, haunted the dark corners of the room, out of sight. He was losing sense of where he was. Who were all these people pressing into the room? He forced himself to focus on the woman across the wide expanse of the cluttered table. At the far end of a long lighted tunnel, Georgette emerged through the haze wearing a loose white, low-necked Chiapas blouse and black slacks as snug as a bullfighter's. Amber and silver Mexican earrings dangled among strands of shiny dark hair tumbling down the sides of her face. Why was he with this woman? And where was Beth?

"How long is this going to go on?" Georgette's voice seemed amplified, part of the song coming out of the living room speakers. Who had changed the CD?

"Do you want dessert?" Jack repeated.

"The question is, do *you*?" Her husky voice grew huskier. She cast an inviting smile. What strong, lovely white teeth she had. Was he getting the drift of this thing right?

Her hand dipped into her purse. A pocket mirror, faceup on a cleared spot on the table, glistened with lines of luminous white powder.

"I don't want to get into this stuff," he said.

"Well, don't then," she said. She bent low to the table with a crisp rolled dollar bill fluted into a nostril. Her pretty nose flexed twice. The line of powder shot up the tube. "You really are just like Billy, aren't you? You don't want to get into this stuff. You don't want to get into me either, do you?"

Jack flung his hand toward her and snatched away the dollar bill. Bent over, he involuntarily rocked backward, plopping down in the chair. He lined up the wavering end of the bill like a gun muzzle at the end of the coke and snorted.

He handed the bill back to her. "What are you talking about?" he said. "You're the one."

"Hey," she said, "I was ready a long time ago. What does a girl need to do with you?"

"You kept putting me off."

"You never asked. You were more interested in Billy than me."

He wasn't going to let this night turn out like the one with Susanna back at Penny's. And he was no Billy Crockett. He intended to let her know there were things he liked better than hunting. He felt a pleasurable dry-ice numbness pressing through his sinuses, but his bladder ached. He stumbled into the bathroom. The sudden bright lights, the whir of the exhaust fan, the yellow jet streaming into the toilet bowl churning up foam brought a sobering alertness to his vision. "This is really happening," he said to himself. "I'm here now. I'm really here right now."

He flushed the toilet and stared at the descending vortex of frothy water.

Back in the kitchen, Georgette was gone. The table was a mess. A toppled wine glass lay on the rumpled tablecloth among abandoned plates streaked with orange remnants of shrimp casserole. The candles had sputtered down to blue stubs. Georgette's pocket mirror glinted in the fluttering light.

"Jack?" Her husky voice called from the living room. She had taken off her blouse and was standing in the darkness in a black bra and tight black pants, changing CDs. She turned away from the portable bookshelf, where the CD player sat between two brass poles. Her tight-waisted slacks pinched a little roll of white flesh around her middle. In her gravelly voice, Janis Joplin sang "Me and Bobby McGee." Georgette unbuttoned her waistband. The front of her pants sprang into an open V, exposing her bare belly. She slid the dark slacks down her tan legs. She wore no underpants. Her thighs were broad and brown. She reached behind her back and un-snapped her bra. Leaning forward, she let the black cups fall delicately into her hands, the shoulder straps sliding down her arms, her full white breasts swinging free.

She tossed the bra onto the couch and stood with one hand cocked on a hip, the other pointing toward his pants. "Why don't you take those off?" she said. "I don't feel like wrestling with them."

Jack had started to slide his pants off before taking off his shoes, so he had to sit on the couch, the pants bunched around his ankles, while he untied his shoes. Too much tequila. If only he'd stuck to wine. Georgette grinned, unselfconsciously naked, the bright outline of her one-piece swimsuit sketched against her deep-tanned arms and legs. Bare strips of skin revealed where she had shaved the sides of her crotch so she could wear one of those new high-hipped suits. The tan on her legs ended in half-moons at the top of her hipbones. Jack found himself staring at this lovely naked woman wondering how she might look in a swimsuit.

In boxer shorts, he faced Georgette, now with both fists on her hips, like an expectant teacher, waiting for an unruly student to fess up. He jerked down his shorts and kicked them free from his ankles. She instantly turned away. He trailed her down the hall toward the bedroom, following her trembling white hips, luminous in contrast to the low-scooped tan on her back, beckoning through the darkness like fluttering, receding marsh lights.

That night, Jack supposed, marked the real beginning of their short, troubled romance. By the end of the month they'd slept together as often as he and Beth had during their last year together. Georgette was the first woman he'd slept with since marrying Beth, and it took getting used to. The second time, in her apartment bedroom, she got undressed in the same backwards manner as on that earlier night, first slipping off a pair of white linen slacks, then her sweater and bra. Again, she wore no underpants. She glided into the bathroom and came out brushing her teeth.

"Why are you still wearing those underpants?" she asked.

He was unaccustomed to her casual self-stripping preliminaries. Even after years of marriage, he and Beth had continued to undress each other in bed, before their love-making had gone completely on the skids.

"Why don't you ever wear any underpants?" he asked, truly curious.

"I never have. At least, not since I started dressing myself."

"Never? Not even on that day . . ." He thought of that troll in Times Square.

"Oh, I did back then, with short skirts. But not with pants. You want a clean, straight line with pants. I don't understand women letting those ugly ridges of their underpants show through."

She went back into the bathroom to rinse out her mouth. He took off his boxer shorts, but before he could get into bed, she had returned. They faced each other naked. She stretched out one leg perpendicular to her body and raised up on her toe in a dancer's move.

"Underpants bind you," she said, seeming to speak to the room in general. "You want to feel free." Then she cast her gaze toward his crotch. "I don't know how men can stand it."

"Boxer shorts are loose," Jack explained. "They're not like Jockey shorts."

"I don't mean that." She did a little dancer's squat, placing both hands, palms upward, fingers interlaced, under her crotch as though she were supporting some invisible genitals dangling between her legs. "I don't see how you can stand it— walking around with that stuff just hanging there."

So much for Dr. Freud's theory of penis envy, Jack thought. He wondered what his old university psych teacher might say in this situation.

They climbed between the sheets, and soon they were coupled, her shaved crotch, scratchy as a man's chin, pricking him as a reminder that the large-boned, eager woman in his bed was not his wife, the mother of his children, the companion and lover of his youth.

Well, who was she then? Hard to call her a lover. Neither

of them wanted to live with each other. She worked late several nights and was "tied up" on others. She wanted to come and go as she pleased. When they did get together, they usually drank as a prelude to bedding down. She was wilder than he'd realized, although she now kept her coke in her purse. As he'd told her on that first night she'd trotted it out, he didn't want to get into that stuff. He had enough problems.

Drinking seemed just fine with her. She drove a red Firebird and loved to gun it. When she came to pick him up, she would hit the horn with a "shave-and-a-haircut" toot. When he appeared at the door, she added the "two-bits." Booze and sex were what they had. A lot of people, he knew, didn't even have that.

Jack asked her once if she ever thought about remarrying.

"I already had one of those," she replied.

"A marriage?"

"No, a husband. Now I want a life."

One night they ended up at some country-and-western bar, sidling up to fenced pasture at the edge of town. Smoke, noise, and blinking colored lights engulfed the joint. A platinum-blond singer in a fringed leather vest and a cowgirl skirt cranked up the band with her big, booming voice and kept all the cowboy types pounding the floor with their shit-stompers. Most of the women were dressed like rodeo buckle bunnies in tight jeans, halter tops, and bare bellies. A lot of men said hello to Georgette. She wore a loose Mexican skirt that bounced wildly against her legs when she danced. She tossed the skirt this way and that, and her legs flashed in and out of view. The Mexican shawl draped over her shoulders flapped around her like broken wings. It was the first time she'd worn a skirt on a date.

Unbalanced from booze, Jack slipped on the dance floor. Georgette helped him up and guided him outside, ostensibly to walk around and sober him up, but she was polluted, too. Maybe not as much as he was, but as much as he'd seen her.

They had their arms draped over each other's shoulders as they swayed together through the dark parking lot singing "El Rancho Grande."

They came to a barbed-wire fence—they were that far out at the edge of town—in front of a dark pasture stretching toward the desert. Vague dark humps rose up from where an immobile herd of cattle huddled in the pasture. Against the far-off hills, casinos blinked their neon.

"Let's go," Georgette said. She dropped to the ground as though doing a pushup and slid under the fence. Jack wriggled between strands of wire, catching his pant leg on a barb as he fell to the other side, hearing a rip. Georgette already swayed toward the cattle, waving her shawl in front of her like a bullfighter's capote, shouting, "Toro! Toro!" Jack caught up with her. Her feet stomped up and down like those of a flamenco dancer as she arched her back, jerked back her head, and glided toward a clump of seven or eight horned steers facing her with dull, dumb, motionless stares of disbelief. A big white-faced Hereford lowered its head and pawed the earth with a front hoof.

Georgette stomped toward it, swaying back and forth, now holding her shawl waist high in one hand like a muleta. "Eat death, fat cow!" she chanted. "Eat death!"

The big Hereford swung its head and led a charge away. All the steers, one after another, turned their rumps and bolted away, joined by more and more unseen beasts. Their hooves thumping against pasture sod sounded like distant rain as the herd vanished into darkness.

Georgette ran laughing back toward the fence. Jack followed, tripping and sprawling into the grass before catching up with her at the fence. They clutched at each other, her tongue in his mouth, her groin pressed hard against his. He pulled at her skirt, hiking it up the backs of her legs until his palms found bare skin, continuing to rise, unencumbered now, all the way up her thighs and hips. She unbuckled his belt, and with one foot placed on a low strand of barbed wire she managed to straddle him, standing up, until she kicked her foot off the wire and her thighs clamped around him. He grabbed a fence wire for balance, pricking his hand, as they danced their hopping dance to a rhythm without music. "Fuck me," Georgette said over and over. "Fuck me, fuck me."

Sometimes he wondered who she was speaking to in these moments, because the next time he would talk to her, she wouldn't pick up where they'd left off.

At the end of that night she must have dumped him off at home, he guessed, because he woke up the next morning alone, feeling as though a hoof had cracked his skull. He uncapped a beer and called her. There was no answer. It was Sunday. He didn't get hold of her until the next day.

"Oh, I had some things planned with friends," she said in a bored, dismissive way.

They didn't talk about Billy anymore. She never offered anything about him, and Jack had ceased wanting to hear anything, but the bastard still flickered at the edge of their lives. One night they were watching a Clint Eastwood cowboy movie called *Pale Rider* when Georgette said, "I don't understand what people see in Eastwood. He seems like a wimp playing a tough guy."

Jack hadn't ever really taken to movie stars, even as a kid. He couldn't understand what the fuss was about, why girls went gaga and boys adulated movie stars. To admire good acting was okay, but to make an actor into an idol seemed crazy. Even in college he'd learned from knowing friends in plays that actors were pretty insecure people, always pretending to be somebody they weren't. What was so admirable about that? He preferred someone who actually was what he appeared to be, like Uncle Pete.

"I hear it's all in his jawline," he said to Georgette about Eastwood's attractiveness. "With his little beady eyes, if he had a weak chin, everyone would think he was creepy."

"Well, you can see who he really is by the way he shoots his pistol. Look. He holds it limp-wristed. A man doesn't shoot a pistol like that."

Then Jack sensed him there, for a moment, in the room—Crockett—holding his pistol in a firm, straight-wristed grip. Did Georgette consider Billy the model of a real man? She measured Eastwood against him. Jack wondered, Am I being measured, too?

Over the weeks, Jack had grown to feel that the woman he'd once identified with Billy—the one in the jumpsuit who had watched him during his trial—no longer really existed. Thanks to the mysterious alchemic powers of sex, he could hardly connect Georgette to her previous self. When they'd begun sleeping together, she'd become a new person in relation to him—just as Beth had done—so that Georgette's past, and the men in her past, became those of a woman different from the one he now knew. How could he feel jealous about a person he remembered as if glimpsed, long ago, in a fleeting, distant dream? The men she had loved in her former life could mean nothing to him.

Or so he thought, until two new books appeared about Billy, one called *Desperado: The True Story of Billy Crockett*, and the other titled *Quick Draw: A True Story of Violence in the American West*. They were anything but true. Jack was interviewed for both of them. Neither writer got much right.

The author of *Desperado* was an old-time newspaper reporter from L.A. who had scarcely listened to Jack because he seemed already to know what he intended to write. In his book, what happened in Little High Rock Canyon came totally from Billy's false testimony. The reporter had simply copied the court transcripts. But at least he'd understood that Billy was trying to live out an Old West fantasy, and everyone was buying into it.

The other writer, a journalist who specialized in true-crime books about psychopaths and serial killers, had spent hours taping Jack. Then he sent his assistant to make some more tapes. He didn't really believe Billy, but a fat lot of good that did. His book had so many contradictory details that it was impossible to know what the author was trying to say. The only thing that emerged with any clarity was a contrast between Jack and Billy. Jack was described as "confused," "bitter," "glowering," "vindictive," "haunted," and "alcoholic." Billy was "determined," "tough," "uncompromising," "violent," "ascetic," "soft-spoken," "baby-faced," "gentle," and "idealistic."

One Sunday night Jack and Georgette were at his place drinking when he started to watch an old B movie about Basque pioneers called *Thunder in the Sun*. Georgette wanted to go to bed early, but he wanted to watch the film. She had been working all weekend and had a lot planned for the next day.

"I thought I was going to see you tomorrow," Jack said. Usually he worked on Georgette's free Mondays, so it was easy for her to be "busy" or "tied up" all day and night with friends. But that Monday—Veterans Day—was also a holiday for him, and he had hoped to spend the day with her.

"I forgot you were off," she said. "I've made other plans."

"Well, go to bed then. I'll be right there—after I finish this movie." And this bottle, he added to himself. A Sunday night of drinking, free from an impending morning of work, was too precious to cut short. Georgette's evasive plans irritated him, but he hadn't pried simply because he didn't want to know the truth. He didn't want to be hurt. He kept hoping her other involvements would just stop, and they would be together.

Georgette came over to kiss him. He clicked off the film with the remote. "I want to ask you about something," he said, "about you and Billy."

"Not now. It's late. I need to get some sleep."

He pulled her onto his lap. "I only want to know one thing, about what happened after the trial." Both new books about Crockett had claimed that when Billy was free on bail, he had illegally shot a protected prize bighorn in the Santa Rosa Mountains while camping with an old girlfriend named Georgette Spinelli. The news had been gnawing at Jack, but he hadn't said a word to her until now. "Why didn't you tell me you were with him after the trial?"

"That's bullshit," Georgette blurted out. "I didn't tell any of these guys shit. That L.A. guy wasn't interested in what I had to say anyway. I didn't like either of them."

"They got the information somewhere. It's odd that they'd both be wrong."

"Well, they are. Somebody told them both the same thing, and they didn't check it out. What do they care, as long as it makes a good story?"

"So you haven't heard from Billy since the trial."

"I didn't say that. He called me when he was out on bail, but I told him I didn't want to see him. He wrote once from prison, but I didn't answer."

"Do you really expect me to believe that?"

"Look," she said, "why would I want to see him? I'm the one who told you he was on King Lear."

He remembered that late-night call and the squeaky, high-pitched voice of the snitch. "That wasn't your voice."

"I had a girlfriend make the call. I told her what to say." As he mulled over this startling news, Georgette went on, "I have to go to sleep. We can talk when you're sober. I need to get some sleep."

Jack filled his tumbler with straight Jim Beam. Images of Crockett pressed into his brain as he tried to concentrate. At times he hoped that word would get to Crockett in prison about him and Georgette. He had Billy's girl now. She liked him, not Crockett. But when sober he expunged those embarrassing thoughts; he didn't want the punk to have anything to do with his feelings for Georgette or hers for him. But the smirking bastard was still there, in his mind and hers. Who was getting the last laugh? Once again, Jack regretted missing his chances at the son of a bitch.

He clicked on the video, rewound the film, and tried to concentrate. In the movie, red-haired Susan Hayward was supposed to be a Basque traveling to California with a wagon train of her countrypeople. Silver-haired Jeff Chandler, with a scar over one black eyebrow, was the immigrants' guide through Indian country. A legend rolling up the screen at the beginning of the movie explained that Basques were a "spirited, lusty people with quaint names and centuries-old customs." Susan Hayward was certainly spirited. She kneed Jeff Chandler in the balls when he tried to put the make on her. She spoke with a French accent and danced a kind of Sevillano flamenco, as though Basques were some sort of French hybrid from southern Spain. How did moviemakers come up with their goofy ideas? These Basques not only spoke French instead of Euskera; they constantly let out wild *irrintzi* howls. "This is the way we communicate in our country," a Basque explained. "We are very proud of it." Jack appreciated how Indians must feel when they see their ancestors portrayed as both primitive savages and New Age clairvoyants with telepathic powers.

He was pretty drunk by the time the Basques decided to make their stand. "We will fight in the mountains as we fought at the Battle of Roncevaux," a leader proclaimed. "The mountains are like home to us." Fight they did. Jeff Chandler, like Clint Eastwood, held his pistol with a kind of limp-wristed weakness, but the Basques unleashed their violence with terrible ferocity. More Indian than the Indians themselves, they leapt from rock to rock, flung stones with jai-alai sticks, threw knives, fired rifles, screeched their Basque yells, and spooked and slaughtered Indians with savage efficiency. This explosion of violence solved everything. Susan Hayward hooked up with Jeff Chandler. Together they headed for their new western home to keep alive the vision of those Basques who had died. "They had a hope," Jeff told Susan, "a dream that carried them six thousand miles. That's what they died for. If you don't keep that dream alive, they'll have died for nothing." The End.

This hokey speech got to Jack, touching something real,

despite its sappiness: these Basques knew there were some things you had to fight for, even die for. No one wanted their loved ones to have died in vain. To live devoid of hopes or dreams was only an existence, not a life.

He went to the bookshelf and pulled down that book by Pablo Neruda, the one he and Beth had used in their Spanish class, *Splendor and Death of Joaquín Murieta.*

He clicked on the light above the stove and sat at the kitchen table. He didn't want to wake Georgette. He drank and read parts of the play. Blurry letters danced in the light. One side of the page was in English, the other in Spanish. Once again he felt that the world of this passionate play made sense. Here were people who knew how to wreak vengeance, to take an eye for an eye, a tooth for a tooth. They lived with honor.

He hit the table with his fist and squinted to make the swarming words settle down. He read how when a wrathful posse murdered his mistress, Joaquín Murieta dropped to his knees in the shadows, kissed her eyes, and swore by the roses and the stars to avenge her. "Whatever is fallen or fouled or betrayed," Joaquín said, "I will redress in her name."

> *Then Joaquín rose up, a bandit, committed in honor and love to wipe out his shame. Every joy vanished. Face to face with his sorrow, wild with his loss, he paid out his lifetime, avenging, opposing, till the wound of her dying was healed, and there in the mud and the gold his blood and his guts were spilled.*

He slammed his hand on the table with the rhythm of the verse as he chanted aloud: "Juró estremecido matar y morir persiguiendo al injusto, protegiendo al caído. . . ." *Shattered with grief, he swore unto his own death to slaughter the unjust and to avenge the violated.*

He thought of Bob and the chances missed to avenge his death—those times in the canyon, on King Lear Peak, at Wyatt Green's trailer.

He felt Georgette's hand shaking his shoulder. "What the hell are you doing?" She stood behind him in a pink shortie nightgown. She squinted in the light, her tired face wrinkled.

He had placed his black .357 Magnum on the Formica table next to the book, along with a box of cartridges. The handle grips of the pistol were damp from the sweat of his hand.

He shouted, "Whatever is fallen or fouled or betrayed, I will redress in his name."

Georgette stepped back, her eyes alarmed, as he picked up the pistol. "You're crazy, Jack. Put that thing away."

"I will redress in his name," he repeated, and put the barrel of the pistol into his mouth. On his tongue the cold metal tasted of dirty coins. He had a vision of fragmented bone and blood spraying out the back of his head, cleaning out the torment, grief, and guilt pounding in his skull. He just wanted it all to end.

"Jack," Georgette shouted. "Wake the fuck up and put that gun away. You're scaring me."

He kept the gun in his mouth but just couldn't bring himself to squeeze the trigger. He felt worse for going so far, but not far enough, than if he'd done nothing at all. He slammed the gun down on the table.

Georgette disappeared into the bedroom and came out dressed.

"What are you doing?" he asked.

"I can't take this. Find somebody else to play your little boy's games."

The front door slammed. Georgette's Firebird exploded into a roar, quieted momentarily as she backed out of the driveway, and peeled out down the street. He poured more bourbon into the glass. He gripped the handle of the pistol. He flipped open the book and read again: "Whatever is violated, I will redress in his name."

After that night, he didn't see Georgette for two weeks. Every time he called she had other plans. He frightened her, she said. He needed help. She just couldn't handle where he was coming from.

Who could blame her? He had scared himself. When he thought back on that night, it was like looking at a different person. He wanted to tell Georgette that he really intended to do something this time; he would cut out the hard stuff and stick to beer. He got her on the phone, but before he could convey his resolutions, she yelled, "Fuck off," and hung up. When he drove over to her place, she didn't answer the door. On the way home he stopped at Barney's. He kept his word about sticking to beer but still found himself slipping over the edge.

One night, after tanking up pretty good, he drove over to her apartment without calling. It was getting late, but he figured she would have just come home from work. He expected to have trouble crossing the lintel, but she opened the door without asking who it was, and he stepped right in. She looked shocked. She wore a short silky Chinese flower-patterned housecoat with a green belt. The hem of the robe rested high on her bare thighs.

"You expecting someone?" he asked, examining the flimsy robe.

"I was just getting ready to take a bath. I wish you'd leave me alone."

"I want to ask you something about you and Billy and your other boyfriends."

"Come on, Jack. Drop it. It's late. I need to get some sleep."

He walked silently past her across the thick wall-to-wall carpet and into the dark living room, not hearing her until he turned and saw her facing him in the shadows, her hair down, her arms folded.

"We can talk, can't we? That's all I want."

She pulled the lapels of her skimpy robe across her chest. "I think you better go home. We can talk when you're sober. I need to get some sleep."

"Why don't I just stay here and sleep, too?"

He had stayed overnight at Georgette's apartment only once, so her response didn't surprise him. "No, I don't want you here."

"Why? Are you 'tied up' tonight? Are you 'busy'?"

"As a matter of fact I am. Someone's coming to see me in a few minutes, and I need to take a bath."

Although he always knew she had been seeing other men, this was the first time she'd admitted that someone else was really in the picture.

"Does he have a name?"

"It's none of your business. Just please get out of here—and leave me alone."

He plopped down on the couch. Georgette leaned her shoulder against the doorjamb of the hallway. The room swirled. Like an image in an unfocused camera viewfinder, Georgette sprouted two heads on a bifurcated torso.

"Is he the bartender at the Hacienda? Is that why he's coming over so late? Or is it that big jock from the White Rose?"

Georgette's puzzled expression showed she didn't know who he was talking about, but his willingness to start a guessing game alarmed her.

"I'm asking you to leave, Jack. I'll talk to you about this when you sober up."

He felt his face consciously contort into the semblance of a smile. He thought of Clint Eastwood and his manufactured thin-lipped sneers. "Just tell me the man's name, and I'll be on my way."

"I'm not telling you anything. Who do you think you are anyway?"

"Who do you think *you* are? Stringing me along for three months, while you're balling someone else."

"Get the hell out of here. I've had it with you."

"I'm busy," he said, mocking Georgette's deep, laid-back voice. "I'm tied up tonight. I'll see you when it's convenient."

Georgette folded her arms tight across her chest. "You don't own me. Maybe if you weren't so damn crazy I wouldn't be seeing other people. But I'm not going to be involved with a man who's insane when he drinks."

"Look who's talking here, Miss Carrie Nation, Miss Shirley Temple Black, Miss—"

"Get out of my apartment."

"Just stringing me along when your real boyfriend isn't around."

"What boyfriend? You're just nuts. I don't owe you anything. And by the way, it's not just one man. I can see whoever I want, I can date whoever the fuck I please, and you can't do a fucking thing about it."

"Oh, you can, can you?"

He grabbed her by the wrist. She tried to wrench away. Despite her strength he got her turned around with his arms clasped around her waist and pushed her with his chest down the hall. She tried to brake herself by planting her feet on the rug, but he pushed her into the bright bathroom where she had started to fill the tub. Fluorescent lights glared off yellow tiled walls and counters. She twisted in his arms and her robe came loose. Her bare breasts looked vulnerable in the startling brightness.

He pulled her onto the cold floor next to the tub. He got the hot water turned on, and steam billowed up. He twisted the other knob, increasing the plummeting flow into the tub.

"Let me go, you fuckhead," she shouted. Her naked legs squirmed on the tiled floor like two vipers.

He rolled her over the edge of the tub, robe and all, and her head cracked against the ceramic soap holder on the wall. She landed in the water sideways. The flowered robe fanned out into the bath. Her broad hip with its half-moon tan protruded from the steaming water.

"Let me get you clean," he said. "Let me help get you clean."

She twisted into a half-sitting position. He pushed her backward. Water sloshed over the side of the tub as her head went under, her hair's fluffiness transformed into black, stringy ropes. She surfaced with her eyes shut, spitting water. He jerked the wet robe down over her shoulders as though skinning a rabbit.

He grabbed the green bar of soap and rubbed it over her reddening breasts and stomach, turning her skin slick and shiny. She kicked her legs up and down. Hot water splashed on his shirt, slopped onto the floor. She was strong, hard to hold. She lunged against him with the hard rubbery density of a slippery seal. He plunged the soap between her legs and scrubbed the black mossy clump at the fork of her thighs. "Here, get clean," he said. "Get clean."

He felt himself washing off all the dirt from every man who had fondled and violated her. He felt himself washing her clean of the grungy little guy who had hitched up her skirt in Times Square, of Mr. No-Name who took her waterskiing and kept her tied up while banging her on Mondays, and even of himself who had pursued her through three months of drunken nights. Most of all, he was washing her clean of Billy Crockett. He rubbed the smear of his murderous hands from her breasts, the touch of his smirking mouth from her lips.

Georgette somehow got her arms free and swung a fist that popped hard against his nose. Blood splattered like bright Kool-Aid on the wet tile and porcelain tub. He thought at first it might be from Georgette's cracked head before he realized it was his. Her sharp red fingernails scratched at his face. She got to her knees in the tub and flung her claws at him, screaming, "Help me, help me! Somebody help me!" Her flushed, anguished face, streaked with water and tears, her wet hair hanging in sad, twisted strands, snapped him from his dreamy daze. He stood up. In the mirror, his mouth and chin ran bright with blood.

Georgette lurched from the tub into her bedroom. The face

of a stranger stared transfixed at Jack from the mirror. He snapped a strip of toilet paper free from its roll and rubbed his face with the wad, leaving his mouth and cheeks smeared pink.

Georgette was talking to someone in the other room, and when he went into the bedroom she was giving her address over the phone. Then she hung up and faced him from the other side of her rumpled bed, her tense naked body squared off to confront him, her dark eyes recessed into frightening hatred. "Don't touch me. I've called the police."

Jack really couldn't believe it. He felt as though he'd just witnessed a vast wrong. It felt as though the floor had opened into a yawning gulf. "Why'd you do that?" he asked.

Georgette looked as shocked as he felt. "Why?" she screamed. "Why? Are you really asking me why?"

Rage distorted her puffy lips and crazed eyes. The bridge of her nose looked more broken than ever. Jack didn't know who she was. He felt as though someone else had been in that bathroom with her.

"I'm sorry, Georgette," he said, but her rage wouldn't let him continue.

"I was wrong about you," she screamed, her words scraping at his face. "You're not like Billy at all. You're a fucking animal."

He was out of the house and in his car, facing a haze of blurry lights on the dashboard, gunning the engine in an attempt to get away from that house, that screaming woman, that horrid night. He didn't know exactly what happened, but he came around a corner and blindsided a parked car, skidded across the suburban street and plowed into the opposite curb, blowing out a tire and barely missing some kid's new customized low rider. When the cops got him, he was already three blocks down the street, on foot, heading home. His forehead was bleeding, his right wrist swollen, but he didn't want to go to the hospital. They took him anyway. Then they booked him and tossed him into the drunk tank because he couldn't think of anyone to call to take him home.

That night turned into a six-month horror. The judge hit him with DWI, a $2,500 fine up front, forced attendance at driver's school, six months of compulsory attendance at AA meetings, and a six-month license suspension. The worst fallout was that his driver's insurance, when he could drive again, would be tripled for the next three years, so the whole bust would wind up costing him over $7,000.

Jack felt that something unfair had happened. A few years ago, if Uncle Pete had been caught drunk, the cops would've driven him home, the car would have been towed, and that would've been that. But Jack was flattened. Wendell called him in to say that he'd been suspended from his job. Except for Wendell's intercession, he would have been fired. Jack had six months to get himself straightened out. If he didn't attend AA during that period and stay off the booze, he could kiss his job good-bye.

The first thing he did after getting this news was walk to Pyramid Plaza and get a bottle. But after filling a tumbler, he just let it sit on the kitchen table. He thought of the .357 Magnum in the bedroom. He thought of the grief he'd caused Georgette and knew that if he pulled the trigger, he could never express the regret for what he'd done to her. But just telling her he was sorry wasn't enough. She hadn't pressed charges against him, and he was relieved for that, but he felt the need to offer some recompense. She had caught the brunt of all his bottled-up rage against Billy, against Cindy, against Beth, and he was sure if the psychologists had their say, against his mother for surviving the death of his father. But he couldn't think of a thing to do for Georgette. He couldn't even bring himself to call her, feeling that an apology, no matter how sincere, masked a desire for some magical absolution, as self-serving as those confessions he'd made as a kid when wiping a sin clean merely cleared the way for its repetition.

He had no car, no wife, no kids, no girlfriend, no job, and he didn't care. The idea of having no life didn't bother him a bit. He didn't know what might happen during those next black days and nights as he contemplated the possibility of ending it with a press on the trigger of that .357 Magnum. The desire didn't arise from pity. He looked at himself from a position of cold, distant emptiness, and he just didn't care. He didn't even care enough to kill himself. That was the problem. There was just no telling what might have happened if Billy, in his bizarre, perverse way, hadn't saved him.

CHAPTER 13

Jim Sandoval called late one night to say that Billy had escaped from prison. Jenny Morrison had visited Crockett that evening, and after a twenty-minute conversation, Billy had left the visiting area at 7:35 P.M. Authorities figured he'd escaped around 7:45, but the breakout wasn't discovered until a routine cell check at 10:05. Billy had cut his way through two heavy wire fences with a pair of bolt cutters.

"How did Jenny Morrison get those wire snips to him?" Jack felt a grudging admiration for the relentlessly resourceful Basque woman who'd earlier raised $35,000 for Crockett's defense.

"She didn't," Jim said over the phone, "or at least we don't think she did. Billy was strip-searched when he left the visiting area. He must've got the snips from the inside, left them out on the grass before he went into the visiting room, then picked them up on his way back. We figure he slipped off into the shadows of the building instead of returning to the cell block."

"It's hard to believe Jenny's visit was just coincidental."

"There's a good chance that she picked him up after the breakout. That's what we think, anyway. Deputies stopped her coming into town a little after eleven, but they had no probable cause to hold her. Around midnight they got a warrant to impound her car. We'll see if the lab boys turn up any traces of Crockett in the car."

An airy lightness swelled through Jack's chest, buoying his heart like early whiffs of spring air, at the news of Billy's escape. Although it was late fall, he felt released from a wintry deadness.

"Where do you think he went?" he asked Jim.

"Anywhere but the desert. We have a report that he was spotted in a car crossing Donner Summit around eleven-thirty. It was a red Firebird. A woman answering the description of his old girlfriend Georgette Spinelli was driving. You know her, don't you?"

Was Jim just playing coy? Since Jim had taken up with Cindy Pritchard, Jack hadn't seen much of him. The affair with Cindy was an on-again, off-again deal. Jim had too many other girlfriends, and Jack feared that one of them might've been Georgette.

"You know her, too," Jack accused him, "don't you?"

"Not really," Jim answered casually. "I interrogated her once. She's a pretty good looker, for a moll."

Jack's relief gave way to the dawning, hurtful realization of Georgette's prolonged affection for Billy. She'd helped him escape. Was it possible that *all* the time she was with Jack, Billy had been on her mind? "Are you sure it was Georgette Spinelli in that car?"

"We're not sure of anything. But if it was, and if Billy was with her, then he's somewhere in the Bay Area right now, and we've got a real mess on our hands. Billy's not going to make the same mistake twice. This time I don't think he'll let himself be taken alive."

The next day, news of Billy's escape was in all the papers, and he was a hero again. More so than before. Escaping from prison added a brighter edge to his image. He was scarier now, more wily and elusive. More exciting. The calls of the coyote and wilderness had beckoned him, and he'd broken out, a free man.

Four days after the escape Jack got a call from Uncle Pete. "Billy was here last night. He's not here now, but he was. I gave you my word I'd let you know."

The next morning Jack boarded a bus out of Sparks to Winnemucca. Uncle Pete picked him up at the station in his battered pickup, once black, now sun-faded and brush-scraped into the streaked, ashen colors of a dead campfire. Pete had turned eighty-three but looked ten years older behind the wheel of the old pickup creeping into the parking lot. His bony hands gripped the steering wheel, his long skinny neck stretched like a turtle's so that his grizzled chin stuck out as he squinted to peer through the dirty windshield. The drooping fringe of mustache around his mouth was tobacco-stained from the Copenhagen he still chewed.

On the way to the ranch he offered Jack a dip. "You haven't given this up, too?" he asked.

"No," Jack said. "But I've given up everything else."

"Even pussy?"

"Even pussy."

Pete grinned. He hadn't put in his dentures. At the ranch house he walked stooped through the picket gate. He poured himself a tumbler of red wine. Jack got some canned grapefruit juice from the fridge and plopped onto the dusty couch. The space in front of the fireplace where Pete's old Australian shepherd had regularly stretched out was empty.

Before Jack had a chance to ask about the dog, Pete said, "Alice kicked the bucket. I buried her out back."

"I'm sorry about that."

Pete nodded. "Yep, she was my friend." He took a sip of wine.

They talked about two Paradise Valley old-timers, Fritz Bellingham and Ed Higgins, who had both died within two days of each other the previous week. They had been Pete's friends for years.

"Fritz died in an old-age home in Sacramento," Pete said. "I hope you'll shoot me before they put me in one of those things."

Jack returned the book Pete had loaned him, the one by his neighbor's boy who'd written about ranching and his repudiation of that way of life.

"I liked it better than you did," he told Pete. "I've had a lot of the same feelings about what's happened to the land around here. You've got to admit, ranching has been pretty hard on this country."

"Not as hard as it's been on us," Pete said.

Jack tried to avert an argument by saying, "It works both ways."

Pete ignored the point. "We busted our asses to tame this country, and you kids all benefited from it. Now you just want to write that it was all wasteful."

"I didn't write that book." Jack could hear himself getting defensive. "I just agree with some of what was in it."

Pete grunted and stared into the darkening afternoon light. The autumnal smell of decaying cottonwood leaves drifted through the screen door.

"Billy came by," Pete said, "to borrow some money. He promised to pay it back, and I knew he'd keep his word."

Jack worried that Pete would now be implicated in harboring a fugitive. "Did you give it to him?"

"No, he already had several thousand dollars. I'm sure he got it from that kook Jenny Morrison. I don't know why he needed more."

"Maybe he just wanted it from you," Jack prodded, "to get your approval."

If Pete agreed, his expression didn't show it. "I told Billy he should've finished out his time like a man and started over again. He was going to get a second chance. Now he's blown all that by escaping."

"Did he say if his old girlfriend Georgette Spinelli helped him escape?"

"He didn't tell me nothing. He wouldn't give any names or details. He's honorable that way to his friends. He's just fucked up in his mind about some other things. Even when he was out here working for me trying to be a buckaroo, he never understood that it ain't toughness that makes a top buckaroo. It's good judgment. That's something Billy's always lacked. This escape deal showed poor judgment, too."

"Where do you think he went from here?"

Pete shrugged. "All I know is he didn't go away happy. I told him his mistake was that he was always trying to be something he wasn't. That's what got him into trouble. Even now, he won't admit in his mind that he's a murderer and ought to pay for what he's done and get on with a new life. No, he's got to pretend he's some kind of mountain man who did what was right and then got a bum rap."

"He's not alone in thinking that way."

"There's nothing you can do about fucked-up people. You're always going to have people like this Jenny Morrison who are bored out of their skulls with their city lives and who're going to make some kind of hero out of Billy. You best just stay out of it."

"How do you mean?"

"Billy knows you want to get him. Maybe it was that Spinelli girl who told him, I don't know. But I think that's part of the reason he came by here. He asked me to tell you not to try to come after him. He'll kill you. And that's what I'm asking you to do. I'm asking you to show a little good judgment in this deal. It looks like you're getting another chance, too, you know, to straighten out your life."

Jack didn't respond, and his uncle didn't ask him to. They ate some leftover tamales the housekeeper, Mrs. Rodriguez, had made. Before turning in, Jack called the Humboldt County Sheriff's Department to report that Billy had been in Paradise Valley, then he spent a wakeful night on a sagging cot in a room cluttered with old spurs, lariats, saddles, and other gear.

In the early morning, the unmistakable straining chatter of a helicopter rattled the walls of the old ranch house. Jack rolled out of the cot. Pete had pulled on a pair of Levi's over his yellowing long johns. Ground fog shimmered against the living-room window like sifted flour. Morning's first gray light filtered into the house.

"You want some coffee?" Pete asked. "Or do you want to see what's up first?"

"Let's see what's up," Jack said. Greeting the early-morning hour without a pounding skull or acid-gurgling stomach was still an unusual enough experience to cause Jack to wonder afresh who he was. He felt heart-tugging ties to that boy who had once got up before dawn to catch horses and round up cattle with Uncle Pete.

"I got to have some coffee," Pete said. He shuffled barefoot across the faded pine floor.

By the time the coffee boiled up, Jack heard the bloodhounds baying outside. When he opened the door, Jim Sandoval stood on the porch in a tan departmental cap and field jacket buttoned to his neck. He wore sunglasses even though there was no sun to shield. The butt of a twelve-gauge pump shotgun rested against his hipbone, the barrel slanted skyward.

"Morning, Jack. The dogs are hitting on the house. Mind if we come in?"

Two men with Century Security insignia held the taut leashes of the sniffing bloodhounds straining to get into the house. A Humboldt County sheriff's car pulled into the yard followed by a van carrying more armed men. Besides two county sheriffs' departments, the security guards and their dogs, the state had also put prison guards on the manhunt. It was standard procedure for the prison to assign at least six correctional officers to a search for any escapee.

Inside the house, the dogs acted confused, sniffing the floor here and there to pick up a scent.

"Things are faint in here," a deputy said.

"No one's here," Pete told Jim. "You're wasting your time."

"The dogs alerted on the house. He must've been here."

"Sometimes these dogs are unreliable," Pete said.

Jim Sandoval whipped off his sunglasses. "Why did they alert to the house then, Pete?"

"Take them outside," Pete said. "I think they're just looking for a tree."

It turned out that Jack wasn't the only person who'd called the department. Around three in the morning the Humboldt sheriff had also received an anonymous call about activity in a empty mobile home near where Billy's old buckaroo buddy Gary Valdez lived at the far end of the valley.

"The dogs really hit hard on that trailer," Jim said. "They were wanting to get in there bad. We found crumpled bedding. We think Crockett was in there last night."

The owners of the empty mobile home lived in Sparks, so when a neighbor had seen lights in the trailer she'd called the sheriff.

"People out here are hesitant to say much," Jim said. "They think Billy's friends are going to hammer them."

"He was here three nights ago," Jack said. "I called the department last night."

Jim turned toward Pete. "Why didn't you tell us that?"

he asked. "That explains why we're not getting much scent now."

"My hearing aid's on the blink and I can't hear too good," Pete said. "That's why I called Jack to handle things. He would know the procedures."

When the Humboldt County sheriff's investigator finished questioning Pete, Jack got a lift into Winnemucca to catch a late-morning bus back to Sparks. He figured that from Paradise Valley Billy would head to Gerlach. Jack wanted to get up there before the cops did. But by the time he got a ride with a sheepman heading up that way the next morning, Jim, the Feds, and the dogs were crawling all over town. The dogs had picked up Crockett's hot scent at Eddie Dodd's bar.

Of course, Eddie Dodd told deputies, "I don't believe Billy's been around here at all. I don't believe he will return for six months or a year. It's a shame what you goons have done to that boy."

At noon, after a sandwich at Bruno's café, Jack walked over to Scotty Larsen's log house. He was surprised to catch the guide at home, since it was fall hunting season.

"I'm expecting some clients to show up in the morning," Scotty said. In the last four years, Scotty's hair had turned grayer, but his blue eyes were still lively. He had taken to wearing bright red suspenders to hold up his Levi's. He was working on a black metal rod on the kitchen table. "Here, look at this gizmo, Jack. What do you think?"

He explained that it was a lightweight gun-barrel support he was marketing with a guy from Pocatello. In the advertising the rod would carry Scotty's signature.

"I think you might make some sales," Jack said.

"A lot of these hunters can't shoot worth beans. When they spot wild game, their gun barrels wiggle all over like a waddling duck's ass. This gizmo will help them bag some meat."

"I'm looking for some game myself," Jack said. "I'm looking for Crockett."

Scotty poured two mugs of coffee. He motioned Jack toward the couch and chair near the front door.

"You're not going to find Crockett around here," Scotty said, settling into the chair. "I think he came through to get some dough from his friends. Hell, you can't hide out in that desert. It's too empty. We know everyone who's out there. It's easier to get lost in a crowd."

"I almost got him out there," Jack said.

"You mean up on King Lear? Well, we all knew he was there. You were carrying a three hundred Savage, I hear."

"Billy was, too." Jack had always liked the shape and feel of his grandfather's rifle, even as a boy, and he'd liked the powerful sound of its name—the .300 Savage—indicating savagery of high caliber.

"The three hundred Savage is such a fucking terrible rifle," Scotty said. "You can't hit a thing with it."

Jack didn't want further criticism. He'd had enough from Beth and Georgette. He also knew better than to talk guns with old-timers. They all had their favorites. To get off the subject, he mentioned that the sheepman who'd given him a ride had been complaining about the proliferation of coyotes around Gerlach, all because the government had banned poisoning with K-40.

"Talking to a sheepman is like talking to a senator," Scotty said. "They're born liars. Poisoning only made coyotes increase. They began dropping bigger litters. Now things are settling down. Stockmen still want to try to exterminate the coyote, but it can't be done. When the last stockman dies, the coyote and the raven are going to be picking over his bones."

"That sheepman said he felt almost exterminated himself."

"Yep. They'll all be gone soon. All of us will. When things change, you've got to change your program. You've got to diversify. That's why I'm making these gun rods."

Ready to leave, Jack said, "Let me know if you hear anything about Billy."

"When they catch Billy," Scotty said, "it won't be out here. It's going to be where there's lots of people."

In January, two months after his escape, Billy appeared on the FBI's Ten Most Wanted Fugitives list. In July he was spotted in California, near Fort Bragg, where his brothers still made a living stripping bark and logging. Jack called his brother-in-law Dave at the Fort Bragg Fish and Game office. Dave confirmed the rumors.

"A lot of people think he's around here," Dave said. "There's just too much smoke."

"He seems to be following the same pattern as before, showing up at all the same places."

"Billy's like a cottontail," Dave said. "A jackrabbit will hightail it into wild country when it's spooked. A cottontail's more timid. It likes to stick close to home."

Just as Beth had said: we're all creatures of habit.

Jack pulled out of town that night, headed for California. He'd gotten his license back and had been driving for a month and a half. He was glad to be on the road. In the July night, the truck droned out of Reno toward the Peavine Mountains, where for two days a wildfire had burned unchecked. A line of flames stretched across the black hills like a glowing strip of blood-colored neon. Jack remembered eight or nine summers ago when the hills east of town had burned. In the warm evenings, he and Beth would drive out of town and park along Vista Boulevard to watch. Where points in the line brightened, they knew that a wall of flame had leaped up thirty, forty, or maybe a hundred feet high. From a distance it was just a beautiful flash. Up close where exhausted firefighters worked, the terrifying flames threatened their lives. He and Beth wrapped their arms around each other and kissed. One night the fire jumped the line and turned into a canyon, disappearing from view. They continued to drive out to watch, changing their lookout, joining dozens of cars parked along Route 80. Now, after eight years, the hills out there still looked like a scorched moonscape, dry and rocky, with no trees, no sage.

Strange how from a distance a disaster like a wildfire could be so exciting, even beautiful. When Jack was a boy, his uncle Ralph in Las Vegas would call to tell the family when an "event," as it was called, was scheduled at the nuclear test site. Uncle Ralph was a member of the city council in those days and got to sit with other VIPs on metal folding chairs to watch the explosions. At the test site they were given tan caps and told to wear long-sleeved shirts and dark glasses for protection against the bomb's blast. Officials distributed whisk brooms for observers to brush off the grit and sand that often covered them after an event. Soldiers rushed into the storm of dust as part of their practice maneuvers in preparation for a real nuclear war, which nearly everyone accepted as inevitable. Now everyone knew that the war had actually happened—against Americans themselves. Jack's uncle had died of thyroid cancer ten years ago.

As a boy, Jack had always wanted his folks to send him to Las Vegas so he could join Uncle Ralph up close at a blast. Instead he got up at 4 A.M. and drove with his parents and sister to K Street in Sparks to search the sky for the mushroom cloud. From three hundred and fifty miles away they usually could only see the sky brighten a bit. One winter day the blast shocked him with its unexpected brilliance. Strong winds roared from the south. Around that time people were beginning to worry about radioactive fallout. Teachers told Jack and other school kids not to eat any snow. But, of course, they did.

The truck climbed up the winding freeway into the Sierra. Off the edge of the road, under the moonlight, nestled the ebony jeweled shape of Donner Lake. Jack thought of his father dying on the dark road when it had been a treacherous two-lane highway. He thought of how his dad would feel if he knew how much his son had messed up his life. "Find something you love," his dad had advised about work. Jack had done that—he found something—but then he'd come close to deep-sixing it, just as he had his marriage. His father had spent most of his life in the casinos, doing what he disliked, watching people chase venal dreams, so that he might pursue his own dream—to spend his last years away from it all on the Mendocino coast. So much for dreams.

Still, who could go on without them? Jack knew that other people attributed his rebound from booze to his finally hitting bottom when he'd lost his wife, his girlfriend, his car, his license, and his job. That was part of it. So was AA. He had been attending meetings regularly, and he'd stayed off the sauce a day at a time—except for one slip, three months ago, when he'd gone to Barney's and slid back to square one. But since then he'd stayed dry. It wasn't easy. But he'd also joined a Tuesday night therapeutic group of ex-alcoholics, or—as he'd learned to say—recovering alcoholics. He liked the group; it helped him stay sober. There was always someone to call when he felt on the edge. It helped to know that he wasn't the only cat who had fallen out of the tree.

But even that wasn't enough. He could've kept losing. He could've easily lost his house, his daughters, even his life. Others had done so. No one could see up when they were looking down. It took more than the fear of failure to make him want to change his ways. That was almost impossible to explain to anyone who hadn't been in the alcoholic pit. He had to believe that a life without booze was possible and better. Billy's escape had given Jack the freedom to imagine a different life, driven by the clear-eyed purpose of finally making things right. When he'd climbed out of the pit, it had been a little like returning to earth from a foreign planet. No one could understand where he'd been except his fellow aliens who'd also known that other world. Jack had failed to track down Billy when he was drinking, but he had no intention of blowing this new chance.

A month earlier, seven months after he'd gone on the wagon, Beth had come to see him about the possibility of getting back together. He didn't know if she had just been doing it for the girls or if she really still felt something for him. "It was the booze," she said, "that came between us. I always loved you—the real you—and I still do."

"I'm the same," he said, "except for the hooch."

"That makes the difference. You didn't drink because you were crazy, Jack. You got crazy because you drank."

"I feel the same way about a lot of things—like Crockett."

"That'll change. Booze is the first step. Giving up the rest comes next. The girls miss you. I miss you. We can do it together."

That week, one of the women in Jack's therapy group asked, "What's Beth doing about herself?"

"She's seeing a therapist," Jack answered.

"About her co-alcoholism. Is she in Al-Anon?"

"No, she's not."

"Stay away from her then."

"I'll decide that," he snapped.

"That's right," the woman said. "And you can both decide to get right back into your destructive game."

Before getting involved in his group, he knew little about co-alcoholism and denial—except that they were trendy, irritating labels—but he'd come to believe in their accuracy.

The therapist intervened. "How long have you been sober now, Jack?"

"Seven months—well, not counting that slip."

"You know the facts. After a year of abstinence, you still have only a fifty-fifty chance of staying sober. You're in a dangerous game."

That was distressing news, but those were the statistics. Trying to replay the past with Beth could be a treacherous move. But he didn't resist her proposal for those cerebral reasons. He went to see her again. They had dinner. They talked. But the spark just wasn't there. Jack had changed more than he thought. That made him sad, but relieved. He wanted a new life.

On the way to Fort Bragg he stayed overnight in a Marysville motel near the town park with its large pond and black swans. When he left early the next morning, the day's coming heat already thickened the valley air. An hour later, he stopped for gas and a cold soda. The heat was palpable. It weighted the air with a burning oppressiveness. The softening black asphalt of the gas station felt sticky on the bottom of his shoes. Along with everyone else during the summer in the Great Central Valley, he walked with head bent, eyes averted, the sun smeared across the metallic sky like a broken egg yoke.

Hot flatlands sped past, broken by canals and irrigation ditches with tall Johnson grass gone to seed. Red-winged blackbirds trilled in the cattails. From a wire fence, the six liquid notes of a yellow-breasted meadowlark singing, *"Laziness will kiiiillllll you,"* whipped on the wind through his open window. In the dry heat he felt no sweat on his face, although the radio said the thermometer was climbing toward the day's high of 108 degrees.

No relief came in the drought-scorched coastal hills where the road lazily curved left-right, left-right, past dry yellow grass and twisted oaks. Following the winding road out of Willits he passed logging trucks loaded with the felled trunks of redwood trees. Then a shadowy green corridor enclosed him among tall, feathery, living redwoods and the pungent smells of a cool forest floor. Fog boiled up against the windshield until a dreary overcast sky broke into view, and he saw and smelled the vast gray desert of the cold ocean. The weepy cries of gulls and cormorants swirled in the wind. Smoke mounted skyward in a dense white column above the Georgia Pacific lumber mill and power plant.

He passed the tourist Skunk Train taking passengers in

white caps, white shorts, white socks, and white legs for a tour of the redwood forest. Little did they know that they would be seeing a false-front grandeur. When Jack had flown over the hills with his brother-in-law, he'd noticed that strips of trees lined the railroad tracks to prevent the tourists from seeing the massive clearcuts behind them. Georgia Pacific owned the whole coastline. The tree farm the company displayed to replenish the forest was a joke compared to what the loggers were destroying.

He crossed the Noyo River rushing into the sea, then Pudding Creek slicing through a beach of smooth black sand. The tide was moving out, leaving a film of water like clear ice on the sand. Jack pulled off the road and walked barefoot along the empty shore, staring out over the rocking ocean. The hard sand chilled his feet. It made him realize how lucky he was to be alive and feel this wet coldness on his skin. The gray sea merged imperceptibly into the overcast sky. In the distance, a jogger ran along the edge of the surf. On the beach, Jack stopped in front of a decomposing harbor seal—a dark, humped corpse, washed ashore, without a head.

That evening, during a dinner of barbecued sablefish, he told his brother-in-law about the headless seal. Dave had worked as a marine biologist for sixteen years, and was constantly worrying about maintaining his job against the annual budget cuts of California's Fish and Game Department. He had short, bristly black hair and drooping Asian eyes. His father had been one of the original Chinese raiders who had almost completely fished out the abalone along this coast. Now Dave was at war against abalone poachers.

"I got calls about that seal," Dave said. "Everyone thinks it's a shark hit. Of course, a shark could've decapitated it and then lost it. Nature's wasteful. I have to go look at it. Several people think they saw a great white at Russian Gulch four weeks ago. But I'd be surprised if it was shark."

Dave and Marlene's thirteen-year-old son and sixteen-year-old daughter stopped eating and listened to their father with open-eyed attention. Jack watched them. They were beautiful kids, the alchemic product of a miraculous Eurasian fusion. Basque and Chinese genes apparently grafted nicely. Kim was already a woman, and Jack thought of how quickly his own daughters would be following her. Tommy wore a black San Francisco Giants baseball cap backwards on his head. He was still a kid, but little cracks in his voice omened puberty, as he reminded his father that they were to go diving in the morning.

"What about the sharks?" Tommy asked. It was clear that he was scared.

"We'll still go. There hasn't been a hit at Van Damm for twenty years. Want to go with us, Jack?"

"Sure. Why not? But then I need your help tracking down Crockett's brothers."

Dave nodded, but he lowered his eyes and began eating. He seemed nervous about Crockett, just as he'd been seven years ago when he'd refused to wear his uniform or to send any of his subordinates into areas around Fort Bragg where Crockett had been sighted.

"We heard someone spotted Crockett in the town post office," Marlene told Jack. His sister's streaked hair with its reddish and blond lights was growing out so that the crown of new black hair formed a kind of dark yarmulke on her head.

"I don't know why it is that fugitives are always being spotted in post offices," Jack said. "I bet the cops and the Feds have received reports of a dozen post offices where Billy has gone to pick up or send his mail."

Marlene seemed annoyed at his dismissal of her report and went on defensively, "Maybe it's because people see his picture there and start imagining people look like him. I didn't say I saw him. I'm just telling you what I heard."

"I know," he replied. "I'm just telling you how people are always fucking up."

Dave looked like a glowering Chinese warlord. "Watch your language, Jack, around the kids."

Tommy giggled, but Kim demurely took a bite of sablefish as though nothing had happened. Something popped under the table as one of the kids kicked the other.

"Knock it off, you two," Marlene told them, "and finish eating."

After dinner, Jack volunteered to do the dishes, but Marlene said the kids would do them. He liked that. He thought Beth pampered Carrie and Sarah too much, as if spoiling them with few responsibilities was a way of making up for the hurt of the divorce.

When he told his sister about Beth's proposal to get back together, she said, "Forget her. She made her choice. There are a lot of women out there. Let Beth stick with her lesbian witches."

"Don't worry," he said. "I'm not going to do it. But you can't blame her for everything that happened, especially the booze."

"Come on," Marlene said. "You let Beth walk all over you. You're too passive with women."

The next morning at Van Damm beach, under another overcast sky, Jack hooked the beavertail of the wetsuit between his legs, activated the saline solution in the body warmer against his stomach, strapped forty pounds of weights around his waist, and kicked off from the shore. He followed the bobbing heads of Dave and Tommy toward the huge rocks jutting from the water. The sea was flat; it was a good day to take a kid diving for abalone. That's what it looked like to anyone watching from the parking lot, three guys with pry bars swimming out on the first Saturday of abalone season.

But Dave was at work. Commercial abalone fishing was forbidden along this coast. An amateur diver was allowed four a day, seven inches or bigger. One of Dave's Fish and Game men had spotted a woven sack full of abalone, several under legal size, pegged at the base of the black rock farthest from shore. A poacher would retrieve the sack at night, then hide it in the hull of a boat or ferret it away in one of the trucks that ran along the coast in darkness. The shellfish would then be brought to shore south of the Farallon Islands, where commercial abalone fishing was legal.

Dave swam out alone toward the hiding spot of the poached abalone while Jack kept an eye on Tommy. Dave disappeared into the water, diving down to put an abalone carrying a planted transponder, the size of a bead, into the sack. When the shellfish were inspected in territory where commercial fishing was legal, the activated chip would reveal they'd been poached in illegal water. At least that's what Fish and Game hoped the judge would believe when they took the poachers to court.

Jack spit into his mask to keep the glass from fogging up, adjusted it on his face, then kicked downward through the cold water. Waves of sand swirled against black rock. A neon green tube glowed where the knife harness was strapped to his calf. He swam down into broad wavering leaves and swaying yellow hoses of kelp. Dave had assured his son that diving here was safe. "Sharks aren't going to swim into the kelp," Dave had said. "Watch him for me, will you, Jack? If his weight belt is too heavy, take it off."

Underwater, Tommy swam up to Jack, his eyes enlarged and frightened behind the mask half-filled with water, his lips bruised and swollen around the mouthpiece of his snorkel—underwater illusions similar to the distortions Jack had seen in Beth's face when they used to dive together. The morning's immersion into the powerful, buffeting waters of the sea brought Jack memories of the happy time in Mexico early in his marriage. The cold water made him feel sad. He'd thought his feelings for Beth were over.

He dove toward the floor of the sea under a rock shelf where an abalone shell clung to dark volcanic stone amid clouds of swirling sand. He held the metal pry bar poised near the base of the shell. If he touched it, the abalone would seize the rock and never come off. He hesitated a moment, like a spearfisherman, then jammed the pry bar home. Yanked up, the shell popped free into his gloved hand.

That evening they pounded and breaded the abalone for dinner. Dave had brought home only the two big ones Jack had gathered. "That's all we need for a meal," he said. "Four is too high a limit. There's too much effort on this coast. The abs aren't going to survive all this effort, especially when you add the poachers and the sea otters. The Friends of the Sea Otter think otters are cute, but those cuddly little animals multiply and multiply. They're taking over the damn coast. They're another bunch of self-interested, voracious predators, just like us."

After dinner, they all crawled into the open-air hot tub on the redwood deck surrounded by old wooden wine barrels full of plants. Forceful underwater jets caused the water to bubble. Rising steam brightened the night air. Jack's red swimsuit captured air from a jet and swelled up like a balloon, pinching the elastic waistband against his skin. Kim and Tommy began splashing each other.

"Knock it off, you two," Marlene warned.

The stretched lycra of Kim's pink swimsuit revealed the bump of a woman-sized nipple protruding from her little girl's breast. Jack thought that Carrie would soon be as developed, and Sarah was not far behind. He felt bad that he hadn't been with them during the last five years. Now that they were on the verge of sexual awareness, they needed a father—a sober, responsible father—more than ever.

Marlene climbed from the hot tub and wrapped a yellow towel around her waist. Kim imitated her mother and followed her through the sliding glass door into the house, where Tommy already had disappeared to watch TV.

Dave and Jack sat in the hot, swirling water. "Mind if I take off my trunks?" Dave asked, already splashing the freed

European-cut swimsuit onto the deck next to the tub. "It feels so much better."

Jack slipped off his own boxer-style trunks, relieved to be rid of their restriction. The warm water massaged his skin. The damp night air carried the rank smell of low tide. Even in the hot tub, the fishy smell of raw abalone clung to his fingers. In the blue lights, underwater, Dave's limp cock wavered like a bit of kelp.

"Kim's already going steady with someone," Dave said. "She's been dating since she was thirteen. It's really disgusting."

Jack thought of Carrie. She'd just turned thirteen, but Beth had said nothing about her dating. He hoped she wasn't. "Kids are starting early," he told Dave. "There's nothing we can do about it. If you try to crack down, they'll just sneak off."

"Marlene thinks it's okay," Dave went on, ignoring Jack's words. "She says Kim has a good head, but she doesn't know what scumbags the boys are in this town. Fucking predators."

"Can't you talk to Kim, you know, like a father? Give her some advice?"

Dave wearily rubbed his eyes. "She hates me," he said. "Didn't you notice? She won't talk to me. She won't even look at me."

After the kids were in their rooms, Marlene pulled out a videocassette, the CBS Movie of the Week about Billy Crockett that she'd taped on Monday. Jack had resisted watching the damn thing at home, but the next morning he'd regretted not seeing it. Marlene slid the cassette into the VCR slot, and with a moan from the machine it slid out of sight. Dave turned off all the lights except one dim standing lamp.

The man who played Eddie Dodd was a joke. A big, burly guy with a Santa Claus beard, he looked about as much like toady Eddie Dodd as a Viking warrior would. Jack almost couldn't watch. The actor who played him was a slight, urbane-looking fellow who seemed out of place in the mountains. Marlene thought he was handsome. "He makes you look good, Jack." She sat on the couch in her white terry cloth robe, her bare feet resting on the glass coffee table covered with magazines.

The young actor who played Billy Crockett was Jed Saunders, the son of Matt Saunders, who had starred in so many cowboy movies in the fifties. Jed was taller, blonder, and rangier than Crockett. With his wire-rimmed glasses he looked like a Swedish Presbyterian God seeker in some foreign film. No smirk crossed his lips. Instead a shy little boy's smile lit up his face with winning innocence. In contrast, Bob's character was an obnoxious bully even Jack couldn't like. The movie had been shot in the Colorado mountains, full of green spruce and fir, rather than in the harsh Great Basin desert.

"This is such a crock of shit," Jack said. "How can they keep making a folk hero out of this punk?"

"Why don't you write your own story?" Marlene asked. "So you can tell it like it is."

Jack felt as though someone had cuffed him on the ear. He'd just never considered such a thing.

"I don't know if I could do that," he said.

"Just tell the truth," Dave said.

"You can't do any worse than this," Marlene added, pointing with her bare toe toward the new *People* magazine on the coffee table.

"Did you read that article?" Dave asked.

Jack nodded. "I glanced at it." But he'd only looked at the photos, relieved to see that his picture wasn't included. A grim snapshot of Bob made him look like a brutal Marine drill sergeant. A full-page picture of Crockett reprinted from the book *Buckaroos in Paradise* showed him in a Boss-of-the-Plains Stetson and Cristóbal Romero boots riding horseback as he had years ago.

Jack picked up the magazine during a commercial. The title

of the article was "An Angry Rebel's Paradise Lost." It was mostly about the making of the TV movie. Under the guise of balanced journalism, the writers asked, "Was Billy Crockett a western legend or a paranoid killer?" They then sneakily gave their opinion in the form of a narrative about this "young, stocky, self-reliant mountain man . . . the ultimate sagebrush rebel . . . symbol of the Old Western ethic . . . fighting a New West of sissified environmentalists and their acronym-laden laws . . . firing two bullets too many . . . an expression of rage and revenge that violated the limits the New West could tolerate . . . as the old frontier values go down fighting."

People went on:

> Even as his odyssey continues, TV is turning it into a movie of the week starring Matt Saunders's son, Jed, as Billy Crockett. All the actors are keenly aware, while making the movie in Colorado, that William David Crockett, Jr.—buckaroo, wild-horse hunter, trapper of coyotes, bobcats, and mountain lions—could conceivably be looking over their shoulders, for the mountain man is loose again, a prison escapee, hunted cautiously by lawmen throughout the Rocky Mountain West. All his pursuers know is that, wherever he is, he is armed and dangerous.

Jack turned back to the TV as the movie mercifully came to an end. It showed Jed Saunders on his belly cutting his way through a prison fence.

Dave sat in the lounge chair, arms folded, chin on his chest, eyes closed. Jack touched his brother-in-law's leg with his toe. Dave raised his head slowly and opened his eyes, completely alert, as though he hadn't been asleep at all.

"Look, Dave, you don't seem to want to talk about this, but I need your help to find out where Crockett's brothers are. If you won't take me, at least tell me where I can find them."

Dave rubbed his eyes as he had in the hot tub. "Why do

you want to do that?" he asked, as if he hadn't been aware of Jack's wishes until this moment.

"You've been doing so well, Jack," Marlene chimed in. "You don't need any more stress in your life. We're all so proud of you."

"You know I didn't come here just to get stroked. Billy has been seen here, and I want to know where he is."

"He's not here," Dave said.

"Come on, Dave. You told me on the phone he's been spotted a number of times. Marlene just said he was seen in the post office."

"We were wrong," Marlene said. "This movie threw us off. Everyone started seeing Crockett, but they were all guys who looked like that actor Jed Saunders."

Even though he hadn't had a drink in eight months, except for that one slip, Jack felt the same familiar rage of years ago when Crockett had eluded him again and again. He felt the old frustration of facing one wild goose chase after another.

"I have to make a call," he said. "If you're not giving me a bum steer, I'll head out in the morning."

Marlene stood up and tightened the cloth belt around her waist. "Don't run off, Jack. We love having you here. You're a different person now. A new man."

Jack used his calling card to ring Jim Sandoval. He didn't want to get back to Sparks only to learn that Crockett really was hiding somewhere in the coastal redwood forest.

"That damn movie has been giving us fits," Jim Sandoval said. "Some guys even jumped that actor Jed Saunders in a Caribbean restaurant. Crockett has been seen everywhere."

"So the trail is cold." The hopefulness he'd felt since Billy's escape started to fade.

"No," Jim said. "It's very hot. We know where he is."

Jack waited through the silence for the deputy to speak again.

"I shouldn't be telling you this, Jack. You don't know where you heard it."

Jim sounded exactly like a deputy in that TV movie, but Jack reassured him. "I've always kept quiet when you've asked me to."

"I know it. I trust you."

"So where is he?"

"He's in Mexico."

Jack hesitated, unable to accept the news. "Get real, Jim. We've heard this before."

"This time it's true."

"We've heard that before, too."

"You can believe it or not, Jack, but his old girlfriend Georgette Spinelli has been keeping track of him for me and she's been telling it straight. There's no doubt about it. Crockett's in Mexico. He's had cosmetic surgery, and he's down in a resort town called Zihuatanejo. That's the truth, Jack."

CHAPTER 14

Engines whined as the Mexicana 727 banked. Jack leaned his head against the scratched Plexiglas window. A strip of beach unfurled along the expanse of the Pacific Ocean. Ixtapa's resort hotels dotted the shore like plastic buildings on a Monopoly board. As they loomed larger, the high-rise hotels and turquoise swimming pools exposed their shabby fragility in the glaring sunlight.

The plane skimmed the tops of trees until the jungle vanished and sun-bleached macadam appeared under the wing. The gray runway jumped up with a hard thud that spit smoke from the rubber tires until the jet, engines roaring, wings rocking, shuddered and hissed to a calming crawl.

As Jack ducked through the door and stepped unsteadily onto the portable stairs, tropical air, smelling of earth and vegetation, slammed into his face. Enveloped in steamy heat, he walked toward the low white terminal building as if through warm water.

A shuttle van drove him into Zihuatanejo. Ponderosa Travel had made a reservation for him at the same small hotel where he and Beth had stayed fifteen years ago. It hadn't changed much. A complex of one-story bungalows, the hotel sat right on the edge of the horseshoe bay. The room was clean and airy with whitewashed walls, four beds—cots really—and a slowly rotating ceiling fan. It was the only room available.

Jack unpacked his duffle and slipped his pistol into the dresser drawer under some clothes. He'd finally been allowed to check it with the baggage. Even as a licensed officer, he couldn't carry it onboard.

From the veranda, he scanned the beach. Bathers in folding chairs gazed out over the water and munched slices of pineapple bought from strolling vendors. Billy Crockett could've been plopped in one of those chairs. Jack's stomach clenched. From now on, he and Billy probably shared the same odds of spotting each other.

That night, as he lay in bed, the waves lapped back and forth, back and forth, outside the bamboo-shaded window. Fifteen years ago he and Beth had sprawled contentedly naked under a single sheet, listening to the soft slaps of water on sand. Now, around midnight, a man with a guitar outside the bungalow began to sing a *ranchera* about lost love. The man had been drinking, but his voice wasn't bad. The song cut off in midverse, then there were just the comforting, sad sighs of the surf.

Early the next morning an old man with a bamboo rake stroked the sand along the beachfront. A white sun peeked above the mountains, chasing away the shadows nestled between the little ridges of raked sand. Fishermen climbed into boats with butterfly mesh nets and shoved off from shore. Fifteen years ago these same fishing boats had crossed a bay spotted with a few anchored sailboats. Now big motorboats and sleek speedboats crammed the bay. Some sort of fishing derby and speedboat derby was in town. As he walked along the beach, Jack passed a number of people speaking German.

The little bungalow hadn't changed much, but everything else in Zihuatanejo was different. The big jetport and the Ixtapa resort four miles away had transformed this formerly somnolent fishing village. Hotels had sprouted up all along the beachfront. The thatch-roofed palapas cluttering the beach sold boiled shrimp and ceviche. T-shirt emporiums and boutiques crowded the main drag. Jack went looking for a little shop that had sold colorful San Andrés huipils and Chamula sashes from Chiapas, to buy something for Sarah and Carrie, but he couldn't find the store. He only found more shops with lettered T-shirts on display.

In the afternoon he bought a newspaper cone of roasted peanuts and rented a rickety beach chair. He sat there cracking shells and watched men and women in swimsuits and garish holiday sports clothes pass back and forth along the surf. The sun, a blood-red disc, dropped behind the mountains on the western arm of the bay, and the fishing boats he'd watched leave that morning returned to shore with their shrimp and lobster. That's how he remembered the rhythm of those days fifteen years ago. The sun came up, the sun went down. The boats went out, the boats came in. His presence there affected nothing. People died and others were born. Fishermen gave up their trade, but their sons took their places. The boats still skittered out and came back as regularly as the sighing waves.

The next three days passed much the same. Jack greased his body with sun cream and bought a white baseball cap with a long bill to protect his nose, already red and peeling. Sunglasses alone had left raccoon rings around his eyes.

Then after lunch one day, while walking along the Paseo del Pescador toward the zocalo to buy peanuts, he saw Billy casually saunter out of a fish restaurant. The rolling duck walk remained unmistakable. Billy wore blue cotton pants and a short-sleeved yellow sport shirt. Under a short-brimmed straw hat, his face was bruised and swollen, older looking, more square and jowly, but still puffy with baby fat. It looked as though he had been whacked with a baseball bat. He sported a thick Marlboro Man mustache. Jack wondered why the Mexican authorities hadn't picked him up. He was such an easy mark. They probably didn't want to. Billy strolled past two teenage federal police in army fatigues who looked as though they were itching to use the pump shotguns cradled in their arms.

Jack dropped behind a family of German tourists as Billy headed east on the beach way. Jack followed him at a distance, finding it easy to keep that yellow shirt in sight even as it wended through crowds.

Past the bungalows on the eastern edge of town, Billy turned up a pathway into the hills toward the hotels that overlooked the bay. Enough people passed back and forth that Jack didn't worry about being conspicuous. He had on his white cap and sunglasses. Billy took a pathway that led up to a hotel. Jack waited about fifteen minutes and then entered the foyer. At the desk he took a chance and asked if a Mr. Atxaga was registered at the hotel. He was. In Room 14. Billy was using the name he'd adopted on the run seven years ago.

Jack left the hotel and walked down to the shore, where he headed south, crossing the brown sands of La Madera beach and the white sands of La Ropa. If he kept walking he'd reach Las Gatas, where he and Beth had snorkeled in the coral reefs and sat on the beach watching wild parrots fly among the palms. It was about three in the afternoon, and the sun blasted the glowing sand and pale water. Sweat streaked his face. He kept clenching his clammy palms as he walked. Everything—the sand, the hillsides, the white bungalows draped with flowering bougainvillea—wobbled in the heat.

He found himself climbing into the hills overlooking the sea, on a glaring white dirt road that snaked past a few thatch-roofed shacks, seemingly abandoned in the siesta hour. Dry coconut palms with drooping fringes stood motionless along the road. All air seemed sucked from the blistered earth. He was alone, mouth dry and head dizzy. A magenta tumble of bougainvillea flamed on the side of a whitewashed stone wall with such brilliance that the wall looked afire. A mangy donkey carrying a crude wooden packsaddle lurched along the road next to him. A burlap saddle blanket lay under the empty cross-buck. The little burro's front hoof was crippled, bent below the knee so that it stumbled with each step as it clopped along the road, all alone, no master in sight, oblivious to Jack's presence. Its dull dark eyes under drooping lids registered only stoic indifference to its plight as it hobbled forward.

For an instant, Jack felt as if he didn't exist at all. He was only a pair of eyes watching a lame animal pass a man in a white baseball cap shuffling through dirt, and that man was him. A panic-driven fear swelled within him. He felt foreign to himself, engulfed in a glaring landscape of white dirt, tortured rocks, and dry grass. He saw himself as just a man, no different from any other person on a road, no different from any other donkey, any other dog, any other palm tree, any other tuft of dry grass, momentarily appearing on a white Mexican road under a mysteriously burning and indifferent sun. He was just a man.

That evening, as the sun dropped, he sat in a shaded palapa on the beach, still shaken. He tried to eat a bowl of ceviche. He couldn't. The electrifying fear was gone, but the memory of it lingered, like a frightening event he'd heard reported about another person. He was tempted to order a glass of wine, just one glass, and then he did. The alcohol helped—for a moment. With the tingling heat of the wine in his face, he knew he couldn't keep drinking. He ordered a Pepsi, barely chilled and fizzy, and with each sip began to feel an unaccountable glow of contentment at the realization that he was still alive. That was the only thought worth thinking: he was alive. He sat in a thatched palapa. The sun was fading, long shadows stretched across the sand, fishing boats crossed the bay's darkening waters toward home, and he was alive to see and feel the water, the warm air, and the coming night. He began slowly to eat the spicy, chilled ceviche and with each bite felt a strange expanding contentment.

By ten o'clock that night, after repeatedly walking up and down the beach, he felt calm. The night air vibrated with *ranchera* and mariachi music. Someone was setting off *cohetes.* The homemade rockets hissed and exploded in the night sky. The dark hills across the bay twinkled with electric lights. He figured Billy would be in his hotel by now. He walked to the bungalow to get his pistol.

He said hello to the hotel manager, who sat shirtless on the veranda cooling himself with a small bamboo fan. He fished for his key and inserted it into its slot, but he'd apparently left the door unlocked—it swung open. He closed the door and felt along the wall for the light switch. Then a man's voice from the back of the room said, "Leave it off, Jack, and sit down."

Billy sat at the far side of the room, his puffy face crisscrossed with shadows and slits of light from the bamboo shade at the window. He wore white duck pants, rolled up at the ankles, and a white shirt. In his hand, a pistol—a .22— pointed at Jack's chest. On the floor, next to Billy's sandaled foot, lay Jack's pistol, its empty cylinder swung open. Jack dropped into the chair facing Billy. Outside the window, the muffled voice of the manager spoke Spanish to someone who had joined him on the veranda.

Billy's bruised face looked a mask of calm resignation. The cosmetic surgery had given his swollen skin a boiled, rigid cast. Even his Marlboro Man mustache hung stiffly on his lip, immobile as on a wax museum dummy.

As if he'd been holding his breath, Billy released air through his nostrils in a long sigh. "You're a fool, Jack," he said in a controlled, sad voice. "A goddamn fool."

What could he say? Admit that Billy was right?

"I told your uncle to warn you not to come after me," Billy went on calmly. "I did everything I could to get word to you. I took a chance to do that. But you're just a fool."

"So I'm a fool," Jack managed to say. "That makes two of us."

"Why, Jack? Why did you have to come down here?" He asked the question like a grieving man authentically searching for an answer.

"I came to take you back—or kill you. I don't care which."

Billy shifted in his seat. "You should've known better. How many chances did you think I was going to give you?"

"So you beat me," Jack conceded. "It could've been different. I had to take that chance."

Billy sighed. "I've been watching you. I can't believe you came here. Why couldn't you just leave me alone?"

Jack felt no desire to talk his way out of this situation. He knew well enough that words weren't going to sway Billy. If he intended to shoot, he would. The only thing to do was to tell the truth. "Because you're a murderer," Jack said. "You killed Bob, and you've got to pay for what you did."

Billy's eyes widened in momentary anger, but his voice remained low and controlled. "You know he brought that on himself. You were there. He had no business doing what he did."

"You're lying to yourself. You lied in court, and you're lying now."

Billy responded coolly, "You lied, too."

The charge shocked Jack. "You can't believe that!"

"You told your story," Billy went on patiently, "and I told mine. If you were in my shoes, you'd see things different. You're trying to make me into something I'm not."

"That's bullshit! You made yourself by what you did."

"Get off it! I did what I had to do. Other people see that. The jury saw it. Why can't you?"

"Because I know better, that's why. They just thought you're someone you're not. So did the judge."

"Fuck him! He was against me from day one."

Jack almost laughed, but it didn't get out. He remembered how scared he'd been in Little High Rock Canyon, how bullying Billy had been on that day. It wasn't that way now. "It took him awhile," Jack said, "but Judge Reilley finally pegged you. Everyone else just wanted to believe you were from another century."

Billy spoke in a raspy whisper, as if to address ghosts in the room. "I don't care what they believe. I'm happy to live in this century, and I'd like to see a little more of it in peace, that's all."

Jack lowered his own voice. "You lost that chance. You played too many games."

Billy sounded sad again. "Other people don't know what I've been through. You don't know either. That time I was on the run was worse than anything you can know. Chased like some stupid animal. Scared all the time. Always knowing someone was out to kill me. I went through hell."

"Then why didn't you stay in prison? You just got yourself into the same damn situation all over again."

Billy placed his pistol flat on his knee, holding it so the barrel still pointed at Jack. "I'm going to tell you something. You don't know what it was like in there—cooped up—working on garbage detail. Always hassled, put on cell restriction and close security. I was singled out. Everyone knew it. I had to leave."

Jack couldn't hide his sarcasm. "So Jenny Morrison slipped you some bolt cutters, and you just walked out and rode away with her."

"I escaped on my own. She had nothing to do with it."

"Jenny Morrison visited you that day," Jack persisted. "You could've got them from her."

"What the hell are you talking about?" Billy's outburst seemed to embarrass him. He collected himself, continuing politely, "Think about it. The guards searched me on the way out of the waiting room. I had to walk through a metal detector. They would've found those snips. They were always watching me."

"So her visit was just a coincidence."

Billy nodded. "That's right. They watched her like a hawk. They would've loved to have me walk in with some cutters. They would've loved to have a cover to shoot me for trying to escape."

Jack leaned forward. "But that's exactly what you did. You made a break and gave them a reason to kill you. That doesn't make any sense."

Billy seemed ready for the accusation. "What choice did I have?" he asked matter-of-factly. "I couldn't stand it in there. Living in fear every day. Always harassed. Those bastards were out to crush me one way or another. I had to take a chance."

According to rumors, Crockett had been labeled an escape risk from day one in the joint. Prison guards were supposedly poised to blast him. Jack couldn't figure it. "Why aren't you dead," he asked, "if what you say is true?"

"I didn't make the break when they thought I would. I hid out, then made my run. I lucked out."

"And Georgette Spinelli just happened to be on hand to help you out. I suppose that was a coincidence, too." Jack knew he sounded less sarcastic and more hurt than he wanted to.

"I don't know what you're talking about."

"You were seen in her car driving across Donner Summit."

"I don't know what you're talking about."

"You know damn well what I'm talking about. You're just covering up again for your idiotic friends, like you always do."

Billy lifted the pistol. "I think you better settle down, Jack."

"For what? I'm tired of all this bullshit. Go ahead and shoot me. I don't give a shit. Be a big man and shoot someone sitting here without a weapon."

"I don't want to do that. I don't shoot unarmed men."

"You did it before. Go ahead and do it again."

"Pritchard had a gun. You know that."

"I didn't. Out on the desert. You shot me." Jack pointed to his chest. "Right here."

He felt as though he was groping to pierce some kind of iron wall that separated this man from who he always pretended to be.

"I've tried to explain to you why I did what I did," Billy replied. "I just wanted to be left alone to live the way I wanted. Nobody lived out in that country the way I did. I liked doing for myself, walking the country, seeing the animals. Living alone. It was never easy. It was always hard. But it was my life. I lived it. I tried the very best I could to keep everything right and to be straight. At least what I was doing was natural. It made me happy—"

"Killing things," Jack interrupted. "It made you happy to kill things."

"Don't be a fool, Jack." He sounded like a mild man growing exasperated with someone's willful obtuseness. "What I did was natural. Animals kill other animals to live. That's all I was doing."

"They kill to eat. You just killed to kill."

Billy let out the irritated sigh of a reasonable man gathering his patience. "See it your way, but you know better. City people just let others do the killing for them. Nobody did nothing for me. I took care of myself. That's all I wanted to do."

"You had plenty of people taking care of you. You couldn't have lived out there without a whole bunch of people coddling you. No way are you as tough as you think you are."

"I was tough enough to live that life," Billy spit back. "It was people like you who ruined it—always wanting to step on a free man just because you can't live like him."

Jack could tell that he'd tweaked a nerve. "No, Billy, you're not tough." He knew he was onto it now. He was getting close to it, to saying what he'd always meant to say.

"So what was I supposed to do?" Billy asked. Nothing plaintive haunted his voice anymore. He sounded hard and angry. "Just let you pussies stomp me down? Just let you take away my traps and hides and everything I worked to get in my life? Just hunker down like some scared rabbit and let you cage me up? Just let you take away my life and make me live like all the rest of you dogs in your slimy cages?"

"Or trailers," Jack interjected. "Isn't that where you lived most of the time? In a scummy trailer behind a bar full of scuzzballs who told lies about what a big, tough guy you were? But you know you're not as tough as they said, don't you?"

Billy raised the pistol. "Don't push it."

"Why don't you throw down that peashooter, Billy, and let's have it out, you and me, like men, without the toys. What do you say, punk? Are you game?"

Billy's grip tightened on the pistol. "You're asking for it."

"Go ahead, Mr. Phony Tough Guy." Jack knew he had it now. "You know it's the truth." Then he said it. "You're not tough, Billy. You're mean, but you're not tough."

In the darkness, a yellow flame spit from the pistol barrel. The bullet ripped through Jack's calf, knocking him to the floor. He sat up and grabbed for his leg. Blood squirted between his fingers. He squeezed his burning calf through the soaked pants. When he looked up, Billy was already walking out the door. This time he hadn't even said, "Sorry, Jack."

CHAPTER 15

Billy was arrested in California four months after he returned from Mexico. Nine FBI agents surrounded him at midafternoon in a San Bernardino parking lot as he came out of a Stop N' Go store with a bag of groceries. He was captured unarmed and without a fight. Two of his buckaroo buddies from Paradise Valley, Gary Valdez and Tommy White, were also arrested in San Bernardino. The FBI charged them with harboring Crockett, but they were released the next day because of insufficient evidence.

The newspaper reported Billy's father as saying that stool pigeons had helped the FBI. "I'm proud of my boy," William David Crockett, Sr., said, from his Memphis mobile home. "He eluded those goons for almost a year. But he would've been better off down here in the hills of Tennessee than out there in Los Angeles. If there was a fight I'd have liked to have been in it. All those damn stool pigeons up there, what chance did he have? People will do anything for a dollar. The FBI's really got them. They're just like fleas on a dog's back."

According to the paper, Billy's capture had shocked Jenny Morrison, especially the news that he'd been living in San Bernardino. She also thought that someone like Valdez or White had snitched on him. "I'm sorry they caught him, but I didn't think they'd ever give up trying. He would've been better off here in Nevada. He's coyote smart and would've been tough to catch in the wilds. I think they're going to do all they can to keep him in jail the rest of his life."

The paper identified Jenny as the woman who had visited Billy a few hours before he snipped through two prison fences and escaped into the desert under cover of darkness. "I had no idea he was planning an escape," Jenny said. About the $35,000 she and her husband had raised for his defense six years ago, she said, "I'd do it again."

Jack told Jim Sandoval that he didn't want to testify at the trial.

"Come on, Jack," Jim pleaded. "Billy shot you again. That's proof that he's violent and dangerous."

"He shot me in the leg," Jack explained. "They'd turn it around like they did last time and say that Billy was just defending himself. They'd say I was down there to kill him and he was just protecting himself."

"But you were unarmed."

"They wouldn't say that."

"Well, it would be your word against his."

"I've been through that before. I'm not going through it again. And anyway, I did go down there to get him."

"So now's your chance to really get him, if you testify."

"They've got enough on him with his breakout. That's indisputable. They won't have any trouble nailing him for escaping from prison."

Jim persisted. "Escape is a continuous crime, Jack. It doesn't end when a guy cuts through wires. Crockett was escaping when he was down in Mexico and shot you. You're living evidence of his crime."

"I don't want to testify, Jim."

"You'll have to, of course, if you're called."

"The prosecutor will wish he hadn't called me."

"You're just being a blockheaded Basco."

"Look, Jim, what you've got to understand is that I'm through with Billy. The game is over as far as I'm concerned."

"And he won, is that what you're saying?"

"No, I wouldn't say that. He shot me, but I wouldn't say he won."

What Jack didn't bother trying to explain was that winning or losing had nothing to do with it anymore. When Billy shot him and walked out of the bungalow in Mexico, he walked off the board as far as Jack was concerned. So did every other tough-guy hero he'd grown up wanting to be.

In Zihuatanejo, the motel manager had rushed into the room and wrapped Jack's leg with a towel while Billy nonchalantly sauntered down the beach way. No one tried to stop him. With bands playing along the way and *cohetes* exploding in the air, only a few people would have heard the pop of the little .22. Fewer would've cared.

A doctor cleaned and dressed the wound. Then Jack spent two hours at the municipal police station while a guy in front of an ancient manual typewriter pecked out a report in triplicate. By the time the police reached the hotel, Billy was gone. He was probably gone from Zihuatanejo. Now Jack wanted him gone from his life.

What he couldn't explain to Jim Sandoval was that when he returned from Mexico and went back to work full time, he no longer felt about Billy as he had in the past. When Billy was caught, Jack experienced an immense relief. His leg ached whenever the weather changed, and he sometimes found himself limping, but the pain and the limp didn't call to mind Billy so much as that gimpy burro on a Mexican road. Jack wasn't about to try to explain to Jim Sandoval his feelings about a crippled donkey.

He did tell Beth, though, at Uncle Pete's funeral. Two months after Billy's capture, Mrs. Rodriguez found Pete dead of a stroke, lying in the pasture, where he had gone to change some irrigation water. Jack regretted not seeing his uncle since the visit after Billy's escape, but he'd talked to Pete a couple of times on the phone. During the last conversation, Pete had come as close as he ever would to saying good-bye, though he didn't use that word. He'd just said, "So long."

On the way to Winnemucca, Jack passed the garish Indian monument, now torched and abandoned.

After the funeral Beth said, "I was always fond of Pete. He was my favorite of your relatives."

"I liked him, too," Jack said. "The old coot."

At the Pyrenees Motel, where he and Beth were both staying, in separate rooms, he told her about what had happened in Mexico. They'd seen each other several times in the past few months, but he hadn't yet told her about his walk on the dirt road.

"It's wonderful," Beth said, "how life always gives us second chances."

He knew she wasn't talking about the two of them. She no longer brought up their getting back together. They both seemed to know that second chances only mattered if past mistakes weren't repeated.

Beth unfolded an article, clipped from the *Reno Gazette-Journal*, that she'd been saving for him. The piece had helped her understand what had happened at Billy's first trial.

"I could never figure why that jury had bought Billy's story," Beth mused. "I knew it didn't have anything to do with the facts. It was just him, the way he came across."

The article reported that in a long study of courtroom trials, a behavioral psychologist had found that the more baby-faced the defendant looked—doe eyes, chipmunk cheeks, and a teddy bear chin like, say, Paul McCartney—the more likely he was to be acquitted of crimes involving intentional misconduct. Such a person, however, would likely be found guilty when charged with negligent behavior, such as falling asleep at the wheel of a ship.

For a tough, mature-faced man with wide cheekbones and a rugged jawline, like Clint Eastwood, the exact reverse was true. He wouldn't be convicted of negligence, but he was likely to get nailed for intentionally killing somebody.

"So it's all in the face," Jack said, reluctant to follow Beth into these pop theories.

Her response surprised him. "Up to a point," she said. "Billy did have that baby-faced look, you know, cute and cuddly. Even you said that if some tough old desert trapper like Jess Nichols had been in Billy's place, he would've got slammed with first-degree murder."

"You bet," Jack agreed. "But now Billy's changed his face. He looks more like the tough guy he wanted to be."

"But not completely," Beth said. "He's kind of half and half."

"So he's ideal." Jack sensed a renewal of agitation about Billy. He'd thought he had rid himself of those feelings. He wished Beth hadn't brought up this subject. He was getting annoyed. "Now he's both manly *and* cuddly, a soap-opera dream."

"Not quite. He's still got those scary eyes. That's why I could never figure what happened with the women on that jury. Sure, he had that baby face, but he has such cold eyes."

They hugged and kissed each other in the parking lot when it was time to leave. Beth touched his cheek. "I'm glad things are this way between us," she said.

"It's better this way, isn't it?"

Beth nodded. "I guess we get what we want when we quit wanting it."

They kissed again, then headed back to Sparks in their separate cars.

Billy's trial was set for late April. Jack planned not to attend. Then he changed his mind. He even began to think that maybe he should testify. He almost called up the prosecutor—he'd already talked to him twice—but decided to stick with his original decision. The prosecutor assured him that the state had a strong enough case against Billy that Jack needn't take the stand unless he wanted to.

The other thing working against Billy was that the public mood had changed. People had his number. Billy's luck seemed to be running out. After his capture the *Gazette-Journal* ran a headline: CROCKETT CAPTURE HO-HUM STUFF IN SAN BERDOO. The headline of another article asked, JUST HOW TOUGH IS BILLY CROCKETT? SOME ARGUE IT WAS FRIENDS, NOT SKILLS, THAT KEPT HIM FREE. "Yes, he shot deer," the article said, "but he swapped most of the game meat for canned food, cookies, and pies. Do we have a true western hero left anywhere?"

A funny column on the op-ed page was titled A CROCK CALLED CROCKETT. "Now, let me see if I got this straight," the columnist asked.

"Mountain Man" Billy Crockett was captured while he was *busy buying groceries in a convenience store in a suburb of Los Angeles where he was being sheltered by some "cowboy" friends.*

I want to know a couple of things—first, what, exactly was Crockett purchasing in the store? I mean, are we talking Twinkies here? Beenie Weenie? Chap Stick? Was this rough-and-tumble Man of the Wild poaching Spam out of season?

And who were these "cowboys" they keep talking

about? If these were indeed riders of the sage, they must have been members of the Drugstore Brigade. It's tough to visualize a buckaroo riding old Lightnin' down Sepulveda and whooping it up in the L.A. suburbs.

When some kid on the mean streets of New York blows away a cop, we call him a menace to society or a crackhead. A jerk, anyway. And we want to see him fry.

Billy Crockett guns down a cop and an innocent bystander, and a cry goes up that he should go free because he represents the Last of a Dying Breed.

The writer ended his column with a ditty called "The Ballad of Billy Crockett."

"C'mon out, Billy," the bullhorn squealed.
"And I mean come out now!"
The Mountain Man, he turned and ran
Behind the Meister Brau.

A shot rang out! Crockett scurried
For another place to hide.
He ended up behind a wall
Of newer, whiter Tide.

The siege wore on throughout the day.
Crockett knew there was no hope.
He sadly found the mouthwash aisle
And drank a quart of Scope.

And when at last the cuffs were on,
Billy said he meant no harmin'.
But the cops tacked to the murder charge,
Five counts—of squeezin' Charmin.

After Billy was extradited back to Nevada State Prison to await his trial, he dropped from the news. Budget cuts had left Jack's office shorthanded, and he was busier than ever with herd counts and strutting-ground surveys. He and the wardens were also having trouble with people poaching bears.

Two bear corpses had been found on Mount Rose, their paws and galls gone. On the Korean black market, galls sold for thousands of dollars. Paws ended up in gourmet soup in San Francisco restaurants, and claws found their way into high-priced silver and turquoise necklaces sold on Indian reservations or at mountain-men rendezvous. Jack knew they were dealing with a hard-core poaching operation that was going to be tough to crack.

Good news came from Wendell that he would support Jack's application for the warden's position that was due to open up with Dale Ellison's retirement. Jack had applied, but with all his past troubles he felt that the state review team would probably weed him out as emotionally and psychologically unstable. But Wendell believed in redemption and went to bat for him, arguing that Jack's triumph over booze demonstrated strength of character. The bad-luck affair in Mexico was not common knowledge—it never made the papers—and Wendell, wily Christian that he was, forgot to mention it. He knew how important it was for Jack to finish the work that Bob Pritchard had begun.

Jack didn't share Wendell's sense of triumph over the hooch. He still met with his group, and he had faltering moments, but he struggled along, as they advised, one day at a time. "It's funny, though," he told Beth one night on the phone. "You were right. Most of the time I've just quit wanting it, and I feel like I'm getting what I used to want."

He'd started giving talks to schoolchildren. He stayed away from gory poaching stories and tried to get kids to think about how birds and animals in their complicated lives made this world beautiful. He always told the schoolchildren about the Indian boy he knew in college who'd said that all animals and humans in the world were part of an intertwined and continuous chain. "The problem is that most people think humans are the center of the chain," the Paiute boy had said. "That's not true. We're just one of the links."

One day an eighth-grader raised his hand and said that his dad was a farrier who claimed that Paiutes and Shoshones were rougher on horses than anybody. They rode them too hard and didn't take care of sores or wounds.

Jack knew that horses with reservation brands were often the most thick-skinned, cantankerous, and broken-spirited in the state, but he told the boy that not everyone treated animals as they should, even Indians.

He avoided the Bambi stuff and showed slides of real animals. He passed around copies of Bob's drawings, which the kids seemed to like. He wondered at times if he might be turning some kids into vegetarians. It could get harder for them to eat a KFC drumstick if they kept imagining the living, breathing thing it came from.

"I'm never going to eat meat," Carrie told him one day after he'd visited her class. Going on fourteen, she was skeleton skinny with sallow cheeks and blue hollows under her eyes. Beth worried about her. So did he. Being a vegetarian was one thing, but Carrie wouldn't even eat Beth's health-food bulgur or greens. Pop-Tarts, rock-salt pretzels, Dunkin' Donuts, and frozen yogurt were the only things she deigned to nibble.

On the weekends she and Sarah spent with him, Carrie responded to anything he cooked, even soybean hot dogs, with one word. "Gross," she said, while wrinkling her snubby nose.

Carrie watched MTV, played with her pet rat named Squeaky, looked at the pictures in *Teen,* and thought about the party clothes she had to buy. Jack could never get her to read a book. A thin, tightly twined braid appeared in her blond hair, and she changed her clothes two or three times a day, usually emulating the fashions of her idol Drew Barrymore, the child actress whose pictures hung on her bedroom wall. In one of them the teenage star sprawled naked in a grassy meadow.

One Saturday, during a window-shopping trip to an antique

clothes store called Wonderland, Carrie had seen a short black velvet dress with a sequined red heart on the front that she wanted her father to buy her for a Valentine's Day party.

"Valentine's Day," Jack objected in a stern voice, "is almost a year away, Carrie."

"This dress is very groovy, Daddy, and it will be gone if I wait."

Everything with her was either groovy, cool, weird, or gross. Jack wondered how it had become hip for these kids to use words from the fifties that he and his friends had used in grammar school when they thought pink and black shoelaces were groovy.

The big poster from *Terminator 2*, also hanging in Carrie's bedroom, worried him. What kind of heroes and heroines did the movies give children to idolize these days?

One night, he asked her about Schwarzenegger. What did she see in him?

"He docsn't take shit from nobody," Carrie said.

"Anybody," he corrected her.

"What?"

"The word is 'anybody.' You can't use a double negative."

"Oh, Daddy, why don't you just let me talk like other people?"

"So this guy doesn't take anything from anybody. Is that what you think is so groovy about that movie?"

"Haven't you seen it?"

"No, and I don't think I'm going to."

"Well, you should. Eddie Furlong plays the boy in it. I'm going to marry Eddie Furlong when I grow up."

He didn't know what he was going to do with Carrie. People in his therapy group told him not to let his own sense of guilt make him too permissive with her. Tough love, he was told, was what kids needed today. He had trouble with that notion, when what he felt for his daughters was just love, without the rough qualification.

One Saturday afternoon, he saw Carrie and Sarah sprawled on the couch with their heads hanging over the edge staring down at the floor where a hand mirror reflected their images back up to them. "What are you doing?" he asked.

"This is very weird, Daddy," Carrie answered. "This is how you can see what you'll look like when you get old."

That night after the girls were in bed he put a mirror on the floor and bent over. It *was* weird. The skin sagged from his face. There was something about the change in his features that was odd. He didn't look like himself anymore. He decided it might be a good idea to grow a mustache, not like Crockett's, but more trimmed and distinguished, like Bob's.

CHAPTER 16

Good news reached Jack that he'd been selected to replace Dale Ellison as a Washoe warden. He was sent to POST for training. A few weeks before Billy's trial, in April of 1991, he received his warden's badge. He felt a need to celebrate and called Beth. They went to Louie's Basque Corner with Wendell and his wife, Sue, for a special dinner of tripe and lamb shanks.

Wendell gave a toast. "Here's to Bob Pritchard and the new man to continue his work."

"The best man," Beth added, "to do that work."

They lifted their glasses of picon punch, Jack his O'Doul's, and clinked glasses.

Billy's trial finally started on a Monday. Jack skipped the first two days and arrived at the courthouse on Wednesday when Billy was scheduled to testify. The courtroom, as expected, was packed. Jack recognized Billy's Belles and some of the women from the previous jury. Georgette Spinelli, wearing purplish rouge and dark eye shadow, sat among the spectators, staring straight ahead with that insouciant look of hers. She'd streaked and curled her hair so that it tumbled to her shoulders much like Beth's. Jack kept looking at her. He wondered if she was still seeing Jim Sandoval. He'd learned that his earlier suspicions had finally been fulfilled. Georgette and Jim had hooked up shortly after Billy's escape.

Jack was sorry Cindy Pritchard hadn't come, for Bob's sake, but she'd moved to Los Angeles and—rumor had it—remarried.

When Billy took the stand he looked husky, almost chubby, and more mature than at his last trial. He also seemed more forthright. Not once did his thickly mustached lip curl into that earlier mocking sneer. He no longer wore glasses. He looked directly at individual members of the jury as he retraced the steps of his nearly yearlong escape from prison. He seemed like someone just trying to tell the truth. He maintained that in escaping he had been trying to protect his life. The law allowed an inmate to escape if he acted without criminal intent and without violence, under duress and necessity, to avoid a specific, imminent threat of death, sexual attack, or substantial bodily harm. That was the legal loophole his defense attorneys were pursuing. The escape, they maintained, was justified.

"I was somewhat worried about getting set up in prison," Billy said calmly. "My feeling at the time, people, was that my life was in danger. The administration tried frame-ups by getting snitches to plant lockpicks and bolt cutters in my locker. They had a kangaroo court to reclassify me. I had thirty days of solitary and a year of close custody. Guards had my picture hanging in the towers. I got reports that they practiced shooting at my picture on the target range. The authorities claimed they had to concentrate on escape risks, but I was afraid how they intended to concentrate their AR-15s on me. Christ, it was persistent. Everybody knew it."

When asked about specific guards threatening him, Billy said, "In October of 1989, inmate Carter reported to me that he'd heard Lieutenant Norris make a statement that if he had the chance he'd be more than happy to take me out. Lieutenant Norris was up in tower four—that's right above where I worked when I was on garbage detail. At that time, I felt a riot was imminent. We had a lot of new young guys in there, a lot of hotheads, a lot of anger and energy. The older inmates tried to keep things calm, but the tension was getting out of control. I felt the place could go off any minute. I knew if the joint blew, I'd be iced. Christ, I had nowhere to turn, nowhere to seek relief. I'd filed lawsuits and complaints, but it was always futile. I made up my mind that it was necessary for me to leave—or I'd be dead. About five days passed while I worked out my plan. Then about 8 P.M., on a Sunday, I escaped."

Billy wouldn't give any details about how he'd got the bolt cutters or eluded the guards. "I just want to make it clear right now, people," he said, raising his voice for the first time. "I did not get into a car in the parking lot. I did not go to a bar in Gerlach."

The qualification *in the parking lot* put iron into Billy's voice. Investigators were almost certain that Billy had climbed into Jenny Morrison's car, not in the parking lot, but somewhere outside the prison grounds. That qualification gave his remark enough truth for him to express it with outraged conviction. Jack felt simmering that old rage at Billy's ability to express half-truths and quarter-truths so credibly. He had to hand it to the guy. He was a good storyteller, a good liar.

"I fled afoot into the desert," Billy went on, "for about eleven days. Like I say, I didn't go to Gerlach. I was afoot. I did eventually make contact with someone. About eleven days from here. That's all I'll say."

During cross-examination the prosecutor asked Billy to reveal the names of people who had helped him during his escape. He refused. The prosecutor asked the judge to order Billy to answer.

"I can't identify people," Billy objected. "They were extremely loyal friends. They placed a great deal of trust in me. They're family people. They know I'm trustworthy. That's why they're not here to testify on my behalf. They could be prosecuted for aiding in a federal offense. I refuse to ruin them."

During a break when the jury was removed and the judge consulted attorneys about a state objection, Jack went into the hall. He longed for a dip, but this time he intended to stay quit. Georgette leaned against a gray wall, smoking a cigarette.

"Hello, Jack," she said, shooting smoke from her nostrils. "I almost didn't recognize you with that mustache."

He involuntarily raised his fingers to his upper lip. "I guess it makes a difference."

"It does on you. Billy and you don't look all that different anymore."

He felt awkward with what hovered unspoken. He hadn't seen Georgette since that bad night over a year ago. He had eventually tried to apologize to her on the phone, but she had hung up. Then he learned she was seeing Jim Sandoval, and he didn't try to get in touch with her again. She'd helped Billy escape, got involved with Jim, then turned around and snitched on Billy. Jack felt a need to understand where she stood.

"What brought you to this show?" he asked. "I don't see many of Billy's other good friends exposing themselves."

"Jenny Morrison's here, so are a lot of the ladies. But I'm not one of the Belles."

"You helped him escape," Jack said, feeling his heart speed up. Georgette's attractive composure made it hard to accuse her. "That's what Belles are supposed to do."

She remained poised. "It wasn't voluntary. Billy showed up at my apartment and told me I was going to drive him to Frisco."

Jack hadn't expected that revelation. "Then you can't be prosecuted for helping him. Why aren't you testifying against him?"

"I was willing, but the prosecutor challenged me. He didn't want me on the stand. I don't know what he was afraid of. That's his mistake. What's your excuse?"

"I didn't think I'd do any good."

"That isn't what Jim said. He said you wimped out."

"Well, Jim's wrong," Jack snapped. "I decided that I was willing to testify if it would help. But the prosecutor said he didn't need me. I don't report to Jim on everything I do. He doesn't know."

Georgette took a drag on her cigarette. "You have bad feelings because I started seeing Jim, don't you?"

"Well, wouldn't you?"

"You and I were quits. I was free to go out with whoever I wanted."

Jack felt himself getting close to the root of his earlier animosity toward her. "But it started before we were quits. That's the problem. There were others."

"But not Jim," she said. "That started afterwards."

Behind Georgette, the eight women and four men of the jury followed the bailiff back into the courtroom. Jack realized he was trying to justify what had happened between him and Georgette to himself, if not to her. But there was no justification. He tried to cut off the tack he'd taken. He was the one who'd been in the wrong. "Well, I'm glad you're happy," he said, "you and Jim."

"We're not seeing each other anymore," Georgette said. "Jim's got problems, but he's trying to take care of them."

"Problems?"

"I probably shouldn't tell you, but it might help your attitude. Jim's joined Sexual Compulsives Anonymous. He's in a group."

Jack felt as though he'd been popped on the skull with a blackjack. It's happening to all of us, he thought. We're all in groups. Maybe Billy would join a group for cop killers. After all, cop killers also had their problems and oppressions. They were probably victimized by their parents, too.

"I want to go back in," Georgette said. "It's been nice talking to you, Jack."

She didn't sound sarcastic. He touched her on the arm, stopping her. "Georgette, hold on a minute. I just want to tell you—I mean, I just want to say that I'm sorry about what happened. I mean it."

She looked past him, gazing at the wall. Grief clouded her eyes. "I've had worse happen," she said in a matter-fact tone, as if addressing no one in particular.

Georgette hadn't said, "That's all right," or "I forgive you," and he was just as glad. Despite all the contrary sentiment and promptings of his group, he couldn't forgive himself either.

She brushed his cheek with the tip of her index finger and turned toward the courtroom.

Jack took his seat among the spectators. He missed hearing the first few questions because he was thinking about Jim Sandoval. He still didn't trust the guy. He was wary of Jim's motive for joining a group. If a person was indeed sexually compulsive, what better place to try to pick up someone than at a group for sexual compulsives?

On the stand, Billy was saying, "My intention when I left the prison was to put the money together so I could fight these people and get my convictions overturned."

Even if Billy's escape had been justified, the law still maintained that he was obligated to notify authorities of his escape after reaching a place of safety. But Billy had never called authorities while on the run. He had stayed hidden for eleven months and twelve days. He'd fled the country. As the prosecutor said, he was so safe from any threat to his life that even the FBI couldn't find him for 353 days.

"I never felt safe," Billy insisted. "I didn't want to be on the run the rest of my life. It was a matter of family. I was over a hundred thousand dollars in debt for my earlier legal fees, and I couldn't pay that back on the run. But first I needed to raise at least fifteen thousand dollars for legal help. I felt it would take about a year for me to put the money together. Just by working. That's what I knew how to do and what I wanted to do."

Jack grew irritated. The yarn mocked the facts. During his year on the lam, Billy had never demonstrated any intention of turning himself in. He'd never even tried.

"It would've been crazy to turn myself in before I had the funds," Billy continued, "what with the propaganda the FBI was putting out on me in their releases and wanted posters. They were saying how I'd demonstrated violence numerous times, shot it out with the FBI, how I swore they'd never capture me, they'd never take me alive. These are statements I never made. I never had a felony conviction before I went to prison. I never shot at the FBI. The FBI shot at *me*. I was very much afraid of the FBI. Everyone I met said that law enforcement people had no intention of taking me alive."

Billy insisted that as soon as he'd escaped he began to carry out his plan to get back on his feet so he could raise money for legal help. He went to the Bay Area to look for work. He got himself pretty well set up there but then had to flee because of a news flash.

"I fled to Nevada—country I knew. I hid out for a while, afoot again. Then I made my way back to California, up to Fort Bragg. I had to start all over. There are all kinds of jobs I can do—run heavy equipment, custom farm work, dig wells, cut timber. That was no problem. But I knew if I was going to get back into the work force I needed a change of appearance. I'm talking about cosmetic surgery now. I put together three thousand dollars, but I was afraid to approach any surgeons in this country. I crossed the Mexican border in June of 1990. I found a Mexican surgeon and stayed down there four months or so while I healed up. I sensed Mexican authorities were onto me and I fled. I could've gone to South America, but I returned with my plan to fight this thing. I went up to Oregon. I didn't want to be in a big city, but I thought that Corvallis was of sufficient size that I could be anonymous. After two weeks, I didn't like the feel of things. I was always reported wearing glasses, wire-rim glasses, that sort of thing, so I got fitted with contact lenses to further my identity change. Then I went down to the L.A. area."

Billy said he'd been in San Bernardino only three or four days before the FBI got ahold of him. He had a motel room and went into a convenience store to pick up some sandwich things. He had a funny feeling something was going on. A black woman had followed him into the store and was carrying on a suspicious conversation with the man at the counter. Billy let the woman go out of the store in front of him, then walked across the parking lot with his bag of groceries.

"A man stepped out of a car and threw down a revolver on me. Then other cars pulled up, and people jumped out with rifles and revolvers. One car kind of squirreled across the lot and almost hit me. They were all yelling different things: 'Drop the bag,' 'Put up your hands,' 'Don't move.' I was very much concerned. I had a jar of crunchy peanut butter in the paper sack and I didn't want to let it drop. I knew it would make quite a pop. I was afraid of what they might do if that happened. I wasn't going to give them a chance."

After his arrest, Billy waived extradition and was returned to Nevada.

The prosecutor asked Billy about the help he had received from family and friends during his first trial. He answered that he had received about $10,000 from a brother in Vermont and another $5,000 from his father. Friends in Nevada had raised $35,000.

"Between your conviction for manslaughter and your sentence hearing you were free on bond," the prosecutor said. "Is that correct?"

"Yes, that's right."

"Who put up that bond?"

"A good friend of mine," Billy said. "Someone I had worked for in Oregon."

"And how much was that bond?"

"A hundred thousand dollars," Billy answered.

"No further questions," the prosecutor said.

Jack had to skip the trial on Thursday because during the night garbagemen had found a dead bear in a Dumpster on the outskirts of Reno. He went to check it out. The carcass lay in garbage, covered with buzzing green flies, its four paws hacked off, its stomach slit open. The bear was a sow, still thin from its winter's hibernation. Somewhere in the mountains a cub probably wandered looking for its mother.

Up in Washington, thousands of bears had fallen to poachers, fewer down here. Bears were shy loners. Except during mating season and with their cubs, they wandered the mountains in solitude. Poachers had to get them one at a time. It wasn't easy, but as long as entrepreneurs in Korea who wore Gucci shoes and drove Porsches still believed in the thaumaturgical cure-all of powdered galls, someone would be willing to pop a bear for a few dollars. Then black-market middlemen in Los Angeles and San Francisco would grind dried gall bladders worth a few hundred dollars into a powder worth thousands. A new day still had to come before it all stopped.

At the office Jack filled out a report. His file on bear poaching was getting thick, but until he got a lead, there was nothing he could do to stop the killing. He made some calls to wildlife people in California to see if they'd heard anything about the illegal sale of bear parts, but they had nothing helpful to report. The other Washoe warden was out of town, working near the Sheldon National Wildlife Refuge on the northern border. Correspondence and paperwork had piled up, and Jack stayed late at the office to get some of it cleared away.

On the way home, he drove by the courthouse. A number of people milled around outside. He learned that the testimony had ended and the jury was in deliberation. "They haven't left the jury room," a woman told him, "so they must be near a decision."

Jack found a bench in the hall to wait. It was about nine-thirty. The woman was probably right. The jury would've quit for the night if a verdict wasn't imminent.

Jack tried to think of what those eight women and four men might be considering. The state had proved the fact of Billy's escape beyond a doubt, but that wasn't the issue. The burden of justification for Billy's escape and for his failure to notify authorities lay with the defense.

At one point during the trial when the jury was out of the courtroom, the judge had commented to the prosecutor that it was irritating to have the prison system put on trial, but counsel had a right to its chosen defense. "A threat to life that is both specific and imminent is at issue here," the judge had said. "I haven't yet heard a report of such a threat, but I expect it to be made."

But it never was. There were only rumors, hearsay. During his years in prison Billy had filed incessant grievances and lawsuits, but not once had he filed a complaint about anyone threatening him. He'd been dauntless in his attempts to get his manslaughter conviction overturned and to render grievances about prison classifications, detentions, and close-security placed on him. Jack had to give him credit. The guy was incorrigible. He had relentless energy. Jack found himself in the awkward, uncomfortable position of admiring a murderer for his drive.

No doubt Billy had focused on escaping prison from day one. He'd probably got the bolt cutters from the prison industries shop where he'd worked as a janitor. He knew he was an escape risk. But his picture hanging in the guard towers was nothing unusual. Twenty to thirty pictures of inmates who were considered security risks hung in those towers.

Billy's yarn that he needed a year of work to put together fifteen thousand dollars for legal fees before he felt safe enough to surrender just didn't hold water. He hadn't worked. He got the dough for cosmetic surgery from friends. No telling how much they'd given him during his year on the run. They had put up a hundred and fifty thousand for his earlier trial. To such friends, legal fees of fifteen thousand would've been a piffle. Billy wanted out, and he wanted to stay out.

It was about ten-thirty when the bailiff announced that the jury had reached a verdict and the court was in session. The jury had deliberated for five and a half hours. They looked haggard. Two of the women sobbed. Others wiped their eyes with handkerchiefs. One man repeatedly blew his nose.

The bailiff handed the written decision to the judge, who glanced at the paper and looked up. "I'm not going to keep you in suspense, Mr. Crockett," the judge said. "You've been acquitted."

As gasps and murmurs rose from the crowd, Billy stammered for a moment, then responded in a firm voice, "Judge, thank you."

The bailiff spoke loudly, "Court's still in order. Take it easy, folks."

The clerk officially announced the verdict, "Not guilty," and the prosecutor waived a poll of individual jurors.

Jack was as stunned as the defense lawyers appeared to be. The judge had invited those who wished to discuss the trial into the jury room, but before anyone moved, reporters circled Billy's attorneys.

"This acquittal is a wonderful surprise," the chief defense lawyer was telling reporters. "The optimum outcome we expected was a hung jury. But Mr. Crockett had reason and justification under the law to leave that institution. He is the best natural witness I've ever seen. He can articulate his own defense better than anyone else can."

Jack tried to find the prosecutor but couldn't. He went up to one of the women on the jury whose cheeks were damp with tears. She was talking to a group of spectators. "This was very hard," she said. "Everyone in the jury felt bad and mad. It was a real close call. We were all teary-eyed. We were cutting really fine lines, but we finally shifted in favor of the defense on the grounds of criminal intent. We felt that the state never really proved that Mr. Crockett had escaped without justification. They never proved beyond a reasonable doubt that he had no intention of returning."

"They didn't have to," Jack said, sounding more angry than he'd intended.

People near the woman glowered, but a man said, "Juries definitely misinterpret judges' instructions. Crockett's lawyers helped them do that."

Jack walked back to where reporters were still talking to the defense lawyers. One of the attorneys from San Francisco, although he never spoke in court, was a noted expert on jury selection. Jack had read in the newspaper that the expert had offered his services to the defense for a reduced fee. He had also been involved in the trial that had led to the acquittal of that New York subway gunman Bernard Goetz who shot four black kids.

"Mr. Crockett is a very charismatic witness," the lawyer told reporters. "He's the type of guy who can be very intimidating if you meet him on the corner, but he speaks very well—slowly and with great conviction. He makes great eye contact. It's quite natural for him. He does it one-on-one. That can be very persuasive in a jury trial."

A reporter asked, "Is that what made the difference in the verdict?"

"Oh, no," the attorney replied. "It was only one of many things. The prosecution used one of his six peremptory challenges on someone who would have been very good for his case. We were also fortunate to have eight good women on the jury. Statistically, women tend to be more understanding and liberal in evaluating a criminal defense." The lawyer smiled at the reporters. "The main thing, of course, is that we were on the right side."

On the way home, Jack tuned in the car radio to a local talk show where callers were already discussing the case. The talk-show host put through a call to a writer back east who had published a book about Billy. "It's the age we live in," the writer said. "Image is all that counts. We have a PR president, PR heroes, and PR prisoners."

When Jack got home, the dark house felt particularly empty and lonely. He was glad his daughters were coming for the weekend. He was grateful for the diversion. He didn't want his embitterment about Billy to get out of control. He tried to persuade himself that the outcome of the trial didn't make that much difference. If Billy had been convicted, the maximum sentence for escape was only another five years. Billy had to return to prison anyway to continue his thirty-year sentence for manslaughter. Plans had already been made to ship him out of state to Nebraska State Penitentiary. After he served some time there, he'd be moved to New Mexico. They would keep moving him around to thwart any efforts of escape. But who knew what would happen when he came up for parole? He was due for review soon. By the mid-1990s, he could be free.

The red light on the answering machine blinked its signal. The message was from Scotty Larsen, saying that Jack could return the call anytime.

It was almost midnight. Jack wished for a splash of Drambuie, just a nightcap. Nothing more. But none was in the house.

He dialed Scotty's number. He could tell from the man's voice that he'd been asleep.

"I just wanted you to know," Scotty said, "that I came across some bear bait when I was photographing up on Mount Rose this morning. There was bear sign and what looked like some blood, too."

These days Scotty was doing more photographing than trapping or guiding. His life had changed direction.

"Will it be hard for me to find?"

"No," Scotty answered. "I can tell you right where it is."

Jack then called Beth to tell her that he planned to be back the next day in time to pick up the girls in the afternoon, but if something developed he might be tied up until a bit later. "I'll call you as soon as I get in."

"Is Roger going with you?" Beth asked, meaning the other Washoe warden.

"He's up north. I'll call Dennis Simmons, our new game biologist. He's been involved in this bear deal."

"I wish another warden was going to be with you."

"It'll be all right. I don't expect any trouble. By the way, did you hear about Billy? He was acquitted."

"I heard it on the news," Beth replied, "just before I went to bed. What a travesty!"

"It doesn't really matter. He still has to go back to prison."

"An escape conviction would've helped keep him there. I just don't want him to get out."

"Even though he did get off, he didn't help his chances for parole. He's more of a security risk now than ever. They'll keep the clamps on him."

"But he will get out someday."

"Someday. But he has to do his time. That's not easy for him. His years in prison have already been hell on him because he fights it every day. Billy wants to be free real bad."

Beth didn't respond for a moment. "It sounds as though you're almost defending the guy."

Her accusation startled him. "I don't want to do that," he said. "But I will say one thing for him. He dreams about more than just money."

"It's a rotten dream."

"A confused one, anyway. The problem is a lot of people have it all confused."

"You be careful, honey," Beth said, "when you go out there."

"I will," he assured her. "I'll call you tomorrow."

He hung up, grateful for her concern. It gladdened his heart. He felt himself a lucky man.

He looked up Dennis Simmons's number and picked up the phone. It was now a little after midnight. Dennis would be asleep. His young wife would be asleep. They had just recently had their first child, a little girl. She would also be asleep. Jack imagined Dennis telling his wife what was happening and kissing her good-bye. Maybe then he would kiss his daughter good-bye. Jack put down the phone. He'd go alone.

Plenty of moonlight lit his way as he followed the Forest Service trail up Mount Rose. Smells of ponderosa and sugar pine spiced the cool air. The trail was dry. It was the fifth year of drought, so bears were coming down into the low country for berries.

Jack picked up some tracks and switched on the flashlight. He knew that sometimes it was hard for people to believe they were seeing bear tracks. Like a man, a bear walked on the entire sole with the heel touching the ground, leaving tracks turned in slightly at the front, as if made by a flat-footed man in moccasins.

Jack switched off the flashlight and cut off the trail, bushwhacking north, so that he would circle to where Scotty had reported finding the bear bait. A breeze blew out of the west, noisily stirring the tall spruce and pines. He stayed downwind as he worked through buckbrush and spotted a five-gallon can in the moonlit clearing. The wind carried the smell of rotted meat. Hunters often put out a can of horsemeat or garbage to attract game, or they shot a goat or dog and dumped the carcass in a shallow pit. Sometimes they used dogs to tree a bear, but more often they used bait. Once a bear found the food, it would return nightly to eat. Sport hunters sometimes liked to watch the animal feed for a couple of nights before flashing on their lights. The startled bear would then look up from its dinner, searching into the glare with its weak, close-knit eyes until a slug knocked it dead and a hunter claimed his kill.

About eight feet up the trunk of a nearby ponderosa, a piece of plywood had been nailed on supports to form a bench. Bears rarely glanced up. They met most threats at ground level, and hunters or poachers overhead wouldn't be noticed unless their scent gave them away.

No one else was around. Jack stretched out on his stomach downwind behind some buckbrush and waited. He pulled the .357 Magnum from its holster and laid it near his face on a dry bed of pine needles. He held the twelve-gauge pump shotgun in his hands. This time he would be ready.

An hour passed. Footsteps came up the trail. A man wearing a short checked mackinaw and a slouch hat broke through the brush. He climbed up the ladder of nails driven into the trunk of the ponderosa and settled into the wooden overlook, cross-legged, with a lever-action rifle slung across his knees. The man turned. Platinum moonlight revealed the tough, bearded face of Jess Nichols.

Beth was right. We're all creatures of habit, making the same mistakes over and over again. Life gave everyone two, sometimes even three chances, to change their ways, but if they didn't respond, life didn't care. It quit giving chances. That was probably the only thing Jack had learned in the eight years he'd spent chasing Billy Crockett. But at least he'd learned it. He hoped Billy would too. Jess Nichols hadn't.

Jack's palms sweated against the shotgun stock. Jess lit a cigarette. The glowing red tip flared and died in the darkness. A half-hour passed, then an hour. Jack thought of making the arrest right then. He might find bear parts stored in Jess's trailer. But he waited. Finally, the sound of rustling brush caught his ear, and a dark bear emerged into the clearing, casually shuffling toward the garbage can. It was a cub, probably the one whose mother had ended up in the Dumpster. Jess wouldn't shoot a cub—or would he? If he did, Jack would have him red-handed, but he wasn't going to wait to find out. Jack fired the shotgun into the air, startling the cub. The little bear reared up on its hind legs.

Jack shouted, "Throw down the rifle, Jess, or I'll blast you."

Four or five seconds passed as Jess squinted in Jack's direction. Jack tightened his sweaty finger on the trigger, and then Jess's rifle tumbled from the tree and thudded onto the pine needles.

Jack eased the pressure of his finger from the trigger. Now that the less dangerous animal had vanished into the night, bounding westward up the mountain, unfettered—and happy, he hoped—free for the moment to unfurl its wild story into a new day, Jack rose from the brush and walked forward with the shotgun aimed at the treed man.

Western Literature Series

■ ■ ■

Western Trails: A Collection of Short Stories by Mary Austin
selected and edited by Melody Graulich

Cactus Thorn
Mary Austin

Dan De Quille, the Washoe Giant: A Biography and Anthology
prepared by Richard A. Dwyer and Richard E. Lingenfelter

Desert Wood: An Anthology of Nevada Poets
edited by Shaun T. Griffin

The City of Trembling Leaves
Walter Van Tilburg Clark

Many Californias: Literature from the Golden State
edited by Gerald W. Haslam

The Authentic Death of Hendry Jones
Charles Neider

First Horses: Stories of the New West
Robert Franklin Gish

Torn by Light: Selected Poems
Joanne de Longchamps

Swimming Man Burning
Terrence Kilpatrick

The Temptations of St. Ed & Brother S
Frank Bergon

The Other California: The Great Central Valley in Life and Letters
Gerald W. Haslam

The Track of the Cat
Walter Van Tilburg Clark

Shoshone Mike
Frank Bergon

Condor Dreams and Other Fictions
Gerald W. Haslam

A Lean Year and Other Stories
Robert Laxalt

Cruising State: Growing Up in Southern California
Christopher Buckley

The Big Silence
Bernard Schopen

Kinsella's Man
Richard Stookey

The Desert Look
Bernard Schopen

Winterchill
Ernest J. Finney

Wild Game
Frank Bergon